the
dancing
master

Books by Julie Klassen

the dancing master

JULIE KLASSEN

BETHANYHOUSE
a division of Baker Publishing Group
Minneapolis, Minnesota

© 2013 by Julie Klassen

Published by Bethany House Publishers
11400 Hampshire Avenue South
Bloomington, Minnesota 55438
www.bethanyhouse.com

Bethany House Publishers is a division of
Baker Publishing Group, Grand Rapids, Michigan

Printed in the United States of America

Library of Congress Cataloging-in-Publication Data
Klassen, Julie.
    The dancing master / Julie Klassen
        p.   cm.
        Summary: "Regency era dancing master Alec Valcourt wants to bring new life to the sleepy little village of Beaworthy in remote Devonshire—and to one young woman's restless heart"— Provided by publisher.
        Includes bibliographical references.
        ISBN 978-0-7642-1070-9 (pbk.)
        1. Dance teachers—Fiction. 2. Young women—Fiction. 3. Mothers and daughters—Fiction. 4. Widows—Fiction. 5. Villages—England—Fiction. I. Title.
    PS3611.L37 D36 2013
    813'.6—dc23   2013032378

Scripture quotations are from the King James Version of the Bible.

Cover design by Jennifer Parker

Cover photography by Mike Habermann Photography, LLC

Author represented by Books and Such Literary Agency

13 14 15 16 17 18 19   7 6 5 4 3 2 1

In honor of

Aurora Villacorta

ballroom dance instructor
at the University of Illinois
for more than twenty years.
Thanks, Miss V.

Your lessons are forever with me. Dance steps, yes, but
so much more—etiquette, manners, respect, and grace.
Your classes were the most enjoyable of my college years.
I will never forget you.

∽

Mr. J. Dawson, professor of dancing and fencing,
has the honour to announce his return from London;
at the same time begs most respectfully to say, that he has profited
by the instruction and experience of the most able professors.
Mr. J. D. has acquired all the new and fashionable dances,
the celebrated gallopades, Spanish dances, etc.
and therefore hopes to merit a portion of public patronage.

—The West Briton, 1829

～⁄◯

Quadrilles, waltzing, minuets, Country Dancing completely taught in
six private lessons for one guinea by Mr. Levien, Dancing Master.
26 Lower Charlotte Street, Bedford Square.
A select Evening Academy twice a week, two guineas a quarter.
Also a Juvenile Academy every Wednesday and Saturday afternoon:
schools and families attended.

—The (London) Times, 1821

～⁄◯

What place is so proper as the assembly-room to see the
fashions and manners of the times, to study men and characters,
to become accustomed to receive flattery without regarding it,
to learn good breeding and politeness without affection,
to see grace without wantonness, gaiety without riot,
dignity without haughtiness, and freedom without levity?

—Thomas Wilson, Dancing Master,
An Analysis of Country Dancing, 1811

Prologue

We observed the first of May as we always did. We dressed somberly and rode in the black barouche from Buckleigh Manor into Beaworthy. It was tradition, my mother said.

But I knew she had another reason for visiting the village on that particular day. Lady Amelia Midwinter wanted to make her presence known—make sure no one dared forget.

We drove first to the flower shop and bought two bouquets—lily of the valley and forget-me-nots.

From there our coachman, Isaacs, halted on the corner of High Street and Green, as he knew to do without being told.

The young groom helped my mother alight. She turned to look back at me, but I ignored her, sullenly remaining in the carriage. This was her tradition, not mine.

She crossed the street and laid one bouquet before the market hall—that center of trade on an island of green amid the cobbled High Street. The place where he died.

Forget-me-nots. *Never forget.*

She returned to the carriage, though we did not immediately depart. We sat for a few minutes in silence, waiting for the church bells to ring at midday.

Clang, clang, clang...

As the last peal faded away, she used one dainty finger to move aside the velvet curtain and survey the street. For a moment her face remained impassive, but then her mouth parted in surprise before stiffening into a grim line.

"What is it?" I asked, rebellious hope rising in my contrary heart. I slid over to that side of the carriage and looked out the window.

There, before the village green, an elderly woman as thin as a sparrow stood. She held her skirt aloft with one hand and raised her other hand high. She looked this way and that, as though waiting for someone, and for a moment I feared she would be left standing alone in the middle of the street.

Then, from behind the market hall, an old man hobbled into view. He tossed aside his apron and bowed before the woman. And she in turn curtsied. She gave him a girlish smile, and decades flew from her face.

He offered his hand, and she placed hers in his. Together, side by side, they slowly walked up the High Street in a curious rhythm—step, shuffle-step. Step, shuffle-step. Then they faced each other, joined both hands, and turned in a circle.

"What are they doing?" I breathed in wonder.

My mother snapped, "What does it look like?"

"Who are they? Do you know?"

She made no answer.

I glanced over and saw an array of emotions cross her face. Irritation. Pain. Longing.

"Who are they?" I whispered again.

She kept her gaze trained out the window. On the couple's retreating figures as they continued their odd shuffle-step up the street.

My mother inhaled deeply, clamping an iron fist over her emotions, whatever they were. "A Mr. and Mrs. Desmond, I believe."

"I don't think I know them."

"No, Julia. You wouldn't. They . . . live outside of town."

I felt my face pucker. "Then, don't they know about . . . the rule?"

"They know."

I glanced at her, but she averted her eyes, using her father's walking stick to knock against the roof.

At the familiar signal, the coachman called "Walk on" to the horses and we moved away.

We returned to Buckleigh and paused at the estate's churchyard. My mother alighted first, waving away the hovering groom and his offered umbrella. I exited after her, and when the young groom offered his hand to help me down, I smiled flirtatiously and enjoyed watching his face redden.

The day had turned pewter grey. A cold drizzle pricked through my thin cape, sending a shiver up my neck.

I followed my mother past lichen-encrusted graves and listing markers. We stopped before the family plot, outlined in brick and set with impressive headstones like dull gems in a macabre bracelet. There I read her brother's epitaph.

> Graham Buckleigh, Lord Upcott
> Born January 4, 1776
> Died May 1, 1797
> Beloved Son & Brother

"One and twenty years old," I murmured. "So young."

"Yes," she whispered.

"How did he die?" I asked as I did every year, hoping she would one day tell me the whole story.

"He was killed in a duel."

"Who killed him?"

"I prefer not to speak his name."

My gaze wandered from the headstone of the uncle I had never met, to settle on that of the aunt I had never met either. She died in childbirth before I was born.

> Lady Anne Tremelling
> Born December 5, 1777
> Died December 9, 1797
> Beloved Daughter & Sister

I nodded toward her sister's headstone. "She died less than a year later."

"Yes."

My mother bent and laid the bouquet of lily of the valley on her brother's grave.

Lily of the valley. *Tears and humility.*

She straightened. "We ought not tarry, Julia. Your father is not at all well."

"Yes, I am surprised you wanted to come today."

"It is tradition."

I sent her a sidelong glance. "You believe in carrying on only your own private traditions, I see."

I referred, of course, to May Day, which had not been celebrated in Beaworthy for twenty years—though I had heard whispers about the old tradition and its demise.

Mother turned toward the carriage without reply, and I tried to ignore the sting of rejection as easily as she ignored my sharp tongue.

"What was the duel fought over?" I asked, following her.

She did not answer. Ahead of us, the waiting groom opened the carriage door.

"Why do you not put flowers on your sister's grave?" I asked. "Why only your brother's?"

With a glance at the groom, my mother said quietly, "We shall discuss the matter another time. Not now. We have left your father alone too long as it is."

I doubted he would mind my absence. But then, I doubted he cared for me at all.

My father left *us* the next day. And in the aftermath of death, of mourners and bombazine, of funerals and the selection of headstones, we buried my questions along with my father, knowing they would someday be resurrected.

Her Ladyship had been out riding and was dressed in a long riding habit . . . She danced capitally and made use of her riding whip in the most playful manner.

—*A New Most Excellent Dancing Master:*
the Journal of Joseph Lowe

Chapter 1

NOVEMBER 5, 1816
BEAWORTHY, DEVONSHIRE, ENGLAND

Julia Midwinter joined the inhabitants of Beaworthy gathered between the village church and inn. Although Julia's mother, Lady Amelia, had put a stop to the May Day celebration years ago, the village continued one long-held tradition. Her mother rarely attended, but she allowed Julia to go along with their neighbors, the Allens. Each year on the fifth of November, the villagers encircled a massive stone, some six feet by four and weighing more than a ton—this estimated by a supposedly renowned man of science no one had ever heard of when he visited Beaworthy several years before.

That long-ago year, Julia had stood at the edges of the crowd, watching as the man of science studied the rock with great interest. He peered at it through a magnifying glass and declared there was no stone like it in all of the West Country, nay the whole of England. He scratched his chin and pondered aloud how it had come to be there.

Julia could have told him. Any of the villagers could. But they enjoyed his befuddlement—that they knew something this learned man did not. Every child in Beaworthy had been told the tale sitting atop his grandfather's knee: The stone had fallen from the devil's pocket as he fell from heaven to hell. And that was why, every year on the fifth of November, the church bell ringers turned the great stone over—to keep the devil away.

But this year was different. The bell ringers could not turn the stone, despite their straining efforts. Julia, standing there with Sir Herbert Allen and his sons, wondered if the bell ringers had grown too old and feeble.

Men from the crowd joined in, using sturdy poles for leverage, and strength built in the clay works, forges, and fields. More stout poles were brought and more men—Sir Herbert and his sons among them. But still the stone would not budge.

Sir Herbert speculated the ground had frozen early. Others shook their heads and decried such an earthly explanation. No, it could mean only one thing.

The return of the devil.

The most superstitious among them declared it a portent of dire happenings to come. But almost everyone agreed on one thing—change was on the way.

Julia Midwinter hoped they were right.

Anything to shake up the plodding days, endless church services, and somber silent meals. Days spent on needlework for charity, and evenings spent reading Fordyce's *Sermons to Young Women*, *The Mirror of the Graces*, and the few boring novels her mother deemed proper for young ladies. Her only diversion was to escape into the company of her bosom-friend, Patience Allen. Or her horse, Liberty.

But November, December, and January passed without the hoped-for change, and nineteen-year-old Julia grew increasingly restless. The mourning period for her father had passed as well, though the pall still lingered. At least now she could quit trying to gain the man's approval.

On a grey February day, Julia and Patience rode together through the extensive Buckleigh Manor grounds. They followed a trail through a wood just beginning to awaken after winter—ivy and moss beginning to green, but the gnarly tree branches overhead still bare. A few brave birds warbled rusty melodies, perhaps hoping, as Julia did, that spring would arrive early.

Ahead of them, the wood opened into a meadow, and beyond loomed the west hedge. A wickedly delicious thrill threaded up Julia's spine, and a grin lifted one corner of her mouth. She leaned low over Liberty's neck and, with posture and voice, urged the mare to gallop—the riding crop she held mere affectation, like a man's walking stick. She would never strike her horse.

She vaguely heard Patience shout that the hedge was too high. But as Julia's horse was faster than hers, and Julia twice the rider, her friend's words were the faintest buzzing in her ears. She rode confidently, as comfortable in sidesaddle as a man riding astride. Exhilarated by the wind, the speed, the sense of freedom, she gave Liberty her head. The beautiful horse galloped for all she was worth, straight for the hedge that bordered her mother's estate—Julia's confinement. Beyond it lay the whole of Devonshire, and England, and the world.

One last time, Patience shouted, "It's too high!"

For a flash of a second Julia regretted risking the legs, the life, of her beloved Liberty, but it was too late.

Liberty jumped, and for a blissful moment Julia felt the weight of the world fall away. She was flying. Escaping.

The horse thudded to the spongy turf on the other side and Julia braced herself, keeping her seat with effort. The horse bobbled slightly, and Julia hoped Liberty hadn't lodged something in her hoof upon impact.

With a "Whoa," Julia reined her horse to a walk, then nudged her to turn back with the slightest pressure of ribbon and knee. A few yards away stood a stile—built to allow pedestrians but not livestock to pass the hedge. She would use it to dismount and check Liberty's hooves, though she would not be able to remount without help. No matter. She could walk her horse back.

She unhooked her knee from the sidesaddle pommel, reached down to grab the top of the stile, and slid to its top step. Tucking the riding crop beneath her arm, she gently picked up one foreleg, then the next, inspecting the hooves.

Patience came riding toward her a few minutes later. She'd had to ride out the west gate a quarter of a mile away to reach her.

She looked at Liberty with concern. "Is she all right?"

"I think so, yes."

"And you?"

Julia grinned. "Never better."

Patience didn't return the grin, but at least she didn't scold—not like Julia's mother was sure to do if she heard of the jump.

Releasing Liberty's leg and untying the rein, Julia began walking her horse home. Patience rode slowly alongside.

Nearing the west gate, voices drew her attention and Julia paused to listen.

Patience halted her horse. "What—?"

Julia held up a hand to silence her. The voices were coming from the other side of the old gate lodge, long abandoned. The voices did not sound familiar. Or pleasant.

Looping Liberty's rein around the branch of a nearby tree, she whispered to her friend, "Wait here."

"Julia, don't," Patience hissed. "It could be dangerous."

Ignoring the warning, Julia tiptoed across the damp ground, holding forth her riding crop like a weapon. She crept along the wall of the stone building and peered around the corner.

It took her eyes a moment to register the scene before her. A beefy man held back a thin young man in workman's attire and flat hat. Meanwhile another man, wiry with lank blond hair, harassed a young woman, taking her hand and spinning her around.

"Come on, love," he urged in an oily smooth voice. "Let's see you hop. Dancin' in the spirit, I believe your lot call it—that right?"

Indignation heated quickly to anger as Julia recognized two of the parties involved. Those infernal Wilcox brothers.

She marched forward, riding crop at the ready. "Unhand her, Mr. Wilcox."

Felton Wilcox turned, beady green eyes narrowing. "Well, well. If it ain't Miss High and Mighty, stickin' her nose where it don't belong."

"I said, let her go."

"Oh, come, miss," Joe, the younger Wilcox urged. "It's only two of them ranters. Just want to hear 'er sing and see 'er prance, as they are wont to do."

"Leave her alone!" the captive young man shouted, struggling against Joe's grip.

Joe Wilcox kneed him in the back.

"Benjamin!" the young woman shrieked.

Felton Wilcox silenced her with a viselike clamp to her cheeks. He squeezed so hard the young woman's lips puckered like a gasping fish.

"Rant for me now, my pretty dissenter. Let's hear it."

"I sing to praise God," she managed, "not amuse bigots."

"Why you . . ." Felton frowned thunderously and reeled back his hand as though to strike her.

Julia slammed her riding crop across his wrist.

Felton jerked back, stunned by the whip's bite and her audacity.

He turned on her, reeled back his hand again, but hesitated.

Julia stood her ground, unflinching, glaring at him, daring him. "Perhaps you think the constable won't bother if he hears you've harassed these people. But I promise you, you will find yourself swinging by the neck if you dare lay a hand on me."

He shook the stringy hair from his eyes and snarled, "Witch!"

In a flash of anger, Julia again lifted the riding crop and sent it slicing through the air. But Felton snatched it from her hand.

Snakelike eyes glinting, he lifted the crop menacingly. "Who says I'd lay a *hand* on you . . . ?"

From a distance came the sound of galloping horse hooves. Julia kept her eyes pinned on Felton Wilcox, but he glanced toward the west gate and frowned. He threw down the crop and turned to his brother. "Come on. This was supposed to be a private party, but our uninvited guests have spoilt it."

With a nasty shove, Joe pushed the young man to the ground and ran with surprising speed for one so bulky, following his brother into the wood.

The slim young man scrambled to his feet and made as though to pursue them, but the girl grabbed his arm. "Benjamin, don't. Let them go. I'm all right."

He pulled his gaze from the retreating figures to scan the girl's face. "Are you sure?"

"Yes. Perfectly." She turned to Julia. "I know you meant well, miss. But you ought not have struck him. We are to turn the other cheek."

Julia felt her brows rise. "You may turn the other cheek all you like. Felton Wilcox will only strike the harder next time."

The girl gave her a pointed look. "As you did?"

Julia was incredulous. "I was trying to help you."

The young man laid a hand on the girl's arm and looked at Julia. "I am grateful, miss. Truly. Only ashamed I could not help Tess myself."

"Don't feel too bad," Julia consoled. "The Wilcoxes are local wrestling champions. You are not the first man to be laid low by them, and you won't be the last."

He picked up his fallen hat and bowed. "I'm Ben Thorne, and this is my sister, Tess. Again, we thank you, Miss Midwinter."

They knew her name, Julia noticed, though she hadn't known theirs. She had seen these two before in passing, she believed, but had never met them.

The riders finally reached them, reining in with a storm of thundering hooves and flying dirt.

"Are you all right?" James Allen asked as he gracefully dismounted, handsome face tense.

"Yes. Quite."

Beside him, his brother, Walter, swung his leg across the saddle to dismount. He caught his boot in the stirrup, hopped to keep his balance, and finally loosed his boot with a desperate jerk, which sent his hat flying to the ground.

Miss Thorne stepped forward, bent to retrieve it, and held it out to him. "Are you all right?" she asked gently.

Walter's face reddened. "Yes, miss. Thank you, miss."

James's gaze remained on Julia. "Patience found us out riding and told us you were in trouble."

Had she? Julia hadn't even heard her ride away. "The Wilcox brothers," she explained. "They were bothering these two. But they've gone now."

Ben Thorne nodded. "Thankfully, Miss Midwinter and her riding crop convinced them to leave."

James Allen's fair brows rose. "Riding crop? Julia, that was not wise. Who knows what sort of revenge those two might resort to."

"Well, thankfully you rode up when you did."

Walter, she noticed, was still staring at the young woman called Tess. The girl was lovely, with a wild, wood-sprite look with long reddish-brown hair tumbling about her shoulders, and big brown eyes.

Poor Walter. The tall young man was ever awkward around females. But a *pretty* female his own age? Heaven help him. With his unremarkable light brown hair, sad eyes, and unfortunate ears, Walter possessed a sweet face, but not one a woman was likely to think handsome.

Before Julia could make introductions, Patience came galloping up. Her hair, even fairer than James's golden locks, danced around her flushed cheeks. Poor Patience. The proper young lady was usually so sedate. Julia had never seen her ride so fast. Even so, she had apparently been unable to keep up with her brothers.

Winded, she called, "Is everything all right?"

"Yes, my dear," Julia said. "Thanks to you. Thank you for calling in the cavalry."

⁂

On Sunday, Julia Midwinter sat in her usual pew in St. Michael's, her mother on one side of her, her friend Patience on the other. The rector, Mr. Bullmore, stood above them in the raised pulpit, droning on about something or other. Julia wasn't really listening. The rector liked using lofty words, and many of them, apparently enamored with the sound of his own voice. Worse yet, the man reminded Julia of her father. Whenever he looked at her, his eyes were cold and disapproving. Like her father's had always been.

Julia noticed the rector's son was visiting again from Oxford. Cedric Bullmore planned to follow his father into the church. She wondered where he might secure a living—somewhere interesting, far away? She decided she would have to make more of an effort to flirt with the young man. In fact, she would begin that very afternoon.

Eligible son or no, Julia preferred when Mr. Bullmore left the sermon making to dear old Mr. Evans, the curate. On special holidays, Mr. Evans still led worship at the church on the Buckleigh estate for any who wished to attend—usually just her, Lady Amelia, the Allens, and a small clutch of servants and tenants. Everyone else, it seemed, preferred the newer village church.

Attention straying, Julia glanced over her shoulder across the aisle. There she noticed a man she had never seen before, sitting in Mr. Ramsay's pew a few rows back. The young man had dark hair and a handsome profile, a good nose, firm chin, and strong cheekbones. But his most striking feature was his unfamiliarity—he was *not* from Beaworthy.

She leaned nearer Patience and whispered, "Who is he?"

Patience, who'd actually been listening to the sermon, roused herself from concentration long enough to follow Julia's gaze. "I don't know," she whispered back.

Without removing her dutiful gaze from the Reverend Mr. Bullmore, Lady Amelia laid her gloved hand gently on Julia's knee, signaling her to sit quietly.

A few minutes later, as the congregation rose to sing a hymn, Julia noticed a woman of perhaps forty-five, in somber black, standing beside the unfamiliar man. His mother, Julia assumed. And on the woman's other side, a slender girl of seventeen or so. His sister, she guessed.

She hoped.

After the service finally concluded, Julia followed her mother down the aisle to thank the rector. Mr. Bullmore's cold eyes slid past Julia to rest on Lady Amelia.

He smiled at her and said, "Your ladyship, might I introduce a few newcomers to the parish?" He gestured toward the trio standing nearby.

Her mother politely inclined her head and turned to face the woman in black.

"Lady Amelia Midwinter, may I present Mrs. Valcourt, Mr. Ramsay's sister."

The woman smiled wanly and dipped her head. Julia saw no resemblance to Mr. Ramsay, the prim, rotund solicitor who stood a few feet away.

"How do you do," Lady Amelia said in a tone that did not invite reply.

The rector continued, "And this is her daughter, Miss Aurora Valcourt"—the pretty girl dipped a graceful curtsy—"and her son, Mr. Alec Valcourt."

The well-dressed man bowed with impressive address. "A pleasure to meet you, your ladyship."

Julia blurted, "Are you visiting Mr. Ramsay, or have you come to stay?"

Her mother stiffened at the forward question, yet turned to acknowledge her. "And this is my daughter, Miss Midwinter."

Again Mr. Valcourt bowed and the ladies curtsied.

Julia smiled at the Valcourt family. "A pleasure to meet you all. Welcome."

Mr. Valcourt's mother was handsome, Julia decided. Though the sad downturn of her cheeks, and even her nose, kept her from being pretty. And black did not flatter her complexion. His sister, however, was lovely, with brown hair and bright blue eyes set in a sweet, fair face. Mr. Valcourt was perhaps an inch or two shy of six feet and athletically built—broad shoulders narrowing to a trim waist. His dark hair was wavy, where his sister's was straight. From the front, his face was even more attractive than it had been in profile. Full lips, well-formed slightly belled nose, and blue-grey eyes. He was not only more handsome on closer inspection but older as well. Perhaps as old as five and twenty.

Julia gave him her most effective smile.

But instead of smiling in return, or blushing, or any of the responses she was accustomed to, he merely blinked and looked away.

"Um . . . and as to your question," Mrs. Valcourt replied, sending a quick glance toward her brother, "Mr. Ramsay has kindly invited us to stay for as long as we like. Just how long, we have yet to decide."

"Ah, I see." Julia nodded, though she didn't see. Not really. It was, after all, a vague answer, but she knew better than to press the matter. She guessed she was already in for a lecture on prying as soon as she and her mother were out of earshot.

Mrs. Valcourt went on to thank Mr. Bullmore for the sermon and his warm welcome.

While the woman spoke to the rector, Julia stepped nearer her mother and said quietly, "Patience has invited me to go riding this afternoon, and then perhaps to do some needlework for the ladies' aid society. You don't mind, do you?"

"On Sunday?"

"Yes, she is most insistent." Julia turned to Patience, who was talking to a little red-haired girl nearby. "Are you not, Patience?"

Patience turned and blinked her pale blue eyes. "Pardon me?"

"I was just telling Mamma that you have asked me over for the afternoon. You have your heart set upon it, don't you?"

Her friend's lips parted. "I . . . I do, yes," she faltered, then added more convincingly, "Nothing would please me more."

"You see?" Julia beamed at her mother. "Girls our age enjoy talking and sharing secrets. Did you not do so when you were a girl?" It was something Julia could not imagine of the woman of three and forty years, but she was determined to win her way.

Her mother's eyes clouded. "I had few friends of such an intimate nature."

"But then, you had a sister, whereas Patience and I do not."

"Yes, I did," Lady Amelia said, her voice strangely clipped. "Very well, you may go. But have the groom escort you."

"Mamma, that is hardly necessary. It's less than half a mile from our stables to Medlands. It would take Tommy longer to saddle his horse than to ride there and back."

"I insist."

"Oh, all right. But don't make him wait for me. One of the Allens can escort me home."

"Very well."

Triumph surged within her breast. As she turned away, Julia allowed herself a secret smirk of satisfaction—only to find Mr. Valcourt watching her.

She paused, and for a moment their eyes met. He held her gaze with a knowing look that told her he had overheard their conversation and was not fooled. She opened her mouth to say something, but he turned away without a word and escorted his mother and sister outside.

By 1706, even dour Philadelphia had a dancing and
fencing school, despite protests by the Society of Friends.

—Lynn Matluck Brooks, York County Heritage Trust

$\mathcal{C}$hapter 2

On his first full day in Devonshire, Alec Valcourt left the village
church still seeing Miss Midwinter's lovely face in his mind.
She was beautiful, yes. And she knew it. She reminded him
of too many spoiled young ladies he had met who enjoyed flirting—
practicing both their seduction and dance skills with him, but only in
hopes of snaring a more suitable gentleman in future.

Alec had overheard enough of Miss Midwinter's conversation with
her mother to know she was up to something. Her coy manipulation
had brought to mind Miss Underhill, and Alec had turned away, determined to put both young women from his mind.

He had more important things to consider.

Already missing London, Alec walked through diminutive Beaworthy
with his mother and sister, and an uncle he barely knew. As they passed
the inn, he glanced at the upper windows, wondering if the inn had
an assembly room. He would have to stop in sometime and meet the
proprietor.

Uncle Ramsay lived outside the village in a two-story whitewashed
cottage capped by a tile roof—with a small stable, paddock, and other
outbuildings behind. As a young partner he had lived over the law

practice on the High Street, he'd explained, but had bought the cottage when he bought the practice. Now his two clerks shared the rooms above his office, while he lived alone, with a cook-housekeeper and manservant to keep the place going.

Shortly after reaching the cottage, Alec joined his family in the dining parlor for a stiff early dinner at the bachelor's meager table. It was not that his uncle was poor—he was after all the only solicitor in town and employed two clerks—but apparently he was exceedingly frugal and his cook-housekeeper had learned to stretch a sixpence into a pound.

Alec was careful not to eat too much of the plain roasted chicken and boiled potatoes so there would be enough to go around. Covert glances at his mother and sister revealed they did the same, slicing a small potato into tiny slices and eating them slowly and delicately, so that their plates did not empty ahead of Mr. Ramsay's. If their uncle ate this way regularly, he should have been a thin, spindly man, but he was not. Rather, he possessed a well-rounded waistcoat that belied his parsimonious table.

The conversation was meager as well. His mother had explained the previous night why they had come, as well as her husband's fate. At the time, Cornelius Ramsay had nodded gravely but said little.

Now, abruptly, he began, "Perhaps we needn't share the particulars of how it happened, hmm? It is enough for people here to know your husband is gone and that is why you've come."

Around the table Alec, his mother, and Aurora nodded in somber agreement.

After the meal, Alec retrieved his violin case. Knowing his music would fill the small house, and unsure whether his uncle would welcome it, he took his instrument outside. The February day was chilly, but he found a sunny bench—the breeze blocked by the garden wall—and felt quite comfortable. Sitting down, he removed his violin, positioned his bow, and began to fiddle. As he played, he reviewed his plans in his mind.

He had a small stack of pamphlets left over from London, describing the fencing and dancing classes he'd taught in private homes or the academy. If he cut off the bottom portion, which listed the Valcourt Academy's address and weekly dance times, he could still use them. Armed with the pamphlets, he would introduce himself to local schools, as well as middle-class families and gentry. He thought he would teach private lessons in homes first. Then, when he had sufficient students and income, he would find and let a suitable place in Beaworthy to open a new academy.

He thought again of the pretty Miss Midwinter he had met that morning at church. He supposed a young lady like her already counted dancing among her many accomplishments, but it wouldn't hurt to ask. . . .

Aurora came out, wool shawl around her shoulders, and sat on the bench beside him. She stared peacefully over the dormant garden and silent road beyond, listening as he played.

After a few minutes, she asked quietly, "That's new, isn't it?"

He shook his head. "Not exactly. It's a variation of Grandfather's 'L'Aimable Vainqueur.'"

"Ah." She stood and began walking through the dance steps in a demure, understated fashion while Alec played.

A horse and cart rumbled by, and the man at the reins turned to stare at them. Self-conscious, Aurora stopped and waited until he had passed before resuming the steps. As Alec added spirit to the tune, Aurora raised her arms and twirled a pirouette, nearly losing her shawl as she did so.

"Stop! What are you doing?"

Aurora whirled again, this time to face a flushed Uncle Ramsay. Did he reprimand her because she had danced on Sunday? Alec had not taught lessons on the Sabbath, but their family had often spent a pleasant hour or two with music and dancing on Sunday afternoons.

Alec lowered his fiddle and stood. "I'm sorry, Uncle. Was the music too loud? We came outside, hoping not to disturb you."

"You do disturb me." Glancing toward the road, he gestured them forward. "Come inside, the both of you."

Alec and Aurora exchanged uncertain glances and followed him through the door and into the sitting room, feeling like naughty children.

Inside, Mrs. Valcourt looked up from the book of sermons she was reading. Her gaze shifted from her children to her brother, worry lines creasing her brow.

Uncle Ramsay turned to face them. "Dancing is frowned upon here."

"On the Sabbath, you mean?" Alec asked. "Aurora was only walking through the steps of a variation I've composed. My fault, I'm afraid, not hers."

"No, not *only* on Sabbath," Uncle Ramsay said. "Dancing is not allowed here in general."

Alec stared at the man, certain he must have misheard. "I don't understand."

Aurora gave a tentative smile. "You must be teasing, Uncle. For you know Alec is a dancing master."

Uncle Ramsay's mouth fell ajar, apparently thunderstruck. "What?"

Alec felt a quiver of dread snake up his spine but steeled himself and met his uncle's gaze directly. "I am a dancing and fencing master, sir. Like my father and grandfather before me."

Uncle Ramsay's face darkened in displeasure. He turned to his sister. "Really, Joanna. You should have told me your son was following the family line before you came."

"I knew you would not approve," she replied, setting aside her book and averting her eyes.

Alec looked from his mother to his uncle, mind reeling. "Surely my profession does not come as a surprise to you."

"It does. And not a happy one. I knew your grandfather was a dancing master, and French in the bargain. But your father vowed to forsake the profession if I would permit him to marry my sister."

"He did give it up," Mrs. Valcourt said, then added, "for a time."

Cornelius Ramsay shook his head, eyes troubled. "He promised. Upon his honor."

Mrs. Valcourt's lips tightened. "Men do not always keep their promises, I find."

Several moments of strained silence followed. The mantel clock ticked. Aurora sent Alec a nervous look. It was the nearest thing to an accusation they had yet heard from their mother.

Uncle Ramsay picked up the fire iron and jabbed at the embers in the hearth. "I suppose your husband's return to the profession, and your son's following him, explains your vague and infrequent letters over the years?"

He sent his sister a challenging look, but she did not meet his gaze.

"Well, well," he said briskly. "If you had divulged your son's profession, I could have warned you there is no dancing here in Beaworthy. And precious little call for a dancing master. In fact, I cannot think of any place *less* in need of one." He shoved the fire iron back into its stand with a *clang*.

"But . . . why?" Alec sputtered.

"A decision of the leading family of the parish. Lady Amelia Midwinter, daughter of the last earl."

Alec's stomach churned. Flabbergasted, he asked again, "But why? Is she a Quaker or some such?"

His uncle shook his head. "It's the way things were when I came here years ago as partner to old Mr. Ley—God rest his soul."

"I don't understand. Are you saying there's an actual law or ordinance that says one cannot dance here?"

Uncle Ramsay's lower lip protruded in thought. "Not an actual law that I know of, though certainly an unwritten one." He shrugged. "I own I've never looked into it. Didn't affect me—I never went in for that sort of frivolity."

"But—"

His uncle laid a hand on his arm. "The *reason* is not the main point here, my boy. The fact is, dancing is not done here in Beaworthy, hasn't been for twenty years, and is unlikely to start now you're here."

Alec looked at his mother, stunned by this unexpected turn of events. "Mamma, why did you not say anything? If I had known—"

Her eyes sparked. "If you had known . . . What? We still would have come. We had no other choice. And thanks to my generous brother, we have a roof over our heads. Let us be thankful."

"But we cannot presume to live on Uncle Ramsay's goodwill for long, Mamma," Alec insisted. "I must earn my own way—support you and Aurora."

His uncle nodded. "Well said, my boy. Well said. A young man of nearly five and twenty must have some skills and abilities to recommend him."

Alec lifted his chin. "I am a skilled and able dancing and fencing master, sir." He hesitated, then added, "Though I did apprentice as a clerk for a time, before Father reopened his academy."

"Ah! A clerk. Now, that's something useful."

"I've never regretted the experience," Alec allowed. "Even after I began teaching alongside Father, I was able to help with the business side of the academy—keeping the books, paying taxes, that sort of thing."

His mother asked hopefully, "Might Alec help you in your law practice, brother?"

His uncle considered this, then shook his head. "Unfortunately no. I have two clerks at present and haven't need of another. Nor have I heard of any such position available nearby. But I shall ask around."

Alec wanted to please his uncle, but he did not want to be a clerk. He said, "Perhaps there is more interest in dancing than you think. And I teach fencing as well. I might find pupils for that skill at least."

"Enough to support yourself? I think that highly unlikely."

"Then I shall go farther afield to seek pupils," Alec said. "I may have more luck in neighboring villages."

"But folks around here are primarily farmers and laborers. Few well-to-do families interested in dancing."

"How do you know?"

"Call it an educated guess. My professional opinion."

"It cannot hurt to ask."

"Actually, it can. It can hurt your reputation and your reception. It won't do me any favors either."

"But—"

Uncle Ramsay held up his palm. "Look. Alec. I am a reasonable man and will not forbid you. However, I would advise you to tread carefully and be discreet. And do not tempt fate by going to Buckleigh Manor or its neighbor, Medlands. Give yourself, say, a week, and if you haven't rummaged up sufficient pupils by then, we shall discuss alternate plans for your future. All right?"

"That sounds reasonable," Alec's mother agreed. "Quite generous, brother. Thank you."

A week? Inwardly, Alec rebelled. He felt his life beginning to spin away, out from under his control, and he didn't like it one bit.

Dismissed, Alec exchanged his violin for a sword and strode back outside. Instead of turning right into the village, he turned left into the countryside. In his uncle's compact cottage, there was precious little room for privacy. He needed a place to exert himself and burn off his vexation with no one to criticize, or scoff. A place where he could toss aside his coat and work himself into an ungentlemanly sweat.

His small sword held inconspicuously to his side, he strode down the unpaved road, eyeing with interest the wooded area ahead.

He passed a walled churchyard, the listing graves and grey limestone church far older than the one he'd attended in the village. Not sure if the place was in use, he walked on. The road entered a copse of trees both deciduous and evergreen. Though only February, birds sang hopefully. Evidently, spring returned earlier here in the southwest. Perhaps all was not as bleak as it appeared.

The vague rumble and wave of two voices reached him. Through the trees, he glimpsed movement. He paused, not wishing his footsteps to announce his presence, or to meet anyone in his current mood. Something about the uncertain shapes beyond the pine boughs drew his attention. He walked gingerly from the road into the copse, careful to avoid stepping on downed branches.

He stopped behind a dense Scots pine and peered around it. The shapes became clearer. Two horses. Two people. Partially shielded by the horses, a man and woman stood, reins in hand, heads near in conversation. A love scene? he wondered. At all events, Alec realized he had no right to intrude.

Alec was about to turn away, when one horse lowered its head to nibble among the brush and he saw the young woman more clearly— Miss Julia Midwinter, whom he had met in church. Who was *supposed* to be out riding with another young lady. Her present companion was young but not female. He was a handsome, well-dressed gentleman in green coat and buff trousers. Miss Midwinter smiled coyly up at him and leaned very near.

Again the image of Miss Underhill appeared in Alec's mind, and his gut pinched with guilt and regret.

Suddenly Miss Midwinter looked right in his direction. Had Alec made a sound after all?

The pretty blonde frowned and murmured something to the man. Then she added more loudly, "What a pleasant surprise to happen upon you, sir. But now I must bid you good-day."

Alec turned and walked away. Her stilted words had not fooled him. Miss Midwinter had clearly deceived her mother. What would he do if he ever came upon his sister in such a compromising situation?

Deep in contemplation, Alec tripped over something in the wood.

"I say, have a care," a man grumbled. "That's my leg you're kicking."

Alec spun around, startled by the affronted male voice. He had not realized anyone else was near.

And no wonder, for the person addressing him was seated on the ground amid the brush, legs sprawled, back reclining against a tree. The offended man was a few years younger than Alec and well dressed, though his cravat was an untidy wad and stained with mud. Or was it . . . chocolate?

"I beg your pardon," Alec said. "I did not see you."

The fire faded from the man's dark eyes. "Well, no harm done."

Alec hesitated, taking in the man's position. "Are you . . . all right?"

"I expect so. Good thing I was wearing my boots."

Alec looked down at the man's riding boots and saw that one of them was clamped between the metal jaws of a trap.

"Good heavens. Are you hurt?"

"Not too bad, I don't think."

"How can I help?"

The man thought. "You don't happen to have a fire iron or crowbar on your person, I don't imagine?"

"I'm afraid not." Alec raised his sword. "I have this, but I don't think—"

"A sword? Handy thing, that. Not every chap carries one these days."

"I fence," Alec murmured. He feared that using his blade as a tool would break the tip, but he couldn't very well leave the young man entrapped. He searched the ground for a sturdy stick, then knelt beside the fallen man.

"Dashed foolish of me, I know," the young man said. "The game-keeper has warned me time and time again to mind his traps. Yet somehow I stumbled into this one."

Alec slid the edge of his sword between the metal jaws and pried the trap open just far enough to insert the sturdy branch.

The young man eyed his sword with interest. "Perhaps we might fence together sometime. Though I fence very ill, no doubt."

"I could help you improve your skills."

"Really? Excellent."

Using the stick as a lever, Alec began prying open the trap.

"Wait 'til James learns of this," the young man moaned. "I shall never hear the end of it."

"James?"

"My brother."

"Perhaps he needn't learn of it."

"You're not from this parish, I gather, or you'd know there's no keeping it secret. Everyone hears everything eventually. Besides, I'd not rob my brother of a good laugh, would I? Have you no brothers?"

"No. Only a sister."

"Ah." The young man nodded. "One ought to be gentler with sisters. Though Patience is quite sporting about our teasing, I will say."

Trap released, Alec held it gingerly while the young man extracted his foot. He woefully eyed his dented boot. "At all events, I fear there's no hiding *this*. Father's valet will throw a fit when he sees all his polishing gone to ruin."

"And your foot?" Alec asked.

The young man rotated his ankle. "Hurts but seems all right."

Alec offered his hand and helped pull the man to his feet. He nearly lost his own footing, so much heavier was the man than he appeared. Standing, the man's lanky height became evident—he was several inches taller than Alec and likely a stone or two heavier.

Tentatively putting weight on his foot, the young man winced.

"Is it broken?" Alec asked.

"I don't think so. But it'll be black-and-blue tomorrow if I don't miss my guess."

Alec offered his shoulder. "Here, lean on me."

"I don't live far. Medlands. Do you know it?"

"No. I've only just arrived from London." Though Alec did recall his uncle mentioning the place. "We're staying with Mr. Ramsay—my uncle."

"I know him—he's my father's solicitor. Well, welcome to Beaworthy. A good show you came when you did." The young man stuck out his soiled hand. "Walter Allen."

Seeing the muddy hand, Alec withdrew his pocket kerchief and placed it in the man's waiting palm. "Landed in a spot of dirt when you fell, by the looks of it."

Walter looked down at his palm, then obligingly wiped his hands. "And so I did." He held out the soiled kerchief. "Many thanks."

Alec smiled and waved away the offer. "Keep it."

The man shrugged and pocketed it. "Didn't catch your name," he said.

"Alec Valcourt. How do you do?"

"About average." Walter grinned. "For me."

He put his arm around Alec's shoulder, and the two walked slowly out of the trees and onto the road. Not far past the walled churchyard, they came to a wrought-iron gate with a lion's head baring its teeth and glaring down at them from atop the metal scrollwork.

Seeing him glance down its long drive, Walter said, "That's Buckleigh Manor."

"Is that where the Midwinters live?"

"You've met them?"

Alec nodded. "At church."

"Ah." Walter lifted his chin in understanding. "Yes. They're our neighbors." He turned his head. "Medlands is just there, on the other side of the road."

Ahead, an open, inviting entrance awaited, with two stone pillars on either side of a gently curved drive, with no menacing lion to warn visitors away.

The house beyond seemed relatively modern and well maintained, or perhaps recently refurbished. It was built of warm red brick with white-framed doors and windows. Its roof of many gables and tall brick chimneys was crowned by a cheerful white cupola.

In spite of the man's humble, self-deprecating manner, he was apparently from a wealthy family.

Glancing up at the house, Alec glimpsed a fair head in one of the upper windows. A flick of a curtain and the figure disappeared. As they reached the front stairs a few moments later, the door burst open and a young woman hurried out, pale face a mask of concern, framed by the lightest blond hair Alec had ever seen.

"Walter!" she exclaimed. "Are you all right?"

"Yes, Pet, I am."

"Then why are you limping? What happened?"

"I shall tell you by and by, or you'll wring it from me, I know. But first, let me introduce my rescuer." He released Alec's shoulder and gestured with a sweep of his hand. "Miss Patience Allen, my sister, please meet Mr. Alec Valcourt, newcomer to Beaworthy."

She turned to him, her light blue eyes round. He found himself comparing her to Miss Midwinter, who was also blond, though that lady's curls were a deeper, honey hue. Miss Allen's eyes seemed wide and innocent, compared to Miss Midwinter's knowing gaze.

"I believe I saw you at church today, Mr. Valcourt," Miss Allen said.

"Allow me to express my heartfelt appreciation on behalf of my entire family. Better yet, come and meet them. I know Mamma and Papa will want to thank you."

Alec hesitated. "I don't wish to intrude."

"Not a bit of it," Walter said.

"They are just here in the drawing room. This way." Miss Allen turned and led the way across the hall. When she opened the broad paneled door, Alec glimpsed a scene of domestic happiness framed in its threshold. A woman of forty or forty-five sat at an embroidery screen before the fire. She had paused in her needlework to regard with fond amusement her husband holding a biscuit before a hound on its rear haunches in eager beggar's pose. Hearing the door open, the man gave the hound his reward and praised him with a fond "Good boy." He then rose and turned toward the door with a ready smile.

He was a tall, handsome man with silver threaded through dark blond hair. His wife was equally attractive with faded blond curls and the dimples of a young girl. She rose and stepped to her husband's side.

Walter introduced Alec and shared the story of their meeting. As he did so, Sir Herbert and Lady Allen gazed at Alec with smiles that lit their eyes and gave him a warm feeling of approval and value. Their expressions of gratitude were instant and genuine, and both took turns vigorously shaking his hand.

Sir Herbert insisted on inspecting Walter's foot and bid him sit in a nearby chair to do so.

As the examination commenced, Walter's older brother, James, came in, dressed in green coat, buff trousers, and tall boots—riding clothes. Alec recognized him with a start as the man he had seen with Miss Midwinter near the wood.

Perhaps then, Alec thought with relief, there had been nothing untoward about Miss Midwinter stopping to speak with a neighbor while out riding. Mr. Allen had clearly not lingered with the young lady.

James Allen's hair was a halo of tawny gold curls, his features finely formed. Even Alec could not miss noticing that he was an exceedingly handsome young man. He was in appearance very like his sister,

Patience. And both resembled their parents. Alec wondered idly who Walter resembled.

Walter repeated the story, and James Allen thanked Alec and shook his hand, though with more reserve than his parents had shown.

But when James turned to his brother, his reserve fell away. His eyes sparkled and a smile played about his mouth. As Walter had predicted, James lost no time in teasing him. "Not another trap, Walt. What does that make—two or three this year?"

Walter ducked his head to hide a sheepish smile.

"You might have called out," James said. "I rode very near that spot."

He didn't mention meeting Miss Midwinter on his ride, Alec noticed, and wondered why.

James continued, "We shall have to ask Hooper to paint the traps yellow to warn you off—and all the foxes and weasels in the bargain. What do you say, Papa. Spare the game birds or poor Walt's foot?"

His father smiled. "There are many birds in those woods, but Walter has only two feet. Better spare those."

James nodded. "I quite agree. The Beaworthy cricket team would be hard-pressed indeed if our best batsman showed up lame." He laid a hand on his younger, though larger, brother's shoulder. "Jesting aside, I am glad you are all right, old man. You must promise to look about you next time you go for a ramble."

Walter grinned. "I shall."

Lady Allen spoke up. "I am afraid it is Cook's half day, Mr. Valcourt, or we should invite you to stay for dinner."

"Thank you anyway, Lady Allen. But no further thanks are necessary."

"You've not eaten Mrs. White's puddings," Walter teased. "Or you'd not be so quick to decline."

"Another time, then," Sir Herbert suggested.

Alec bowed. "Thank you, sir."

Alec recalled his uncle's admonition to avoid soliciting pupils at Buckleigh Manor and Medlands, yet even had he not, Alec would have been reluctant to press his advantage—to spoil the moment by asking for their patronage. His father's critical voice, saying, *"You must be more persuasive and assertive . . ."* echoed in Alec's memory, but he ignored it.

"And I hope we might fence together one day," Walter added. "James and I had a few lessons, but it's years ago now."

Alec explained, "That's why I was wandering about today. I'd hoped to find an out-of-the-way place to practice, but . . ."

"But instead you found me." Walter chuckled, then added, "The churchyard isn't used much. Or you're welcome to come here."

"Perhaps after your foot heals," Alec suggested.

"Oh, I'll be right as a trivet in a day or two." Walter gingerly replaced his stocking.

"You mustn't rush things, Walter," Lady Allen said. "And I don't know that playing with swords is, um, the best pastime for you."

"Worried I'll cut off my own head?" Walter turned to grin at Alec. "You see how my reputation precedes me."

Learning to dance was an important accomplishment for ladies and gentlemen, so was included in any genteel or semi-genteel education.

—Susannah Fullerton, *A Dance With Jane Austen*

Chapter 3

J ulia led her horse back to the Buckleigh Manor stables and there removed Liberty's bridle while the groom unfastened the saddle and carried it away. Julia insisted on grooming Liberty herself, first with currycomb, then brush, putting off returning to the house as long as possible.

"There, my sweet girl. My beauty," she murmured, stroking the mare's forelock.

Finally she went inside and up to her room, removing her hat as she went. Then she rang for the upper housemaid to help her change from her riding habit.

While she waited, Julia slumped onto her dressing stool. Noticing the brass mermaid on the table, she picked it up and fiddled with it while she thought back over the afternoon. The outing had certainly not turned out as she'd hoped. She had ridden, not to Medlands, as she'd told her mother, but rather toward the stream where Cedric Bullmore liked to fly-fish. The rector was forever bragging about his son's angling prowess, mixing fish stories into his sermons on "fishers of men." And Julia had planned to do a little fishing of her own. . . .

∽⃘

Julia rode alongside the wood, allowing it to conceal her approach until she could observe the scene unnoticed. If Cedric's father was there with him, she would turn and ride home. She did not wish the rector to report to her mother that he'd seen her out riding alone. Nor would she dismount until she was certain.

She halted at the edge of the wood and peered toward the stream. There he was. Standing on the bank in his boots, broad-brimmed hat shielding his face, fly rod bent as he worked to land a fish.

Cedric Bullmore was not as handsome as either James Allen or the new man she had met in church. He was extremely thin, had a long nose, and tended to blather on like his father. But he was a gentleman, and better yet, he had recently returned from his grand tour, and she longed to hear about his travels on the continent.

For a moment, Julia imagined herself married to Cedric Bullmore and traveling the world with him. . . .

Together they journeyed through Spain, France, and Italy. He had filled out under her nurturing and learned to curb his tongue. Arm in arm, they toured art galleries, palazzi, and Roman ruins. Cedric introduced her as *mi esposa, ma femme,* or *amore mio,* with pride and affection wherever they went. They dined in lovely cafés and were invited to fashionable balls. They stayed in quaint *pensiones,* where they enjoyed breathtaking views from separate rooms. . . .

Blinking away the daydream, Julia lifted her knee from the pommel and slid to the ground. Keeping hold of the reins, she watched from behind Liberty's neck as Cedric netted the obstinate fish. She would wait until he had placed it in his basket, and then—

"Julia?" a male voice called.

She turned, her stomach dropping.

James Allen came riding up, looking none too pleased to see her. "Where is your groom?"

"Hello, James." Julia forced a smile. "And how are you on this beautiful day?"

"Relieved I came upon you when I did—that's how." He jerked up his hand. "For there stands Cedric Bullmore. What would the rector's son have thought had you happened upon him unchaperoned? Do you not care a whit about your reputation?"

Julia lifted her chin. "It is perfectly respectable to ride on one's own land, I think."

James dismounted. "Then why are you off your horse? Tell me you did not plan to go over and speak to the man alone."

"Why not?" Julia changed tack, stepping nearer and lowering her voice. "I am speaking to *you* alone."

"I realize that. And if Mr. Bullmore sees the two of us together, he might think we . . ."

"He might think we . . . what?" Julia smiled into the young man's angelic face. If everyone expected them to marry one day, she might as well see if there was any spark of attraction between them. Especially since he'd ruined her other plans.

She leaned toward him, nearer yet.

James stiffened and pulled back. "He might conclude we are . . . engaged."

Irritated, Julia pulled a face. "Which we are not, of course."

"No. But even so . . ."

Some slight movement snagged the corner of her eye, and Julia glanced toward the wood. There through the trees stood a figure, partially hidden by a pine bough—the new man she had met in church. Embarrassment singed Julia's ears but was quickly overpowered by indignation. Was everyone spying on her today?

She gritted her teeth and murmured peevishly, "Very well, James, you have made your point. Now, will you give me a leg up?"

He hesitated. "I am no groom, Julia. I'd probably toss you over the other side. Better walk her back."

She huffed. "Some gallant you are." Then she added more loudly, for the benefit of the eavesdropper, "What a pleasant surprise to happen upon you, sir. But now I must bid you good-day."

Even now, in the privacy of her room, the memory provoked an uncomfortable wave of embarrassment, irritation, and . . . disappointment. Must James Allen be such a dull stick? So suffocatingly proper?

She hoped the newcomer, Mr. Valcourt, would keep his mouth shut about seeing her alone with him. Not that her mother would suspect gentlemanly Mr. Allen of impropriety, but she might see it as the excuse she'd been waiting for to prod him into declaring himself. And Julia wasn't ready for that. She wasn't sure if she ever would be.

She looked down at the old brass mermaid in her hand. Half woman. Half fish. The only gift she'd ever received from her father, odd though it was.

Too bad it was the only fish she'd managed to land that day.

⸿

Alec returned to his uncle's house, without having taken as much exercise as he would have liked, but feeling oddly invigorated by the brisk walk and the encounter with the Allen family. *At least one potential fencing pupil,* he thought. Or even a friend.

Perhaps things in Beaworthy weren't as bleak as Uncle Ramsay declared, Alec thought. It was time to put his plan into action.

His uncle's cook-housekeeper had Sunday afternoons off, but Alec found his manservant and borrowed a pair of scissors and an iron. With the former, he carefully trimmed his pamphlets. Then he heated the iron and smoothed a shirt and his finest cravat.

Dressing well to meet prospective pupils had served him well in the past, so he would do the same on the morrow. He brushed his best frock coat, laid out buff pantaloons and his most fashionable waistcoat. He missed his father's manservant, Lester, who had kept all their dancing slippers, shoes, and boots in excellent condition, and had helped Alec on with his tight-fitting coats and tied his more complicated cravat knots. But they'd had to let Lester go last year, and Alec had learned to do for himself.

Thinking ahead to the next day's unannounced and likely unwelcome calls, nerves pricked Alec's stomach. He always detested this part of the job. And his father had always criticized him for it. To buoy his spirits, he thought not of his pushy father, but of his charming, gentle grandfather. His grandfather truly believed dancing added to life's joys and satisfaction. He believed his lessons in both dancing and fencing helped people physically as well as socially, and he genuinely cared about his pupils' success. In his younger days, his grandfather had been one of the strongest men Alec knew. Beneath his fashionable coat and polished manners lay solid muscles and strength built from hours of fencing and dancing every week. Because of him, Alec knew a man could be strong and yet graceful and caring. That was the sort of dancing master Alec wished to be, whether soliciting pupils or teaching them.

Lord, be with me, he murmured as he lay down to sleep. If half of his uncle's warnings were true, he'd need all the help he could get.

※

In the morning, Alec dressed with care, and helped himself to a breakfast of tea and toast in the quiet dining parlor alone, as no one else was yet down. Then he set off, pamphlets and a map his uncle had provided in hand.

Taking his uncle's advice into account, Alec decided to bypass Beaworthy proper and start on the outskirts of town.

He walked to the Sheepwash Road and headed east out of the village. A hedgerow lined one side, a stream and meadow the other. The ding of cowbells and bawl of sheep announced his passing. He came first to a small house with an outbuilding—a forge, perhaps. He didn't think a blacksmith or his offspring likely clients and walked on without stopping.

Some distance farther, he saw a tidy white cottage with a thatched roof. It reminded him of his uncle's house. Perhaps a merchant or a professional of some sort lived there. A rope swing suggested children—promising indeed. Steeling himself, he walked up to the front door and knocked.

A neat middle-aged woman answered.

Alec doffed his hat. "Good day, madam. I am Mr. Alec Valcourt, lately of London, but newly arrived in Beaworthy. I am a dancing and fencing master, and am well acquainted with all the new and fashionable dances. Have you children, madam? Dancing is an important accomplishment for young ladies and gentlemen, you know."

The woman frowned. "No, sir. We want nothing to do with dancing here. Now be on your way and don't come back." She shut the door before Alec could say another word.

By midday, Alec had knocked at four more promising-looking houses, with similar results. *Don't give up,* he told himself. *You can do this.*

He saw a prosperous-looking farmhouse across the field, flanked by a barn and woodshed. *One more,* he told himself. He was met by a friendly dog that wagged his tail and offered his head to be patted. Alec didn't oblige him, but still thought it a good sign. He knocked, and the door was opened by a mustachioed man of perhaps forty years.

Again Alec introduced himself and offered lessons, tensing as he awaited the man's reaction.

"Ohhh . . . !" the man said as though Alec had given him the answer to a deep mystery. "Saw you stop by the Williamses' place across the way. Wondered what you was sellin'. Sent you on yer way and sharp-like, did they?"

"Yes," Alec admitted.

"Coulda told ya that. The Williamses and most folks in these parts are tenant farmers—workin' Buckleigh land. Not me." His chest puffed out as he spoke. "I own my land outright. And my son Bertrand helps me farm it."

"So . . ." Alec began hopefully, "might you be interested in dancing lessons for yourself or your son?"

The yeoman farmer considered this, then asked, "Will dancin' help me farm my land? Help Bertie plant our crops?"

"Not directly," Alec allowed. "Though it is excellent exercise and develops grace—"

"Me and Bertie get plenty of exercise round here, I can tell you. And we have precious little need of grace. But I thank you just the same and wish you well."

Alec swallowed the rest of his argument. "Then, can you think of anyone who might be interested in dancing or fencing lessons?"

The farmer crossed his thick arms and pursed his lower lip. "If I were you, I'd go see the Stricklands out Holsworthy way. Always did think they were better than the rest of us. Just your sort, I imagine. No offense."

Alec forced a smile.

It was too late in the day to start off for Holsworthy on foot, so Alec decided he would call in at the private girls' school—one of the few places Uncle Ramsay had pointed out on his map as a potential client.

Alec walked back toward town and took the side lane his uncle had marked. A square stone house with a tiled roof came into view. A small plaque on the gate read *Miss Llewellyn's Boarding and Day School for Girls*.

Alec's heart lifted. He'd taught regular dance classes at several girls' seminaries in London. Such schools were always hiring drawing and dancing masters to enhance their curriculum. He would be well received here, he thought.

The schoolmistress—a plain, slender woman in her late twenties—received him in her parlor with reserved civility. She accepted one of his pamphlets and regarded it wistfully. Looking up from its text, she sighed. "While I would very much like to offer my girls the opportunity to learn dancing, I am afraid I can't."

Alec's stomach fell, but he managed to keep his expression neutral. "May I ask why not?"

She nodded. "Lady Amelia Midwinter is our primary benefactor, you see. She offers scholarships for worthy girls who could not otherwise afford tuition. And she and her daughter tutor my younger pupils in reading from time to time."

Alec was surprised to hear it.

Miss Llewellyn pointed across the room. "Lady Amelia even gave us that harpsichord for my pupils to play. She has been generosity itself, and I could not go against her wishes in this."

The schoolmistress rose, her long-lashed eyes sad. "But thank you for thinking of us."

Alec returned home, tired, hungry, and discouraged. The meager dinner at his uncle's table did little to cheer or strengthen him. Nor did having to relay his utter lack of success.

After dinner, Aurora and their mother withdrew to the sitting room. When they'd gone, Uncle Ramsay said, "Alec, I've been thinking. If you're going to seek pupils in Holsworthy or farther afield, you ought to have a way to get there." He rose and gestured for Alec to follow. "Come with me."

Alec followed his uncle outside to the stable around back. His uncle unlatched the stable door and stepped inside. As Alec entered, the sharp, musty smell of hay, leather, and manure struck him. Inside were three stalls, two occupied with horses and one with straw and hay.

His uncle turned and beamed at him. "He's all yours, if you can manage him."

"What?"

Uncle Ramsay pointed to the sandy brown horse in the first stall. "The dun horse. The Cleveland bay is my carriage horse."

Alec narrowed his eyes. His practical, penny-wise uncle was *giving* him a horse? There must be a catch. He asked, "What do you mean, *manage* him?"

"He isn't terribly well trained, or behaved for that matter," his uncle allowed. "I should have known, when a client signed him over to cover my fees."

"You've ridden him?"

"Once." His uncle pulled a face. "It was not a long ride. I own I haven't taken the time to work with him. My offices are within easy walking distance. And I take the carriage for longer trips. Besides, I have little interest in pleasure riding . . . and less in breaking my neck."

"I am surprised you haven't sold him."

Uncle Ramsay shrugged. "Probably should have. Oddly enough I think my bay likes having a friend. I don't take the carriage out as often as I once did. I imagine he'd get lonely living out here all alone."

A strange bleakness lit his uncle's eyes. Cornelius Ramsay knew something about living alone, Alec realized. He wondered if his uncle had been lonely before they'd arrived. Was he lonely still?

As if sensing his nephew's scrutiny and the direction of his thoughts, the man cleared his throat and said brusquely, "Well?"

Alec considered the prospect. "I am sorry, Uncle. But I cannot afford a horse's upkeep. Not until my financial situation improves."

"I realize that." Uncle Ramsay waved a dismissive hand. "Have you experience with horses?"

"Not much, I'm afraid."

"Know how to saddle one?"

"No."

"Well then, more for you to learn." He clapped Alec's shoulder and inhaled. "It's time you discovered there's more to life than dancing."

Perhaps, Alec thought. Though he doubted he would like it as well, or be half as good at it. Even so, the idea of having his own horse appealed to him. Very gentlemanlike, horsemanship was. He was no expert, but this seemed a fine-looking animal, with a dark line along its spine and black points in sharp contrast to his sandy coat. This was no old nag he should be embarrassed to be seen riding. But then again, he had no desire to break *his* neck either.

His uncle added, "Abe can even saddle him for you, if you like."

"Thank you, Uncle. What's his name?"

"His original name was Apollo. But I simply call him Dun. Fitting, don't you think? Since my client was in *dun territory* when he handed him over to settle his debts." His uncle's mouth quirked in a rare display of humor. "Well. I shall leave the two of you to become acquainted."

Once Uncle Ramsay returned to the house, Alec approached the stall tentatively, hand extended, wondering if he appeared as foolish as he felt. *A horse is not a hound, Valcourt,* he thought, but did not know if there was a better way to greet an unfamiliar horse. The creature stiffened, then turned its long muzzle in Alec's direction and whickered an airy trill of question. Its watchful, long-lashed eyes reminded him of the sad-eyed schoolmistress.

"It's all right, boy. I mean you no harm," Alec said in a low voice.

The horse did not jerk away as he feared. Instead Alec was able to reach out and touch its coarse forelock. The horse sniffed his outstretched hand, and Alec felt the velvety lips, wiry whiskers, and warm breath. He wished he had a carrot or a lump of sugar in his pocket.

Alec wondered if he could manage to bridle him, or at least get a lead around his neck. He looked this way and that for a halter or hackamore and instead saw his uncle's manservant, Abe, walk into the stable, eyeing him curiously.

"Hello."

The old man nodded his grizzled grey head and began polishing harnesses.

"My uncle said you might saddle him for me tomorrow."

Abe nodded. "Aye. Saddlin' him is the easy part. What time do you want him ready?"

"I'd like to arrive in Holsworthy by nine. Shall we say . . . seven thirty? Is that enough time, do you think?"

"Oh, plenty of time, I'd say. More than enough."

Alec didn't like the knowing look in the man's eye but said nothing more.

Dance developed strength and began a basic training that was foundational for lessons in fencing and riding. Indeed fencing masters often doubled as dancing masters, which demonstrates the proximity of the two arts.

—Kate van Orden,
Music, Discipline, and Arms in Early Modern France

Chapter 4

In the morning, Alec rose early, washed, and dressed. Since he planned to ride, he selected a pair of cord breeches and his caped Carrick coat. Then he pulled on a pair of Wellington boots he'd purchased last year because they were fashionable, not because he rode. They would certainly come in handy now that he had a horse.

As Alec buttoned his coat, he glanced out his small window down into the paddock. Abe stood there with the dun horse. The old man-servant reached up and forced the bit between the horse's large teeth and the leather bridle over its head and black ears, though the creature jerked up his chin in silent protest. Then Abe went to work on the saddle. Perhaps the horse was better behaved than his uncle had led him to believe.

Alec finished dressing and combing his hair, then went downstairs for another solitary breakfast of toasted bread and tea. Remembering his resolve to make friends with the horse, he helped himself to a few lumps of sugar from the sideboard and pocketed them.

He also wrapped a thick slice of bread and another of cheese in a table napkin, in case he was absent for the midday meal, as he'd been the day before. His uncle's cook-housekeeper strode in from the kitchen while he did so, and he felt like a thief, caught. Mrs. Dobb gave him a suspicious, resentful look, then returned to the kitchen with a sniff.

Alec would be glad when he'd begun earning money and could contribute to the household funds—and eat without guilt.

He quietly left the house and walked back to the paddock. He let himself inside the fence and approached the horse cautiously. The horse looked over his shoulder and watched him in wary interest, nostrils flaring. Did he smell the sugar?

"Good morning, boy," Alec said quietly.

He saw his uncle's manservant hovering in the doorway of the adjacent stable. "Thank you, Abe," he called.

"Don't thank me yet."

Alec offered a lump of sugar on his flat, open hand. The horse sniffed it, then puckered his lips and took a tentative nibble that tickled Alec's palm. The horse managed to get the sugar into its mouth, the bit clearly little hindrance. *So far so good.*

Alec reached up and grasped the saddle with one hand, then raised his foot to the stirrup. The horse stepped to the side, taking Alec's captured boot with him, causing Alec to hop on his grounded foot to keep from falling. "Steady, steady on," he quietly urged.

"Shall I hold him for you, lad?" Abe offered.

"No, I'm all right, thank you."

Alec managed to yank his boot from the stirrup, tugged his coat back into place, and patted the horse's withers. "You're all right," he murmured. "I won't hurt you. You don't mind the saddle, see? And I am not such a heavy man. Not like my uncle."

He wondered again why his uncle, who ate so abstemiously, managed to remain portly.

He tried once more to mount, but the horse again shied to the side. The tied rein limited his range of motion, yet his rear end fanned nearly to the fence. Thinking the horse could not back away farther,

Alec tried to mount again, but the horse sidestepped in the opposite direction—forcing Alec to leap backward to stay out from under his hooves and finally pressing Alec against the fence.

Oof. Alec felt the air pushed from his lungs.

"Doesn't like to be ridden," Abe observed.

"You don't say," Alec murmured dryly.

Alec met the horse's big brown eyes. "All right. You win for today." He pushed the horse away to gain a breath and a foothold on the fence. The horse yielded and resumed its original position with an air of offended dignity.

Alec decided he would put off the trip to distant Holsworthy until the following day, hoping by then the horse would have grown more accustomed to him and allow him to ride. For today, Alec would walk west out of town, as he had walked east the day before.

Leaving his uncle's property, Alec walked into the village, passing the inn and several shops, all relatively quiet at this hour. As he neared the bakery, he noticed an old man asleep on a bench outside. *Sleeping it off?* Alec wondered. He tried to ignore the warm savory smells coming from the shop as he passed.

The bakery door opened with a jingle, and a woman with faded ginger hair emerged. She looked vaguely familiar, though Alec didn't think he'd met her before.

"Halloo! Mr. Valcourt?"

Alec paused, and the short, buxom woman asked, "Venturing out again today, I see?"

"Um . . . yes," he replied.

"And what has my sister given you to eat?"

"Your sister?" He didn't even know the woman.

"Martha Dobb, of course. Works for your uncle."

"Oh!" Perhaps that explained why she looked familiar. There was a slight resemblance between the two, though Mrs. Dobb was painfully thin while this woman was pleasingly plump. Alec faltered, "She . . . em . . . allowed me to, um, choose as I liked."

She eyed him shrewdly, hands on hips. "Which means she gave

you exactly nothing, and allows you very little indeed." She held out her palm. "Let's have it."

Alec felt like a wayward schoolboy producing a frog from his pocket as he pulled forth the bread and cheese.

She eyed it with displeasure and wrinkled her nose. "As I suspected. Wait here." She walked away with his meal.

"But I—"

"No buts."

She returned a few moments later, holding forth a thick, fragrant pasty lying on a square of brown paper within the same table napkin.

Alec salivated at the sight and aroma.

"But I can't afford—"

"Psht," she shushed him. "We'll call it a trade." She placed the meat-and-potato-filled pastry into his palm. Still warm.

She tsked and shook her head. "That sister of mine. A young man needs more than a slice of bread and cheese to see him through the day."

"I am not certain how long I shall be gone, or—"

"Never mind. I doubt you've had a decent meal since you arrived. You stop by and see me every morning before you head out. You hear? It shall be our secret."

"I . . . Thank you, Mrs. . . . ?"

She pointed at the sign above the door as though he were daft. *Tickle's Bakery.*

"I am Mrs. Tickle, of course. Famous throughout the world for my pies and pasties. Or at least throughout the parish." She winked.

Alec found he hadn't the heart or iron will to refuse the woman's gift, though he wondered at her reason. Apparently she had taken pity on him. Whatever the case he—and his stomach—was grateful.

He thanked the woman again and walked away. Glancing over his shoulder, he saw her hand his bread and cheese to the old man sleeping on the bench outside her bakery. "There you are, Mr. Gawman. Breakfast!"

Late that afternoon, after another fruitless day, Alec trudged back through Beaworthy. He noticed flower baskets filled with dry, dead flowers hanging listlessly from lampposts. He continued along the walkway, detouring around the greengrocer's crates and giving way to a shoemaker carrying a roll of leather into his shop.

Returning to the walkway, something in the window of a second-hand shop caught his eye and Alec paused to look. There beside a display of old toys, tinware, and copper kettles, he saw a flute. Its price card bore two crossed-out numbers, leaving a third, pathetically low price. Alec wondered whose it had been. He could guess why the owner no longer had occasion to play it. For a moment Alec stood there looking at that instrument: tarnished, silent, and sad. Like Beaworthy itself.

With a sigh, Alec forced himself to walk into the inn to ask about an assembly room. He entered the beamed taproom with several open fireplaces and crossed the flagstone floor.

The short, slight innkeeper looked up from behind his counter.

"Good afternoon." Alec removed his hat. "Are you the proprietor here?"

"I am. Jones is the name."

"And I'm Alec Valcourt. New to Beaworthy."

"You don't say," quipped a thin man slouched on a stool nearby. "And I'm Alvin Deane. *Old* to Beaworthy." He chuckled at his own joke.

Mr. Jones rolled his eyes. "Ignore him. What can I do for ya, Mr. Valcourt?"

"I was . . . em, admiring your inn from outside and wondered if you had an assembly room."

The two older men shared a look, smiles fading.

Jones said, "In a manner of speaking, yes."

"May I see it?" Alec asked.

"Suit yerself." Jones nodded toward the stairwell. "Top of the stairs."

Mr. Deane, a man with a gentle face and thinning hair, unfolded his tall self from the stool. "I'll go up with ya. Miss seein' it."

"Take a lamp," Jones advised.

Mr. Deane did so, and Alec gestured for him to lead the way.

At the top of the stairs, Mr. Deane crossed the passage to a set of double doors. He pulled one open with a squeak and led the way inside. The candle lamp projected an arc of light into the dim, musty room. Boxes and crates were stacked haphazardly about, and a row of barrels blocked their way. "Become a storeroom, sad to say."

They stepped around the barrels, and Alec surveyed the long, modest-sized room, like so many used for public balls. On one side stood a shrouded harpsichord. Chairs lined the opposite wall and at the far end lay a raised platform for musicians.

It was perfect. Alec wondered if Mr. Jones might allow him to clean up the assembly room and use it to teach lessons, assuming he ever found any pupils.

"How long since it's been used?" Alec asked.

"Oh . . ." The man puffed his cheeks and blew out a breath. "I think it was December four or five years ago. Had ourselves a Christmas concert. Used to have one every year, before the old rector died. He organized the affair and gathered us together to rehearse."

"And the last dance?"

Mr. Deane gave him a sharp look. "Back before you were breeched, I'd wager."

Alec shook his head. "That is a long time."

"Don't I know it. Should have seen this place then. . . ." His eyes took on a distant wistfulness. "Men from shops and forges turned gentlemen-musicians in Sunday best. Ladies in frocks every color of springtime. Hopeful spinsters dancin' with our rector. Schoolboys with their mums. Pretty girls and eager lads . . ."

"You're quite the poet, Mr. Deane."

"Hardly. Just cursed with a good memory." He turned. "Let's go down. Jones'll wonder what became of us. And the missus will scold if I'm not home in two shakes."

When they returned to the taproom, Mr. Deane retrieved his hat and bid them both good-night.

Alec turned to the innkeeper. "An excellent room, Mr. Jones. How sad to see it sit idle. I don't suppose you would consider letting it out?"

Mr. Jones shook his head. "Not for dancing, son. I've heard what you've been about this week, and yer wastin' yer time, I can tell you."

"It certainly feels that way."

"Don't you know dancing isn't done here? I'm surprised yer uncle hasn't told ya."

"He told me, but I don't understand why. Do you?"

A horn blew outside, announcing the arrival of a coach. In a matter of moments, the innkeeper was busy filling pints and taking orders for supper. Alec knew his questions would have to wait.

He waved to a harried Mr. Jones, who acknowledged the gesture with a terse nod. Replacing his hat, Alec took his leave.

As he crossed the High Street, a man stepped from his uncle's law office. "Mr. Valcourt?"

Alec paused. "Yes?"

"Milton Pugsworth. Your uncle's senior clerk." The stout, homely man appeared to be near Alec's own age.

"How do you do, Mr. Pugsworth."

"I am well, thank you. Listen, I hear you mean to teach dancing lessons. Is that right?"

"I hope to, yes. It was my profession in London."

Mr. Pugsworth nodded. "Your uncle confided as much. He's worried you'll have your eye blackened going door to door. And vex a few important personages in the bargain."

"So he has said."

"Between you and me, I'd be keen to improve my own dancing skills, would it not irk your uncle and no doubt several clients. And I'm afraid there is scarce little space in the rooms I share with Bixby." He pointed to the windows above. "But if you ever open a place of your own, do let me know."

"I shall."

Mr. Pugsworth chewed his thick lower lip. "Do I understand correctly that you called in at Miss . . . at the girls' school?"

"I did." Alec nodded. "Yesterday."

"And . . . may I ask what the schoolmistress said?"

"Miss Llewellyn declined my offer."

"Oh." The man looked surprisingly crestfallen.

Alec added, "I will say she did so regretfully. Even . . . wistfully."

"Did she?" Pugsworth's eyes brightened. "I am glad to hear it." He added apologetically, "Not glad that she refused you, of course. But that she was sorry to do so."

"It eased the sting, I admit. But why should that please you?"

"Oh, it's only that . . . Well, I met Miss Llewellyn at a public ball in Holsworthy. Only the once, you see. She hasn't been back."

"Ah. I understand," Alec said, thinking again of the schoolmistress's reluctance to go against Lady Amelia's wishes. *Generous benefactor, indeed.*

After dinner that night, Alec went out to the stable to spend time with his horse. He plied the dun gelding with sugar as before and patted his neck. Again Abe saddled the horse for him, and again Alec tried to mount the skittish creature. He managed to get his leg over the gelding's back only to be tossed onto his backside. He looked up in time to see old Abe bite back a grin.

Alec gingerly rose, dusting off his backside, disgusted to find he'd got more than dirt on his trousers. Inwardly he sighed.

It really wasn't his day.

❦

By Saturday night, Alec found himself longing for the Sabbath with a zeal due less to the prospect of worship than the thought of an extra hour of sleep, and rest from another round of disheartening calls. Even strengthened by Mrs. Tickle's pies, it had been the longest week in Alec's memory, and at the end of it, he had very little to show for his efforts. He had been set upon by dogs and a vicious goose. Thrown from his horse and forced to walk many miles each day. He'd been scoffed at and stared at like a man with two heads. True, he had been received civilly by several others, though declined just the same in the end.

He did have a few nibbles from the calls he'd made farther afield.

A few families said "someday" but had little time or money to spare at present. The most promising among them were the Stricklands—a wealthy family who lived between Beaworthy and Holsworthy. They were interested in lessons for their son, although not until he returned from school for the Easter and summer vacations. The Millmans, a merchant family from nearby Shebbear, were also interested in lessons for their twins, but they preferred to wait until Alec had acquired other pupils with whom their children might practice.

Even if the latter two possibilities came to pass, Alec knew three pupils would not be enough.

On Sunday morning, Alec forced aside the temptation to stay in bed, and rose with a groan. He knew it was his duty as the man of the family to escort his mother and sister to church—and his obligation to his uncle, who had been so generous in hosting them and who expected them to attend. As newcomers, he'd said, they must do all they could to establish respectable reputations.

It wasn't that Alec didn't deem God worthy of worship. But his view of the Almighty had taken a blow of late. Alec had grown up believing God was someone like his kindly, benevolent grandfather—at least hoping that was true. Though there were times he feared God might be more like his disapproving father, who was as parsimonious in serving up morsels of praise as Uncle Ramsay was in serving food. Colin Valcourt had never been satisfied with Alec, always remonstrating him for his reticent manner, his reluctance to push more lessons on families who could ill afford them, or in soliciting business from strangers. And then, of course, came the disillusionment over Miss Underhill.

Since then Alec had attended church, prayed, read Scripture, and did his best to obey it, because he feared God's judgment and was keenly aware he needed forgiveness. But the love of God felt very distant.

Seated in his uncle's pew a short while later, Alec glanced across the nave and noticed that all five of the Allens were in attendance, though he did not recall having seen them the week before.

In the pew in front of them, he glimpsed Miss Midwinter, lovely in profile, with pert nose and full lips and a dangling coil of honey hair artfully escaping a lacy pink bonnet. Lady Amelia sat ramrod straight beside her, a small veiled hat atop a tight coil of dark auburn hair.

Throughout the service, Alec continued to observe Miss Midwinter, subtly he hoped, though he did catch his sister regarding him quizzically when he turned his head at last. He met Aurora's raised-brow gaze with an innocent smile. He doubted he fooled her but had no intention of explaining why he watched Miss Midwinter. He barely understood it himself.

After the service, the curate exited down the center aisle, and the congregation began filing out after him. Alec lingered, making a show of looking for a lost glove. He watched as Lady Amelia greeted the Allens. Behind her, Julia Midwinter stopped to greet several young girls clustered around the schoolmistress like ducklings. Then Julia took Miss Allen's arm and walked with her down the aisle.

Patience Allen's face lit up when she saw him. "Mr. Valcourt! How good to see you again."

He bowed. "Miss Allen. How do you do. And . . . ?" He looked at her companion expectantly. He knew very well who she was but had an illogical longing to give her a setdown.

Patience quickly responded, "Miss Midwinter, have you met Mr. Valcourt? Forgive me, I thought you had been introduced."

"We have," Miss Midwinter said dryly. "Evidently it was not a memorable occasion."

"Of course. Now I remember." Alec smiled. "Miss Midwinter, a pleasure to see you again."

She coolly dipped her head.

Patience said, "I told Miss Midwinter how you came to Walter's rescue last week. She was most impressed."

Miss Midwinter did not *look* impressed. She asked, "Do you make it a habit to trespass in our woods?"

So she *had* seen him last Sunday. And she wasn't happy about it.

Patience looked from him to her friend in confusion. "Surely you jest, Julia. It is not as though he is a poacher. And I thank God he did happen by, for poor Walter's sake."

Julia eyed him shrewdly. "And what is it you do when you are not prowling about the woods, Mr. Valcourt?"

"I . . ." He hesitated, uncertain he ought to mention his profession.

He was saved from answering by the hearty greetings of Sir Herbert and Lady Allen. They reiterated their gratitude and assurance of a future dinner invitation and then departed.

When the Allens had left, Alec found himself standing alone with Miss Midwinter, while her mother conversed with an elderly parishioner several yards away.

He suddenly felt tongue-tied.

She said, "Patience mentioned you are a Londoner."

"That's right."

"How dreary and boring you must find Beaworthy."

"It would be impolite to agree with you, miss."

She gave him a wry glance. "And dishonest to disagree?"

He felt a grin quirk his lip, and she grinned in reply, eyes sparkling.

Alec's chest tightened in attraction. *Don't be a fool*, he told himself. Had he learned nothing?

"I would enjoy hearing about your life there," she said. "All the social events and theatre and balls and routs. Shocking as it may seem, I have never been."

"That is a shame, indeed."

Emboldened by her mention of the word *ball*, he admitted, "I am afraid I was not at my leisure to enjoy all that London has to offer. Though balls, yes. Often. You see, I was a dancing master there." He steeled himself for her reaction.

"A dancing master?" she echoed, fair brows rising.

"Yes. I know that is not—"

"In Beaworthy?" she interrupted.

"Well, we didn't know about—"

Miss Midwinter tipped back her head of curls and laughed. The rippling peal of gleeful amazement boomed across the reverent nave.

He might have found the sound charming, were it not so humiliating. Across the pews, parishioners still clustered in hushed conversation turned, mouths gaped. Lady Amelia, he saw, frowned darkly.

Unaware of the stir she had caused, or not caring, Miss Midwinter chuckled. "That is too rich. You do know where you've landed, don't you?"

"My uncle has since told me about the unwritten law. And I've seen for myself the disapproval and even fear caused by the mere mention of dancing."

She shook her head, eyes bright with mirth. "Poor Mr. Valcourt."

Lady Amelia appeared at her daughter's elbow, her smile tight. "Julia, it is past time we took our leave."

As they departed, Alec glanced about for his family, but his mother and sister had preceded him out of the church while he had lingered. He picked up his hat and gloves and walked down the aisle. At the open doorway, he shook the curate's hand and stepped outside.

The Allens were climbing into their chaise. Walter raised a hand in greeting before ducking his head to enter the carriage—but not low enough—and had to make a mad grab for his hat before it fell. With a sheepish grin, Walt disappeared inside, the whole carriage lurching under his weight. Alec was glad for a reason to smile.

∽✑

A driving rain kept Alec home on Monday morning. He used the time to review his grandfather's book on the positions of the German waltz, and then decided to compose an advertisement for the *West of England Journal and General Advertiser*, or the *West Briton*.

> *Mr. Alec Valcourt, professor of dancing and fencing,*
> *has the honour to announce his arrival from London;*
> *where he taught all the traditional and fashionable dances.*
> *He therefore hopes to merit a portion of public patronage.*
> *Quadrilles, minuets, and country dancing completely taught in*
> *six private lessons for one guinea. Schools and families attended.*

By midday, the rain had cleared and the sky brightened. Alec's mood had not, however. He wondered—even began to doubt—whether an advertisement would do any good when personal calls had not. Perhaps he ought to wait until he found a place to let.

Alec and his mother and sister had just sat down to a sparse midday meal, when Uncle Ramsay unexpectedly entered the dining parlor. He had walked home to join them, though he usually remained in his office all day and had a bite at his desk.

His eyes shone and his thin mouth quirked in an eager smile. "I have just learnt of an opening at the clay works outside of town. Mr. Kellaway is a client of mine, and I am quite certain he'll take you on if I ask him."

Alec blinked, dread filling his gut. Tentatively, he asked, "In the office, you mean? As a clerk or . . . ?"

Uncle Ramsay shook his head. "Advancement may be possible eventually, perhaps even to assistant assayer. But first you'll need to start in the yard as a cutter." He regarded his well-groomed nephew. "Not afraid of getting your hands dirty, I hope."

Alec noticed his sister bite her lip and send him an apologetic look.

"Afraid, no," Alec replied. "But I make every effort to avoid doing so." He winked at his sister. It *was* one of his foibles, he knew. But, dash it, gloves were expensive.

"Please, Alec," his mother said softly. "At least try."

"But a clay works, Mamma? Manual labor?" It would be a waste of his talents and skills. It wasn't what he was good at. Made for.

"Good honest work, my boy. Nothing to be ashamed of." Cornelius Ramsay sat down and tucked a table napkin into his waistcoat.

Alec was not afraid of hard work. He would gladly work tirelessly to build a business or to train others. And he loved nothing better than dancing or fencing until every muscle ached. Yet he had always considered himself a gentleman. A coattail gentleman, perhaps, but at least he had always looked the part. Like his grandfather and father before him, he was well educated, well spoken, and well dressed.

His uncle sat there looking at Alec, awaiting his reply.

Keenly aware of his mother's pleading expression, Alec swallowed a hot retort and managed, "I shall think about it, Uncle."

After the meal, his uncle left to return to his office, and Alec retreated to his small room beneath the eaves. He wanted quiet solitude to think, hoping to formulate some alternative plan to taking a job at the clay works. Or failing that, to lie down and sleep to forget his troubles for a while.

But he had only just removed his coat when Aurora knocked and announced they had visitors—Miss Midwinter and Miss Allen had come to call, bearing gifts. Suddenly Alec forgot his plans for a nap. He put his coat back on, checked his appearance in the small mirror above the washstand, and followed his sister downstairs.

His mother smiled up at him from the entry hall. "Miss Midwinter and Miss Allen have brought us jam and a lovely tin of China tea."

"To welcome you." Patience Allen smiled shyly.

Alec said, "That is very kind."

Miss Midwinter added, "And we thought we would offer you and your sister a proper tour of Beaworthy, if you are interested. It is a lovely afternoon."

Alec had thought knowledge of his former profession might repel Miss Midwinter. Apparently, it had worked the opposite effect. "Thank you. That sounds quite . . . edifying."

"Will you join us as well, Mrs. Valcourt?" Miss Allen asked, all politeness.

"Thank you, no. You young people go ahead."

Aurora gathered her bonnet and gloves. Alec his hat, gloves, and stick. Together they strolled from his uncle's cottage, and up the Buckleigh Road into the village.

Alec had been through Beaworthy several times, but now he saw it with more interest. How different to walk at his leisure, in the company of two beautiful, accomplished young ladies—three, if he counted Aurora.

As they walked up the High Street, Miss Midwinter pointed out her favorite shops. Alec noted his uncle's office and waved to Mr. Pugsworth, apparently returning from his midday meal at the inn. Outside the greengrocer's, Alec saw Mr. Deane arranging bundled stalks of rhubarb in a raised crate. A woman's shrill voice called from within, and Mr. Deane scurried inside.

Patience pointed out the market hall, which sat on a small green amid the cobbled High Street. The half-timbered structure was supported by columns like a house on stilts over an open-sided pavilion beneath. She explained that on market days, sheep were driven through, and stalls were set up where merchants and farmers sold wares and produce. The room above was used for village council meetings and other parish gatherings.

A young man in workman's clothes plodded wearily up the street. His coat was worn, short at the sleeves, and dusted with white, as was his flat cap. Noticing their party, the man stepped onto the street to give them a wide berth as they passed.

Alec was surprised when Miss Midwinter turned and addressed the young man.

"Mr. Thorne, is it not?"

The workman turned, surprised and wary, but then his eyes lit with recognition.

"Miss Midwinter." He smiled, swiped the cap from his head, and bowed. Alec saw that his black hair was speckled with white, like a serious case of dandruff.

"Thank you again, miss, for coming to our aid that day. You were a godsend."

Miss Midwinter smiled and dipped her head. "I was happy to help."

Self-conscious, the man said, "Please forgive my appearance. I've just come from the clay works."

So that was what a man looked like after working there. Alec shuddered.

While Miss Midwinter spoke with the young man, Patience stepped nearer Alec and Aurora and quietly explained, "A couple of ruffians threatened him and his sister last week, and Julia intervened."

Aurora breathed, "What did she do?"

Patience sighed. "I will just say, don't anger her when she has her riding crop in hand."

Alec felt his brows rise and made note to remember that.

He heard Miss Midwinter politely ask the man, "And how is your sister? Those two have not bothered you again, I trust. You both fare well?"

He momentarily hesitated, then said, "Yes, Tess is quite well, thank you. She will be much obliged when I tell her you asked."

"Yes, please do greet her for me."

The man bowed again and went on his way. At the wheelwright's, he turned down a narrow side street.

Once he had disappeared from view, the tour continued. But Alec would not soon forget the young man's appearance.

On the small patch of turf beside the market hall stood an unusual fountain. At least Alec assumed the statue was a fountain, though he saw no water.

Patience explained, "My father says water from an underground spring used to flow through it, but the spring has long since dried up. Now its only function is ornamental."

"What is it, exactly?" Aurora asked, her brow puckered.

They all squinted up at the female figure, with arms reaching upward but head bowed. She stood barefooted on a sandstone base, into which links of a chain had been carved.

"Looks like a captive to me," Miss Midwinter said. "See those chains at her feet? She's a prisoner here."

"But the chains are broken," Aurora observed.

"And look at her bowed head and raised hands," Patience said. "I think she's praying."

Alec murmured, "Looks like a dancer to me."

He felt Miss Midwinter's gaze on his profile. "Yes, you would see that," she said in a quiet aside.

Apparently, she had not shared news of his profession with her friend Patience. He wondered if she had told Lady Amelia.

"Don't tell my mother it looks like a dancer," she said, as if reading his mind. "She'll have the thing dismantled."

She grinned slyly, and they walked on.

"See that large stone there?" She pointed to a massive stone between the church and the inn.

Alec nodded. "Yes, I've noticed it before."

Miss Midwinter told them the legend of the stone falling from the devil's pocket, the tradition of turning it every autumn until last year's failure, and the predictions of doom to come.

Then she smiled at him. "Perhaps *you* are the devil come to visit us."

"Julia!" Patience looked stricken at her friend's words. "You ought not tease about such things." She turned wide eyes to Alec. "She didn't mean it, Mr. Valcourt."

"I can think of one person in particular who would think him devilish," Miss Midwinter insisted.

"Julia, stop," Patience pleaded. "Besides, Mr. Valcourt cannot be the . . . em, you know. The prediction is about the *return* of . . . said being."

"Have you ever been to Beaworthy before, Mr. Valcourt, to visit your uncle?" Miss Midwinter asked.

"No, I had never been here before in my life."

"Hmm . . ." Miss Midwinter studied him through narrowed eyes. "Very well. Then I shall keep looking."

William Turner, Lately arrived from LONDON, Begs Leave to acquaint the Gentlemen and Ladies of the Town and Country, that he continues to teach the polite Art of Dancing and Fencing in the newest and most approved Method.

—*Boston Gazette & Country Journal*, 1774

Chapter 5

A t dinner that night, Uncle Ramsay again broached the topic of the clay works, urging Alec not to wait too long or the position would be snapped up by someone else. Alec thanked his uncle for his concern, even as he still inwardly chafed at the notion. Was there really no other way to support his mother and sister? He didn't want to give up his profession, his dream, so easily. There had to be something he could do.

Agitated by the prospect of working in the clay pits, Alec took himself out for another walk that night. He strode back through the village, determined to check every shop window for hiring notices, hoping to find a way of escape.

At that hour the High Street was quiet. Most of the shops had closed, and the rooms above rumbled with dinnertime conversation and the occasional clatter of pots or cutlery.

Remembering fondly his village tour with Miss Midwinter and Miss Allen, Alec again walked past the shops, reading the signs over their doors or in their windows—wheelwright, shoemaker, greengrocer, bakery—but finding no one advertising for help.

The next window drew his attention by the conspicuous absence of either sign or wares. The lower windowpanes were papered over, obscuring any clues to the shop's identity. He had not noticed it before. He paused, stood on tiptoe, and peered inside. There was just enough twilight to see into the mostly empty room. A hodgepodge of crates stood stacked on wooden floorboards. A few mismatched chairs circled the perimeter, and a large dusty mirror hung on one wall.

His chest tightened. Exactly the kind of place he had hoped to find to start an academy, before he'd learned of the unwritten law against dancing.

Alec walked to the shop door, saw the padlock and above a small hand-lettered notice.

For let. Reasonable terms. Inquire at the inn.

Might it be possible? Would the innkeeper even rent to him? Alec had a little savings. Was it worth the risk? Anything would be better than working in the clay pits. . . .

As he stood there contemplating, he became aware of carriage wheels and the *clip-clop* of unhurried horses. He glanced over his shoulder at a fine barouche making its way up the High Street. Through its window, he saw Lady Amelia Midwinter, apparently on her way back to Buckleigh Manor. She looked from him to the deserted establishment behind him and back again. Her face appeared somber. Perhaps even disapproving. Was her expression due to whatever call she had just made, or from seeing him? Had she learned of his former profession? She did not smile or lift a hand in greeting. So neither did he.

The carriage moved on, past the church and inn, past the village green and market hall, and then turned down the Buckleigh Road. But even after the carriage had disappeared from view, Alec could still see Lady Amelia's somber face watching him. He shivered, then dragged himself home.

⌒⊙⌒

On Tuesday morning, Alec rose early with lead in his stomach. He had agreed to his uncle's request that he at least go out to the clay works, meet Mr. Kellaway, and see what the job entailed. Alec hoped he could still find a way to teach evening classes, but he accepted the fact that he might have to work during the day to support his family.

Time to gird up your loins, Valcourt, he told himself. *You can do this.*

While Alec cleaned his teeth, he pondered his wardrobe. He wasn't certain what one wore to seek a place at a clay works, so he selected one of his older coats, a pair of dark trousers, and boots, and he made do with a simple barrel knot for his cravat.

He breakfasted alone, as usual, took a piece of bread and cheese in case he was expected to start work straightaway, and left his uncle's house as quietly as possible.

He walked through the village and passed by the bakery and a slumbering Mr. Gawman. Alec didn't expect to be gone long, so he did not plan to stop and trade up his lunch, but the jingling bell of the bakery door and Mrs. Tickle's voice stopped him in his tracks.

"Halloo! Are you not forgetting something, Mr. Valcourt?"

He turned and saw the baker, one hand fisted on her ample hip, the other cradling a meat pie wrapped in brown paper.

Alec smiled. "Morning, Mrs. Tickle."

She said, "Off to Kellaway's today, I understand."

The woman seemed to know his business before he did. Apparently she and her sister spoke daily.

"Yes. I am going to take a look around, at least."

She held out her palm. "Well then, let's have it."

He hesitated. "But I'm not certain I shall even take the job."

She waved a plump, dismissive hand. "And if you do get hired on, you stop by and see me every morning, you hear? The work is hard at Kellaway's. You'll need to keep up your strength."

"Very well. Thank you, Mrs. Tickle." Alec handed a drowsy Mr. Gawman his bread and cheese, accepted Mrs. Tickle's pasty with a warm smile, and went on his way.

As Alec followed the main road west out of town, a gig rattled up beside him. Thinking the vehicle wished only to pass, Alec stepped farther to the side of the road.

The driver slowed his horse to match Alec's stride. Alec looked up curiously, but he did not recognize the man of some fifty years at the reins, with dark hair and long side-whiskers as black as his suit of clothes.

"A moment of your time, Mr. Valcourt."

Alec paused. He was quite certain he had not met the man before. Still, he stopped and waited as the man halted the horse and small gig.

"I am afraid you have me at a disadvantage, sir," Alec said. "For I don't know your name."

"I am Mr. Barlow—estate manager at Buckleigh Manor. You are acquainted with Lady Amelia Midwinter, I trust?"

"We have met, yes."

"Right. Well. Her ladyship wishes you to call in at Buckleigh Manor. This morning at ten."

Alec frowned. "Why should she wish to see me?"

"That is for her to explain," the man replied. "But I will say, it could very well be worth your while."

Had Lady Amelia read his mind when she saw him standing outside the empty storefront last night? Did she wish to warn him—make sure he understood dancing was unwelcome in her domain? As if his uncle hadn't already told him at every turn.

Alec said stiffly, "I am on my way to see Mr. Kellaway. I don't know that I shall have sufficient time to return and change by ten."

Mr. Barlow's eyes hardened. "Make time, Mr. Valcourt. This is not a lady you want to keep waiting."

The gig moved on, but Alec remained where he was, thinking. Then he made his decision. He would postpone the trip out to the clay works and see what Lady Amelia wanted first. His uncle would not want him to disappoint the lady of the manor.

He turned and made haste home, wishing again he could ride his horse. At his uncle's, he set aside his pie for later, and changed into his Sunday suit of clothes. He told himself he was not out to impress the woman, but knew he would feel more confident for whatever lay ahead if he were well dressed.

As his pocket watch marked the hour, Alec jogged through the estate gate, tipping his hat to the glaring lion as he hurried up the long drive. When the manor came into view, he slowed to a long-strided walk, hoping to appear at ease to anyone who happened to observe his approach.

Alec surveyed Buckleigh Manor in awe. It was a magnificent stone structure with a front portico supported by massive granite pillars. The manor overlooked an ornamental lake and was surrounded by luxurious lawns and topiary gardens scattered about in pleasing negligence. In the distance, he saw more trees and glimpsed the Dartmoor hills beyond.

In the vestibule, a stiff-lipped butler took his hat. "Her ladyship has been expecting you these two minutes gone."

"I am sorry," Alec panted, trying to catch his breath, and wondering why he was apologizing to the butler.

The black-suited man led him through the inner hall and showed him into the library. "Mr. Valcourt," he announced and then backed from the room, closing the door behind him.

Alec tried not to gape at the two-story library, with a gallery above. Two walls held floor-to-ceiling bookshelves, the third was primarily of windows, and the fourth was dominated by a broad marble hearth, framed by panels of rich green silk. He had been in impressive homes before, he reminded himself. But houses in town were not usually built to such a sprawling scale.

Lady Amelia looked up from an ornate desk near the fireplace, laid with a tasteful arrangement of silver writing implements, sealing jack, and a vase of silk flowers. Seeing him, she replaced her quill in its holder and gestured him closer with a regal hand.

Alec bowed. "I am sorry to have kept you waiting, your ladyship."

She waved away his apology with that same pale hand. "You do not yet work for me, Mr. Valcourt, so a delay of two minutes is of little concern."

Not yet work for her?

She regarded him with eyes that were either green or blue—it was difficult to tell. She appeared to be several years younger than his mother and would be quite a handsome woman, he thought, if not so severe. Discomfited by her imperious gaze, he glanced down at his hands.

"I understand you were formerly a dancing master." She said the words as though distasteful.

"That is correct, your ladyship. I taught dancing and fencing in London."

She studied him thoughtfully. "You are well spoken, Mr. Valcourt," she said. "May I ask about your education?"

He felt both eager and wary at once, not certain he wanted to work for this woman. "I was educated from a young age by my grandfather, and was later apprenticed as clerk to a London solicitor."

One thin brow rose. "Were you indeed?"

"My mother's idea."

"She hoped to interest you in another profession?"

"Yes."

A ghost of a smile. "As do I."

Alec shot her a look, trying not to frown. "I don't understand."

"I saw you standing outside the empty shop on the High Street. I hope you were not considering opening a dancing school of your own. You have undoubtedly learned by now that Beaworthy is not a propitious place for a dancing master."

"Thanks to you?" he asked before he could curb his tongue.

"Thanks to me," she acknowledged graciously, as though a compliment.

"May I ask why?"

"I am under no obligation to explain myself. Suffice it to say I have good reason to believe dancing—and dancing masters—to be insidious and dangerous."

"Dangerous? Not all dancing masters are corrupt or lecherous, your ladyship. If that's what you mean."

"I hope not. For I am prepared to offer you a position here in

Buckleigh Manor. As clerk. Assuming your uncle will vouch for your character."

His mind spun. It was a good offer. A good position. And the only mess he would get on his hands was the occasional smear of ink. But was it a bribe? Would he, by accepting, be agreeing never to teach dancing again? That he could not do.

Seeing him hesitate, Lady Amelia said, "I prefer not to speak of anything as vulgar as money, but Mr. Barlow will make certain your wages are more than fair."

Alec faltered. "But . . . why would you want me here?"

She entwined her slender fingers. "It is not that I particularly want you *here*, but that I don't want you elsewhere, doing . . . other things." She held his gaze.

He exhaled a dry laugh. "You mean to reform me, then?"

"By offering you an alternative livelihood, yes. That is the plan."

"You recall my saying that my mother tried that once already?"

"I do. But I think you will find I am nothing like your mother."

Their gazes locked, each weighing the expression, the fortitude, of the other.

"Very well," Alec said. "I accept. Gratefully."

Lady Amelia leaned back fractionally. "Good. You may start tomorrow." She stood and pulled a cord on the wall nearby.

The library door opened, and Mr. Barlow entered.

"Mr. Valcourt has agreed to join us," Lady Amelia announced. "Please advance his salary so he might purchase a suit of clothes befitting his new situation." She glanced at Alec. "Mr. Gilbert in the High Street will know what you need."

He was offended by the condescending suggestion but knew better than to object. He turned to follow the estate manager from the room.

Lady Amelia's voice reached him at the threshold. "And Mr. Valcourt?"

He turned back.

She ran her fingers over the highly polished desk. "I hope it goes without saying that, even though you are to work here under my roof, you are to have as little to do with Miss Midwinter as possible. You are not her social equal, you understand. She is destined for . . . greater things."

Alec's stomach soured, but this time he managed to hold his tongue.

❦

There was an air of celebration in his uncle's dining parlor that evening, as the family lifted glasses and offered prayers of thanksgiving for Alec's new position. There was even a cake from the bakery. Alec wondered if Mrs. Tickle had slipped inside and left it on the sideboard herself, or if Mrs. Dobb had actually purchased it for the occasion. He thought it wiser not to ask.

His uncle smiled broadly, and seemed in danger of popping the buttons off his waistcoat. Alec could imagine him boasting to his clients. "My nephew is clerk at Buckleigh Manor. Engaged by the earl's daughter herself. And how well he looks in his new black coat!"

His mother was all relieved happiness. Only Aurora, the sister who knew him so well, watched him with concerned eyes, clearly testing his outward appearance of gaiety and wondering if it was genuine.

Alec *was* glad to have a way to support his family that didn't involve dirty manual labor—that relief was genuine enough. Yet he had his reservations about working for the woman who had single-handedly laid waste his career and plans for the future.

At least for the present.

After dinner, Alec decided to walk to the bakery, hoping to catch Mrs. Tickle and let her know not to set aside any more pies for him. The stroll would also ease his stomach after the unusually filling dinner.

He walked into Beaworthy and up the High Street but found the bakery already closed for the evening. Turning back, he glanced once again at the unusual fountain—dry and lifeless. Like the village.

As he passed the wheelwright's on the corner, he recalled the young man Miss Midwinter had spoken with during their tour the day before. Curious, Alec turned down that side street. Ahead, he saw a narrow green tenement and that very young man sitting on the front stoop, whittling.

The dark-haired man looked up with a welcoming smile. "Hello. Fine evening, isn't it?"

"Yes, it is." Alec hesitated. "May I ask what you are making?"

The man shrugged. "Nothing really. Just an excuse to step outside and have a few moments to myself."

Alec nodded. "That I understand. It's why I'm out for a walk."

The man stuck out a strong hand. "Ben Thorne."

Alec glanced at it, trying not to notice the soiled nails, and shook it. "Alec Valcourt."

Following the direction of Alec's gaze, Ben said, "Sorry. Never clean these days, no matter how I scrub them. And I forever have white dust in my hair. I'm a cutter at the clay works, you see. Bring a bushel of clay dust home with me every night. My poor mother."

"Oh, I see." Alec was relieved all over again to have escaped that fate.

The man squinted up at him. "I don't think I've seen you around here before."

Clearly, he'd had eyes only for Miss Midwinter when they'd spoken on the street.

"I've only recently moved here with my mother and sister," Alec explained. "We are staying with my uncle, Mr. Ramsay."

"Ah yes. I've heard the name." Ben set aside his whittling and asked conversationally, "And what do you do for work, if I may ask?"

"I've just been offered a place at Buckleigh Manor."

"Have you, now?" Surprise lengthened the man's thin face. "Well, good for you. What sort of position?"

"Clerk."

Ben's eyes widened. "You don't say? I'm impressed. Well acquainted with her ladyship, are you?"

"Not really. I met her at church." *And her beautiful daughter,* he added to himself.

"Ah." Ben nodded in understanding. "My family are Bryanites. We have our own services. You should come along sometime. Far more lively than what you're accustomed to, I can tell you. Singing and dancing..."

"Dancing, you say? That's intriguing."

"Well, I don't mean a reel or minuet. Still, you won't be tempted to sleep through the service, I promise you."

Alec chuckled. "Have you been spying on me on Sundays?"

Ben grinned. "No. But my family attended St. Michael's before we joined up with the Bryanites, and I remember nodding off more than once. Come with us sometime. Sundays at four and Wednesdays at seven. We meet in the room above the market hall."

"Thank you. I'll think about it."

A young woman stepped out onto the stoop. "Who are you talking with, Benjamin?"

Thick, reddish-brown hair tumbled over her shoulders and framed a heart-shaped face with a hint of freckles. Dark chocolate eyes met his. Goodness, she was beautiful.

Ben rose and said, "This is Alec Valcourt. New to Beaworthy, and new clerk at the manor. Mr. Valcourt, my sister, Tess."

"How do you do, Mr. Valcourt." She did not smile. Yet her long-lashed eyes shone.

Alec bowed. "A pleasure to meet you, Miss Thorne."

Ben turned to his sister. "I was just inviting Mr. Valcourt to visit our services one of these days."

"Were you?" His sister nodded her approval. "Indeed I hope you shall, Mr. Valcourt."

She smiled then, the expression emphasizing her prominent cheek-bones and lovely teeth. Suddenly Alec thought he just might visit one day after all.

From the corner of his eye, Alec noticed two men sauntering up the street. Glancing toward them, Ben instantly stiffened. He said between clenched teeth, "Go inside, Tess."

Following his gaze, Tess paled and hurriedly complied.

The two men paused before them, one stout, one wiry, both muscled.

"Where's your sister gone in such a hurry?" the wiry one asked.

"To help our mother inside," Ben replied.

"Too bad."

The stout one eyed Alec. "Who's your friend, Ben?" His round cheeks and dark curls made him look boyish, but a man's muscles were evident beneath his layers of fat.

"Ain't he pretty?" the wiry one added, shaking the dark blond hair from his face. "Never seen such a pretty lad. Have you, Joe?"

"No, Felton. I ain't."

Alec held out his hand. "Alec Valcourt."

"Felton Wilcox," the wiry one said. "You probably heard of me."

Felton gripped Alec's hand hard. Too hard. Alec tried not to wince. "And this is my little brother, Joe."

"Valcourt?" Joe Wilcox asked. "Ain't that a French name?"

"Sounds like it," Felton agreed. "We're not partial to the French here."

Alec lifted his chin. "I was born in London, Mr. Wilcox, as was my father before me."

"No Frenchie accent," Joe observed.

"No, he speaks good English," Felton agreed. "And has a fine hat. Isn't it fine, Joe?"

Joe smirked. "That it is, Felton."

Felton knocked the hat to the ground before Alec could react.

Alec's muscles tensed to pounce on the man, but Ben caught his arm. "No, Alec," he hissed. "You don't want to cross that lot."

The Wilcox brothers snickered and sauntered away, yet Alec kept his wary gaze on them until they disappeared up the High Street.

Finally, Ben released him, and picked up Alec's hat. "I see what you're thinking, but forget it. Felton Wilcox is a champion Devon wrestler, and his brother fights for pleasure. You've no chance against them, as I've learnt the hard way. So steer clear."

Caper Merchant: A dancing master, or hop merchant; [also] to cut capers; to leap or jump in dancing.

—*The 1811 Dictionary of the Vulgar Tongue*

hapter 6

On Wednesday morning, Julia walked beside her mother on the way to the breakfast room. She would have preferred sleeping in, but Lady Amelia kept a strict schedule of rising and devotions before breakfast and insisted Julia do the same. Lady Amelia explained that, as heiress to Buckleigh Manor, Julia would one day assume her responsibilities—meeting regularly with housekeeper, cook, estate manager, rector, and charitable committees. Such duties were incumbent upon the leading family of the parish.

From the half landing, Julia had a good view of the vestibule below. There she glimpsed Alec Valcourt disappearing into Mr. Barlow's office.

"What is he doing here?" she asked in surprise.

"Mr. Valcourt is our new clerk. He shall be assisting Mr. Barlow."

The news filled Julia with conflicting emotions. "Since when does Barlow need help?"

Continuing down the stairs, her mother said, "Perhaps it is not Mr. Barlow who needs the help."

Julia felt comprehension dawn. "Oh, I see! You are trying to help Mr. Valcourt resist the temptation to return to his former wicked pursuits. Is that it?"

"Of course I would like to see any man gainfully employed." Her mother gave her a curious look. "And how did you know about his former profession?"

"Oh . . ." Julia shrugged. "You know there are no secrets in a place like Beaworthy."

"No, I don't know that."

Julia halted midstride, feeling her mouth fall open. "What do you mean, Mamma?" But Lady Amelia continued across the hall. "Mamma!" Julia hurried to catch up.

Lady Amelia sent her a sidelong glance. "Not a thing, my dear. Only that at your age, you cannot presume to know everything." She changed the subject. "Is Patience coming over to knit stockings for the poor this afternoon?"

"Yes." Though knitting wasn't the only thing Julia had in mind. She had a secret or two of her own.

That afternoon, Patience came over as expected, needlework bag in hand. They settled in the drawing room with their knitting wool and needles, and one of the maids served tea.

For a few minutes the only sound in the room was the *click-clack* of knitting needles. But Julia soon set aside her work. She lit a candle lamp, picked up a folded lap rug, and gestured for Patience to follow her out of the room. With a quizzical look, Patience complied. Checking the hall and finding it quiet, Julia led the way up one flight of stairs, then another, her friend trailing reluctantly behind. They passed servants' bedchambers, and the old schoolroom where she and Patience used to play school. At the end of the passage, Julia started up the dim stairway to the attic storeroom.

"Are you certain we should be up here?" Patience asked in a timid voice.

What a proper mouse her friend could be.

"Why not? It is my house, after all."

"I thought you said your mother doesn't want you up here."

"Oh, she warns about the dust, and a certain trunk she doesn't wish me to disturb, which is of course the one I most wish to investigate."

"Julia. We mustn't. Not if your mother said not to."

"No, of course not." Julia changed tack. "But I did think it would be amusing to look through her old gowns. From her coming-out days."

Lap rug under one arm, and candle lamp in hand, Julia opened the attic door and led the way across the dim storeroom, head slightly bowed to avoid brushing the low ceiling, in case any cobwebs should lurk there, so far from the housemaids' diligent campaign against them.

She paused before an ornate trunk of dark mahogany. "This trunk, I believe."

"Is this the one your mother asked you not to touch?" Patience asked in alarm.

"No, Patience." Julia sighed. She turned and nodded toward a smaller trunk in the corner. "That one."

Patience looked at the plain, stout trunk. "I am surprised she mentioned it. She had to know it would make you want to look inside all the more."

"You *would* think she'd realize. But my mother doesn't know me as well as she thinks."

Julia set her lamp on a discarded side table and laid the lap rug on the floor. The two young ladies knelt before the first trunk, lifted the lid, and began looking through the layers of gowns within.

Julia lifted out a pretty sprigged muslin and sighed again. "I shall never have a proper coming out. Never even attend a ball. Not trapped here so far from the London season."

"I went to London once." Patience shuddered. "I should never want to stray so far from home again."

"I should," Julia insisted. "London and farther afield. And had I money enough, I should never come home."

"Never come home?" Patience looked at her, aghast. "What a horrid thought."

"I suppose if I had your family, I should think it horrid as well."

Her friend's eyes took on a wistful glow by candlelight. "There is no place I should rather be than Medlands."

"How self-sacrificing of you to come here, then," Julia quipped.

"Oh, Julia. I didn't mean anything by it," Patience apologized. "You know I enjoy spending time with you."

Julia nodded. "Too bad I wasn't born into your family. Then I could live at Medlands too."

"There are ways to join our family," Patience teased. "And one of those ways is spelled J-a-m-e-s."

"Why, Patience Allen," Julia exclaimed. "That is almost improper of you to say. I'm quite proud of you." She opened a brittle Chinese fan and waggled her eyebrows over the top of it.

Patience grinned.

Julia was well aware of the expectation, even hope, that she and James Allen would marry one day. As the Allens' eldest son and heir, even Lady Amelia would approve, which was of course, a strike against him in Julia's eyes. James was very handsome, she allowed. Nearly prettier than his sister, who shared his fair coloring and good looks. Poor Walter. Almost an ugly duckling among swans, though none of the Allens seemed aware of the discrepancy.

And Julia liked James. She did. She was fond of him, as she was fond of Walter and Patience. They were like cousins to her, nearly as close as brother and sister—or so she imagined, never having had siblings of her own.

For a moment there in the dim attic, Julia imagined herself married to James Allen, playing man and wife. . . .

They lived in Medlands with his parents, for only death would remove them from its premises. Since she had become family, Sir Herbert often embraced Julia and doted on her as her own father never had. James doted on her as well, like a fond friend or kissing cousin. She and Patience were closer than ever, and Patience, as the spinster aunt, managed the children and the house, leaving Julia free to read and travel at her leisure. . . .

There the imaginings faded. She could share a life with James, but a bed? Children? No. It was no good. At all events, Julia was far from ready to contemplate marriage, especially to a man permanently tied to Beaworthy and one her mother approved of.

She thought of Mr. Valcourt—a forbidden man installed under her very roof. *My, my.* Life at Buckleigh Manor had suddenly become more interesting.

Half an hour later, Julia and Patience had inspected and admired the best of the gowns, while chuckling over a few gone horribly out of fashion.

Near the bottom of the trunk, they came across a gown carefully folded in layers of tissue. She and Patience had played dress-up with some of her mother's gowns as girls, but Julia had never seen this one. She stood, holding the ivory satin gown to herself, admiring its dainty pink-and-green embroidery. "A gown like this . . . It had to be a ball gown," Julia said. "You know very well Lady Amelia danced when she was my age. It doesn't seem fair that she forbids me to do what she no doubt did."

"It might not be a ball gown," Patience said tentatively. "Though it is pretty, to be sure."

Julia rewrapped the gown and prepared to return it to the trunk. Looking inside, she noticed the paper lining the trunk's bottom had become bunched at one end. Julia leaned in to spread the papers back evenly. As she did, a rectangle of yellowed newsprint caught her eye. She picked up the clipping and read the advertisement printed upon it.

Mr. J. D., professor of dancing and fencing,
has the honour to announce his return from London;
where he has acquired all the new and fashionable dances.
Reels, minuets, and Country Dancing taught in
private or group lessons.
A select Evening Academy twice a week, by subscription.
26 High Street, Beaworthy

"Can you imagine?" Julia breathed. "A dancing master here in Beaworthy? Right there on the High Street?"

"It is difficult to imagine. It must be a very old advertisement."

Julia turned the clipping over but saw no date.

"I wonder why she kept it," Patience mused. "Or maybe she just forgot about it."

"I wonder if she took lessons from him . . ." Julia said. "How can I ask her without letting on where I found it?"

"Julia! You said this trunk wasn't forbidden."

"It's not . . . specifically. Though she has asked me not to go rummaging about up here making a mess."

"Then let's put everything back just as we found it," Patience urged.

"Very well," Julia agreed. She slipped the clipping up her sleeve. *Everything but this . . .*

After Patience left that afternoon, Julia strode into the library.

Her mother had taken it over after Arthur Midwinter had fallen ill and been confined to his bed. Julia didn't like the ornate, formal room. It reminded her of her father, who had not wanted a young girl in his domain, who always winced in martyr-like pain whenever she skipped in to retrieve a nursery book or an errant ball, warning of the breakable vases, children being seen and not heard, and a library full of valuable books not being a place for sticky fingers.

Walking toward the desk, Julia held up the clipping. "Mamma, what is this?"

Lady Amelia glanced up distractedly. "Hmm? What is what?" Then her eyes focused on the faded print and her eyes widened. "Where did you find this?"

"In your trunk of old gowns. Don't worry, that's the only trunk we looked in, and we put everything back just so. Patience made sure of it."

"I hope you haven't dirtied your hems." Her mother flicked a glance at her skirt. "You know I have asked you not to go up there. You might have at least changed your frock first."

"Never mind about my frock. Where did this come from?"

Lady Amelia waved her hand dismissively. "Heavens, I don't know. You know Doyle takes care of my gowns and packs my trunks. She always lines them with paper, does she not?"

"Tissue paper, yes, and sometimes old newsprint. But this has been cut out."

Her mother held out her hand for the clipping. "Let me see it." She accepted it and flipped it over. "Perhaps it was cut to preserve this article here on the reverse. This bit of parliamentary news."

Julia shook her head in vexation. "I knew you would never admit to having any interest in dancing. I'd like to hear you explain away that carefully preserved ball gown as easily."

Lady Amelia lifted an expressive hand. "Of course I had gowns of every description when I was young. My parents took us to London for several seasons. But all of that was before my brother died."

"And how do you expect me to find a suitable husband, since you refuse to take me to London?"

"London society is no place for either of us, Julia. Not with all its airs and immorality. Besides, you need look no further than Medlands to find a suitable mate."

That again. "But—*you* went to London to find an advantageous match."

"Yes, I suppose that was the plan for Anne and me. And my brother did meet a very suitable young lady. They might have married, had he lived." Sadness dulled her eyes.

Julia asked, "Is that where you met Father?"

Her mother hesitated. "No. Mr. Midwinter did not enjoy the social season. My father had long been acquainted with him—he lived in Torrington with his mother and older brother. Father invited him here to meet me."

"Then did your sister meet her husband during the season?"

Lady Amelia scoffed. "Not likely."

"What do you mean?"

"Julia, I am sorry, but my mind is full of plans for the charity event for the poor fund. Can we talk about this later?"

"Oh, all right," Julia huffed. She was used to being dismissed, her questions ignored, and being less important than her mother's many charitable organizations.

She flounced from the library, not realizing until later that her mother still had the clipping.

After her daughter had left the library, Lady Amelia Buckleigh Midwinter picked up the rectangle of yellowed newsprint and allowed her gaze to linger on the words. And to remember . . .

When Amelia saw the dancing master standing in the threshold of the salon, she felt her eyes widen and her lower lip droop. She closed her mouth quickly and did her best to hide her surprise—her jolt of feminine awareness and attraction. Good heavens, he was much more handsome than she recalled. His time studying under an experienced professor had clearly added polish as well as any new dances he may have learned while he was away.

He bowed smartly, and then straightened to his full height. He cut a dashing figure in his rich blue tailcoat, buff breeches, and buckled shoes. She forced her gaze away from the muscled calves so effectively displayed in snug white stockings. His shoulders seemed broader than she recalled. Perhaps he had gained a great deal of strength from a new fencing regimen since she had last seen him. Or it may have simply been the precise cut of the well-made coat, but she doubted it. His patterned waistcoat and cravat were fashionable, yet he managed to look not at all effeminate or foppish. No, he was decidedly masculine. . . .

He was staring back at her, she realized. Had he noticed her impolite survey of his person? Her neck heated, and she lowered her gaze yet still felt his intent scrutiny. Had she changed as well? She doubted her looks had improved as his had, at least not by any marked degree. She certainly hoped he did not find her much aged. Or perhaps there was something on her face. Her skin itched by suggestion, and she brushed self-conscious fingers across her cheek.

Amelia had told her father that she was perfectly comfortable meeting the dancing master alone. She would leave the door open and the lady's maid might join them when she was able. Her siblings had awoken with colds, but it had been too late to send word to cancel the lesson. He was here now. It would be rude to send him away and rob him of his fee. Besides, though they were from different stations in life, she knew him well enough to feel no discomfort in his presence. No concern about inappropriate attention or impropriety.

She swallowed.

Perhaps she should have canceled the lesson.

She remembered him as a pleasant young man of average height, wiry and athletic, and a surprisingly skilled dancer for a person near her own age. But now . . . Was it only the heel of his dancing shoes? He certainly seemed taller. His face was less boyish and more defined, with strong cheekbones and dark eyes capped by thick brows.

Stop it, she told herself. *Stop it this instant.*

"Forgive me—come in." She gestured him into the room, indicating the sideboard where he might leave his walking stick and instrument.

"Thank you," he said. "It is good to see you again. You look beau— That is, you look to be enjoying good health."

She glanced up quickly, studying his face. Had he almost said she looked beautiful, or had she imagined it? No other man had ever said so. Not even the wealthy older man her father wished her to marry. Good heavens, she was becoming as romantically fanciful as her sister, or some of the giggling debutants she had met during the London season.

She reminded herself he was a dancing master—known for flattery. Had she not heard highborn mothers warning their daughters against the charms of caper merchants? Surely that was all it was.

"I am afraid it is only me today," she said, unaccountably nervous. "A slight malady making the rounds. Nothing of concern, but . . . Well, I hope you don't mind."

He set down his things and stepped closer. Again he seemed to be staring at her, and now at closer range she was struck by the intensity of his brown eyes, deep and warm and inviting.

He slowly shook his head. "Not at all."

He held out his hand to her. No gloves? She had not thought to wear any either. This was not, after all, a ball or any sort of formal event. And he was only the dancing master. . . .

Only? She looked down at his hand—long fingers, smooth and strong. Her heart began beating a little harder than it should.

In a low voice he asked, "Shall we begin?"

Amelia felt flushed and light-headed and full of illogical hope. With one last shy glance into those deep, admiring eyes, she placed her hand in his.

Wrastling is full of manliness, for you shall hardly find an assembly of boys in Devon and Cornwall, where the most untowardly amongst them will not as readily give you a muster of this exercise as you are prone to require it.

—Richard Carew, 17th century historian

Chapter 7

On Thursday, Alec returned to Buckleigh Manor for his second day as clerk.

The estate manager's office was not large yet boasted a high ceiling, as did the other ground-level rooms. High on one wall hung a clock. And on another, a large map of the estate, showing the manor, gardens, outbuildings, finely timbered park, and a thousand acres of surrounding farmland.

The office held bookshelves, cabinets for important papers, and two desks—Mr. Barlow's large one at center, and a smaller clerk's desk in the corner.

Alec hunched over the latter. There he summed figures in a ledger column, his concentration hindered by Mr. Barlow pacing behind his chair, now and again glancing over Alec's shoulder. Then he cleared his throat.

"Yes, Mr. Barlow?" Alec asked testily.

"Are you not finished yet, Valcourt?"

I would be, were you not looking over my shoulder, Alec thought, but said only, "I am simply rechecking my work."

"I shall do so." Barlow held out his hand for the ledger.

"Then what shall I do, sir?"

Alec had already reorganized the files the day before. Today he had alphabetized the bookcases, worked through the bills, and taken a batch of letters to the inn for posting.

Barlow looked around the tidy office. "Um, let's see. . . . What else needs doing. . . ."

Alec's gaze was suddenly drawn to the window. He glimpsed Miss Midwinter walk past in a blue riding habit, on her way to the stable, no doubt.

Alec picked up a notice from his desk and said, "I have a question about this saddler's invoice for a new sidesaddle. Do we know if Isaacs has received it and is satisfied?"

Barlow considered. "Good question, I shall go and ask him."

"I'll go, sir," Alec said, rising eagerly.

The man looked about to refuse, so Alec hurried to add, "I thought you were expecting the thatcher any time now?"

Barlow glanced at the clock. "Oh, right. Very well. Go and ask."

"Happily, sir." Alec was happy indeed to escape the office with its heavy silence and constant scrutiny.

Taking the notice with him, Alec let himself out the side door, forgoing hat and gloves on the temperate late-February day. He crossed the back lawn toward the stable block. In the adjacent paddock, Miss Midwinter sat sidesaddle atop a glossy brown horse, the long skirt of her riding habit splayed over its rear and side like a royal sash. She began riding a course of modest rail jumps, the scarf around her hat brim sailing behind her as she did so. Her posture and graceful ease were beautiful to behold. Her confidence and skill admirable. He tried to imagine himself riding Apollo with that competence someday, and chuckled to himself at the thought.

Entering the stable, dim after the brightness of outdoors, Alec allowed his eyes to adjust, then found Mr. Isaacs's small office beyond the tack room. He reviewed the bill with the man and then, assured all was as it should be, took himself back outside.

There Miss Midwinter came riding toward the stable. She noticed him and urged her horse toward the fence.

"Hello, Mr. Valcourt."

"Good day, Miss Midwinter." His hand lifted of his own accord to remove his hat, only to remember he wasn't wearing one. Would he always make such a cake of himself with this woman? He made a show of brushing away an invisible fly, then glanced at the sleek mare. "Beautiful lady you've got there."

She patted her mare's neck. "Yes, she is."

Yes, she is, Alec echoed to himself.

The groom came out and helped Miss Midwinter dismount.

Straightening her skirts, she asked Alec, "Do you ride?"

"No, not really."

"I suppose you haven't a horse . . . being from town."

She'd added the last phrase with the tact of good breeding, he realized. She must assume he could not afford a horse. And she'd be right, but still he was proud to be able to correct her.

"I do, actually. And I'm keen to ride him." He sighed, then added, "Unfortunately he's not keen on the idea himself."

She laughed—a lovely sound—and he smiled, glad he'd admitted the truth.

Eyes shining, she said, "We shall have to see what we can do about that."

When Alec returned to the office, Mr. Barlow told him that Lady Amelia wished to see him before he left for the day.

Alec was instantly on his guard.

At four, he crossed the hall to the library, knocked, and entered when bid.

Lady Amelia looked up from her desk and gestured him nearer. She did not, however, offer him a chair. "May I have an accounting of how you spent your time today, Mr. Valcourt?"

Alec stiffened. It wasn't his fault if Barlow was reluctant to delegate many duties to him, save the most elementary.

He cleared his throat, and began. "I reconciled the bills to the purchase orders, summed the quarter's household accounts, purged the mail of trade advertisements, and took a batch of letters to the inn for posting."

"The hallboy posts any letters that miss the morning pickup."

"I know. But I needed to stretch my legs."

"We are not paying you to stretch your legs."

"I realize that, of course, but Mr. Barlow is busy and doesn't always have time to delegate sufficient duties to me."

He worded his explanation carefully, not wishing to criticize Barlow. But nor did he want to talk himself out of a job.

She arched an auburn eyebrow. "And did you also go to the stables today to 'stretch your legs'?"

So she had seen him talking with her daughter. He'd wondered if she might have, when Mr. Barlow delivered her summons.

"I went to see Isaacs about an invoice for a new sidesaddle."

She considered this. "I see."

She dismissed him, and he left feeling, for the most part, relieved. He knew he had not impressed her with his day's accomplishments, but he determined to do better on the morrow.

The next afternoon, he was ready for her. Before he left for the day, he stopped in the library and handed Lady Amelia a list of all he had worked on and accomplished.

She raised an eyebrow, scanned the list, then looked up at him. "Thank you, Mr. Valcourt. I see Barlow found more to delegate to you today."

More accurately, Alec had wrested duties from the older man's grasp. But he said only, "Yes, my lady. I believe he is finding me useful."

"I should hope so. Well, good evening, Mr. Valcourt."

"Good evening." He bowed and departed.

He'd won that day's bout. But Alec knew he had more battles ahead in winning both Barlow's trust and hers.

Taking his leave, Alec met Walter Allen in the churchyard to fence together as Walter had requested. Alec began simply, reviewing the fundamentals, most of which Walter had clearly forgotten. Then they attached leather guards and practiced an easy pattern of advance, lunge, retreat—striking their blades on every pass. Walter was rangy and raw, but if he ever mastered those long limbs of his, Alec thought he would make a fearsome opponent. When he told him so, Walter flushed with pleasure.

Alec had been tempted to offer the young man formal lessons, but decided he would teach Walter gratis. He found himself growing fond of the young man and liked having someone to take exercise with and talk to—and true friendship was always impeded, he'd found, when money changed hands. If Walter's father were to offer to pay him, that might be another matter . . . but Alec decided not to suggest it. He had his wages as clerk, and that was enough.

Alec had begun demonstrating a more advanced movement, when applause interrupted them. He looked over midlunge. There stood Miss Midwinter and Miss Allen, who must have come in through the churchyard's rear door. He wondered how long they had been watching.

He straightened, feeling self-conscious. But both women were smiling at him with, if he was not mistaken, admiration in their eyes.

"My, my, what gallants," Miss Midwinter teased.

"Indeed," Patience agreed.

Walter rolled his eyes. "I think that is enough for today, Valcourt. I'm done in."

He extended his family's invitation to dinner Saturday evening, and Alec accepted.

Alec was only expected to work half a day on Saturday. It was one of the advantages of working at Buckleigh Manor. Glancing again at Miss Midwinter, he thought, *But not the only advantage.*

❧

On Saturday evening, Alec dressed with care. At his mother's insistence, he took the last bottle of the elder wine she had made last autumn as a gift for his hosts.

At Medlands, a footman took his hat and stick and showed him into the drawing room. The Allens had already gathered—Patience playing the pianoforte, the parents listening, the brothers bent over a game of draughts at an inlaid game table. The scene made Alec miss his home in London, his old life.

The Allens rose and welcomed Alec warmly. Lady Allen accepted the elder wine with effusive gratitude, begging Alec to pass along her thanks to his mother.

Together they all strolled into the dining room without precedence or ceremony. The family took their customary seats, except for Walter, who insisted Alec take his seat in the middle of the table, where all could converse easily with him.

They ate family style, with Lady Allen ladling the soup from a silver tureen to begin the meal. "And how do you like Beaworthy so far?" she asked, passing him a bowl.

"Oh, it's a charming place, and the people are friendly . . . for the most part."

"But much smaller than London. I hope you are not disappointed with our society?"

"Not at all."

James eyed him speculatively. "And how, if you don't mind my asking, did you occupy yourself in London?"

His mother gently chided, "James, don't pry."

"I don't mind," Alec assured his hostess. "I hope you don't mind when you hear my answer. In London, I was a dancing master, as was my father. We taught lessons in private homes, schools, and our own academy."

The family members hesitated, spoons or glasses halfway to their mouths, exchanging glances with one another.

Alec continued, "I did not realize until we arrived that dancing was not . . . popular . . . here in Beaworthy."

"That's putting it lightly," Walter said.

"Oh good, you *know*." Lady Allen breathed in relief. "Not good that you've been disappointed, but good that you've already learned of the . . . restrictions . . . here. I would hate to be the one to break the news and disappoint you."

"Never fear, my lady. That has been done already." He added, "I do hope you are not offended by my vocation."

"Heavens no. Not offended in the least," Sir Herbert assured. "Lady Allen and I took lessons from the old dancing master. Mr. Sharp, his name was. And Lady Allen and I danced at no few balls when we were younger. Did we not, my dear? In fact, I am not boasting if I tell you I won the heart of the belle of the ball. Many gentlemen went away disappointed when our engagement was announced. Now, I take no pleasure in delivering pain to anyone, still I cannot but thank God every day that she agreed to marry me."

"I thank God as well, my love." Lady Allen reached over and pressed Sir Herbert's hand.

Seeing their affection caused a wistful pain in Alec's breast.

"We hold no scruples against dancing personally," Sir Herbert continued, "but have abstained these many years out of respect for Lady Amelia. And, well, because there have been no balls to decline, it has been relatively easy to do so, with little personal sacrifice." Sir Herbert sighed. "But I have always regretted my children have never danced in the High Street on May Day, as we did when we were young."

Lady Allen added, "And Patience never the belle of a Beaworthy ball."

Patience blushed prettily and ducked her head. "I don't mind, Mamma. I should not like everyone breaking their hearts over me."

"Sure you would, Pet," James said. "If we had a ball, Papa would have to beat back the hordes of eager gentlemen with a stick."

Patience blushed again. "Oh, James. Don't be ridiculous."

James patted her hand, then said, "I did learn to dance at school. Well, a bit. Did you not as well, Walt?"

"Um, no. I can't say that I ever learned." Walter grinned. "Doesn't mean they didn't try to teach me."

Sir Herbert looked across at Alec as he carved the roast. "What say you, Mr. Valcourt? Would you do us the honor of teaching James, Walter, and Patience here? We would make it worth your while, of course."

Satisfaction and pleasure surged through Alec. He opened his mouth to accept wholeheartedly, when the image of Lady Amelia's face flashed in his mind. A few private lessons would never replace the regular income he earned as clerk. He had to think about his mother and sister, and not only his own wishes.

"I would like nothing better, sir. Truly. But . . . as I am employed by Lady Amelia . . ." He let his words trail away.

Sir Herbert nodded. "I take your meaning."

Lady Allen said, "You are kind to think of the feelings of others, Mr. Valcourt. We strive for that ourselves. I wonder though . . . Perhaps if I spoke to Lady Amelia, explained that we only want private lessons in our own home, not a public dance. Could she really object?"

Sir Herbert shook his head regretfully. "She could. But let us think on what is best to do. For now, we shall hold off on the idea. All right?"

Alec nodded. "Thank you for understanding."

"You will continue our fencing lessons, I hope?" Walter asked eagerly.

"They're not really lessons, Walter," Alec demurred. "We have been two friends, practicing."

"You can say that all you like, but it's clear you're the master and I'm the fumbling pupil."

Remembering the admiring glances of Miss Midwinter and Miss Allen, Alec smiled. "Well, whatever we call it, I too hope we shall continue."

❧

On Monday morning, Alec stood before the postal log Barlow kept on a lectern near the tradesman's entrance for convenience sake. The post had arrived, and Alec's task was to record the letters that arrived postage due—which was most of them, actually, save for some franked pieces from London. He enjoyed this duty, for it allowed him to stand— a relief after sitting so long. Alone in the office, he found himself humming a tune, and before he knew it his feet began a little shuffle step.

"Must you, Mr. Valcourt?" Mr. Barlow's voice caught him unaware, and Alec felt his neck heat. He'd not heard the man enter.

"Where is the rent from the Reddaways?" Barlow asked.

"I'm sorry, sir. Mr. Reddaway didn't have it."

Barlow sighed in his long-suffering manner. "Must I do everything myself?" He turned and left the office.

Alec followed him out into the hall to explain, and hopefully save the man a trip. "Mr. Reddaway's daughter has just had a child. They haven't the money this quarter, what with buying things for the babe, but he promised to pay once Miss Tabitha is able to return to work."

Barlow turned in stunned wonder. "Little Tabby's had a child? Seems like only yesterday she was a wee imp in long plaits—"

Lady Amelia's frosty voice interrupted them. "Tabitha Reddaway has always held too high an opinion of her own charms. She had every man in the village eating from the palm of her hand. And now she finds herself with child without benefit of marriage and we are to forgo a quarter's rent?"

Mr. Barlow stared at his mistress, clearly taken aback by her bitter tone. "Shall I send Mr. Valcourt back then, my lady? And demand the rent now?"

She pressed her eyes closed, brow furrowed, her whole face tight. She looked away, out the hall window at the slowly falling drizzle, or perhaps some distant memory. "No," she said on an exhale. "It isn't the child's fault." She straightened and said briskly, "But next quarter. No excuses."

"Yes, my lady."

Alec breathed a sigh of relief.

Too soon.

She turned to him, her officious expression back in place. "I do hope this isn't an indication of your ineffectiveness, Mr. Valcourt."

He defended, "I did not realize rent collecting would be one of my duties as clerk."

"I expect you to help Mr. Barlow in whatever duties he sees fit to assign you. I hope I make myself clear."

"Perfectly," he said, though inwardly he chafed. At Medlands he was treated as a guest. Here, as little higher than a servant on trial.

Alec looked up. A flash of movement and color had caught his attention. Glancing toward the stairs, he was chagrined to see Miss Midwinter there on the half landing. He felt indignant and embarrassed to have her witness the unfair reprimand. There she stood, expression inscrutable, looking down at him from on high.

She already looks down at you, he told himself. *So what does it matter?* But it did.

❧

Alec's feet drummed beneath him, his shoes tattooing on the old paving stones. Their report echoed against the gravestones of the ancient churchyard adjoining the manor grounds. Perspiration beaded and trickled down his back. His breathing became labored. He had not danced in far too long.

He danced the hornpipe. The solitary dance of flying feet and still upper body, arms at sides. The hornpipe had long been danced on naval ships to provide regular exercise for men living in cramped quarters. That was how he felt, living in his uncle's small house, having to be on his best behavior at all hours. That was how he felt, working in Buckleigh Manor, at the small desk in Mr. Barlow's office. Trying to be what they wanted him to be. No space of his own. No freedom.

His coat and sword lay on a bench nearby as he danced in his waistcoat and shirtsleeves. He meant no disrespect to the old church or graveyard, though he doubted the dead would mind. It was only the living who would reprimand him if they knew.

This broad, even path, surrounded by concealing stone walls and with an audience of only headstones, was the best place he could think of to dance without censure. He wondered how far the sound of his shoes would carry—hopefully not to the manor, though it wasn't far away, nor to Medlands opposite.

No one played the pipe for him that afternoon, nor the fiddle. But the music of years, engraved in his memory from countless rehearsals, surged through his muscles. The exertion exhilarated, released and relieved, even as it exhausted. His shoes pounded out his frustrations:

his father, Miss Underhill, his uncle, Mr. Barlow, Lady Amelia, Miss Midwinter . . .

Suddenly Joe and Felton Wilcox came lurching through the church-yard gate. *Thunder and turf.* Could he get no peace? Alec stopped danc-ing, but it was too late. The Wilcox brothers had seen him.

"Well, well, and what have we here, Joe?" Felton smirked. "A fairy dance, was it? I thought a woodpecker had gone mad with all that pounding. And here it was only you."

"Gone and joined the ranters, have ya?" Joe asked. "Though that lot don't dance in public."

"I didn't realize I had an audience," Alec said.

Joe gestured with an emphatic hand. "Go on. Show us more of that fancy steppin.'"

"Thank you, no. I've had all the exercise I need for today."

"We wasn't askin', Valcourt," Felton said. "We was tellin.' Dance."

"I have no interest in performing for you," Alec said. "But if you'd like to learn, I'd be happy to teach you."

Joe shook his head. "Won't catch us caperin' about like that."

"Well"—Felton drew himself up—"if you won't give us a dancing exhibition, we shall be obliged to give you a wrasslin' demonstration instead."

Felton looked at Joe. "Cornish or Devon wrasslin', do you think?"

"Perhaps a bit of both."

Felton grinned at his brother. "And people call you slow. Excellent notion."

Alec tensed, wishing he'd kept his sword nearer at hand. Not that he would in good conscience strike unarmed men, but the threat of it might dissuade the pair. Before he could move, however, Felton sprung. He grasped him around the torso, and with a whirl and a thrust, Alec felt his feet fly from the ground and the world tilt. Then he banged onto the stone path flat on his back in a bone-jarring thud, the air whooshing from his lungs and stars tingling before his eyes.

"He's down, Felton," Joe exclaimed. "That's a back scored for you!"

"Your first lesson in Cornish wrasslin.'" Felton's face twisted into a predatory smile. "How'd ya like it?" He jerked a thumb toward his beefy younger brother. "Joe here's the welter champ." He smirked. "No one can get 'im off the ground."

Alec struggled to draw breath. Before he could answer or react, Felton swung back his leg and delivered a vicious kick to his shin. Pain surged, and Alec cried out, blinded in shock.

"And that's Devon wrasslin'," Felton added. "Be glad I don't have my baked boots on. Didn't know I'd find an opponent today." Felton swung back his leg once more.

Unarmed maybe, but that foot was a deadly weapon if ever Alec had felt one. "Baked" or not.

Alec rolled away, desperate to avoid another blow. Reaching the bench, he stretched out his hand for his sword.

Anticipating his aim, Joe lunged for it and snatched it from his reach. In a flash, the brute broke the sword over his knee as though it were a dried twig.

"No!" Alec yelled. Sickening regret and fear filled him. These men were not only strong—they were without conscience.

As if to prove the point, Felton delivered another kick as Alec lay stretched across the ground, punishing his side with cruel impact. Alec felt as though his ribs had caved in, and he couldn't breathe. *God help me. . . .*

"My turn," Joe said, tossing aside the broken sword.

Unable to move, Alec tensed for another blow.

Crack. A gunshot exploded.

"Dash it!" Joe yelled.

"What the blazes do you think you're doing?" Felton shouted at someone.

Alec opened his eyes and tried to turn his head. He twisted onto his back, the pain in his side excruciating, and saw the churchyard, gate, wall . . . And over the wall, a man astride a horse, double-barrel flintlock pointed in their direction, still smoking.

"Leave him be," the man ordered. "That was a warning shot. Next time I shan't shoot above your heads."

"You wouldn't dare," Felton snarled. "Don't you know who I am?"

Joe supplied, "He's Beaworthy's champion wrassler, he is."

"A champion wrestler who kicks an opponent when he's down? Who kicks above the waist? Your sponsors would likely take back your gold-laced hat if they learned of it. Not to mention your title."

"They would not." Felton scowled, eyes flashing. But there was a thread of doubt in his voice.

"I'll give you thirty seconds to leave here unharmed."

Neither Wilcox moved. The man cocked the gun's second barrel and sighted on Felton's chest.

"Let's go," Joe said, grabbing his brother's arm. "We'll get him later."

Felton stood there, glaring at the man, likely weighing his chances against an armed man on horseback. One second. Two. Three.

"Come on," Joe hissed.

Finally Felton turned and followed his brother across the churchyard and out the rear door, sending one last scorching look over his shoulder.

When they had gone, Alec tried to sit up, grasping his throbbing ribs in a futile effort to stem the pain. The man dismounted, tied a rein to the gate post, and strode toward him, his gaze shifting to the rear door and scanning the wall as he approached.

Satisfied they were alone, he lowered himself to his haunches and looked from Alec's clenched hand to his perspiring face. "Are you all right?"

"Been better. But I'll live. Thanks to you."

"There's blood seeping through your trousers there. Can you stand? Or shall I fetch the surgeon here?"

"I think I can stand."

The man laid aside his gun and offered his hand. Alec took it, and the man pulled him to his feet. Alec's head swam. His side screamed and his leg felt as though it might buckle. He hoped he wouldn't thank his rescuer by being sick all over his boots.

"Steady," the man said, holding Alec's arm. "That lot threaten you before?"

"No. Nothing like that. Thank God you came along when you did."

"Thank God, indeed."

Alec winced. "Do you always carry a gun?"

"No. I've been out hunting. No luck, though. And here I'd thought I'd brought the old thing along for nothing."

Alec blinked away the pain to focus on the man's face. "I've not seen you before, I don't think. Do you live nearby?"

The man hesitated. "I'm . . . ah, visiting."

He was tall with longish brown hair and dark eyes. His skin was tan from days in the sun, or perhaps Spanish or Italian blood. His accent was also difficult to place. Northern, perhaps, or Scottish. His coat was well made and well cared for, yet clearly old.

"I hate to leave you alone," he said. "But I think I ought to ride for the surgeon."

"Valcourt?" a voice called. "What's happened?"

Alec looked over the church wall once again, relieved to see familiar, friendly faces. Walter and James Allen on horseback.

"We heard a gunshot," Walter said. "Are you all right?"

The two men looked suspiciously at the man holding Alec's arm.

Alec quickly explained, "This man came to my rescue. I had an . . . unfortunate wrestling lesson from the Wilcox brothers."

Both men tensed and looked about them, surveying the churchyard.

"They're gone," Alec said. "For now."

Walter handed his brother his reins and quickly dismounted. As he hurried into the churchyard, his anxious gaze swept Alec's disheveled form. "Devil take it. You're bleeding."

Alec winced. "The leg is nothing to my ribs, I'm afraid."

"Broken?"

"I don't think so. Dashed painful, though. I'm afraid our fencing lesson will have to wait."

His rescuer spoke up. "I was just about to ride for the surgeon, if you two will stay with him."

"I don't think I need a surgeon, thank you," Alec said. "I may, however, need a little help getting home."

"Too far in your state," James said, dismounting and tying both horses to the gate. "We'll take you to Medlands. Father will know if the surgeon is needed or not."

Walter turned to the stranger and said kindly, "You are welcome to come with us, sir, if you like. We can offer you a good meal and the hearty thanks of our family as reward if nothing else."

The man hesitated, considering.

James looked at Alec. "But perhaps you would rather go to Buckleigh Manor. It is a bit closer."

Beside him, the stranger stiffened and released Alec's arm. "I'll be on my way if I'm no longer needed. You two can help him from here, I trust?"

"Yes, of course," Walter said, taking his place beside Alec.

The man retrieved his gun, untied his horse, and mounted.

The brothers stood on either side of Alec and insisted he wrap an arm around each of their shoulders. With Walter being markedly taller, this made for an awkward and painful half walk, half carry out of the churchyard. Realizing this, Walter held Alec's arm from underneath to even the way.

"Who was that man?" James asked, turning his head to watch him ride away.

"I don't know. Don't you?"

Both brothers shook their heads.

Alec frowned. "Dash it. I forgot my sword. Wilcox broke it, but I shouldn't like to lose it just the same. Or leave it lying about for some lads to find and hurt themselves with."

Walter jogged back into the yard and retrieved the two pieces. "Tough luck, that," he said. "Perhaps the blacksmith can repair it."

"Perhaps," James said. "But for now, let's worry about repairing our friend here. We'll return for the horses later. Unless . . . Shall we boost you up on one of them?"

"Please no," Alec rushed to say. "At the moment, I can bear the walk far better than a fall from a horse."

In the Medlands drawing room, Sir Herbert and Lady Allen examined Alec's injuries with concern and attention. Patience had excused herself, in consideration of modesty. Lady Allen wished to send for the surgeon, but Sir Herbert assured them nothing was broken and wrapped Alec's shin and ribs himself. Evidently Herbert Allen had gallantly served the wounded, especially a certain nobleman, in a previous war, hence earning his knighthood.

Sir Herbert did insist, however, in sending for the constable. An hour later, George Lamont arrived begrudgingly and listened without apparent concern to Alec's report. His response was far from satisfactory.

"Boys will be boys, sir, as you know. No doubt meant to wrassle 'im in good sport and things got out of hand, that's all."

"Good sport? This young man was on the ground bleeding and might well have been seriously injured had a passerby not interfered."

"Who was it, by the way?" the constable asked Alec.

"I did not get his name."

"Too bad. Not many are brave enough, or foolish enough, to interfere with our wrasslin' champions." Mr. Lamont chuckled.

Sir Herbert frowned. "This was no wrestling bout, Lamont. No fair fight. And I would hope you or I or any man of honor would have stepped in to help, regardless of risk to his own person."

"Lofty words, sir. Lofty words." The constable rocked on his heels and fiddled with the hat in his hands. "Well, I will talk to the boys. Make sure they're more careful in future. No doubt they don't realize their own strength." He bowed and replaced his hat. "Gentlemen. M'lady."

After the constable departed, Sir Herbert insisted Alec rest awhile longer. Then the family made preparations to deliver Alec home in their best sprung-and-padded carriage. Lady Allen offered to send word to Lady Amelia, explaining what had happened and letting her know Alec would be in no fit condition to perform his duties the next day.

"I am certain I shall be well enough by tomorrow," Alec said. "But thank you for the offer." Alec was not certain he would be sufficiently recovered. Far from it. But he was loath to display weakness before either Lady Amelia or her daughter.

Later, in his uncle's sitting room, Alec had to endure the sputtering protestations of an unhappy host.

"You must have done something to provoke them," Cornelius Ramsay insisted, his tone nearly accusatory.

Alec did not mention the Wilcox brothers had come upon him dancing. He had little interest in adding fuel to his uncle's fiery arguments against the activity, and no desire to hear his uncle say, "I told you so."

Nearly worse was the smothering concern of his mother and sister. All kindly meant, Alec knew, but he was exhausted and wanted nothing more than to be left alone to figuratively lick his wounds.

Remember to take the best dancing master . . . more to teach you to sit, stand, and walk gracefully, than to dance finely. The Graces, the Graces; remember the Graces!

—Philip Dormer Stanhope, 4th Earl of Chesterfield

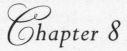

Chapter 8

The next day, despite his mother's protests, Alec forced himself to get up and dress for work. She insisted on redressing his leg wound to assure herself no infection had begun to set in. She grimaced at the purple bruise and nasty gash but was pleased it had stopped bleeding. His uncle tightened the bandage around his ribs, and helped him on with his coat, clearly approving of his stoic determination to attend to his duties despite discomfort.

Aching from his injuries, his walk to Buckleigh Manor seemed twice as long as usual. Each step, each breath hurt.

As he passed the old Buckleigh church on the way to the manor, he glanced through its gate—the scene of his painful humiliation. The churchyard appeared empty. Yet he heard something. . . .

Movement from above caught his eye, and he looked up. His stomach clenched. There atop the church tower, twice the height of the church itself, stood a figure. A woman, in billowing skirts and bonnet, balanced on the parapet, arms outstretched, stepping gingerly toward the corner pinnacle.

Julia Midwinter.

"Stop! Be careful!" he yelled instinctively.

High above him she gasped and lurched, arms windmilling wildly to regain her balance.

"Thunder and turf," Alec grumbled under his breath. What was the fool woman doing?

Above him, Miss Midwinter overcompensated and with a little cry fell backward toward the tower roof.

Ignoring the pain lancing his side, Alec bolted up the path, through the arched doorway, and into the dim Norman church. Grabbing a pew back, he sharply rounded the corner, and pushed through the creaking door into the tower. He ascended the steep, narrow stairs as quickly as his injured leg would allow, calling upward, "Miss Midwinter! Stay there, I'm coming!"

One flight, then another, past draping cobwebs and dust-shrouded bells. The last flight was more ladder than stairs, steeply pitched rungs leading through an opening in the roof. He climbed, his ribs protesting and leg throbbing with every step.

He pushed his head through the open hatch, feeling like a mole emerging from its den. He looked about him, fearing to find her injured. Instead, he found the roof empty. She had already climbed back onto the parapet.

Alec was reminded of a high-wire walker he had once seen in Astley's Amphitheatre. Poised and graceful, Miss Midwinter walked to the corner pinnacle and then pivoted in the opposite direction with barely a wobble. Heaven help him, he would love to see the woman dance.

"Miss Midwinter," Alec said, forcing his voice into moderation, not wishing to startle her again. "What are you doing?"

"What does it look like?"

"Like you are trying to break your neck. Or give me an apoplexy."

"I did not know anyone was watching. I should be vexed at you for startling me. I thought you were staying home today."

"Oh?" Alec sat on the edge of the hatch and swung his legs up. How had the young woman managed it in long skirts? He rose gingerly to his feet, the pain in his leg and side returning in full force now that the panic had passed.

"Lady Allen sent over a note. Told us you'd been injured and not to expect you. Which reminds me . . . Mother asked me to inform Barlow that you'd been trounced, but I quite forgot."

"I am perfectly well," he said through gritted teeth, hoping she had not heard his involuntary groan, nor noticed the sweat trickling down his hairline.

She smirked. "So I see."

He crossed the roof to where she stood atop the parapet wall, four feet or so above him. He stretched up his hand to her. "Please come down."

She placed her hand in his. "You needn't worry. I often come up here." She hopped down as nimbly as a cat.

For a moment, she kept hold of his hand, studying his face. Then she released him, and turned to look out over the lichen-spotted ledge.

"This moldering church has been my playground since I was a girl," she said. "Especially since it was all but abandoned in favor of St. Michael's."

Alec stood beside her. He looked out past the churchyard, over the meadows and trees to the rolling hills beyond.

"I like it up here," Julia said wistfully. "I can see for miles . . . and imagine I'm far away."

Watching her pensive profile, he asked quietly, "And why would you want to do that?"

She slanted him a look but made no reply.

He said, "I did not realize life in Buckleigh Manor was such a hardship."

"No, you would not." Pain flashed across her eyes, and she looked away. "When I was younger, I would sometimes stand here and shout at the top of my voice. If the wind was in the right direction, no one heard me. Though once five estate workers came running, sure I was being torn limb from limb by wolves."

She chuckled at this, but he did not think it amusing.

"What did you have to shout about?"

She shrugged. "I don't know. Sometimes this feeling of—" she circled a hand near her abdomen as she searched for the word—"restlessness . . . vexation . . . grows and churns until I feel I will explode if I don't do something." She glanced at him defensively, as though daring him to scoff. "Do you never get frustrated? Never need to vent your anger?"

"I do, actually. And I understand you, to some extent. But I don't shout or jump about rooftops scaring people half to death."

Her mouth quirked. "What do you do?"

He looked at her, then away.

"Tell me," she insisted.

"You'll laugh."

"Is it worse than shouting or jumping about rooftops?"

"It all depends on your perspective, I suppose." He inhaled. "Sometimes I fence. And sometimes I . . . dance."

She turned fully toward him, her fair brows rising nearly to her hairline. "You dance alone?"

"You don't approve?"

"It's my mother you're thinking of. I don't disapprove of dancing. How could I?" She lifted her chin and placed a solemn hand over her heart. "I, Julia Midwinter, have never danced." She glanced at him, eyes twinkling. "And if you tell my mother otherwise, I shall deny it to the end."

They shared a grin. Then Alec felt his grin fade.

Tentatively, he asked, "Why is your mother so set against dancing? Some people object for religious reasons, I know. Some Methodists and Quakers and . . ."

She shook her head thoughtfully. "I don't think my mother's reasons are religious. At least not primarily."

He waited for her to explain, but instead Julia pointed down into the churchyard.

"Do you see those large headstones?"

Alec followed the direction of her finger and nodded, though from this height the headstones appeared small indeed.

She said, "That's the family plot. My grandparents are buried there. My aunt and uncle. My father."

He glanced at her, surprised at how many close relatives she had lost, but unsure how this answered his question. He nearly joked, *"Don't tell me they all died dancing,"* but knew such a jest would be tactless. Instead he asked, "How long has your father been gone?"

"Two years."

He watched her face, afraid she might cry. When she did not, Alec ventured, "But apparently your mother did not dance even before she lost her husband. Is that right?"

"It has nothing to do with him—my father, I mean. It has to do with her brother. My mother has never divulged the details, but I gather he died in a fight at the last village fair twenty years ago. During the May Day dance."

Alec frowned. "So . . . she blames dancing for her brother's death?" He tried not to sound as incredulous as he felt.

"That's part of it, I believe. I've asked her several times, but she refuses to talk about the past in any great detail. Nor to yield in her stance."

Alec sighed. "Too bad." He drew himself up. "Well, I had better be on my way. Otherwise I shall be late and Mr. Barlow shall box my ears."

"Oh, Barlow is a lamb, for all his gruff ways. Tell him you were helping me and he shall forgive you anything."

Alec hoped that was true.

"My mother, on the other hand, will not."

"Right." Alec tipped his hat and hurriedly descended the tower.

Fortunately, Alec did not encounter Lady Amelia when he let himself in through the tradesman's entrance and slipped into the manager's office. Inside, Mr. Barlow stood at his desk, pointedly regarding the clock high on the wall.

"You are nearly a quarter of an hour late," he announced, his hound dog face sagging in disappointment.

"Sorry, sir. I stopped to . . . help Miss Midwinter."

His eyes widened, then narrowed. "Did you? And where was this?"

"In the churchyard." Alec looked about him, then lowered his voice. "Balancing atop the church tower."

The man winced, then nodded. "Very well, Valcourt. I take your meaning. Now, not a word about that to anyone. Understood?"

"Perfectly, sir."

"Good. Now. I've got a batch of rent receipts for you to add to the ledger and then there's the window tax to figure . . ."

Alec suppressed a groan. It was, after all, better than cutting clay bricks all day. And after his wrestling "lesson" yesterday, he was glad no backbreaking tasks awaited him. He felt broken enough as it was.

∽○

After Mr. Valcourt left, Julia remained atop the church tower for some time, thinking about their conversation. She couldn't blame him for believing her life a charmed one, but there was more to life than ease and advantage. Especially when that advantage came with strings—and an anchor—attached.

"For to whom much is given, much shall be required," her mother never tired of reminding her, paraphrasing Scripture.

Julia's life might have been enviable—had her father not disliked her, and her mother not begun grooming her to take her place at such a young age. When Julia thought back over her childhood, she recalled being trapped indoors with her governess or mother—practicing her curtsy and manners, learning to differentiate seven different types of forks, orders of precedence, and correct forms of address for the ranks of nobility—and glancing out the window and seeing James,Walter, and often Patience, riding together or heading off with fishing poles or cricket bat in hand.

No. Julia had no interest in assuming her mother's role as prim-lipped matriarch of Buckleigh Manor. She did not want to spend her days in interminable meetings and answering endless correspondence. She wanted to live her own life. Charmed or not.

Looking out over the estate grounds that morning, Julia felt uncomfortable in her own skin, and empty inside. Something was missing—

had been missing her entire life. And she was quite certain she was not going to find it within the walls of Buckleigh Manor.

⁓

After his duties were completed for the day and Mr. Barlow had gone to his dinner, Alec put on his hat and left by the rear door.

He was pleased to see Walter Allen leaning against a tree outside. Walt pushed himself upright and hailed him.

"There you are. Wanted to stop by and see how you are getting on today."

"Sore and stiff, but not too bad, considering. I'm surprised you came over—your mother seemed certain I would be recuperating at home today."

"I knew better, didn't I?" Walter winked. "She doesn't yet know how strong and stubborn you are. Not as I do." He extended two lengths of steel in his large hands. "I've brought your sword. Such as it is. You left it at our house last night."

"Thank you." Alec accepted the pieces with a sting of regret.

"Papa says to tell you to see the old smith. His forge is less than a mile out along the Sheepwash Road. There's a newer forge behind the inn, but Papa says the old man is the best and the very man to mend your sword, if anyone can."

"Then I shall go and see him. Thank your father for me."

"I shall. Hurry and get better—you and your sword." Walter grinned. "Your fencing partner is eager to continue his lessons."

After dinner and evening prayers with his family, Alec decided to take his sword and stroll to the blacksmith's. It was after regular hours, and he doubted anyone would be working the forge, but he was stiff after sitting at his desk all day and thought a bit of exercise would do him good. And if the man *was* there . . . Well, Alec was eager to have his blade repaired as soon as might be. He judged his injured leg equal to a mile walk but hoped he would not encounter anyone named Wilcox on the way.

He thought again of the dun horse his uncle had given him. Perhaps he ought to try to ride him again. *After* his ribs healed.

Dusk deepened the sky as he left the village behind, taking the Sheepwash Road as Walter had instructed. A chorus of whirring frogs accompanied his steps. Ahead in the distance he saw the orange-red glow of a fire. And as he neared, the dim outline of a small building came into view. An open-sided porch extended from an enclosed workroom at the rear. The old forge, he assumed. He remembered passing it when he'd come this way on his initial calls.

Within, a man sat over the fire, alternatively heating something and then shaping it with pliers. No sound of clanging metal rang out. No sparks flew. Alec wondered what he was working on. No everyday horseshoes, apparently.

Alec was surprised the old man was not inside having his supper or preparing for bed—but thankful too.

"Hello," Alec called as he neared, not wanting to startle the man by emerging from the darkness unannounced.

"Evening," the man returned, glancing up from his work.

Alec was the one to be startled. This man was not old. Nor a stranger. It was the man who had rescued him from the Wilcox brothers the day before.

"I say . . . you are not who I was expecting."

"Oh?"

"I was told an old man owned this forge."

"That's right." He nodded toward the house. "Old Mr. Desmond."

"Ah, I see. Is he . . . ?" Alec followed the direction of his gaze toward the house.

The man grimaced. "He's taken ill, I'm afraid. I'm helping out."

"Sorry to hear it. I am Alec Valcourt, by the way. I'm afraid I never got your name when you came to my rescue."

The man didn't immediately reply, his focus drawn back to the tool and metal in his gloved hands. "Sorry. Give me a minute to finish this before it cools."

"Of course. Forgive me; I don't mean to intrude."

"Have a seat, Mr. Valcourt." The man nodded toward a finely crafted bench.

Alec sat as bid, laying the sword pieces across his lap and watching the man's actions with interest. He asked quietly, "May I ask what you are making?"

"A hunting knife."

Alec felt his brows rise. "You don't say. For I've brought my own blade to be repaired. Those scoundrels broke it."

The man's eyes glinted. "Not planning to run them through, I hope."

Alec shook his head. "It's a French small sword. Still, sharp enough if need be." He looked over at the man and asked quietly, "Would you have shot them, by the way?"

The red-hot metal reflected eerily in the man's eyes. "I don't know. I hoped it wouldn't come to that."

Alec considered, then inhaled deeply. "I have never physically injured anyone in my life. But I have a mother and sister to support. Next time I will do what I must to protect myself."

Watching the man handle the sharp blade with such single focus, Alec bit his lip, then asked tentatively, "Have you . . . ever injured someone?"

"That's quite a personal question, friend."

"Sorry. Never mind."

The man looked up from his work and sighed. "Yes, I have hurt several people in my life. And one physically. I'm not proud of it."

He returned his focus to the blade. Alec watched as the man's gloved hands plunged the knife into a barrel of water. He then regarded the glinting blade in the light of a lamp, and set it in the curing rack.

He pulled off his thick leather gloves. "All right. Let's have a look at this blade of yours."

The man took the pieces Alec proffered, studying the break, the lines of each.

"Can you mend it?" Alec asked.

"Maybe. Though she'll never be quite the same. Leave it with me, and I'll see what I can do."

"Very well. Thank you." Alec rose. "You still haven't told me your name."

The man looked down. "I know. I'm sorry, it's just that I am not eager for news of my return to get round. I know it will eventually in a small village like Beaworthy, but I'm not keen on helping spread the word."

Alec remembered how the man had stiffened when James had mentioned Buckleigh Manor, and felt foreboding prickle over him. He asked, "Why?"

The man stared at the severed blade in his hands, and slowly shook his head. "I am not a popular person here. That's all I'll say for now."

The legend Miss Midwinter had told them about the large stone in the village echoed in Alec's mind. The story of how the bell ringers had failed to turn it last year and what it supposedly meant: the return of the devil. Alec looked at the strange man before him—red embers reflected in his dark eyes—and felt a shiver snake up his neck.

I shall be told that a person has no bent for dancing; to which I reply we can always learn when we wish to do so.

—Pierre Rameau, *The Dancing Master*, 1725

Chapter 9

The following day, Alec and Mr. Barlow inspected the estate's tenant cottages—noting which cobbed exteriors, thatched roofs, or stone walls needed repairing. Alec wrote as fast as he could with a stubby drawing pencil, taking notes as Mr. Barlow poked and prodded, reporting his findings for Alec to inscribe.

On their way back to the manor, they passed the paddock where Miss Midwinter was again putting her brown mare through a course of rail jumps. Today she wore a deep green habit with a short snug spencer that accentuated the curve of her waist, often lost in the shapeless fashions of the day. Her black brimmed hat was nearly as tall as a man's topper.

She trotted her horse toward the fence when she saw them. "Hello, Barlow. Mr. Valcourt tells me he has a horse but cannot ride it. I told him you were the very person to remedy that."

The last bit about Barlow was news to Alec, but he did not contradict her.

The estate manager's brows rose. "And why would you say such a foolhardy thing, miss?"

"It is not foolhardy, Barlow. As well you know." She turned to Alec.

"Mr. Barlow is too modest to own it, but he is an excellent horseman. Father put him in charge of selecting and training all our horses." Her eyes twinkled. "I think he used to bewitch them with that violin of his."

Alec looked at the man in surprise. "Do you play, Mr. Barlow?"

"Not anymore," he gruffly replied. "No time for it."

Julia continued, "Of course, that was before Mother raised him to his current lofty position, and now he believes himself far above the notice of mere horseflesh."

"Not at all, miss. But Isaacs runs the stables now. Not I."

Ignoring his demur, she continued, "Barlow rose through the ranks like no one I've ever known. Stable hand when just a lad, then groom, then coachman, then estate manager. Apparently he enjoys spending his days sitting in cramped, airless offices with solicitors and trades- men. I'm sure the thought of a grassy paddock on a fine spring day with only a promising horse and birdsong for company no longer appeals to him."

"I didn't say that, miss," Barlow objected. "It's true that now and again I miss the old days, but you'll not hear me complain."

"Of course not. You are all goodness. So you will help poor Mr. Valcourt, then? Say you will, Barlow. For me?"

He regarded her lovely, earnest face. "Oh, very well, miss." He glanced dourly at Alec. "Always could get me to do anything she wanted."

"So I see," Alec said. "And in this instance, I am grateful."

❧

The next day, his uncle's manservant bridled and saddled the dun horse for him. But Alec didn't bother trying to mount. Instead he led the horse by the reins to Buckleigh Manor, ignoring the questioning looks of those he passed on his way. Reaching the estate, Alec led the horse back to the stable yard, where a young groom offered to remove its bridle and saddle. They decided to leave the horse in the fenced paddock for the morning. He and Barlow would have their first les- son at midday.

At the appointed time, Alec returned to the paddock, where the groom had the horse saddled and waiting. Mr. Barlow nodded. "All right. Let's see what he does."

While Miss Midwinter and Barlow looked on, Alec approached the horse's left side, hoping to mount, but the wary-eyed creature sidestepped. Alec advanced again, and the horse sidestepped again.

"Are you trying to teach him to dance?" Julia teased.

Alec grumbled, "I would make a better job of it."

Perhaps a muzzle rub or chin scratch would help. He stepped forward toward the horse's head. The gelding stepped back. He extended a placating hand. "It's all right."

Another step forward. Another step back.

Ready to give up, Alec backed away. But the fool horse stepped forward, toward him.

"He is following your lead!" Julia exclaimed.

Alec regarded the horse. "I've had slower pupils."

Elbows on the rail, Barlow asked, "Where did your uncle say he got him?"

"A client of his."

Barlow said dryly, "A client from a circus?"

"Very funny. Look, if you don't want to help, just say so."

"No, I never said that. Now that I've had a look at him and see what we're up against, I am ready to take a turn." Barlow let himself in the gate. "May I?"

Alec gestured toward the horse. "Please. By all means."

"What's his name?"

"Apollo. Though my uncle had been calling him, simply, Dun."

Barlow frowned. "How would Mr. Ramsay like it if I began calling him silver side-whiskers?"

Julia stifled a laugh. Alec, however, was torn between offense on his uncle's behalf and laughing out loud.

"Horses are smart," Barlow continued. "He knows his name, assuming he's been called more than 'Hey, you.'"

"Easy, Barlow," Julia soothed. "Not everyone loves horses as much as you and I do."

Barlow pursed his lip in disapproval. "A pity too." He drew himself up. "Well, leave him to me for the time being. I'll introduce myself and let him get used to me. Call him Apollo from now on, mind?"

Letting himself from the paddock, Alec said, "I shall. Thank you."

Alec walked alongside Miss Midwinter back to the house.

"You are clearly very fond of Mr. Barlow," he began. "And he of you."

She nodded. "Yes. He has been more like a father to me than my own father was in many ways. Mother respects Barlow but doesn't like me spending too much time with him—with anyone in her employ, for that matter." She sent him a pointed look. "I think she keeps him busy to spite me."

"I don't know. There is a great deal to do to keep an estate of this size running smoothly, as I am learning."

"Then, I wonder Mother didn't hire a clerk long before now."

"Oh, I think Barlow, busy though he may be, was handling things fairly well without me. Some of my tasks seem like busywork. But hopefully he'll come to trust me and allow me to do more real work."

"I hope so too. Then perhaps he'll have more time for me." She grinned. "And your horse."

Alec sat at his small desk a short while later, balancing the postage log at Mr. Barlow's request. The manager was meeting with Lady Amelia in the library, so the office was quiet, save for the ticking of the wall clock. Alec relished the rare moments of solitude, as well as the task at hand.

Mr. Barlow, following the precedence of the estate manager before him, kept a log of all outgoing and incoming postage paid. It seemed an onerous task to log every letter, but in the case of servants, if an excessive number were received postage due, the amount was garnished from their wages.

Sally Jones, upper housemaid, received frequent letters from a gentleman in Bodmin, Alec noted, wondering if the sender was a doting relative or a sweetheart.

Lady Amelia received several newspapers, letters from a London solicitor and a modiste, as well as regular letters from Plymouth, notated as *Tremelling, Royal Navy*. Alec idly wondered what business Lady Amelia had with the navy, or if this Tremelling was some relative. Reading on, he noted that she also posted replies to the same name. Did Lady Amelia—a widow—have a sweetheart? She was not too old. And if she were not forever looking stern and disapproving, she would be a handsome woman. But even so, it was difficult to imagine.

A few minutes later, Mr. Barlow returned from his meeting. But before Alec could ask him any questions, the estate manager informed him that Lady Amelia wished to see him directly.

Alec knocked on the paneled door and entered the library when bid. Afternoon sunlight spilled through the wall of windows onto the carpet and bookshelves. The many windows afforded a great deal of light for reading but also cost a great deal in taxes, as Alec now knew.

Lady Amelia, seated at the wide mahogany desk, gestured him closer.

"Please. Have a seat."

Alec sat in a chair facing the desk, unsure if he should feel like a wayward servant, as usual, or perhaps even a criminal on trial.

"Mr. Valcourt, now that you are in my employ and under my roof each day, I don't think it unreasonable to ask more about your background."

Alec felt his heart rate accelerate. "Oh?"

"May I ask why you and your family have come here to Beaworthy?"

This again? "As you know, this is where my uncle lives."

"Yes. But is he your only living relation?"

"We haven't a large family." Alec faltered. "And he was willing to . . . That is, he offered to take us in and—"

"Why had you the need to be, as you say, 'taken in'? Were you unable to support yourselves in London?"

Alec squirmed. "We thought it best. That is, my mother wished to quit town for several reasons."

Her fine brows rose. "What reasons?"

He hesitated. "My father, having recently . . ." Alec swallowed. "Gone. We—"

She said briskly, "I see that your mother still wears mourning. When did Mr. Valcourt pass on?"

"He has been gone these five months." *God forgive me*, Alec thought.

"Why could you not continue on without him?"

Alec squeezed the arms of the chair. Tightly. "Your ladyship, if you are unhappy with the discharge of my duties, please say so."

She leaned back and lifted a dismissive gesture. "Not at all. Barlow seems quite satisfied with your work. In fact, it seems to have freed his time to visit the stables." She gave him a pointed look.

Alec considered how best to answer. "I did have several clients— pupils who would have continued their lessons with me—but not enough to keep the place going and support my family. And my mother thought it best to leave the scene of our . . . unhappiness."

"But to leave an established academy?"

Alec felt frustration mounting. "I do not see that I am obligated to air all of our personal problems, your ladyship, but if you must know, my father left behind debts. We had to sell our property to satisfy them."

She considered this. "Be that as it may, to come to a small, unfamiliar village in hopes of establishing a new following . . . Well, pardon me for saying so, but it seems very unwise."

He clasped his hands together and struggled to constrain his emotions. "Perhaps, in hindsight, it was. But here we are."

"Yes." Her gaze took in his features, his clasped hands. "Here you are."

She entwined her fingers on the desk and asked, "You would have no objection, I presume, were I to write to a London acquaintance to inquire into your reputation there?"

He stared at her, his cravat suddenly seeming too tight. "You asked for no character reference beyond my uncle's when you engaged me, but now . . . ?"

She lifted her chin. "When I engaged you, I thought I made it clear that you were to have little to do with my daughter. But apparently, the two of you have decided to ignore my wishes in that regard. If you are going to continue to spend time in my daughter's company, then yes, I feel it my right, even my duty, to know precisely whom I have hired."

He swallowed. "I was not such a popular dancing master that I flatter myself to think an acquaintance of yours would have heard of me. Let alone be able to comment on my character or reputation."

She formed a small smile. "Leave that to me. I have many acquaintances in town." She pulled a sheet of paper from her top drawer, slid it across the desk toward him, and held out a quill. "If you would be so kind as to provide your former direction or at least the street where your academy was located?"

Alec stared blindly at the quill, his mind as empty as the blank page before him. The trap had been set and he was about to place his foot squarely into it.

What could he do? He wouldn't give a false address. Should he try to preempt her? Explain away what she might discover? Perhaps she would find nothing. But somehow, glancing into those speculative blue-green eyes of hers, he doubted it.

He stood over the desk, dipped the quill, and wrote the number and street of the former Valcourt Dancing and Fencing Academy, quite certain he was sealing his fate in the bargain.

Alec walked home that afternoon, feeling as though a fuse had been lit. It was only a matter of time now. His past would catch up with him, and his future vanish with it. He wanted—needed—to support his mother and sister. He was the man of the family now. It was up to him. He'd planned to give his uncle half of his earnings for their upkeep, and divide another quarter between his mother and sister, so they would each have a little money of their own. It would not stretch far enough to cover folderols or new clothes, but he had so looked forward to ensuring his mother would not have to ask her brother for spending money as well as a place to live.

What should he do now—begin looking for another place, giving up excellent wages on the chance someone she knew was acquainted with their academy? And if a negative report did arrive—what then? Lady Amelia would lose no time in dismissing him, and likely make certain everyone in the village knew not to trust him or engage him for any sort of position, let alone dancing lessons.

Why did this have to happen? Alec asked his father—both earthly and heavenly.

Why?

The next day, Alec returned to his duties as though all were well. Maybe it would be. Maybe his bluff would stand. Maybe she wouldn't even bother to send a letter—perhaps she had been bluffing as well.

His hopes were dashed, however, when he saw the day's outgoing letters stacked on the hall table, ready for the post.

On the top: one addressed in a fine hand to *Mrs. Leticia Garwood, 14 Queen's Square, Bloomsbury, London.* Queen's Square . . . only a few blocks from their former academy. They were doomed.

He decided then and there that he might as well accept the Allens' offer to teach private dancing lessons at Medlands. With the hatchet destined to fall someday soon, he could not afford to turn down any paying position.

❧

After Alec worked his half day on Saturday, he took his borrowed sword with him into the churchyard. Walter had insisted he use one of their neglected swords, until his own had been repaired. Alec was still sore from the beating he'd taken from the Wilcoxes on Monday, but he thought he would at least stretch his aching muscles.

Making his way to the paved path outside the church doors, Alec set down his hat and sword on a headstone and gingerly peeled off his snug frock coat, his side protesting with each tug. He draped the coat over the headstone and removed his cravat as well. He carefully stretched his arms and upper body, then lunged low, one leg forward, then the other, his injured leg aching as he did so.

He picked up the sword and slid it from its scabbard. The hilt was gilded and decorative, likely far more costly than his own, but he missed having his grandfather's sword and hoped the smith could repair it.

He determined to walk out to the forge sometime soon to check on its progress.

He faced the headstone that wore his coat and hat, as though an actual foe. Blade in ready position, he slowly began his routine: Advance, lunge, retreat, retreat. Strike, parry-riposte. Feint, attack, parry-riposte . . .

He hoped the Wilcox brothers would not make another appearance, but if they did, this time he would be better prepared.

At the sound of a voice, Alec jumped and whirled about.

Julia Midwinter stood there, eyes wide. "My goodness," she said, with a glance at his sword. "A good thing I was not standing closer."

"Miss Midwinter." He lowered the weapon. "Forgive me."

Her gaze skated from his face to his shirtsleeves and open collar and back again. "Fighting phantoms again, are we?"

"You could say that." He sheathed the sword and picked up his coat from the headstone. "Please excuse my appearance."

She squinted at the name carved in the stone. "I remember Ezra Greenslade. I don't think he'd mind holding your coat."

As Alec slipped his hand into the sleeve, he observed her appearance—her lovely face framed by honey curls and a straw bonnet. A figure-hugging spencer over her gown, with ribbon trim on the sleeves and beneath her bosom. His mouth went dry to even think the word in her presence.

"What?" She looked down at herself, as though to flick away an offending insect or speck of soil.

"Nothing." Self-conscious, he struggled into the frock coat. A difficult feat, considering the snug cut, his aching ribs, and his audience.

She watched him with mild amusement. "You do not shock my maidenly sensibilities, Mr. Valcourt. Have no fear."

"May I help you with something, Miss Midwinter?" he said officiously, hoping to chase the self-satisfied grin from her face. And quell his own nerves in the bargain.

"Yes, actually." She clasped her hands. "I've come for a dancing lesson."

"Pardon?"

"A dancing lesson. Here—since Lady Amelia would never allow it in the house."

He licked dry lips and felt his pulse rate quicken. His mind whirled with conflicting emotions. Part of him relished the notion of being alone with Miss Midwinter. Enjoying her company and her undivided attention. Taking her hand in his to lead her through a private dance in a deserted churchyard . . . His chest tightened at the thought.

But he knew all too well the possible consequences of such stolen moments. Such seemingly innocent beginnings.

She took a step forward.

Alec took a step backward, reminded of his horse.

Again she stepped forward, and he stepped back. She performing the *chassé*, and he performing the dance of retreat.

"What is it, Mr. Valcourt?" She grinned. "Don't tell me you are afraid of me."

"You know Lady Amelia would not approve."

"What has that to say to anything?" She stepped toward him, but he sidestepped. A matador avoiding the charge.

"Miss Midwinter. Before we proceed any further, I must tell you that I have a strict policy against any romantic . . . uh, personal involvement with my pupils."

She blinked, momentarily taken aback. "In that case, perhaps I ought to reconsider becoming a pupil of yours."

"Perhaps you should."

She propped a hand on her waist. "My goodness, Mr. Valcourt. How proper you've become all of a sudden. Do you not like women in general, or is it just me you dislike?"

Alec recognized a trap when he saw one. "I like women in general, Miss Midwinter. But . . ."

"But I make you nervous," she suggested.

Alec nodded. Had he just admitted it? He had not meant to.

"Do I?" One fair brow rose high. She clearly took pleasure in the confession. He had not intended that either.

"It is only natural," he insisted, attempting nonchalance. "After all, you are the daughter of my employer. You have the power to see me put out of a favorable post."

"Is that all? I shouldn't worry about that if I were you. I quite like having you about the place. Life has become much more interesting since you've joined us."

"Perhaps you would not intentionally have me dismissed. But your mother has made it quite clear she doesn't wish us to spend time together. And we both know she would not approve of our dancing together."

"True." A shadow fell over Julia's face. "But then, she often disapproves of me." She sobered, her flirtatious manner falling away.

There it was again. That rare glimpse of vulnerability. He felt as if he'd been given a fleeting look into the soul of the real Julia Midwinter. Or was he fooling himself, seeing what he wanted to see? Imagining depth and substance where only shallow vanity existed?

A moment later, her guard went back up and vulnerable Julia was gone. She smiled coyly. "What do we do first?"

Her smirking innuendo suddenly reminded him far too much of scheming Miss Underhill. His defenses rose. If she wanted a lesson, he'd give her one she really needed.

"First, you must learn the etiquette of the ballroom."

"Etiquette? That's not what I had in mind."

Obviously. Alec cleared his throat and began, "A lady may not ask a man to dance. She must wait for him to ask her." He gave her a pointed look. "A gentleman, you see, prefers to do the pursuing."

She self-consciously lowered her eyes.

"And when he does ask," Alec continued, "she must not forget her engagement and dance with someone else. A lady must dance neatly and with decorum, no capering about or bumping into others. And no noisy talking or boisterous laughter."

Julia frowned. "All these rules for ladies. It hardly seems fair."

"Don't worry. Gentlemen have a long list of their own rules to follow. Now, where was I . . . ?" Alec thought, then continued, "Yes. Always wear gloves while dancing, preferably white. Ladies and gentlemen may not dance together unless they have first been introduced. And a couple should dance no more than two sets together in one evening."

He turned to the nearest headstone, still wearing his hat. "And, say Mr. Ezra Greenslade here asks you to dance—"

"Mr. Greenslade!" Julia interrupted. "A kindly undertaker to be sure, but not someone I should like to dance with." She shuddered theatrically.

"Very well, but if you refuse poor Mr. Greenslade, saying for example that you are too tired to dance, and then some dashing fellow asks—"

"Like you?" She fluttered her lashes.

He ignored that. "You would not be at liberty to accept. You must sit out the entire set."

"Can't have that," she said, turning to the headstone. "All right, Ezra. Wash your hands and I shall dance with you."

He bit back a grin. "The proper response to 'May I have this dance?' is 'I would be delighted' or 'With pleasure.' Something of that nature. Let's try again." He tipped the hat atop the stone and asked in a raspy accent, "May I 'ave this dance, Miss Midwinter?"

She curtsied and said sweetly, "I should enjoy it above all things."

The woman was a quick study. It was too bad, really. Because it seemed unlikely Miss Midwinter would ever attend an actual ball.

He would have liked to invite her to the dance lessons he hoped to begin at Medlands but knew it wasn't his place to do so. Nor was he sure it would be wise to tempt fate by including Lady Amelia's daughter in the forbidden activity. At least not as long as he was clerk at Buckleigh Manor.

❧

In the Medlands music room late the following Tuesday afternoon, Alec faced his pupils—James Allen, Patience Allen, and Walter Allen. His sister, Aurora, stood off to the side, ready to demonstrate, assist, or play the pianoforte as needed.

As Alec led the Allens through the beginning exercises, it became quickly evident that James possessed a natural athletic ability and

Patience, feminine charm and willingness if not an abundance of grace. Walter, however, stood stiffly and sullenly, frozen in a mockery of the first position.

"Come on, Walter," Alec urged. "At least try."

"This is ridiculous. I look like a fop. Who stands like this?"

"Dancers do."

"I am no dancer."

"That's the truth," James teased. "We spent a fortnight in London a few years ago, and attended a ball while we were there. I roused my courage and asked two young ladies to dance. But old Walt here spent the entire evening holding up the wall."

"Even though gentlemen were scarce," Patience added gently, "and several young ladies were sitting down in want of a partner."

"Don't you start, Pet."

"Try again," Alec said. "Heels together, feet turned outward."

"I look like a dashed waddling duck," Walter grumbled.

Alec bit back a grin at the apt description. "And now the second position. Move the right foot to the side, and rest your toes on the floor."

"Must I?"

"These basic positions form the fundamental steps of many dances."

Alec demonstrated the position, and Walter tried to force his feet into submission.

"Stand up straight, Walter. Don't slouch. Relax and stand comfortably—"

"Well, which is it?"

"Stand with your arms hanging naturally at your sides. You are not a soldier at attention."

"I feel like an idiot."

"Come, let's have a smile," Aurora encouraged. "Dancing is meant to be enjoyable."

"It's torture—that's what it is. I only wanted to learn fencing, not dancing."

"Come on, Walter." Alec lowered his voice. "Don't you want to impress the ladies?"

Walter blushed and looked at his large feet. "As if I could."

Alec continued to intone instructions, hearing his grandfather's voice, with its lingering French accent, echo through his mind.

"In the ballroom, steps should be performed in an easy graceful manner, with minute neatness, and in a rather small compass. . . ."

How many times he had heard his grandfather give these introductory comments to a new group of pupils. Alec and his father had not acquired his accent, which, considering the recent war and public opinion against foreign teachers, was fortuitous.

"Ladies, particularly, should rather seem to glide along with easy elegance, than strive to astonish by violent action. . . ."

"Come on, Valcourt," Walter begged. "Enough with the pomp and airs. If we must dance, let us have a lively jig or reel. Not this foppish nonsense."

"This is not foppish nonsense."

James winced apologetically. "It is a bit boring."

"Oh, very well." Alec set aside his notes. "As there are only four of you, including Aurora, the Foursome Reel, it is."

He and his sister demonstrated the opening steps. Then Alec instructed the women to stand back to back, facing their male partners.

They walked through the steps slowly, Alec tapping out the tempo with his grandfather's walking stick—a tool first he, then Alec's father had used to mark time. *Oh, Papa,* Alec thought, the bitter regret pinching his gut as it always did when he thought of his father's fate.

James and Patience learned the steps and patterns quickly, while Walter was slower to master them, and even then was ungainly when performing them. Fortunately, Aurora was excellent at leading when need be, and in encouraging the most challenging of partners. But even for her, nudging and cajoling and gesturing Walter through the dance was no easy feat.

Finally Alec thought they had reached a point where words would do no more good. Only one thing would help: music.

There was something about music that transformed rote steps into natural, fluid movements, that clarified the timing and turning like instructions alone never could. When Alec felt the music inside, his body and feet began to move of their own accord, puppets to the strings of notes. But he had learned to dance so long ago, it was difficult to recall a time when he had to think about the steps. In fact, it was sometimes a challenge to teach something one did without conscious thought. This was good for him, he decided. He was out of practice.

He walked to his case and took out his fiddle. He hoped he wasn't as rusty in playing as he'd become in teaching. He positioned the instrument—handed down from his grandfather, who had taught him to play—between jaw and shoulder, then lifted the bow. "Eight-count introduction, then begin. I will call out the steps the first time through to remind you. Watch Aurora if you forget what to do."

Striking bow to strings, he launched into the jaunty introductory bars, then said, "Ready, and . . . set to your partner."

Aurora and James began the coy little side-to-side step, which James performed remarkably well for a beginner. As they danced, Alec thought he noticed James Allen's eyes lingering on Aurora once or twice. Or was he imagining it? A man like James Allen—eldest son and heir of Medlands—was not likely to take a respectable interest in a dancing master's daughter. Aurora glanced over, and finding James looking at her, ducked her head self-consciously. Also strange, for Aurora was accustomed to partnering male pupils of every description.

Patience, craning her neck to watch Aurora, joined in a few seconds late but quickly recovered. Walter looked like an ox treading grain, but with a wild eye on his brother's movements, shadowed them a few beats after the fact. The first intertwining pattern looked more like a knotted lace than a figure eight. The women were supposed to switch partners before returning to their original places, but Walter ignored Patience, likely not even seeing her, as he followed Aurora with dogged determination.

Alec stopped playing, reminded them of the pattern, which Aurora demonstrated again, and then he played once more. This time, with a little push and whispered reminder, Aurora managed to nudge Walter toward his sister at the appropriate interval.

Walter grinned, sheepish and self-conscious. "Thanks, Miss V."

The simple pattern repeated itself and the dancers became more confident. Faces relaxed as the need to concentrate lessened and the enjoyment of the dance took over.

Alec began to remember why he enjoyed teaching. The pleasure of seeing the light of understanding spark in a pupil's eyes—the thrill of learning a new dance, of mastering steps at first deemed too difficult. Alec thought he might challenge himself to learn a few new dances from one of his books by famed dancing masters in London or Edinburgh. Not that there would be any call for all the new and fashionable dances here in Beaworthy with all of three pupils.

At the thought, Alec sighed inwardly, then forced a smile. Things were looking up, he told himself. After all, he was teaching dance in Beaworthy, and the world had not come to an end.

❧

The next day, Alec performed his duties gingerly, on edge, waiting for a summons to the library to meet with Lady Amelia, afraid she had somehow heard about the dancing lesson at Medlands and dreading the consequences. Patience might easily have mentioned it to Julia—the two young ladies were fast friends. And if Julia mentioned it to her mother in passing . . . Or perhaps a Medlands servant might have mentioned it to someone who worked in Buckleigh Manor, and word had got back to the mistress. . . .

The clock struck the hour and Alec started.

Barlow looked up from the letter he was signing. "Good heavens, Valcourt. You're as jumpy as your horse. What's got into you today?"

"Nothing, sir. Sorry. Too much coffee."

Barlow hmphed at that excuse and bent back over his work.

"How is Apollo?" Alec asked.

"He's coming around, I believe. Come out before you leave for the day and I'll show you."

After work that afternoon, Alec left the manor feeling relieved and hopeful the dance lessons could continue, undetected, his job as clerk secure—at least until Lady Amelia received a reply to her London letter. As he strolled toward the stable, the late-afternoon sun shone on him and cautious hope filled his chest.

Mr. Barlow, already standing in the paddock with Apollo, called Alec over. "All right, Mr. Valcourt, your turn."

As Alec approached, Barlow patted the gelding's neck, trying to keep the dun calm enough for Alec to mount.

Alec lifted his left foot into the stirrup, grasped the saddle leather, and pulled himself off the ground, swinging his right leg up and over. Apollo lurched in a violent sidestep worthy of the Highland Reel. Alec felt himself falling back as the horse slid out from beneath him. He landed on his backside in the paddock mire.

Alec was relieved Miss Midwinter was not on hand to witness his mortification.

Barlow sighed. "We shall try again next week."

For some weeks past the town has been disturbed by frequent assemblies of Bryanites, in a room over the marketplace. What with the ravings of the disciples within, and the laughter of the crowds without, the place has been a perfect Babel, disturbing the comfort and repose of the more rational inhabitants of the neighborhood.

—The West Briton, 1827

Chapter 10

Patience planned to spend Saturday afternoon with Miss Strickland, leaving Julia bored and lonely. So she arranged a diversion for herself—and hopefully Miss Valcourt as well. The early March day was cool but sunny. A lovely day for an excursion.

Soon Julia sat at the reins of the lightweight, speedy curricle pulled by a pair of horses. Their young groom sat on the back—her mother had insisted. With a lift of reins and an eager "Walk on," Julia urged the horses across the grounds and up the Buckleigh Road.

She halted in front of Mr. Ramsay's house. The groom hopped down and helped her alight.

"Hold them for me, will you? I won't be long."

Aurora Valcourt must have seen her drive up, for she opened the front door before Julia reached it.

"My goodness, Miss Midwinter, you are quite the whip."

"Thank you, Miss Valcourt. Come with me and I'll show you just how well I handle the ribbons."

"Oh? Where are you off to?"

"Shopping, I think. If you will accompany me."

Mrs. Valcourt appeared at her daughter's elbow.

Aurora turned and asked, "Mamma, Miss Midwinter has invited me to go shopping with her. May I?"

"Shopping? We don't . . . That is, I don't think you . . . need anything, my dear."

"Only window-shopping, Mrs. Valcourt," Julia clarified, guessing the Valcourts had little spending money. "The millinery has a new shipment of bonnets for spring."

"Oh. Very well, then," Mrs. Valcourt said. "But don't be gone too long, Aurora. Mr. Bullmore plans to call at four."

Aurora smiled with pleasure. "Yes, Mamma." The girl disappeared inside and returned a few moments later with bonnet, gloves, and reticule.

The groom gave both ladies a hand up and then climbed back onto the rear box. Once he was settled, Julia lifted the reins and urged the horses up the road and into the village. But as they clattered along the High Street, Julia made no effort to slow down.

"I thought you said the millinery?" Aurora asked as they passed it by.

"I did. But not the Beaworthy millinery. The bonnets there are for spring all right—spring of 1801."

Aurora chuckled.

They drove to the larger town of Holsworthy, some six or seven miles away. There they stopped at a livery, where Julia handed over the reins to a hostler, instructing him to make sure the horses had plenty of water while they rested. She gave the young man her name, a silver coin, and a warm smile. He blushed as red as his hair.

Julia gave their own groom a coin as well and told him to buy himself some refreshment at the inn and then wait for them at the livery.

Arm in arm, the two young ladies walked along the Holsworthy High Street and paused before the millinery window to take in its display of hats and Easter bonnets.

"Very nice," Aurora murmured.

"Don't be polite, Aurora. I can see you are not impressed. I'm sure no shop in Devonshire could compare to the London shops you are used to."

"I don't know. Some of these are lovely. Have you set your heart upon one in particular?"

"No . . ." Julia turned her head, her attention snagged by a flash of red. "Any of them will do."

Aurora turned toward the sight that had captured Julia's attention—not the assortment of hats, but the assortment of men clustered at the end of the street. Men in lobster-red uniforms.

"You see, Aurora," Julia said. "Holsworthy has not only more bonnets than Beaworthy, but more men as well. A regiment of Devon militia is training nearby. And the officers are allowed a half day's leisure once a week."

"So I see," Aurora said.

"There is something about a man in uniform." Julia sighed. "Handsome, are they not?"

Aurora squinted. "It is hard to tell at this distance."

"Good point." Julia hooked Aurora's arm and walked forward. "Come on."

"Julia!" Aurora whispered, voice trembling in fear and excitement.

"Don't worry. I promised we would only window-shop." She winked at the younger girl.

As they approached, the men in red coats parted like the Red Sea to allow them to pass. Hats were swiped from heads, gallant bows were made, compliments given—a few wolfish whistles punctuating the more gentlemanly addresses.

After they had passed through the gauntlet, Julia smiled at her blushing, starry-eyed companion. "Now, was that not worth the trip?"

"Indeed. . . ." Aurora breathed, and Julia gave the girl's arm an affectionate squeeze. She knew they would be fast friends.

Later, as the girls left Holsworthy, they were followed by two officers giving mischievous chase on horseback, hands to their hearts, vowing undying devotion. Julia soaked up the admiration and laughed at their antics, urging the carriage horses faster. When she finally tore her gaze from the young men long enough to glance at Aurora, she noticed the girl's smile seemed stiff and determined, and her gloved hand gripped the wooden side rail.

When they left the town limits, the young men reined in, lifted their hats, and waved them overhead. Determined to impress both the officers and Aurora with her driving skill, she urged the horses into one final burst of speed as they drove from sight. Ahead, the road curved sharply.

"Miss!" the groom called a warning, hanging desperately to his rear perch.

With a thrill of pleasure, Julia rounded the corner on one wheel. *Crack, thwing!*—the wheel hit a rocky hole in the road, and careened to one side.

Beside her, Aurora cried out.

The vehicle lurched back down onto both wheels with shuddering force. Alarm for the first time gripped Julia's stomach. She reined in the horses and guided the vehicle to the side of the road, sensing in the rattling vibration that something was wrong. She hoped they had not broken a wheel or axle.

She tied off the reins and hopped down without waiting for the groom to assist her. She didn't see the young man on the rear ... but spied him sprawled on the verge several yards back.

She called, "Are you all right?"

"I think so, miss." He rose to his feet and wiped at his coat and trousers.

"Sorry about that, Tommy."

Together they inspected the undergirdings and discovered one of the spring straps had snapped off, but thankfully the axle and wheels appeared sound. Still, it would be a slow, jarring ride home.

When they returned to Mr. Ramsay's cottage late that afternoon, they were met by a white-faced Mrs. Valcourt.

"Aurora, there you are! I was becoming frantic. You've been gone for more than three hours. You have missed the rector's visit, though he came expressly to become acquainted with our family. Your uncle has sent Abe to the milliner's and Alec back to Buckleigh Manor, but no one had seen hide nor hair of you. You don't know how I've been praying for you—certain you'd been set upon by highwaymen or were dead in a ditch somewhere."

Inwardly, Julia groaned. *Wonderful. Now Mamma shall scold me as well. . . .*

"I am sorry for worrying you, Mrs. Valcourt," Julia said. "It is my fault. There was nothing in Beaworthy to suit my fancy, so we drove into Holsworthy. On the way back, we lost a spring strap and had to slow down considerably, or we would have returned sooner."

A horse came galloping up the road, and Julia recognized Barlow on Raven, his favored black horse. He did not look pleased.

"Miss, there you are. Your mother sent me to look for you. We were worried."

"You all worry too much," Julia said, forcing a chuckle to lighten her complaint. "I am well. Miss Valcourt is well. We were only window-shopping."

Barlow hesitated. "Well, I shall ride on ahead and let her ladyship know you're safe. Promise you'll follow directly, miss."

Julia stayed only long enough to thank Aurora for accompanying her, and to apologize yet again for returning her late, before lifting the reins and turning the curricle toward home. She dreaded the pending argument with her mother. That's all they seemed to do these days— Lady Amelia reprimanding or lecturing. Julia sniping or defending.

It hadn't always been that way between them. When she was young, Julia and her mother had enjoyed each other's company—reading together or strolling through the gardens, visiting the students at the girls' school, or occasionally driving into Holsworthy to shop or attend a concert. If the weather was pleasant they had sometimes taken a picnic into Dartmoor or some other lovely place. They had talked about everything. Though, thinking back, Julia had prattled on while her mother mostly listened. She rarely talked about herself, about her past or her family or her marriage. Julia had not given it much thought at the time—the self-centeredness of youth, she supposed.

Her father, however, had not spent any time with her. And the harder Julia had tried to gain his attention, the more he seemed to withhold it. Her mother never acknowledged his disinterest, but she had tried to make up for it.

Whenever Mr. Midwinter had refused to play dominoes with her or to read her a story, her mother had said nothing would please her more. She remembered once asking her father if she looked pretty in a new dress, and he told her not to be so vain. Her mother had consoled her, saying, "Of course you look pretty, Julia. Your father simply wants you to remember not to put too much importance on outward beauty. Character and behavior are so much more important." She'd turned to Mr. Midwinter. "Is that not what you meant, my dear?" And he had emphatically agreed.

But somewhere along the line, Julia had come to resent her mother's cheerful interference and attention, and begun to push her away. Was it an urge to reject as she had been rejected? To hurt as she had been hurt? She wasn't sure.

Whatever the case, Julia now sighed and steeled herself for the clash to come.

Reaching the house, Barlow and her mother came out to meet the carriage.

Barlow knelt to inspect the broken spring, then frowned up at her. "Those were brand-new spring straps, miss. How fast were you going?"

Julia shrugged. "Heavens, I don't know. Don't scold me, Barlow. No one was hurt."

He scowled at the groom's filthy trousers. "No? Then why is Tommy covered in mud?"

"I'm all right, sir," the young man said sheepishly.

Her mother shook her head. "One of these days, Julia, your reckless-ness is going to end in more than mud and broken springs. Someone is going to get hurt."

Julia swallowed a pinch of guilt. She hadn't done anything so very wrong. She was tired of being chastised every time she came home. Perhaps it was time to try harder to encourage a marriage proposal from a man who lived somewhere else. Anywhere else.

◦⁄◦

On Sunday after church, Alec saw Miss Midwinter exit the building alone. Lady Amelia had stopped to talk with the churchwarden, leaving Alec the perfect, if brief, opportunity to speak with Julia without the disapproving presence of her mother.

With a smile of thanks to the clergyman, Alec hurried outside.

There she was, standing alone amid chatting parishioners, watching the doorway, apparently waiting for someone—for him?

But then she suddenly turned away as though to avoid him. Alec frowned. She had been eager to seek him out before. . . . Perhaps she had simply not seen him.

"Miss Midwinter," he called as he caught up with her on the church path.

She turned and asked politely, "Mr. Valcourt. How are you?"

"I am well, thank you. And you? Dangled off any church towers lately?"

She pursed her lips and looked up as though estimating. "Only twice."

"Ah. Good. You've reformed, I see."

That earned him a lovely grin. Seeing it lightened his heart.

But at that moment something snagged her attention and she turned abruptly. "Pardon me, Mr. Valcourt. I see someone I must speak to."

Alec's mouth opened in surprise, but before he could reply or attempt a witty farewell, her heeled slippers were already tapping away down the paved path.

She hailed a young gentleman Alec only vaguely recognized. "Mr. Bullmore!"

In response to her call, the thin gentleman turned and joined her a few yards from where Alec stood. "Oh. Hello, Miss Midwinter."

She beamed at him. "Going fishing today?"

"Not this time. I am off to Bath this afternoon."

"What a pity. I wish you were staying longer. I hoped to hear about your grand tour."

"Perhaps another time." The young man glanced back at Alec and asked, "And who is that young man you were talking to?"

"Oh, that's Mr. Valcourt, our clerk," she said with a dismissive wave of her gloved hand. She fluttered her lashes at the man. "How exciting Bath must be. I suppose you know many people there . . . ?"

Alec turned and walked away. He told himself not to let her snub bother him. As a dancing master, he had been used to society ladies looking down at him. A caper merchant was beneath the notice of highborn females and certainly their parents, who were busy planning advantageous matches with heirs or second sons of nobility. The girls might flirt with him—all the more if he ignored them or appeared oblivious to their beauty. Most couldn't stand that. And seeing them try all the harder to dance well, to flirt with him and gain his notice had somewhat assuaged the slight to his pride—until it had all but ruined his life and his entire family. No, he told himself. All the better if Miss Midwinter ignored him and he treated her with nothing more, and nothing less, than common civility.

His uncle came and stood beside him, and the two men watched as Julia Midwinter chatted away, apparently unaware that the young gentleman was trying to extract himself from her company.

"Mr. Bullmore's son," his uncle explained. "Recently engaged to a lady from Bath, I understand. Apparently Miss Midwinter has not yet heard."

"Ah."

"Don't take it to heart, lad."

Too late, Alec thought. "I know I should not," he said. "After all, what do I expect? A lady like her and a man like me . . ."

His uncle clapped his shoulder in a rare display of affection. "Now, don't say that, my boy. The Midwinters are no better than they should be."

Alec looked at Uncle Ramsay in surprise. "What do you mean?"

"Normally I wouldn't say anything," his uncle continued. "But in this case, the client in question is no longer living."

"What are you talking about?" Alec asked. "What client?"

"Halloo!" a female voice called. "Mr. Ramsay!"

Alec glanced over and saw Mrs. Tickle, the kind widow from the bakery.

At the interruption, Cornelius Ramsay seemed to remember his surroundings. As he lifted a hand to greet the woman, he said quietly, "We'll talk later, all right? In my study, after we dine."

"Of course."

Mrs. Tickle walked over to them. "'Tis March, Mr. Ramsay, and you know what that means."

"No. What?"

"Only three months 'til gooseberry season. Can you believe it?"

"I am flummoxed, madam. But what has that to do with me?"

"Goose!" She smacked his arm with her prayer book. "Three months until gooseberry tarts, as if you didn't know." She smiled conspiratorially, then turned to Alec.

"Hello, Mr. Valcourt. My sister tells me you are working at Buckleigh Manor now. I suppose that explains why you haven't been by for one of my pies."

He bowed. "Exactly so, ma'am. Nothing else would have kept me away." He hadn't had an opportunity to return to the bakery since he'd begun working every day.

"I suppose they feed you there?"

He nodded. "I share the midday meal with Mr. Barlow."

"That Mrs. White is known to be an excellent cook. Would be, working at the manor as she is." She bit her lip. "I suppose her pies are far superior to mine?"

"Why no, Mrs. Tickle. Far from it. I never ate a pie as delicious as yours in my life."

She beamed a closed-lip smile that puckered her lips and bulged her cheeks until her face seemed about to burst like a squeezed berry. "You are too kind, sir. Too kind. What a charming nephew you have, Mr. Ramsay."

His uncle eyed him dourly. "Indeed."

Uncle Ramsay tipped his hat to the woman and quickly excused himself, telling Alec he would go home straightaway to see how dinner was progressing, but that he and his mother and sister should return at their leisure. The man was clearly uncomfortable in social situations. Or perhaps only women made him nervous.

Seeing his mother and sister talking to Miss Allen at the edge of the church path, Alec bid Mrs. Tickle farewell and hurried to join them.

He bowed to Miss Allen and was welcomed into the pleasant conversation. She explained that she had ridden with the Midwinters that day, as her parents were home nursing colds. They all stood speaking for a few minutes longer, and then the Valcourts bade Patience farewell, asking her to pass along their greetings and get-wells to her family.

As they crossed the High Street together, Alec saw Felton and Joe Wilcox loitering in the deserted market hall, watching the churchgoers depart.

Felton leaned against one of the columns. "Well, if it ain't Valerie Valcourt, the pretty boy," he called with a lazy grin.

Joe said nothing, his attention snagged by Aurora.

Misgiving filled Alec.

Not willing to risk the Wilcox brothers approaching his mother and sister, Alec whispered for the two of them to go on without him and turned to the dangerous pair.

Felton's brows rose in surprise as Alec walked over. He pushed himself upright and elbowed his brother. "Looks like he wants another wrasslin' lesson."

Alec told himself to be polite. At least until his family was out of sight and harm's way. "Hello, Felton. Joe. How are things at Kellaway's?"

Felton tsked, shaking his head. "Ben Thorne seems to lose his balance and fall into the pit at least once a week. His hat even oftener." The two brothers shared a smirk.

Then Joe asked a question of his own. "Who's that pretty girl you were walking with? Your *lover*?"

Alec stiffened at his innuendo and quickly corrected the crude man.

"No, my sister." But he regretted the words as soon as he'd uttered them. Even more so when Joe's eyes widened.

"Your sister?" he breathed. "Why, I'd say she's nearly as pretty as you are."

"Maybe more so," Felton agreed.

Alec glanced at Felton but saw that his gaze was firmly fixed on Miss Allen across the street, still waiting to enter the Buckleigh barouche.

Meanwhile Joe watched Aurora's retreating figure. "Come on, Valcourt. Introduce us."

"Ah . . . sorry, Joe. Our uncle is expecting us. Perhaps another time." To himself he added, *After I'm dead and buried.*

Alec joined his uncle in his study after a buffet meal of cold meats, breads, pickled beets, and leftover pudding.

He was curious about Miss Midwinter, of course, and longed to learn more about her, but something in his uncle's eyes told him he wouldn't like what he had to say.

"I can see you're interested in Miss Midwinter. A pretty girl, I don't blame you. But I want to give you a word to the wise, that there's no sense pining after her."

"Because she is above me, you mean?"

"Well, of course you are not her social equal. And certainly in terms of rank, wealth, and connection, she is out of your reach, but that is not what I refer to."

You mean there's more? Alec thought acerbically. He prompted, "You mentioned a client?"

"Yes. Arthur Midwinter."

"Julia's father?"

"Well . . . um. Perhaps. You see, my former partner, Mr. Ley, was his solicitor. He acquainted me with the particulars when he retired."

Lady Amelia, Alec knew, retained a London solicitor.

"Mr. Ley had been called in to compose the marriage settlement for a quickly orchestrated union between Mr. Midwinter and Lady Amelia," Uncle Ramsay explained. "Her father, Lord Buckleigh, was on his deathbed, and apparently eager to see her settled before he died—especially since he'd recently buried his son and there would be no man to lead the family otherwise. Arthur Midwinter was from a family of landed gentry. He was wealthy and well respected. But his older brother had inherited the family property, so he was at liberty, as it were, to become master of Buckleigh Manor."

Alec still didn't see what his uncle was driving at but did not interrupt him.

"Mr. Ley confessed to me that when he heard of the birth of a child seven or eight months later, he was quite surprised. He'd heard nothing of the impending birth, though the Beaworthy rumor mill has its tentacles everywhere and is usually quite accurate. However, that particular summer and fall—after her brother's death—Lady Amelia sequestered herself indoors, I understand. The wedding was private, the vows said right in the earl's sickroom. There was no wedding trip. Lady Amelia didn't even attend church for months, in her grief, everyone supposed. But apparently in her confinement as well."

Uncle Ramsay paused to draw breath, then continued, "Mr. Ley called on Mr. Midwinter a few months after the child's birth, but the new father saw no need to update his will. Years later, when Mr. Midwinter's health began to decline, and I was then his solicitor, I again asked about his will and whether he wished to leave anything to his daughter. He said there was no need to mention the girl. I believe he hinted, although subtly, that the child might not be his. I was shocked, as you can imagine, though professing to be a man of the world, I pretended not to be."

Uncle Ramsay shook his head. "Lady Amelia is widely respected as a paragon of sense and virtue. But apparently public opinion is not always accurate. After I spoke with Mr. Midwinter myself, the rushed wedding Mr. Ley had described made more sense. I thought it quite generous of Mr. Midwinter, assuming he married Lady Amelia knowing she carried another man's child. Though perhaps he found out later.

"Either way, he clearly had no intention of exposing his wife or the girl to gossip or humiliation, but nor did he wish to remember the girl in his will. He did remember his wife, and of course the marriage settlement had long ago assured that Buckleigh Manor would remain in Lady Amelia's possession and then pass to her heir. Fortunately for Lady Amelia, Buckleigh Manor has never been entailed away to the male line."

Alec's mind struggled to credit the story. He'd seen nothing in Lady Amelia's character to suggest she was capable of such a moral lapse— none of the recklessness he'd seen in her daughter. But he also recalled Miss Midwinter saying that Mr. Barlow was more like a father to her than Mr. Midwinter had been. . . .

"So you see, my boy," his uncle concluded. "The girl has little reason to believe herself too good for you."

Alec knew that even a hint of illegitimacy could ruin a person's reputation and prospects in some circles. And respectable people, like his uncle, would not approve of a woman whose birth had been tainted by scandal. But she was still an heiress, still Lady Amelia's daughter—if perhaps, not Mr. Midwinter's—and still beautiful. Besides, if he didn't miss his guess, Julia Midwinter had no inkling that scandal may have overshadowed her birth. And he preferred to keep it that way.

"I would appreciate it, Uncle, if you would not tell anyone else what you have just told me. I have a high regard for both Miss Midwinter and her mother and would hate to see them suffer should the rumor mill, as you call it, get wind of this."

"I've not said a word since I first heard of it until now. Nor will I again. But I wanted you to know that your high regard may be misplaced."

"Thank you," Alec said stiffly. "Considering the strikes against my own family, I don't know that I consider this a fatal blow to my hopes— such as they are. Especially as none of it is certain."

"Very well, my boy. But don't raise your hopes too high. They are proud women, for all that. And from what I hear, everyone expects her to marry James Allen."

Marry James? Alec's heart sank.

His uncle added, "I'd hate to see you disappointed again."

So would I, Alec thought, but he made do with a nod and reassuring smile.

Later that afternoon, Walter Allen surprised them all by stopping by unannounced.

He apologized to Mr. Ramsay for disturbing him, greeted Mrs. Valcourt and Aurora, and then with a glance at his pocket watch said, "Valcourt, um, let's take a walk."

Puzzled, Alec nevertheless picked up his hat and followed Walter outside.

"Where are we going?"

"Just come along. I want to show you something." Walt grasped his arm and quickened his pace.

Alec had to scramble to keep up with his long strides. "All right. All right!"

The tall lanky man released him and led the way into the village toward the market hall. The stalls below were deserted, but the room above was brightly lit and unaccompanied singing streamed from windows left open to the cool evening air.

Alec remembered Ben Thorne saying this was where the Bryanites held their meetings and guessed that was the gathering he was hearing.

He glanced at Walter and found the young man looking up at the windows with an expression both openly earnest and pinched with frustration.

"Can't see anything from here. Come on."

"Where now?" He hoped Walter didn't plan to dash up the outside stairs and join the assembly there and then.

But instead Walter crossed the narrow side of the divided High Street, and pushed through the door of the inn nearby.

With a wave to Mr. Jones, Alec followed Walter up the side stairs. He thought he heard a teasing taunt of "Peeping Toms," but hoped he was mistaken.

At the top of the stairs, Walter turned down the narrow passage, past sleeping rooms and the sadly unused assembly room. At the end of the passage, he stopped at a window facing the High Street.

"You can see from up here."

Following Walter's example, Alec looked through the window into the market hall meeting chamber across the way. The room was lit by candle lamps and filled with people. A man at one end of the room stood with arms raised, while those facing him sang, jumping in place, and . . . dancing? Alec could not see their feet, only the swaying movements of their torsos and the graceful fan of hands.

Mixed emotions filled him. On one hand he was taken aback, discomfited by their strange behavior—their boisterous singing, shouts of "Hallelujah" and eye-shut abandon. No wonder some unkind people called them "ranters."

On the other hand, they *were* dancing. . . .

"Now, this is my sort of church," Alec murmured teasingly.

Receiving no reply, he glanced at Walter, saw him vaguely nod, his eyes focused straight ahead. Rapt. Alec followed the direction of his gaze, and realization dawned.

Tess Thorne. There she was, clustered with several other young women. Her eyes were open but focused upward on some distant place. On God, he supposed. Her arms were extended in graceful lines, long hair falling loose over her shoulders and down her back. Fair face serene, she seemed unaware of those around her, of anything but the object of her adoration.

Guilt swamped Alec in double measure. First, it seemed wrong to be watching such an intimate, reverent act—and it *was* reverent, he realized, for all its lack of quiet solemnity. And second, how long had it been since he had communed with his Creator with half the sincerity and fervor of these people?

The Bryanites, as they were known, were an offshoot of the followers of John Wesley, Alec had learned, begun by a man named William Bryant. But their services were certainly unlike any other Alec had ever seen.

Within the meeting room, the volume increased: voices raised in song and shouts, and thirty or forty pairs of feet jumping up and down on wooden floorboards.

"Do you often watch them?" Alec whispered to his fellow voyeur.

Walter shrugged. "Now and again."

"Have you ever gone up and joined them?"

Walter shook his head.

"Have you ever even talked to her?" Alec asked, earning himself a quick glance of worried surprise from the young man.

"I . . . No," Walter said. "But I have met her. At least, I was there when Patience and Julia met her."

Alec rolled his eyes, then looked again at the window display of worshipers.

CRACK. A great bang shot the air and shook the building. For a second Alec thought the inn was collapsing and grabbed for the window ledge. Was it a cannon? An explosion? The market hall beyond shuddered and the worshipers' praise turned to cries of alarm. Several figures framed in the window suddenly disappeared while others looked down in shock.

"Come on," Alec shouted, pulling a stupefied Walter by the arm and rushing down the stairs. Walt's heavy tread thudding behind him, they dashed through the main level, past men clustered at the front window.

"The floor's collapsed!" one of them shouted.

Heart banging, Alec pushed through the door and ran across the lane to the market hall. He quickly assessed the scene before him. A beam under the meeting room had given way. A tumult of splintered beam, floorboards, and tangled bodies had fallen to the market floor below. Alec prayed a frantic, *God help them!*

A cry from above drew his attention upward. A young woman hung from the edge of the gaping hole above, holding on by her hands, skirt torn and billowing, stockinged legs dangling.

"It's her!" Walt cried, face stricken.

Alec recognized her at the same moment. Tess Thorne.

The ceiling of the market hall was at least twelve feet high. He didn't think anyone would die from such a fall, but injuries were likely. Alec thought they might be able to reach Miss Thorne, hanging by her hands as she was, and help her down. He leapt over the fallen beam and sidestepped to avoid a man groaning over an injured ankle and a woman cradling her arm. Reaching the spot, he stretched up, reaching to her ankles, but he could not get a good grip on her. "Walter, come quick!"

Walter blinked awake from his shock-induced daze and bounded over. "You're taller," Alec said. "Help her down."

Walter extended his arms, his large hands reaching about midleg, though it was difficult to tell through her full skirts. He froze, his hands suspended near her skirt, just shy of touching her. He looked at Alec uncertainly.

"Take hold of her," Alec urged.

"But, I . . ."

"Go on, man."

Walter did so and was rewarded with a gasp from above.

"Miss Thorne," Alec called up, "we've got you."

A flash of pale face. Wide eyes. "I'm slipping!"

"It's not so far down. Mr. Allen and I will catch you."

He felt Walt's panicked look but ignored it.

"You'll be all right," Alec assured. "Let go now."

"Promise?" she cried.

Alec looked at Walt pointedly.

"Oh. Right." Walter craned his neck. "Promise!"

They looked at one another, tightened their grips, and hoped to God they could catch her.

With a little squeal she fell. Alec gauged her fall and took a half step to the side. Walter lumbered to match his position and *whoomp* she landed. For a slight creature she weighed a surprisingly great deal when dropped from such a height. Alec, still tender from his injuries, nearly lost his hold on her, but Walter held tight.

Together he and Walt held Tess Thorne in their arms. For some reason, she looked at Alec, and her eyes locked on his.

"Thank God. And thank you!"

For a moment Alec allowed himself to sink into those deep chocolate eyes, to relish the admiration and approval there. Around him, the other people and sounds faded away. She really was pretty. . . .

Then he remembered Walt.

"Um. Just glad you're all right." He nodded toward his friend. "Walt here is the real hero. He's the one who bore the brunt of your weight—" He faltered and hurried to clarify, "Not that you are heavy, Miss Thorne. It's only that, well, I could not have caught you without Mr. Allen here."

She turned her head to look at the silent Walter.

"Thank you, Mr. Allen."

He stared. Managed a jerk of a nod.

"I . . . think you can put me down now."

Still Walter stared. Then he blinked, startled. "Oh! Right. Sorry."

As she regained her feet, her brother and a middle-aged couple rushed down the outer stairs.

"Tess! Are you all right?" Ben called. "Are you hurt?"

"I'm well. Thanks to these two gentlemen. They caught me as I fell."

"Well, praise God," the man said, and pumped first Alec's hand, then Walt's. "Erasmus Thorne. Tess's father. And this is Mrs. Thorne."

Walt said nothing, so Alec replied for both, "Alec Valcourt and Walter Allen. How do you do."

Around them the chaos—calls of panicked family members, groans of pain, and villagers arriving to help—returned to Alec's awareness. "If you will excuse me, I'll see if there's anything I can do."

Mr. Thorne nodded. "Good man."

Again he felt Tess Thorne's admiring glance but looked away. He had not meant to sound gallant; he simply thought his help might be needed elsewhere.

Alec soon discovered that three people had fallen without warning and had no chance to try to catch themselves or break their fall as Miss Thorne had been fortunate enough to do. The surgeon arrived and examined the victims. The woman's arm was indeed broken, the man's ankle only badly sprained. A young man had suffered a concussion, but Mr. Mounce thought he would be fine in a few days.

Before taking his leave, Alec glanced over his shoulder and saw Walter still deep in conversation with the Thornes. As he had guessed, his friend did not at all mind having their sole attention.

On Sunday last a congregation of Ranters assembled in a large loft over a stable. In the course of the service, the fervour of the devotees was so strongly excited, that they commenced jumping, in imitation of David's dancing before the ark. The beams suddenly gave way, and the minister and his dancing congregation, were suddenly precipitated into the stable beneath them.

—*The West Briton*, 1827

Chapter 11

Alec went to Buckleigh Manor on Monday as usual, and spent half an hour answering Barlow's questions about the collapse. Miss Midwinter sought him out as well, eager for an eyewitness account. He was relieved, however, that Lady Amelia did *not* seek him out. More than a week had passed since she'd posted her London letter. She could receive a reply any day now.

The next day, Uncle Ramsay told Alec that the village council had met—choosing the public house over the meeting room for obvious reasons—and appointed a carpenter to inspect the hall. The man had quickly reported that portions of the main beam—an old ship's mast—were riddled with deathwatch beetle. Some disregarded his findings, blaming instead the bell ringers' failure to turn the devil's stone. Those less charitable, especially neighbors who had found the loud singing and foot stomping vexing, held to their own explanation of the cause of the collapse.

On Tuesday afternoon, Mr. Barlow again hailed Alec from the paddock. "All right, Mr. Valcourt, let's try again."

Alec was both pleased and uneasy to see Miss Midwinter standing at the fence, there to witness the proceedings. She would likely enjoy his humiliation. He hoped he wouldn't be thrown again or injured. He had another dance lesson to teach at Medlands in an hour.

As Alec let himself in through the gate, Barlow patted Apollo's neck, again trying to keep the gelding calm enough for Alec to mount.

Alec grasped the saddle leather and placed his left foot in the stirrup. Again Apollo lurched in a violent sidestep, but this time Alec managed to land on his feet.

Barlow still held the bridle, though the horse's back end had shifted far to his left. He gently chastised the horse and encouraged him to be kind to the poor, inexperienced sot.

"He has to trust you, Mr. Valcourt," Barlow said. "You must embody confidence and garner trust."

"I am not confident."

"As we are all aware—including Apollo. A horse is very sensitive to the moods and confidence of its rider."

The calming process repeated, Alec again made ready to mount.

This time when he put his foot in the stirrup, Apollo reared up onto his back legs, tossing Alec to his seat. Barlow's arm flew up to shield his face, and the gelding's front hooves collided with his forearm in a nasty crack.

"Botheration!" the man exclaimed, managing to keep hold of the reins with his other hand.

"Barlow!" Julia cried, swinging her leg over the paddock gate with the same ease she mounted a horse.

Wincing, Barlow held his arm close to his chest. He gritted between clenched teeth, "Shuttle-headed, hog-grubbing sapskull . . ."

Julia hurried over to him. "Are you all right?"

Barlow's whole body tensed in an effort to control himself. Jaw pulsing, lips tight, he said, "Unfortunately, I believe my arm is broken."

"Oh no."

Alec pushed himself to his feet. "I'm so sorry, Barlow."

"It's my fault," Julia said. "I should never have insisted."

Alec shook his head. "It's my horse. I'm to blame."

"You two go on and quarrel," Barlow said, brow perspiring. "But I take full responsibility. I knew better. I grew lax and wasn't on my guard. Now this spoiled brute needs to learn fussing and fighting isn't going to get him his way."

Again Barlow spoke to the horse, looked him in the eye, and told him he meant to ride and ride he would. He draped the rein over the saddle, gripped the leather with his good hand, and swung up and onto Apollo's back with fluid grace.

"Now then, my friend, shall we go?"

At some invisible signal, the horse turned and walked on.

"Barlow, you shouldn't ride with that arm," Julia called.

"Shall I go for the surgeon?" Alec asked.

"I think not. Arm hurts like the blazes, and I'd like it set directly. Apollo and I shall ride for Mr. Mounce ourselves."

Alec opened the gate, and he and Julia watched the man ride off, tall in the saddle, Apollo docilely heeding his every unspoken command.

Alec shook his head in wonder. "He's quite a man, your Mr. Barlow."

"Yes," Julia breathed. "I used to wish, even pretend, he was my father."

Alec looked at her in surprise and noticed her faraway look. "Did you?"

"Mr. Midwinter didn't like that. Once when I was young, he caught me twirling and hopping about while Barlow played his fiddle. He scolded me and taunted Barlow, saying, "Like father, like daughter, ey?" Julia exhaled a humorless chuckle. "I wish."

Alec said quietly, "I'm sorry."

Her expression clouded. "Oh, well . . . I knew he wasn't. I was just an imaginative girl. And my own father was not exactly . . ." She faltered, struggling to find the word.

"Close? Affectionate? Loving?" Alec suggested.

"Heavens, none of those. I was searching for . . . aware of my existence. I don't think he even liked me."

Alec thought of his uncle's revelation that Midwinter may not have been her father but said only, "I am certain he did. Probably just didn't know how to express what he felt. Many men don't."

"Is that so?"

He nodded.

She smiled coyly. "And you, Mr. Valcourt. Do you know how to express your feelings when you like a girl?"

Alec did not take the bait, but instead cleared his throat and continued with the previous topic. "Did your father's coldness extend to your mother as well?"

She seemed disappointed that he did not return her flirting with flattery, but then she tilted her head to one side as the question struck her. "You know . . . he didn't seem terribly fond of her either, come to think of it."

"Have you ever asked her about their marriage?"

"Goodness no. What child wants to delve into that mire? Better left behind closed doors, I'd say." She looked at him. "Were your parents fond of one another? Was their marriage one of affection . . . or convenience?"

It was Alec's turn to consider an uncomfortable question. "Had you asked me a year ago, I would have said they were quite fond of one another—that their marriage, while not perfect, was one of mutual respect and affection. But . . . things changed in the last year. And now . . . I don't know what to think."

Julia inhaled deeply and looked into the distance, though Barlow had already ridden out of sight. "I don't care if I ever marry. I don't need to, you know. Buckleigh Manor will be mine one day. It is not entailed to a male heir."

He regarded her profile. "There are other reasons to marry, you know, beyond financial ones."

"For men, maybe." She shrugged. "If I do marry, it will be for the adventure of it. If I meet a man who can sweep me off my feet and away from Beaworthy, then that's the man for me."

He nodded toward the manor. "But what about your home, your inheritance?"

"The old place will still be here, waiting for me. Like an anchor around my neck. A blessing and a curse."

"A curse, how?"

She looked at him, eyes glinting. "You really have no idea, have you, what it's like to be tied to a place from birth as lord or lady of a manor, with a duty to its tenants, servants, and villagers. Buckleigh Manor—and Medlands, to some degree—is the financial hub of the entire parish. They farm our land. We buy their produce and their meats, their goods and services. We hire their sons and daughters as servants and estate hands, sponsor the charity school, the poor fund, and the church. If we go, they go. If we die, the village dies with us—at least figuratively speaking."

"That seems dire and a bit dramatic," Alec said. "Are you certain you are not overstating the case?"

She slowly shook her head. "Not to hear my mother tell it. I only wish I were."

A door opened and closed nearby, and Alec turned.

Lady Amelia had stepped out onto the back terrace, and looked none too pleased to see Alec and Julia standing close together in private conversation.

"Speak of the devil," Julia murmured on a sigh.

Lady Amelia's expression tightened. "Julia, come into the house, please."

Julia lifted a hand to acknowledge her mother's request, then looked back at Alec. "Pray excuse me, Mr. Valcourt. Duty calls yet again."

◈

The second dance lesson at Medlands had gone even better than the first, and Alec found himself humming a waltz melody as he walked to Buckleigh Manor the following day.

Barlow did come into the office that morning, but he was later than usual. His arm was wrapped in a sling, and it was clear from his rigid, clammy countenance that he was in pain. He confessed that Mr. Mounce had remonstrated with him for riding so soon after his injury and insisted he travel only by foot or by carriage—with someone else at the reins—for the rest of the week, at least, and ideally a fortnight. The good news was that the break did not seem as bad as the swelling and bruising suggested, and the surgeon prognosticated that the arm would heal well given time and care not to reinjure it.

Barlow pressed his lips together in thought, then said, "Valcourt, I must ask you to do something for me."

Alec straightened in his chair. "Anything, Mr. Barlow. I am at your command." Was he going to delegate an important task at last?

"I need you to travel down to Plymouth. I would go myself, but—"

"No, of course you must not go. In fact, perhaps you ought to go home, where you can rest."

"I don't need rest. I need this dashed pain to stop." He winced and lowered his voice. "Sorry. Don't mean to heap coals of guilt on you. I know you feel bad already."

"Don't apologize." Alec hated to see the man in this state. "Cannot Mr. Mounce give you something for the pain?"

"He did, but it makes me devilish sleepy. I'll take some tonight before I go to bed." Barlow waved his good hand dismissively. "Enough about me. If you leave now, you can ride into Hatherleigh in time to catch the Plymouth coach. Stable the horse at the coaching inn there. Here's my card. Just tell them I sent you. They know me there."

Alec's mind raced to absorb the details, but one stuck him like a sharp pin. "Ride?"

"Yes. It is only eight or nine miles. You may take Albina, a docile mare. She'll give you no trouble. Not the fastest horse, I grant you. But even at a trot, it should only take you an hour or so. If you leave now, you'll reach Hatherleigh with time to spare. Do you still have your boots in the tack room?"

"Yes."

"Good. I shall send word to your mother not to expect you for dinner."

Alec swallowed. At least Barlow didn't expect him to ride the horse that had just broken his arm.

"What do you need me to do in Plymouth?" Alec asked. He had never been there, and hoped it would not prove difficult to find his way around.

"I need you to deliver something for me. A letter." He nodded toward the folded paper on his desk.

Alec rose. "Very well, but . . . could not the Royal Mail do that? Or a messenger?"

"I cannot risk the post for this. Nor a messenger I don't know or trust." He enclosed a bank note within the letter, sealing it carefully. He held it out, then retracted it. "Valcourt, I must ask for your utmost discretion in this matter. Her ladyship would not be pleased to know you are going in my stead, but I don't think it wise to mention it, considering the reason I cannot go myself is out there helping himself to Buckleigh oats as we speak."

Alec nodded. "I understand, sir."

"I also must ask if I can trust you not to speak of this errand to anyone else, not even to your family."

Alec nodded, proud to be considered trustworthy by this man. "You have my word."

He looked at Alec from beneath bushy brows. "That includes Miss Midwinter."

Surprise flared through Alec that he should be taken into Barlow's confidence when Julia was not. Good heavens, what was in that letter?

"I understand."

Handing it over, Barlow explained, "I need you to deliver this into the hand of Lieutenant Tom Tremelling. He is on shore leave at present. You will find him at—" he consulted a scrawled note on his desk—"the Admiral MacBride, an inn near the old port." He nodded toward the front of the letter. "He's lodging in one of the rooms there. I've written down the direction."

Alec glanced at the letter. The direction—*Number 1, the Barbican,* was not familiar. But the name *Tremelling* triggered a memory. The postal log. The quarterly and sometimes monthly letters between Lady Amelia and a Lieutenant Tremelling. Why were posted letters good enough in the past but not now? Noticing the solemnity of Barlow's manner, he did not ask.

"Is there . . . anything else I need to know? Anything about the man or the contents of the letter?"

Barlow shook his head.

"Is he expecting you? Expecting this?" Alec fanned the letter.

"Yes. I imagine he has very little doubt of it."

"How shall I answer if he asks who I am or why I've come?"

Barlow grimaced, whether from the pain in his arm or because Alec was being a pain in the neck with all his questions, Alec wasn't sure.

"No need for a social call, Valcourt," Barlow said. "You find the man, confirm his name, and hand over the letter. You can tell him I have been . . . indisposed or would have come myself. Don't engage him in conversation. If he asks for . . . or about anything else, simply tell him he may write to me or her ladyship. But that"—he nodded toward the letter—"should be self-explanatory. More than sufficient."

A prickling of foreboding crept up Alec's spine. Something was going on here beyond a simple errand, but what was it? Even with the problems Lady Amelia had caused him, he hoped she was not in any trouble—that nothing untoward was going on between her and this lieutenant—for her own sake, for Julia's, for loyal Barlow's, even for his own.

Don't be an idiot, he told himself. Why had he jumped to such dire conclusions? It could be anything. A letter to a distant relative, soon to leave port with no time to wait for the post to send greetings. But he'd seen Barlow slip a bank note into that letter. Had he not seen other payments recorded to the same name in the ledgers? He believed so. Payment for what? Services rendered? A naval officer was not a tradesman with a bill to present, like a mantua maker or greengrocer. Or was the man one of Lady Amelia's many charity projects— perhaps injured in the war and unable to return to his duties? But then why all the secrecy? Did she—or Barlow—fear every injured sailor would come knocking, palm outstretched, if word of her almsgiving spread?

Supposition would get him nowhere, Alec realized. He would meet the man and find out for himself.

Half an hour later, Alec strode into the paddock, wearing his boots, greatcoat, hat, and gloves. There, a stout, swaybacked mare stood saddled and waiting. The smug young groom who had witnessed Alec's ill-fated attempts with Apollo held the reins. The horse's coat of light grey had likely once been snowy white. The old mare swished her silver tail but otherwise stood resigned and still while Alec mounted, and the groom adjusted the length of the stirrups. What had Barlow said? Ooze confidence and earn trust? Something like it at any rate.

"She's the sweetest of the lot, sir," the groom said. "She'll give ya no trouble."

"Thank you."

Remembering Barlow's previous instructions, Alec clicked his tongue and gently shifted his weight and lifted the rein. Albina sighed and turned as commanded and plodded to the gate the groom held open.

"She may resist a faster pace, or try to stop and eat. But don't let her have her way. Show her who's in charge."

What happened to "She'll give you no trouble"? Alec wondered, though he nodded to acknowledge the advice, trying not to resent the youth of its giver.

Albina's silver-maned neck and hopeful muzzle—its hair so thin her skin shone through—turned now and again toward a brittle stalk or bramble alongside the road, but with a pull of the reins and a stern word, Alec was able to keep the old thing on course. As Barlow had assured him, the road to Hatherleigh was easy to follow and the turn well marked. The weather that mid-March morning promised to be fine, which lifted his spirits.

A little more than an hour later by his pocket watch, he reached the outskirts of the town. He allowed the horse to leave off its bone-jarring trot and walk the rest of the way. It was a relief to them both.

He saw the coaching inn ahead on the main thoroughfare. Reaching it, a hostler hailed him. Alec handed over Albina with relief, dismounting onto shaky legs the consistency of warm jelly. He gave the young man Barlow's name and card as instructed.

The hostler nodded. "How is ol' Mr. B.? Not ailin', I hope?"

"Oh, nothing serious. He'll be good as new in a week or two."

"Glad to hear it. Well, don't worry about this old girl. I'll take good care of her 'til you get back."

The hostler directed him where to find the booking clerk, and with word and coin Alec thanked him for his help. Inside the inn, Alec paid his fare and even had time for a cup of tea and a hot bun. From a table near the front window, he drank his tea and watched as the coach was readied for departure outside: horses changed and harnessed, wheels checked, and deliveries loaded.

They were soon underway. Alec felt rather important sitting inside the coach with two well-dressed gentlemen and a lovely young lady traveling with her father.

Apparently noticing his daughter's interested glance stray to Alec again and again, the father asked him, "And you, young sir. Traveling to Plymouth to visit friends or . . . ?"

"No, sir. On estate business."

"Ah. May I ask which estate?"

"Buckleigh Manor." Too late Alec wondered if he should have refrained from naming his employer.

"Buckleigh Manor," the gentleman echoed, lips pursed and clearly impressed. "I have heard of it. Are you a member of the family?"

Here we go, Alec thought, anticipating his reaction with little relish. "No, sir. I am clerk there."

"Ah," the gentleman said significantly, with a pointed look at his daughter.

She looked away in a sullen huff.

Alec should have probably left it at that, but he had been taught to reciprocate polite inquiry, so he said, "And you, sir. What takes you to Plymouth, if I may ask?"

"We are meeting my son there. My youngest. He left us a cabin boy and comes home a lieutenant. And him not yet one and twenty. Not bad, ey?"

"Not bad at all, sir. You must be proud."

"Indeed I am. Too bad the war is over, elsewise he might yet make captain, as I did. Ah, well." He sighed ruefully.

Alec found it odd he should regret the end of the war, when so many welcomed it. He thought the man should be glad his son was coming home alive and in one piece, when so many were not as fortunate. But he held his tongue.

Alec pried no further, and the conversation lagged.

They stopped at an inn along a local turnpike in Tavistock to change horses and have a bite to eat. Soon they were on their way again. Through the left-side carriage window, Alec watched as they passed a sprawling wilderness of rolling hills and open moorland dotted with strange rock outcroppings, wild horses, and sheep. Dartmoor.

The journey consumed the greater part of four hours and Alec's pocket watch read half past three by the time he disembarked. The porter in the stable yard directed him to the Admiral MacBride and offered to call for a chair, but Alec declined, preferring to stretch his legs after sitting so long. A brisk walk to the inn would allow him to see a bit of Plymouth as well.

He strode past the old port with its ships and sails, dinghies and docks. The boardinghouses, public houses, and houses of ill repute. He heard the clank of tackle and mooring lines and the cries of gulls. He breathed in the smells of fish and tar.

Walking up a steep lane away from the harbor, he quickly reached the Admiral MacBride, a two-story whitewashed inn with black-framed windows and an anchor above the door.

The taproom was not crowded, but he saw several uniformed men.

Alec approached the barkeep. "Lieutenant Tremelling?" he asked. The aproned man looked up from uncorking a bottle to lift his chin toward an officer sitting alone at a table near the rear door.

The man had a pint before him and a tricorn hat. He looked up at Alec's approach, but seeing him, his interest quickly faded.

"Lieutenant Tremelling?" Alec asked.

The man surveyed him skeptically. "Who's asking?"

"My name is Valcourt. Mr. Barlow sent me."

The lieutenant eyed him, his expression part amusement and part suspicion. "Why'd he send a stand-in? I'm not important enough to warrant a visit from the estate manager. Is that it?"

Alec was surprised by his tone. The man had a hooked nose and cleft chin. His eyes were flat—grey or dull green, he couldn't be sure. His hair was a nondescript bronze. His skin was weathered, but he had been handsome once, Alec thought. And near enough in age to Lady Amelia that he *might* have been a suitor of hers. . . . He stopped, chastising himself for his foolish imagination and concentrated on the task at hand.

"No, sir. Not at all. Mr. Barlow has broken his arm and the surgeon forbids him to ride. That's the only reason he sent me in his place."

The man studied him, taking his measure. Amused irony quirked his lips. "Any idea what you've waded into, lad?"

Alec opened his mouth, then pressed his lips together. He said officiously, "Mr. Barlow has apprised me of all the information he deemed necessary."

"Which is what? Nothing?"

Alec could not resist returning the man's wry grin. "Exactly."

Tremelling chuckled dryly, shaking his head. "Very careful, our Mr. Barlow. Lady Amelia too, for that matter." He hesitated. "Is she . . . Is everyone at Buckleigh Manor in good health?"

"Um, yes. I believe so."

"Good. Good." He exhaled, took a long swallow of ale, and then sat back. "Well, let's have it."

Alec was tempted to ply the man with questions, but recalling Barlow's warnings, he withdrew the folded letter from his pocket and slid it across the table.

Lieutenant Tremelling eyed it without eagerness, with a look of resigned fatalism that surprised Alec.

The man glanced up. "Know what's inside?"

Alec shook his head. "I . . . am not privy to the contents, sir."

"Haven't stolen a peek?"

"No, sir."

"I haven't either, but I can tell you what it says. It says stay away, we don't want you here." The man shrugged. "Not that I blame her."

Alec swallowed. He should leave. Get up and leave. *"Don't engage the man in conversation,"* Barlow had said. *"Don't entertain his questions."*

But what about my questions? Alec wondered. He was so curious. Yet he knew it was not his place to ask about the letter. Instead, he said, "Well . . . A lieutenant, are you?"

"Aye. Had hoped for more, but now that the war is over . . ." Tremelling shrugged. "We're all adrift here. Hundreds of men have already been let go from the dockyard. Who knows when the next commission, the next ship will come, or if it will. Enough to make a man stop and think about his future . . . and his past. The navy is all I've known."

"But . . . surely the navy keeps men on in peacetime, just in case."

"Oh, aye. To patrol and whatnot. But that holds little appeal to a fightin' man like me."

Alec thought of the fine gentleman in the coach, whose son had already reached the rank of lieutenant at one and twenty. Tremelling was easily twice that age but the same rank. Alec wondered what had kept him from progressing up the chain of command.

"So, what will you do—try out civilian life and see how it suits you?" Alec asked it lightly, sneaking a look at his pocket watch beneath the table and already calculating how soon he would need to leave to make the six-o'clock coach back to Hatherleigh.

"Well . . ." The man tapped the letter against the table. "That depends on this."

The lieutenant's steely gaze held his. There was something about the man, about this situation, that intrigued Alec. But he knew it was time to leave if he was to return with his mission successfully and discreetly achieved.

"Well then, I shall leave you to it." Alec rose and picked up his hat. "A good day to you, sir."

"Thanks. That would make for a welcome change."

On the return journey to Hatherleigh, a pair of elderly spinster sisters were his only companions inside the coach. Alec exchanged a few polite words with them, accepted a piece of overbaked shortbread from their basket, and then allowed himself to close his eyes and feign sleep. He was tired from the long day and wanted to review his meeting with the lieutenant, his mind conjuring various scenarios to explain the man's role in Lady Amelia's life. He thought again of what his uncle had told him—that something had been amiss about her ladyship's rushed marriage to Mr. Midwinter. He hoped his uncle's former partner had misunderstood the situation.

After they changed horses and continued on, Alec nodded off in earnest and slept for most of the second leg of the trip. He arrived back in Hatherleigh around ten, and still had an hour's ride on Albina to reach Buckleigh Manor. He wished he had thought to ask Mr. Barlow if he might sleep at the inn if the hour grew too late. But he had not. Thankfully the moon was full and the sky clear, or he would have a treacherous ride back indeed.

When he finally walked Albina back into the stable yard, no one came out to greet him, which he supposed was not surprising considering the late hour. He dismounted stiffly and—keeping hold of the reins—opened the stable door and led the horse inside. An oil lamp, hanging from the low rafters, emitted enough light to see by. Ahead of him, Apollo whickered at him, or perhaps at Albina, from his stall. Alec supposed he should take Apollo back to his uncle's—but not tonight. Walking nearer Albina's stall, he was stunned to see a man slumped on a bale of straw, dark head lolling against a stall, mouth ajar, sound asleep.

"Mr. Barlow?"

The man did not respond. Concern flooded Alec.

"Mr. Barlow," Alec repeated more loudly and gently shook the man's shoulder, too late realizing it was the shoulder of his broken arm.

The man winced, then slowly opened bleary eyes. He murmured, "Master Graham?"

Alec stiffened. Was the man foxed?

Barlow blinked more fully awake, straightening as he did so.

"Sorry, Valcourt. Didn't mean to doze off. It's the dashed laudanum Mounce gave me."

Ah . . . that explains it. Alec said, "You called me Master Graham just now." The name of Lady Amelia's brother, Alec believed, dead these many years.

"Did I?" Confusion tinged Barlow's voice. "Sorry. I was dreaming."

Barlow ran a hand through his dark, slicked-back hair and rose unsteadily to his feet.

Regarding the man's drooping figure, Alec asked, "What are you doing here, sir? You ought to be home sleeping."

"I did go home, but then I came back and sent young Tommy to bed. Thought I should be here to meet you myself. See how it went. I couldn't sleep at home for wondering. Though apparently I had not the same problem here. Arm began throbbing something terrible, so I took a bit of the stuff. It certainly did its job—and then some."

Alec grinned. "As I saw."

"So you found him all right?"

"Yes. He was in the Admiral MacBride, just as you said he'd be."

"Just as *he* said he'd be, in the note he sent to her ladyship."

So Tremelling had instigated the meeting? Odd then that he seemed almost disappointed to receive the letter.

"He was expecting you, of course, but he seemed to accept my appearance in his stride."

"Good. Did he . . . read the letter then and there?"

Alec shook his head. "Did you want him to? You didn't ask me to wait for a reply."

"No. As I believe I said, the contents of that letter should have been self-explanatory and more than sufficient."

More than sufficient for what? Alec wondered. To set the officer up for civilian life? And why would Lady Amelia fund that?

Barlow grimaced, apparently choosing his words carefully. "He didn't . . . didn't say anything about . . . coming here, did he?"

"Coming here, to Buckleigh Manor?" Alec repeated in surprise. "No."

Alec tried to remember the man's exact words. "He said something about the letter being his answer. Telling him to stay away."

"Good." Mr. Barlow expelled a sigh of relief. "Well done, Valcourt."

With Barlow's guidance and one-armed assistance, Alec removed Albina's saddle. He pulled bridle straps over her ears, and the bit from between her long yellow teeth. At last, he led the mare into her stall and patted her sparse-haired neck. "Thanks, ol' girl."

"It's late," Barlow said. "I'll ask Tommy to give her an extra-thorough grooming tomorrow."

"Thank you."

Barlow extracted a few lumps of sugar from his pocket and handed them to Alec. "A present for the lady."

Alec thanked him again, then had the pleasure of offering the horse the treat and watching her nibble and chomp it with evident relish.

Again, Apollo whickered from his stall.

"Jealous, boy?" Barlow patted the gelding's sandy brown neck. "You'll have your chance soon, if I don't miss my guess."

They secured Albina's stall and extinguished the lamp. "Head on home and get some sleep, Valcourt. Take the morning off, since you worked so late tonight."

"But might Lady Amelia not wonder why and ask . . . ?"

Barlow grimaced. "I am afraid she has already learned that I dispatched you to make the journey in my place—and was none too pleased about it either. She came to the office while you were gone, and I could not lie."

"Is she . . . very angry? After all, she wanted you to begin delegating more tasks to me."

"But not this particular task, my boy." He drew himself up. "Now, not a word about it to anyone, remember. You can say I sent you to make a delivery, though none of the particulars."

"Don't worry, sir. You can trust me."

But apparently Lady Amelia did not. Alec doubted she ever would.

We remarked with pain that the indecent foreign dance called the Waltz was introduced (we believe, for the first time) at the English Court on Friday last.

—*The* (London) *Times*, 1816

Chapter 12

The next afternoon Barlow insisted Alec leave the office early, since he had arrived that morning at the regular hour, even after his late return the night before. Alec was tired, but before he went home to take his rest, he would take exercise with Walter Allen.

Alec gathered up his things and walked into the adjoining church-yard to wait for his fencing opponent. As usual, he peeled off his snug frock coat, noting the act didn't pain his side as it had only a few days before. Since he found himself there earlier than expected, he would use the time to stretch and limber up until Walter joined him.

"Here I am, Mr. Valcourt."

Alec looked up, surprised to see Miss Midwinter standing in the church doorway, arms crossed. Had she been waiting for him?

She walked toward him. "I've come for another private dancing lesson, since I was not invited to join in at Medlands."

So she had heard about the lessons. And wasn't pleased to be left out.

He said, "I don't think James Allen would approve of private dance lessons. Do you?"

Her eyes flashed. "Touché. But I don't answer to Mr. Allen. We are not engaged."

Alec was glad to hear it, yet still he resisted. "I will speak to the Allen family," he said. "I am certain they will be happy to include you in their next lesson."

"When is it?"

"Tuesday."

Her lower lip protruded in a pout. "I confess I have never been good at waiting, Mr. Valcourt. I haven't the patience Patience has. May I have just a brief lesson now? And not etiquette again." She locked her beguiling blue gaze on his, drawing him in. "Please?"

Thunder and turf, this woman was desirable. And she knew it.

He swallowed. "Had you a particular dance in mind?"

She nodded, and her voice lowered in register. "I have been hearing a great deal about the waltz. A dance that raised even Lord Byron's eyebrows cannot fail to intrigue a sheltered country girl like me."

"That is not how one thinks of you, Miss Midwinter."

"No? How does one think of me?"

Too often, Alec thought but did not say so.

Instead he said, "The waltz is considered quite scandalous by some, it's true. . . ."

"Why do you think I wish to learn it?" Her eyes twinkled with mischief.

Alec went on quickly, "But I teach a style of German waltz my grandfather learned on the continent. Personally, I find it graceful and exhilarating. And not, as the naysayers claim, indecent."

She feigned a theatrical sigh. "Too bad." Boldly, Julia stretched out her hands toward him. "What's the first step?"

The first step, he thought. The first step down a slippery slope? He realized he had already taken that first step, as far as Miss Midwinter was concerned—at least in his heart. Now his feet were eager to follow.

He sighed, giving in. "First I shall demonstrate the basic step." Ignoring her outstretched hands, he turned his back to her. Anything to give himself a moment to gather his wits and resolve. "Step forward with your left, extending your heel. Then with your right. Now pivot."

He pivoted to face her, his left foot now forward, then drew it back over his right, crossing his legs at the ankles. "Now you try it."

She stepped forward.

"Your other left, Miss Midwinter."

"Oh, right. I mean . . . left." She stepped forward with the correct foot, then the other, then pivoted, which was no easy feat on the rough stone path. But then again, this *was* the woman who balanced atop church parapets. She wobbled as she crossed her left foot over her right, extending her arms to steady herself. She craned her neck to look back at him. "Now what?"

"Repeat, until you do it correctly."

She repeated the step several more times, Alec offering crisp instructions as she did so. "Again . . . Concentrate." He was determined to remain impersonal and professional.

Then he showed her the simpler second half of the step. "From the crossed position, step backward with your right foot. Then turn in place, bringing both feet together."

She watched intently as he demonstrated. He was relieved to see her concentrating, taking him seriously, and leaving off with the flirtation.

When performed together, the two parts of the basic step turned the partners around and around each other. One partner moved forward, propelling the pair into the whirling spins, while the other partner served as pivot. Then their roles were reversed.

"Now for the primary body position," Alec began. "The only potentially scandalous aspect of the dance as I teach it is this—the lower halves of our bodies must remain fairly close together, while our upper bodies lean back, creating the effect of a child's spinning top."

She hesitated, perhaps imagining standing so close to him. "I see," she murmured—for the first time looking mildly self-conscious.

"We don't have to proceed, Miss Midwinter. We may stop the lesson any time you like."

"No, thank you. Pray continue."

"So we stand facing one another." He stepped closer, his shoes nearing hers. "You put your hands here on my upper arms. Lightly. Not a vise grip, please."

He frowned at her splayed fingers on his right bicep and pressed them together, imitating his grandfather's prim admonitions. "No claws, Miss Midwinter. Fingers together."

She nodded her understanding and placed a carefully cupped hand on each of his upper arms.

"Better. Now, I place my hands . . ." He swallowed. "Here." He felt her give a little start as his hands pressed beneath her shoulder blades.

"Now, stand a little closer . . ." He drew her nearer. "Our feet toe to toe."

"Oh!" she breathed.

A becoming blush heightened her color. He found he liked it, liked being the one to disconcert her for once, when it was usually the other way around. "Keep your shoulders back. . . . Excellent."

"Now, we will try the basic step. You will step backward with your right, while I step forward with my left." Alec pivoted, turning her with him, and crossed at the ankles. "See how I propel us around? Now it's your turn. Step forward with your left, heel leading. Now pivot . . ."

She wobbled, and he steadied her in his arms, finding he liked the sensation a bit too much for comfort. Or safety.

"It will actually be easier when we dance at full tempo, Miss Midwinter, as you will see."

"I hope so," she murmured.

They walked through the steps again. When it was her turn to move forward, she stepped on his toe. "Sorry!"

"Nothing to apologize for. My fault. I didn't extend my toe out of reach."

She looked unconvinced. "Are you certain I didn't hurt you?"

"Not at all. Now, let's try it faster." He began humming a Joseph Lanner *waltzer* in three-quarter time, a tune his grandfather had loved to play.

"One, two, three. One, two, three . . . Now you step, now I step. . . ." Soon they were spinning down the churchyard path.

"Wonderful!" she cried, giving herself over to the thrill of the whirling dance. "I am flying!"

Alec smiled. This was why he loved to teach. This was what made all the jeers and taunts of "caper merchant" and "macaroni" worthwhile.

Applause interrupted them. Startled, Alec drew his partner to a lurching halt, afraid they had been discovered by Lady Amelia or the Wilcox brothers.

"Bravo!" Walter Allen stood in the churchyard gate, sword under his arm, watching them with a boyish grin. "Doesn't look like any fencing I've ever seen, but good show all the same."

Alec released Julia and took a step back. A long step. He cleared his throat. "Perhaps, Miss Midwinter, we should continue our lesson another time—"

He looked at Walter. "Would your family mind, do you think, if Miss Midwinter joined our next dance lesson?"

"Not at all. Julia knows she's always welcome at Medlands."

Julia looked from him to Walter and back again, brushing aside a curl that had fallen from its pins. "Very well. Thank you." She curtsied and added sweetly, "I should enjoy it above all things."

⁓

Two weeks had passed with no reply to Lady Amelia's letter. Alec began to hope that her London acquaintance had somehow not heard about the Valcourt scandal.

On Tuesday, Alec and Aurora walked together to Medlands for the Allens' third dancing lesson. Alec was looking forward to it, and to the prospect of Julia Midwinter joining them. Though he knew if he were wise, he would avoid her like the plague.

They met again in the Medlands music room—Alec and his sister, Patience, James, and a reluctant Walter.

Alec announced, "We shall begin with a fairly simple country dance called Knole Park—a longways dance for two couples."

He walked the four through the steps—James partnering Aurora, and Walter with Patience. Alec was surprised Miss Midwinter had not yet arrived when she had seemed so eager to do so, but made no comment.

He began, "Circle four hands once around. Then first corners change places."

James and Patience did so.

"Second corners change places."

With a nudge and a whispered word from Aurora, she and Walter followed suit.

"Now, first couple leads down the center, then back, then cast down one place. Well done, James. Walter, step forward with Patience. Good."

Alec continued his instructions, then he picked up his grandfather's walking stick to tap out the time while he called the steps. "Let's walk through it again."

Walter struggled, but Patience gestured and prodded her brother through the steps.

Even smooth James faltered once or twice, but graceful, experienced Aurora gave him whispered reminders and gentle leads as well. Again, Alec thought he saw admiration in James Allen's eyes, but he hoped he was mistaken. He feared no good could come of it. Especially considering what his uncle had told him about James Allen and Miss Midwinter. Julia had said they were not engaged. Yet would they be, eventually?

Alec set aside the walking stick. "Now, let's try it to music."

"But I shan't remember what to do," Walter groaned.

"Aurora will call out the steps the first time. All right?"

Walter grinned at her. "Thanks, Miss V."

Alec positioned his fiddle and lifted the bow. It felt good to play, though no doubt imperfectly. He began the introduction, and Aurora called out the first steps. Fortunately for him, the couples were too busy concentrating on the dance to pay his lack of precision any mind. Soon the dancers relaxed and smiles appeared as they mastered the simple sequence and began to enjoy themselves.

The door opened and Julia Midwinter walked in.

Alec's pulse accelerated. He finished the final measures and ended the tune with a squeak instead of the flourish he'd intended.

"Miss Midwinter," he said. "Nice of you to join us."

The others turned to warmly greet the newcomer. James, however, stepped quickly away from Aurora, and walked over to welcome Julia personally.

At that moment, Sir Herbert and Lady Allen came in "only to watch," but their children insisted they dance as well.

So Alec moved on to the Ramsgate Assembly, another longways dance, but this one written for three couples. He walked them through the similar steps, with him and Aurora demonstrating as needed. "First and second couple set . . . Lead down the middle and up again. Now turn opposite corners. . . ."

Sir Herbert and Lady Allen mastered the dance quickly, with grace and obvious pleasure. Walter less quickly and with less grace, but with good humor.

They walked through it twice without music, then Alec picked up his instrument once more and Aurora sat down to accompany him on the pianoforte.

With three couples dancing and the lilting harmony of the two instruments, the mood became nearly as festive as a real ball.

Finally, Lady Allen threw up her hands in breathless girlish delight and declared she'd had quite enough. She insisted on playing in Aurora's stead. Her husband patted his chest and said he would turn the music for her while he caught his breath.

He smiled at Alec. "Surely you have earned a chance to dance with the other young people, Mr. Valcourt."

"But as the dancing master—"

"Come on, Valcourt," Walter urged. "Show us how it's done."

"Yes, do dance with us, Mr. Valcourt," Patience added with a sweet smile.

Only Julia said nothing either way, which somewhat surprised him, yet at the same time, made him feel more at ease in accepting their invitation to dance.

James once again claimed Aurora, and Walter asked Julia, leaving Patience without a partner.

"Very well. I would enjoy that," Alec replied. "Miss Allen, would you do me the honor?"

She curtsied. "I would be delighted, Mr. Valcourt."

Lady Allen played what should have been an easy tune with more enthusiasm than precision, her eyes often straying from the sheet music to admire the dancers.

Alec's feet followed the steps of long familiarity, and he felt no discomfort in looking into Patience Allen's face and letting himself enjoy the dance and his partner.

When the tune ended, Sir Herbert applauded. "Now why not change partners and try again?"

But at that moment, the music room door opened, and a housemaid entered with a tray of tea things and a footman followed, carrying a large silver teapot. The Allens insisted the Valcourts take refreshment with them, and they all paused to rest and quench their thirsts.

Lady Allen gestured toward the tray. "Not as grand as a midnight supper at a London ball, I'm afraid. But I hope it will do."

They all assured her it would do very well. Patience began pouring tea for everyone, while they helped themselves to a variety of small dainties.

As Julia accepted a cup from Patience, she said plaintively, "Oh, to experience a London season as you have."

"We took our children only the one time," Sir Herbert said. "What was that—two or three years ago now?"

"Three," Patience replied.

Finished pouring, she joined the other ladies seated in chairs pushed to the room's perimeter, while the men stood about, teacups and saucers in hands.

"We attended a ball whilst we were there," Lady Allen commented. "Patience was a bit young, but James danced once or twice, I recall."

Alec asked James, "Is this the ball you mentioned during which Walter stood and held up the wall?"

James nodded. "For the entire evening."

Walter quipped, "And quite successfully, I might add."

"At all events," Lady Allen said, "all of us soon longed for home. We left London after only a fortnight away and have never returned. There is no place we'd rather be than Medlands."

Around her, the other Allens solemnly nodded.

Julia, Alec noticed, turned her head to discreetly roll her eyes. But a strange ache lanced Alec. "How blessed you are. How fortunate."

"Yes, we are," Sir Herbert agreed. "And are you similarly blessed, now that you've come to live with family?"

Alec looked down into his teacup, then inhaled. "My uncle is very kind. And I have my mother and sister with me, which is a great comfort." He sent a smile to Aurora. "But it isn't home. And likely never shall be."

"You lost your home?" James asked.

"Yes. When we lost my father."

Aurora, he noticed, ducked her head.

James looked at her in sympathy. "I am very sorry."

"As am I," Patience said. "I cannot imagine what we would do if we ever lost Papa."

Alec gave her a sad smile. "Hopefully you shall not need to worry about that for a long, long time."

She brightened. "If ever!"

Alec felt his brow furrow at that, but Sir Herbert chuckled and reached down to give his daughter's arm an affectionate pat. "I cannot promise immortality, my pet. But I shall do my utmost to live as long as I can."

He looked at his wife warmly. "We really ought to host a ball here at Medlands, my dear."

"Indeed we should, my love. I shall think on it."

Refreshment taken, the dancers returned to their positions in the center of the room. Lady Allen sat once more at the pianoforte and launched into another vigorous round of Ramsgate Assembly.

This time Walter claimed Aurora, and James Patience, leaving Alec to dance with Julia. As he'd hoped for. Though with some trepidation.

"Miss Midwinter, may I have this dance?"

"Indeed you may. It is why I have come, after all."

She smiled at him, and he allowed himself to smile back. From the corner of his eye, he caught James Allen observing this exchange with a slight frown.

As they danced, Alec was amused by Miss Midwinter's playful swish of her skirt as she set to him, side to side. He enjoyed taking her hand in his to lead her down the center and back. A few steps later, he took her right hand again, balancing forward, then back, before changing places with her. She really was graceful. However, when she looked at him, he suddenly felt as though he had two left feet. It was both relief and deprivation to release her to turn Aurora. Then again to turn Patience, before returning to Julia once more.

Finally, the tune ended and Sir Herbert clapped his hands. "Well done, one and all." He glanced at the mantel clock. "Good heavens, we have kept Mr. Valcourt far longer than the agreed-to time. He shall be doubling his fee, and with good reason!" He smiled good-naturedly.

"Not at all, sir," Alec assured him. "We were only enjoying ourselves for the last bit."

"And enjoyable it was. Well done, Mr. Valcourt, Miss Valcourt. And thank you for joining us, Julia. I take it your mother does not know what we are about over here today?"

Miss Midwinter gave Sir Herbert a sheepish little smile. "No, sir."

"Perhaps that is for the best. Well." He rubbed his hands together. "It is nearly time to dress for dinner. Will our guests stay to dine with us?"

"You are too kind, sir, but no," Aurora answered. "We will not overstay our welcome. Our mother is expecting us."

"Perhaps another time, then. And your mother would be most welcome as well. Do tell her so."

"We shall. Thank you again."

Julia said, "I will take my leave as well."

"Perhaps the Valcourts would be good enough to walk you home? I don't like the thought of you walking alone this late in the day."

"Of course," Alec blurted. "Our pleasure."

A few minutes later, the three of them walked up the Medlands drive and through its gate. Aurora, Alec noticed, trailed several paces behind them, casually gathering early wild flowers along the way, probably giving him time to talk to Miss Midwinter in relative privacy. Was his interest in Julia so painfully obvious?

"I enjoyed hearing you play, Mr. Valcourt," she said. "You are quite accomplished. Reminded me of Barlow. Many a Sunday afternoon I sneaked out to the stable to listen to him play when I was a girl."

"I should like to hear him sometime," Alec said, then asked, "Did you enjoy yourself today, Miss Midwinter?"

She gave him an amused, sidelong glance. "Fishing for compliments, Mr. Valcourt?"

Embarrassment rushed over him. "No, I—"

"I am only teasing you," she said. "It is what you get for asking an obvious question. I had a glorious time, as well you know."

Alec nodded in relief. "Good. I am glad to hear it."

"And you, Mr. Valcourt? Did you enjoy yourself?"

He smiled. "Above all things."

⊘⌀

Alec rode Apollo around and around the Buckleigh paddock.

Mr. Barlow, arm still in a sling, looked on encouragingly. When Alec rode by the fence, he called out, "You've got the way of it now, Valcourt."

"Or Apollo has," Alec called back.

"You make a good team, the two of you. As it should be."

Alec signaled Apollo to slow from a canter to a trot, and the horse obeyed. "Good boy, Apollo," Alec murmured, for the horse's black ears only. For it seemed the horse liked hearing his own name, or at least that particular fond tone of voice.

When he again approached the gate where Barlow leaned, the manager said, "I think you're ready for a ride out in the open. What do you say?"

"The open?"

"Around the manor grounds. You and Apollo need to grow accustomed to riding outside the protection of this paddock—he must be able to trust you and learn not to bolt when a pheasant flies up or a dog barks."

Both sounded like prospects better avoided. Perhaps Alec and Apollo would remain in the paddock for the time being.

But then Alec recalled something Tommy had said earlier when helping him saddle Apollo. The young groom mentioned that he had just returned from escorting Miss Midwinter over to Medlands to ride with Miss Allen.

Alec considered this. Might he cross paths with the ladies if he rode out now?

He decided it was worth the risk and willed all flying and scurrying creatures to keep their distance from Apollo's hooves.

Barlow opened the gate for him, and out into the open he rode. Around the paddock, past the kitchen garden and flower gardens— beginning to green up and sprout—past the outbuildings and over the gently rolling lawn until he reached the manor's long drive. He trotted through the gate, tipped his hat to the scowling lion, and crossed the Buckleigh Road.

When he neared the Medlands gate, he saw Patience and Julia, as he'd hoped, but they were accompanied by James and Walter.

"Hello, Valcourt," Walter hailed. "It's good to see you in the saddle."

"And staying there," James teased.

"How is he handling?" Julia asked.

"Better. Barlow judged us ready for a ride beyond the paddock today."

At the moment, however, Apollo pranced and jigged, perhaps nervous around the unfamiliar Medlands horses. Alec tried to keep him still with steady pressure on the reins.

Miss Midwinter smiled. "Well . . . the horses are anxious to go." She kindly refrained from pointing out it was only his horse who refused to stand still.

"Join us, Valcourt," Walter invited.

"No, thanks. I'm due back at my desk in a few minutes. Another time?"

"We shall hold you to it!"

The four turned their mounts south and rode off together.

Something about the sight—the four well-dressed ladies and gentlemen of leisure riding off on their well-trained horses—formed a lump in Alec's stomach. Distracted, he forgot Barlow's instructions and jerked the reins, startling Apollo. The horse shied and reared up, and Alec found himself thudding to the road with an *umph*.

Picking himself up with a groan, he noticed with relief that Apollo had trotted a few yards ahead and stopped. He now gazed back over his shoulder at Alec with big brown eyes, patiently waiting for Alec to catch up. With a sigh, Alec walked over, grasped Apollo's reins, and walked the animal back to the paddock, where he belonged.

When Alec left the manor that afternoon, Miss Midwinter followed him into the churchyard.

"I wish I'd known you planned to ride Apollo today," she began. "I would have ridden with you."

"The ride didn't last long," he said. "But longer than usual before it . . . ended."

"Oh no. Sorry to hear it." She caught up with him on the churchyard path. "I have invited the Allens on a little adventure. And I'd like to invite you as well."

She pulled something from the reticule hanging from her wrist and unrolled a printed notice. "There is to be a public ball in Holsworthy."

She handed him the notice and he briefly glanced at it. "Yes, I'd heard about it. I was thinking of borrowing my uncle's carriage and taking Aurora."

"I think we should all go together. You, me, your sister, the Allens . . ."

Alec tried to ignore the flash of excitement that leapt in his chest at the thought.

"But I feel ill prepared to attend without another lesson," she continued. "I am happy to pay you for your time. What is the going rate?"

She again reached into her reticule, but he stayed her with a raised palm. "No, Miss Midwinter. I will not accept money from you."

She fluttered her lashes, looking at him in wide-eyed innocence. "Then what reward might I offer you?"

Alec clenched his jaw. Had the woman no idea how a lesser man might take advantage of such an offer? "That is not necessary," he said.

He steeled himself and began her lesson, which progressed for several minutes without mishap. Then he began to demonstrate the allemande position. Keeping hold of both of Julia's hands, he turned her under his arm until they stood side by side—her shoulder tucked to his rib cage, hip to leg. Was it his imagination, or did she press against him? Heaven help him. He had danced with dozens of females, but this position had never felt so intimate before.

He glanced down at Julia, hoping to see simple concentration or even blank indifference. Instead, she looked up at him, lifting her chin to gaze into his eyes, leaning more firmly, more warmly into his side. Her eyes were soft, her lips curved in a slight smile. Was she inviting him to kiss her? Did he want to? Of course he wanted to. And he was sorely tempted to do just that.

Irritation and longing vied within him. He inhaled through his nose, telling himself to remain calm. He was the instructor, after all. The master to her pupil.

"Partners must keep a proper distance apart," he primly intoned. "Bodies must not actually touch."

"Pity," she breathed, her face tipped toward his.

Oh yes, she wanted him to kiss her. His heart pounded at the thought.

Instead, he unwrapped her from under his arm and cleared his throat. "All right. That's . . . plenty. You have clearly mastered that maneuver."

She looked up at him steadily. "Thank you again for lending me your grandfather's book on the German waltz," she said. "I have been struggling to grasp position four, and hoped you might help me."

He watched her cautiously. What was she up to?

Miss Midwinter raised her left arm over her head, and he reluctantly did the same.

She grasped his uplifted hand in her own, creating an arch above them. "Position four requires, I believe, the man to place his hand about the woman's waist. And the woman to place hers about his. Is that not correct?"

He swallowed. "Yes."

Alec kept his expression neutral but relished circling his arm around her small waist and drawing her close to his side. Regarding her under their upraised arms, he noticed her cheeks blush becomingly. It was all he could do not to kiss her then and there beneath the arch of their entwined arms. . . .

This was Lady Amelia's daughter. A pupil, he reminded himself. What was he doing? He had promised himself to keep his distance—never to become involved with a student again.

"No." He released her hand and stepped away from her.

She faltered. "Don't you want—?"

He shook his head. "Not like this. Not sneaking around and playing games. It is beneath you. Beneath me. You, Miss Midwinter, are a lady. Don't allow any man to treat you as less than you are."

Dancing was the recognised way to meet young eligible partners and escape for a moment from the watchful eye of their chaperones. The great country houses held lavish balls and every middle-sized town with any pretensions to gentility had its own Assembly Room.

—Jane Austen's House Museum

Chapter 13

A s Julia walked to Miss Llewellyn's school the next day, she thought about the scene in the churchyard. The lesson she'd asked for, and the very different lesson she'd actually received. She flushed in embarrassment to recall how she'd tried to work her charms on Mr. Valcourt, to chip away at his self-control, to find a chink in his armor. How different Mr. Valcourt was from the fawning, flirtatious officers she'd met. Not as much fun, perhaps, but certainly more noble.

On the other hand, Alec Valcourt was also different from James Allen, who embodied restraint and propriety. But, she thought, it was easy for James to behave like a gentleman, because he wasn't attracted to her. She believed, or at least hoped, Alec was. She had been so sure he'd wanted to kiss her, but he restrained himself. She'd been disappointed even as she begrudgingly admired his stance. His words echoed through her mind and warmed her heart, *"You, Miss Midwinter, are a lady. Don't allow any man to treat you as less than you are. . . ."* The less he gave in to her, the more it seemed she admired him. But that didn't mean she was ready to give up.

Reaching the school, Julia spent an hour reading with the two youngest pupils, visited with Miss Llewellyn, and then began the walk back.

On the way, she stopped at Mr. Ramsay's house to see Aurora Valcourt and relay the plans and departure time for the following evening. She knew she might not have an opportunity to see Alec all day, because he and Barlow had gone somewhere on estate business. Ah well, she would see him tomorrow. She couldn't believe she was going to her first ball. She could hardly wait.

When Julia returned to Buckleigh Manor, she was surprised to find James Allen sitting with Lady Amelia in the drawing room. He rose politely as she entered.

Her mother beamed. "Look who has come to call."

Julia glanced about the room. "Where are Walter and Patience?"

"Must we always travel as a pack?" James chuckled self-consciously. "I thought I would call on you ladies myself. It has been some time since I have done so."

Lady Amelia rose abruptly. "Well, I shall leave the two of you to talk." She smiled at one, then the other before departing the room.

Oh no. Julia felt her palms begin to perspire. Was she reading too much into his formal call and James's nervous demeanor?

"Shall we ride?" she blurted, eager to escape the sudden tension in the room.

A little frown line appeared between his golden brows, marring his otherwise angelic face. "Not today, I don't think. And not just the two of us." He gestured for her to sit in the chair her mother had vacated.

Julia sat on a different chair, a little farther from his. "We have done so before, when your siblings were unable to join us."

He reclaimed his seat. "When we were children, yes. But we are not children any longer."

Julia swallowed, then laughed nervously. "I am told I still act like a child some days."

He did not disagree. "But you are young and, yes, sometimes a bit . . . foolish, but you will settle down, as we all must eventually."

"That sounds dire."

He crossed his legs and entwined his hands over his knee. "Miss Midwinter . . ." he began.

The Allens usually called her Julia, but she was in no hurry to encourage him by insisting he use her Christian name.

"You . . . like Medlands, don't you?" James asked.

"Of course I do, but—"

"And you are fond, I think, of . . . my family?"

"Of course I am."

"And we are both aware, I trust, of the . . . expectations surrounding our futures."

"James," Julia interrupted, longing to dispel the stilted, stifling atmosphere. "May I ask, how you envision *your* future?"

He brightened at this apparent opening she'd offered, but she hurried to continue.

"I mean, as far as Medlands is concerned?"

Again that little frown line. "Well, I am Father's heir, as you know. I shall be master of Medlands eventually."

"Yes, and in similar fashion, Buckleigh Manor shall someday come to me."

"I am aware of that, yes. But your mother will live here for decades yet, Lord willing."

She nodded. "As your family will no doubt live in Medlands for many years to come."

He nodded as well. "And if we . . . That is . . . were you to marry, you and your husband might go on living here for a few years, if you liked. But eventually, you might, mm, give the place to a second son, for instance."

Julia felt her neck heat to hear James speak of their future offspring, even in such an indirect manner. Goodness, he had certainly given this some thought.

Or had he? A sudden suspicion pricked Julia. "Did Lady Amelia put you up to this?"

"No." James uncrossed and recrossed his leg. "That is . . . She may have encouraged me to begin . . ."

"Negotiations?" Julia suggested.

"To clarify my . . . feelings."

"What are your feelings, James?"

"I . . . I am very fond of you, of course," he said, not quite meeting her eyes. "We've known one another all our lives."

"That is hardly reason to marry."

"There are many worse reasons." He pressed his lips together. "Do you wish me to express my ardent love for you? It is not within my nature to do so. How foolish I should feel. We know each other too well."

She said gently, "James, I have seen how you look at Aurora Valcourt. You do not look at me that way."

He blushed and ducked his head. "Miss Valcourt is just a girl. A pretty girl, to be sure. But not someone I would seriously consider as my future wife."

He looked at Julia earnestly, almost defensively. "Is that why you hesitate? Because of how I look at Miss Valcourt? I could say the same of you—I've seen how you look at her brother."

Julia suddenly recalled his concerned expression when she'd danced with Mr. Valcourt two days before. Had that precipitated this call?

"Yes. I admire him," she said. "I make no secret of that."

"No, you don't. Discretion has never been one of your virtues, Julia. And no doubt that is why your mother thought it time to exhort me to action."

Julia sighed. "James, you are a good friend. And I am well aware of the honor you do me." Even if the manner in which he broached the subject was less than flattering or romantic. "You have done your duty, and I promise to consider what you have said. Why do we not leave it for now—both of us think on it further. And in, say, six months or a year from now if we are both unattached and ready to consider matrimony, we raise the subject again then?"

He looked about to object, then seemed to think the better of doing so. "Very well."

He rose, and she followed suit. He regarded her, made a halfhearted move as though to embrace her or kiss her cheek, then paused, uncertain.

She held out her hand to him. "Thank you, James."

He bowed over her hand, bringing it to his lips for a quick, chaste kiss.

Later that day, Julia breezily entered the library, hoping her mother would not interrogate her about James's call, but at the same time thinking it might facilitate her plan. "Mamma, Patience has asked me to go with her to visit her grandmother tomorrow."

"Mrs. Hearn?"

"Yes." Julia hoped her mother had not heard about the public ball to be held the next night in Holsworthy, near where Mrs. Hearn lived.

"With her parents?"

"And both of her brothers," Julia hedged. Sir Herbert and Lady Allen knew about the excursion but would not be joining them.

Her mother's brows rose. "Their chaise shall be crowded indeed."

"I believe James and Walter intend to ride alongside. If the weather is fine."

"Is Mrs. Hearn ailing?"

"Not that they mentioned. I gather they haven't seen her in some time and wish to pay a call. Patience thought the drive would pass more quickly with me along."

"I have not seen Mrs. Hearn in years," mused her mother. "Do be sure and pass along my greetings. Oh, and have Cook send along a jar of her rose hip jam. I remember Mrs. Hearn being especially fond of it."

Jam? Must she? Julia forced a smile. "Very well."

❧

The next afternoon, Julia asked Doyle, her mother's lady's maid, to dress her hair. The woman then helped her on with a soft green evening gown with embroidered flowers, ribbon sash, and short puffed sleeves. Her cameo necklace and long kid gloves completed the ensemble.

"Such a fine dress to pay a call on an old widow?" Doyle asked, dark eyes glinting.

"Well, I will be in the company of James Allen, after all," Julia said, taking advantage of the fact that people expected a courtship between them.

"I see." Doyle gave her a pointed look. "And in who else's company, I wonder?"

Julia rose and stepped to her dressing chest. "That reminds me, Doyle. Here's a little gift I've been meaning to give you." She extracted a bottle of sherry she kept there for this very purpose. It wasn't the first time she'd had to persuade a servant to cooperate and, hopefully, keep silent.

Later, before she went downstairs, Julia was careful to put on a long cape and tie its hood under her chin. She did not want her fine evening gown or elegantly curled hair to raise her mother's suspicions.

The Allens' chaise arrived on schedule, and Julia went out without waiting for a servant to announce them. As she'd told her mother, James and Walter rode alongside the carriage.

She tried to look objectively at James Allen in his dark coat, gold threaded waistcoat, and frilly cravat. Yes, he was very handsome. In fact, he was in danger of being prettier than she was.

The coachman stopped at Mr. Ramsay's house to pick up Aurora and Mr. Valcourt. In this instance Julia thought it a good thing Mr. Valcourt did not think himself equal to such a long ride on horseback—at least not as long as the horse was Apollo. For with him and his sister inside the chaise with her and Patience, and the curtains drawn, no one was likely to see Mr. Valcourt and report his presence to her mother.

Miss Valcourt looked charming in a pale yellow satin gown with a crossover bodice. But it was the sight of Mr. Valcourt in full evening dress that stole her breath. Fashionably tied white linen cravat, brocade waistcoat, black tailcoat and breeches, white stockings, and black leather shoes. The dark hair falling across his brow framed his striking blue-grey eyes. Julia tried not to stare.

When they reached the outskirts of Holsworthy, they stopped at

Mrs. Hearn's house as promised. The Allens were honest by nature. Mr. Valcourt and his sister offered to wait outside, but Patience insisted they come in and take refreshment. Her grandmother shared the unfailing cheerfulness of the Allen family but was not encumbered with a long memory. After she had repeated the same story for the third time, Patience rose, and upon her cue they all followed and excused themselves. The rose hip jam was given and sweetly received, as was a basket of baked goods and jarred delicacies from the Medlands kitchens.

Duty discharged, the young people continued on into the center of Holsworthy to its assembly rooms above the Red Lion.

Mr. Valcourt descended before her and offered his hand to help her alight before the groom could do so. She placed her gloved hand in his, enjoying the warm pressure of his fingers on hers. He held her hand a moment longer than necessary, but she did not mind in the least.

Looking up, Julia noticed light and music streaming from the inn's upper windows. Hearing it, her heart tingled with excitement. Her first ball. She was not without some trepidation as well, for she knew only a few dances. She took consolation in the fact that Patience and James knew only a handful more than she did, and Walter . . . ? Well, at least she would not be the least skilled dancer there.

Alec recognized the music as "The Caledonian Highland Reel." His pulse accelerated. He'd had his reservations about attending the ball as a member of Miss Midwinter's party, especially after his lofty speech about not sneaking around. But in the end, he found he could not resist. In his pocket, he had brought several pamphlets, in case he met any prospective pupils.

Leaving the horses and carriage in the care of the Allens' coachman and hostlers, the party of six took themselves indoors and up the stairs. In the vestibule, Miss Midwinter removed her wrap. Alec's attention was snagged by the elegant, soft green evening dress. The short sleeves displayed her lovely upper arms. The wide embroidered neckline, her fine collarbones and décolletage.

He met her gaze. "You look beautiful, Miss Midwinter," he said, before he could stop himself.

She smiled. "Thank you. So do you."

Mirth and pleasure warmed his chest, and he smiled in return.

The assembly room was crowded and stuffy—no wonder they had opened the windows. Musicians sat at one end of the room, while a line of men and another of women faced each other at the center. The couples—their cheeks flushed with exertion or perhaps wine punch—smiled at partners made prettier by the dance. Men young and old wore Sunday best, and females wore their finest frocks of various levels of fashion. Older folks not dancing sat opposite the musicians, along with single ladies in want of partners.

"What is it?" Walt asked of the tune, voice tense. "I don't think I know it."

Alec gave him the name of the reel. The dance ended a few minutes later and a second reel was called.

Patience and Julia joined the throng of unclaimed ladies. With their fashionable gowns and regal bearings, Alec thought the men might be intimidated to ask them to dance. If only they realized the ladies' aloof expressions hid anxiety—afraid to be asked to dance, afraid not to be. James Allen stood between them—another hindrance, no doubt.

James asked Miss Midwinter to dance, but she shook her head.

"Not yet. I'm too nervous. Let's watch for a while first."

Unable to seek out a partner for herself, Aurora stood off to the side as well, hiding her restlessness behind a patient smile. It was difficult to stand still when the music was good and the dance a favorite.

"Come, Aurora. Do me the honor, will you?" Alec asked. "No one dances as well as you do."

"But wouldn't you rather ask one of the other ladies?"

He smiled. "Another time."

He offered his arm, and his sister took it, eyes sparkling.

Alec did not mean to show off, truly he didn't. He could not help it if they were the best dancers there. He was aware of admiring and perhaps a few envious looks. But moments into the dance, Alec forgot about the observers and gave himself over to the enjoyment of the reel. He focused on his sister, who was clearly relishing every step, and smiled at his neighbors with sincere warmth whenever the figures of the steps brought them face-to-face.

Afterward, Alec escorted Aurora to the side of the room where the other members of their party stood.

"You two make it look so easy," Miss Midwinter said.

"Thank you," Alec replied. He noticed Mr. Pugsworth, his uncle's senior clerk, standing against the wall, looking around hopefully. He also saw a young woman he recognized.

"Look, there's Miss Thorne."

Walt's head snapped to the side. "Where?"

Alec was surprised to see Ben's sister, Tess, in attendance. He was glad to know dancing was not limited to worship for her family—or at least for her. Alec did not see Ben or their parents.

Tess looked fresh and pretty in a simple ivory gown, her reddish-brown hair pinned to the back of her head in a thick coil.

Alec was torn between asking Miss Thorne or Miss Midwinter to dance, when another man settled the question for him. A militia officer in red bowed before Miss Midwinter, and how she beamed and fluttered her lashes at him, quick to accept his offer. Alec doubted they had even been introduced.

James Allen frowned and asked Aurora to dance. Alec was about to ask Tess, when he remembered Walter. He looked up at the tall man and found his eyes clapped longingly on the young woman. Tess glanced over at him, but Walter quickly averted his face, neck reddening. Alec delivered an elbow to Walt's side, which earned him a glare but nothing else.

With a significant look at Miss Thorne, Alec asked Patience Allen to dance.

As he and Patience danced to "Comical Fellow," with its two-hand turns and cheerful claps, Alec now and again glanced over at Walter standing ramrod straight, staring ahead. Several yards away, Tess stood, unconsciously swaying to the music, watching the dancers with a small smile. Had she any idea of the effect she had on the man?

After the dance ended, Alec escorted Patience back to the others. Finding Miss Midwinter already engaged for the next set, Alec asked for the following, and she agreed with a lovely smile.

Then Alec walked over and greeted his uncle's clerk. "Hello, Pugsworth. Why are you not dancing?"

The man pulled a regretful face. "You haven't seen her, I trust? Miss Llewellyn?"

"No. But there are plenty of other ladies in need of a partner."

"I don't know . . ." Pugsworth shrugged. "I'm not very good at talking to females."

"Come over and I shall introduce you to a few." Alec nodded toward Miss Midwinter, Miss Allen, and his sister.

The man's Adam's apple bobbed. "Thanks, Valcourt. But . . . maybe later."

"Very well."

Realizing Walter had still made no move to talk to Miss Thorne, let alone dance with her, Alec approached her himself and bowed before her. "Miss Thorne, good evening."

"Mr. Valcourt. I didn't expect to see you here."

"I am surprised to see you as well. Though a pleasant surprise, of course. Your brother is not here, I take it?"

She shook her head. "I have taken a place as companion to the Strickland family. They brought me along as chaperone for their daughter. But I don't think she is in much danger of needing one."

She nodded toward her charge, a sweet girlish creature dancing with a rotund young clergyman, head to toe in black, save his snowy tabbed collar.

"So I see. I hope that means you are at liberty to dance?"

Her eyes shone. "I believe so, yes. Though I've had little experience, as you can imagine."

"Then may I have the pleasure of this dance?" he asked, earning himself another glare from Walter and a sweet smile from Tess. Alec could not in good conscience allow the woman to stand there without a partner all night, regardless of Walter's feelings. Besides, the young woman was very appealing, and he longed to dance with her, to discover if her enthusiasm in church might be matched with her enthusiasm on the dance floor.

He was not disappointed.

He was disappointed, however, when he observed Miss Midwinter dancing with yet another dashing officer. Her partner danced with abandon, exaggerating the steps and giving Julia smoldering looks whenever the dance brought them in close contact. Rather than discouraging him, Julia mimicked his boisterous capering and met his flirtatious looks boldly. The officer whispered something in her ear, and she laughed, too loudly, at whatever he had said.

Alec returned his attention to his own partner. Together he and Tess danced their way down the line of couples. When they reached the bottom of the set and waited to rejoin the dance, they were free to converse. He had her undivided attention for several minutes, yet couldn't help but wish he had another lady's attention instead.

When the set ended, Alec eagerly went to find Julia to claim her for the dance he had previously requested. He looked this way and that but could not find her. The music started, and he saw her walking arm in arm onto the floor with yet another officer, their heads close in conversation. Alec's stomach clenched in disappointment. Had she simply forgotten? Or had she found this man too appealing to pass up?

Alec glanced over at James Allen. Did James really cherish marital hopes for Miss Midwinter? Observing him throughout the evening, Alec had seen little evidence of such feelings as the young man danced with one elegant young lady after another. James, or at least his position as heir of Medlands, was clearly well known, for several fathers sought him out for introductions with their daughters. This left Alec to partner Aurora and Patience for much of the evening.

Finally, several dances later, a sheepish Julia appeared at Alec's side. "I am sorry I forgot our set earlier." She winced. "I have broken one of the rules, haven't I?"

Alec knew another rule of etiquette was to accept an apology with grace, so he said pleasantly, "No harm done."

He offered his arm and led her onto the floor. Oranges and Lemons was called, a square set dance for four couples. Around the room, couples grouped together. Alec and Julia found themselves with James and Miss Strickland, Patience with—surprisingly—Mr. Pugsworth. And Tess with a gentleman they did not know.

"Where are you folks from?" the gentleman asked, with a general smile at them all.

"Beaworthy," James replied, as self-appointed spokesman.

The gentleman's bushy brows rose. "Beaworthy? I didn't think anyone there danced."

"Well, as you will soon see, sir, we don't—at least not well. We are novices. At least most of us."

Patience spoke up, nodding toward Alec. "But Mr. Valcourt here is our dancing master. If you should ever need his services, we would not hesitate to recommend him."

"You don't say," the man replied with a thoughtful look at Alec. "I shall keep that in mind."

Dear Miss Allen, Alec thought gratefully. He glanced around for his sister, and glimpsed her trying to cajole Walter to dance, without success.

The music began. Alec reached out and took Miss Midwinter's hand, and around the square the other couples joined inside hands as well. He liked the feel of her hand in his, though with both of them wearing gloves, the act lacked the warm intimacy they'd enjoyed in the churchyard.

The couples stepped forward and back twice, then released hands. Each honored his partner, then turned to honor his corner. The men joined hands and circled around before bowing to their partners, then their corners once more. Then the ladies followed suit. The pattern was repeated, this time turning in the opposite direction.

When Alec reclaimed Julia's hand at last, he said, "You are doing very well, Miss Midwinter. I knew you were a natural."

"Not at all." She grinned. "I've had a good teacher."

All too soon, Alec's set with Miss Midwinter ended. And with all the officers lining up to dance with her, he did not have another chance to stand up with her all night.

For the final Boulanger of the evening, Alec danced with Aurora again, as he had for the first. When the music ended, Alec turned toward the musicians to offer appreciative applause. He started, nearly stumbling. One of the musicians looked familiar. He knew that man playing the pipe. It was the man who had come to his rescue with the Wilcox brothers, the man from the forge. A smith who played? Unusual, but not unheard of, he supposed.

"Alec?" Aurora asked in concern.

"Forgive me. I recognized someone. That's all."

Aurora Valcourt and Patience kept up a steady flow of pleasant conversation on the ride back to Beaworthy, but Mr. Valcourt remained quiet, staring out the window at the passing countryside. Julia sat quietly as well, regretting how the evening had gone. She had thought she could enjoy the attention of Mr. Valcourt *and* all those dashing men in uniform. But with a sinking feeling, she realized she had probably alienated Mr. Valcourt by flirting with the officers, forgetting their dance, and then dancing with him only once. Nor had she enjoyed seeing Mr. Valcourt dance with that pretty Miss Thorne—smiling into her face with rapt attention. At the sight, Julia had felt an unfamiliar knife of jealousy prick her heart.

Mr. Valcourt had been perfectly polite when they had danced, but Julia had spent so much time honoring her corner, joining hands with the other ladies, and passing each gentleman in a circular hey, that she'd barely had opportunity to smile at Mr. Valcourt, let alone converse. And now this cool reserve in the carriage. He was not rude—he answered any question put to him but then returned to silence.

The evening had not been quite as delightful as Julia had envisioned. She wondered if it would be worth the price she would no doubt pay for it.

They dropped off the Valcourts, and then the Allens' carriage stopped at Buckleigh Manor. James dismounted and escorted her to the door. There Julia thanked him, and waved farewell to the others.

She entered the vestibule, and as she'd feared, there sat Lady Amelia in a straight-backed wooden chair. Waiting for her.

She was clearly not happy. "There you are, Julia. I began to wonder what had become of you. I called at Medlands to see if you had stayed for dinner, perhaps, after calling on Mrs. Hearn. Sir Herbert and Lady Allen seemed surprised to hear I thought they had accompanied you to Holsworthy."

"But James and Walter did, as I mentioned they would," Julia defended. "In fact, James escorted me to our door just now."

Lady Amelia hesitated at that, then went on. "So you went to visit Mrs. Hearn. I became concerned when I learned there was an annual festival in Holsworthy on this very night."

"Oh? Who told you that?"

"I hardly think the source important. I began to worry you might be caught—unaware—in the unruly crowd of revelers."

"I am perfectly well, as you see. Still, I would like to know who thought it so important to worry you needlessly."

"Needlessly? I don't agree."

Doyle stepped from the shadows. The lady's maid had likely been listening all along. "I happened to recall the annual ball in Holsworthy, miss. Always the third Friday in March, is it not? I mentioned it to your mother without thinking, really."

"Right," Julia said sharply. "No harm intended, I'm sure."

"Of course not." The lady's maid dipped her head and floated up the stairs like a dark specter.

"That woman," Julia said, regretting she'd bothered to give Doyle the sherry. "She loves nothing more than to see the two of us at each other's throats."

"As do you, I think," Lady Amelia mused, then continued, "I even called in at Mr. Ramsay's house—and was unhappy to learn that Mr. Valcourt and his sister were not at home, but had gone with the Allens to Holsworthy."

At the thought of her parent checking up on her so publically, mortification heated Julia's neck, but she forced herself to hold her mother's gaze.

"I don't expect Mr. Valcourt to understand my scruples," her mother said. "But I did expect him not to lead my daughter astray—persuading you to attend a ball of all things."

Julia held up her hand. "Stop, Mamma. Mr. Valcourt didn't lead me astray. I wanted to go."

"I hardly think you would have gone on your own, or that you plotted the covert outing yourself."

"Then you think wrong. It was my idea."

Lady Amelia gaped. "Then you lied to me. How could you?"

"Quite easily. And why not? It was a public dance outside the Beaworthy village limits, and without a single unruly reveler. In fact, it was attended by a whole host of respectable people, like Mrs. Vanstone and the Stricklands and many officers."

"Officers?"

Ignoring that, Julia asked, "Do your principles make you better than they?"

"Not better, but where you're concerned, more important, yes." Her mother studied her face. "I hope you at least comported yourself with modesty and decorum?"

Julia shook her head. "As a matter of fact, I did not. I had a blissful time."

"And James?"

"He was the belle of the ball. All the mammas were eager for their daughters to dance with the heir of Medlands."

"Julia . . . if you are not careful, you are going to miss your chance with him."

"Perhaps." Julia shrugged. She hoped she had not spoiled her chances with Mr. Valcourt as well.

Her mother shook her head. "I am disappointed in you, Julia."

Julia held her gaze. "And I expected nothing less."

Amelia wished her final words back as soon as they left her mouth. She had promised herself long ago she would do everything in her power to fill the void left by Mr. Midwinter, who had made no secret of his disapproval of Julia, always expecting her to make some grave moral mistake. To fall. Like her mother had done.

She remembered the time Mr. Midwinter had come upon fifteen-year-old Julia flirting with a young footman—and wearing rouge no less. He had rebuked her right there in the passage. Amelia had come out of her own room to see what the matter was, and heard him order Julia to go wash her face that instant and let the footman get about his work. Julia had stalked away, cheeks flaming.

Then he'd noticed Amelia in the passage and boomed, "You had better tighten the reins on that wild child while you can. The apple doesn't fall far from the tree, you know."

Amelia had hushed him, hoping Julia had not heard the crass comment, let alone all the servants. "She is only fifteen," she'd defended. "Were you not a bit wild when you were young?"

"No, I was not. I have always been sensible and responsible, which is why your father approved of me."

Amelia had bit back the hot retort on her lips, and turned away, going to Julia's room to try to comfort her.

Her daughter sat at her dressing table, and glanced up at her in the mirror. Tears filled her eyes, but she blinked them away. "I don't care what he says. I don't like him either."

Julia's lip began to quiver, followed by her chin. Despite her best efforts to control them, tears spilled down her cheeks and rolled through the painstakingly applied circles of rouge. Julia snatched up a facecloth and began scrubbing at her cheeks.

Amelia's heart twisted at the sight. She walked up behind her and leaned down to put her arms around her.

"Mamma . . . don't." Jerking away, Julia's shoulder collided with Amelia's chin. A mild impact, but it stung beyond proportion, tearing a little piece of Amelia's heart. It was the first time Julia had physically rejected her—pushed her away.

For a moment, Amelia stood frozen, staring at Julia as though a stranger. Then, she turned on her heel and strode from the room. She returned to her own bedchamber and closed the door. Her own chin trembled; her throat tightened and ached. She pulled a handkerchief from her sleeve, but too late. Fat, hot tears fell onto her green bodice, staining it black.

When had it happened? she'd wondered. When had her little girl become a cold, distant stranger?

Looking back, Amelia realized that she had begun erecting her own brittle shell of protection after that. She began to stop herself from reaching out, from trying to embrace Julia, to touch her, knowing her daughter would recoil. But perhaps she should not have stopped, perhaps the ever-widening distance between them was her fault. Was it too late? *Oh, God, please help me. I cannot bear to lose Julia too. . . .*

❧

The next morning, Alec was sitting alone in the office writing rent receipts, when someone knocked at the open door. He looked up, surprised to see Julia Midwinter standing there.

He set his quill into its holder and rose.

"Mr. Valcourt," she began, looking unusually nervous. "Might I have a word?"

"If you like."

She remained in the threshold, as if unsure of her welcome. Hands clasped, she chewed her lip, and awkward silence stretched between them.

Concerned, he crossed the room to her. "Is everything all right?"

"Mamma found out where we went last night."

He nodded. "So I heard. My uncle told us she'd called while we were out, and was clearly not pleased to learn where we had gone and with whom."

Julia sighed. "She is vexed with me as well. But I am used to it." She glanced up at him from beneath her lashes. "But I am not used to *you* being vexed with me. I wanted to say that I . . . I am sorry for my behavior last night. All the attention went to my head, I suppose." She attempted a lame little chuckle, then swallowed. "I hope you will forgive me."

He took a step nearer, regarding her closely. She certainly appeared sincere.

"Of course I forgive you. You don't owe me anything, after all. Though I admit I was disappointed to have only the one dance with you."

She nodded, then tentatively asked, "Did I break *every* rule of ballroom etiquette, do you think?"

He tilted his head as he considered. "No. . . ." He added, "You wore gloves."

Her mouth parted in surprise, but her eyes twinkled. "Surely I was not as bad as all that."

He shrugged easily. "Who am I to judge? I broke one of the rules as well."

"Oh? Which?"

"I complimented your appearance."

"Why is that wrong?" she asked. "I rather liked it."

"As I understand it, one's modiste and lady's maid need not be praised for doing their jobs. But I couldn't help myself—I could not take my eyes off you. Nor could half the regiment, apparently."

She blushed under his playful praise. She reached out and laid her fingers on his sleeve. "Well, I shan't tell if you won't."

He looked from her hand to her face but did not pull away. His foolish heart warmed under her touch.

At that moment Lady Amelia appeared in the doorway behind Julia's shoulder. Noticing his gaze stray and his smile fall away, Julia quickly removed her hand.

As if guessing who stood behind her, Julia said formally, "Thank you, Mr. Valcourt. Do tell Barlow I am looking for him." She turned on her heel. "Oh. Good morning, Mother."

Brow furrowed, Lady Amelia remained in the doorway but turned her head to watch Julia stride away.

Then she looked at him and asked, "What did she want? I suppose the two of you were talking about how you deceived me last night. Probably a big joke for you both."

"Nothing of the kind, your ladyship. In fact, she was apologizing for the entire evening."

"Was she?"

"Yes. Now, may I help you with something? If you are looking for Mr. Barlow, he is meeting with the housekeeper in her parlor."

Lady Amelia stood there a moment longer, eyes boring into his. Then she turned and walked away without another word.

For the rest of the day, Alec waited on edge, sure he would be summoned into the library for a private reprimand . . . or worse. But the day passed, and the summons did not come.

At the end of the day, Alec walked through the churchyard on his way home. There he spied a figure leaning against the gate. He stiffened, until he recognized the dark-haired man from the forge, his horse tethered nearby. Alec raised a hand in greeting, and the man nodded in acknowledgement. He turned toward his horse and pulled a sword from his long saddlebag. His own sword, Alec assumed.

As he neared, Alec asked, "You were able to mend it?"

"Aye." The man pulled it from its sheath. "With my father's help."

He offered the hilt to Alec. Alec accepted it, looking at the sword closely, rotating it to view the blade from every angle.

"Can't even see where the break was," Alec observed. He corrected his grip and gave a tentative thrust.

The man removed a second sword from his long narrow saddlebag. He turned to Alec, eyes glinting with humor. "Care to test it out?"

Music and fencing? The man was certainly full of surprises. Alec's spirits lifted at the thought of a new opponent.

"Is testing included in the repair fee?" Alec asked.

The man grinned, spreading his hands in an expansive gesture. "All part of the service."

The two men attached leather guards and then faced off a few yards apart, each assuming a ready stance. Swords raised, they began fencing slowly, tentatively, each measuring his opponent and the reaction of the newly mended blade.

Alec advanced on the path, while his opponent retreated. Then the man advanced and Alec retreated. They repeated this slow, stately dance several times, but then his opponent increased his speed, advancing more quickly, his blade picking up tempo with each strike. Alec retreated, struggling to parry as the man drove him backward. Aha! The man was better than he'd let on. Alec was pleased by the discovery. The man of perhaps forty years held himself well, displayed impressive grace and style, and a wickedly fast blade.

After several minutes, the two men circled one another, catching their breaths.

"How's the blade?" the smith asked.

"Good," Alec said. "The play is a little different, perhaps a little less flexible, but excellent nonetheless."

The man gave a little bow. "We humble smiths aim to please."

He lifted his sword and the bout resumed. Advance, lunge, retreat, retreat. Feint, attack, parry-riposte . . .

Knowing he was expected at home, Alec decided to try to score a hit and end the match. He advanced quickly, driving the man closer to the church wall with every lunge. But the man managed to parry his every strike. Finally Alec jumped forward and lunged in a balestra. The practice tip hit its mark at last, and his opponent touched his chest in acknowledgement.

"Touché," the older man panted, wiping a sleeve across his brow. "I see I am out of practice. And out of condition."

"Lucky for me, or I'd have been done for. You are a worthy opponent, sir."

"As are you." The man straightened. "I suppose it's time I introduced myself." He offered a strong hand. "John Desmond. Though most folks call me Desmond."

Alec gripped his hand. "A pleasure to meet you, Desmond. And to fence with you." He grinned. "Any chance we could make this a regular occurrence?"

The man grinned in return. "Thought you'd never ask."

As the Quakers have thought it right to prohibit music, and stage-entertainments, to the society, so they have thought it proper to prohibit dancing, none of their children being allowed any instruction in the latter art.

—Thomas Clarkson, *A Portraiture of Quakerism*, 1806

Chapter 14

On Sunday afternoon, after church and dinner, Julia went out to spend time with Liberty. Half of the indoor servants, and nearly all of the outdoor staff, had Sunday afternoons off, leaving the grounds quiet as she walked from the house and into the stable block. The interior was quiet as well. The coachman and grooms had quarters nearby, but no one was in the stables themselves to disturb her peace.

Just as she liked it.

She groomed Liberty, pouring out her heart to the beloved animal as she did so—her discontent with life in Beaworthy, her frustration with her mother, her growing feelings for Mr. Valcourt. As she worked a snarl from Liberty's mane, she imagined herself married to Alec Valcourt. . . .

They lived in a fashionable square in London. Whatever problem had necessitated his family's departure had been cleared up. Alec was renowned and respected. Successful and wealthy. Called on by the nobility to teach their sons and daughters and invited to every ball of the season. Together, she and Alec traveled a great deal but only visited

Buckleigh Manor at Christmas and Easter. Alec was as dashing and handsome as ever—and how he loved her. They danced together every night before falling asleep in each another's arms. Their children were beautiful and graceful. She and Aurora were the best of friends, raising their children as close cousins, in one happy, affectionate family. . . .

As the daydream faded, Julia inhaled deeply. *Now, that would be a charmed life indeed.*

Finally, she put away the brush and currycomb, stroked Liberty's forelock once more, and left the stable.

As she walked past the paddock toward the house, she saw Alec striding in her direction, head down. Her heart raced. Had he read her mind?

He looked up in surprise. "Miss Midwinter."

"Hello, Mr. Valcourt. I was just thinking about you."

"Oh? Thinking what?"

Julia's cheeks heated. Instead of answering she asked, "Come to visit Apollo?"

"Yes. I thought I might take him for another—hopefully longer— ride." He squinted up at the grey clouds above. "If the rain holds off, that is."

Julia nodded. "I just gave Liberty a good grooming myself. There was no one else inside, and I find she is the best listener." She tried to smile but felt it waver.

He looked at her in concern. "Is something the matter?"

"Oh, no more than usual. Another London season is soon to begin, but Mother has again refused to take me." She tilted her head and studied his face. "And you? Are you well?"

"Not bad. Waiting for the axe to fall, but otherwise fine."

"What do you mean?"

He grimaced. "Never mind."

Suddenly the hovering clouds above parted, and rain fell in torrents. Julia looked up and squealed. "Come on!" She grabbed Alec's hand and ran toward the stable, pulling him along behind her.

They dashed inside through the double door. Her wet shoes slipped on the hay-strewn floor, and his arm quickly came around her, catching her before she fell.

Even after he steadied her, his arm remained.

Julia smiled up at him. She liked the way his arm felt around her. Yes, Alec Valcourt was attracted to her. But would he resist her once again?

Looking at her, his eyes darkened, and he reached up and brushed a damp curl from her face.

She shivered.

"You're cold," he murmured. He tugged off his coat and settled it over her shoulders.

She was warm, actually, but did not correct him.

"Thank you," she whispered. The aroma of spicy, masculine bay rum enveloped her, and she breathed it in. Around her, the smells of leather, horse, and hay faded.

"Better?" he asked.

She nodded.

Mr. Valcourt looked around the quiet stable and then through the open doorway, at the rain falling in sheets. "So much for my ride."

Julia slipped her arms into the sleeves. The coat was too large for her, and she felt small and feminine inside it.

He looked back at her, his gaze slowly roaming her face. The air between them thickened and coiled. From somewhere behind them, Apollo whickered.

"Apollo wants you," she whispered.

"Apollo can wait."

Self-conscious under his scrutiny, she teased, "Does it suit me, do you think?" She gave a roguish yank on the coat's lapels.

She expected a laugh or at least a smile, but his expression was unreadable—his mouth a firm line, his eyes intense.

He leaned near, and Julia's breath caught. His hand reached up and stroked her cheek.

"A raindrop," he murmured by way of explanation.

His face was so close that Julia felt his sweet breath on her temple.

Her skin prickled into gooseflesh. She found her gaze lowering from his eyes to his well-shaped lips.

Was he going to kiss her? Julia's eyes began to drift closed.

But then he abruptly released her and turned toward the tack room.

Julia swallowed her disappointment and said brightly, "I shall help you groom Apollo."

He made no reply as he came out with a brush and let himself into Apollo's stall. Julia retrieved her own favorite grooming tools and joined him there, watching as he ran the brush over Apollo's back and side.

She said, "Barlow taught me to use the currycomb first to loosen dirt and hair, then follow with the brush to remove it. Here, let me show you."

Julia stood beside him, just behind his right arm. She handed him the rough-toothed comb, then laid her hand over his, demonstrating the circular motion. "That's it."

Liberty gave a jealous snort from her stall.

As Julia removed her hand, her shoulder brushed his arm.

Alec stilled and whispered, "You're killing me. You know that, don't you?"

She looked up at his tense profile. So close. Her breath came fast. "Am I?"

He turned toward her, circling her waist with one arm, and pulled her close.

Julia's heart hammered.

Dropping the brush to the floor, he raised his free hand to cradle the side of her face. His head lowered. Nearer. And then his lips touched hers. His mouth pressed hard. Fervent. Not the soft, tentative kiss she might have expected from a proper "dandy." This kiss was passionate and overwhelming. He angled his head the other way, his kiss deepening, his thumb caressing her cheek, his lips caressing hers.

Julia kissed him back, her mind swimming and languorous, her body growing breathless and full of longing.

Abruptly, he broke away with a strangled cry, lifting a hand high in a claw of frustration.

His face tightened in mirror image of his hand. He rasped, "I am sorry." He inhaled through flared nostrils, then exhaled a ragged breath. "Please forgive me."

He hurried from the stall, through the stable door, and into the driving, drenching rain.

Shaken, Julia watched him through the open doorway. For a moment Alec stood, face lifted to the heavens, hands fisted, letting the rain run over his face. Then he strode away.

He had disappeared from view before Julia remembered she still wore his coat.

⁓

Late the next afternoon, Lady Amelia sent a housemaid to summon Julia into the library.

Oh, bother. Julia felt her defenses rise and her mood plummet as she made her way across the hall.

Her mother glanced up when she entered and refolded the letter she had been reading. "Julia, please sit down."

Julia's stomach clenched. What now? Her mother already knew about the Holsworthy ball. Had she found out about the private lessons with Mr. Valcourt as well? Or their time alone in the stable?

"Another inquisition, Mamma?" Julia sighed. "What have I done this time?"

"This is not about you. At least, not directly. This time, all you have done is befriend the wrong person."

Julia stiffened. "What do you mean?"

"Mr. Valcourt is not to be trusted. I regret placing him here under our roof. Exposing you to his company. Had I known what I know now, I would not have given him a position here in the first place."

Julia's mind struggled to keep up. She asked, "Is this about the ball again?"

"No."

"Then what has Mr. Valcourt supposedly done now?" Her mother couldn't know about that kiss, could she? Julia's body warmed all over again at the memory.

"This is not mere supposition, Julia. Have you not wondered why a dancing master would leave London and come here to small, remote Beaworthy, where no one dances?"

Julia shrugged. "I wonder why anyone should want to live here, but what has that to say to anything? There is no law against moving in with one's uncle, even if he is as dull as ditchwater."

"Julia, that is not kind."

But Julia continued, "And if no one dances here, whose fault is that? I understand Mr. Valcourt did not know before he came." She paused to consider, biting her lip in thought. "I wonder why his uncle did not warn him."

Her mother nodded. "I wondered as well. I also wondered why the Valcourts would give up an established academy even if his father had died. Were times really so hard for dancing masters, or had he some other reason for fleeing London?"

"Fleeing? You make him sound the criminal."

"I am afraid he is just that." She held up a hand. "No, he has not stolen anything or killed anybody—at least as far as I know—but he is not innocent either."

Julia tensed in anticipation. "What has he done?"

Lady Amelia tapped the folded letter on the desk. "Apparently, he seduced one of his pupils. I'm sorry to say it so bluntly, but there it is."

"I . . . I am hardly shocked, Mamma," Julia lied. "I am not a child."

"You should be shocked. She was a young lady from a good family. A wealthy, accomplished girl."

"How do you know she didn't seduce *him*?" Julia asked tartly, though inwardly she quailed. Mr. Valcourt . . . intimate with another young woman? It hurt to contemplate.

Her mother frowned. "Really, Julia. I hardly think that likely."

Julia rose up in his defense. "How do you know all this, Mamma? Have you sent in your spies? Are you so determined I not have any friends who have tasted life beyond Beaworthy? That I shall never leave? Never be happy?"

"What has any of that to do with Mr. Valcourt?" her mother asked. "He is not your friend. Not really. His station in life is too far beneath yours. And worse than that, he is not the honorable young man we thought him." She inhaled and set her face in resolve. "And so I must ask you not to spend any more time with him. And take care never to be alone with him. For your own safety and reputation. Do I make myself clear?"

"How do you even know any of this is true?"

"I wrote to an old friend who lives not far from Mr. Valcourt's London academy. She was away when my letter first arrived, but her reply reached me this afternoon. She writes that everyone knows why the academy closed. Mr. Valcourt was being sued by the girl's father. He probably came here to avoid the civil suit and a hefty settlement he could not pay."

Julia's stomach clenched, but she lifted her chin. "It is all hearsay."

Her mother shook her head. "I wish it were."

"Do you? I doubt it. You have been set against Mr. Valcourt since he arrived. Simply because he was a dancing master—not because of anything else he may or may not have done in the past."

"If I was so set against him, why did I offer him a position here?"

"To keep him from hanging out his shingle as a dancing master and ending your iron-fisted reign."

Her mother stared at her, lips parted, a sheen in her eyes. Tears? Julia had never seen her mother cry. Not even at her father's death.

"How you speak to me," she breathed, slowly shaking her head. "Do you not realize that everything I do, I do for you? To protect you?"

"I don't want to be protected! I am not a little girl any longer. I want to live. I want to breathe. I want to leave this dreary, stifling place forever!"

Julia whirled and ran from the room, unsure where the anger, the tears, the desperate longing for escape came from but slave to its call. She ran from the manor, through the estate grounds, and into the churchyard. Pushing through the old heavy door, she fell into the nearest pew and sobbed until her throat ached.

Was she crying because of what her mother had learned or because of what Alec had done? *Oh, Alec . . .*

Julia thought she had finally found an honorable man to love who admired and respected her. Had she been so mistaken in his character? She prayed the report about him was wrong.

Why couldn't her mother have left well enough alone? Had she never made a mistake? From her distant memory rang her father's voice, snapping at Lady Amelia about something Julia had done. *"The apple doesn't fall far from the tree,"* he'd said. And not for the first time, Julia wondered what he'd meant.

༄

The next day, when Alec returned from a midday visit to Apollo, Mr. Barlow met him at the office door, somber faced. "Lady Amelia wishes to see you straightaway."

Alec's muscles tightened. Was she going to reprimand him about the Holsworthy ball? The dancing lessons? Kissing her daughter in the stable? His pulse thudded. Or had she finally received a letter from London?

With a heavy sigh and a heavy heart, Alec turned and walked across the hall. He removed his hat but did not bother to leave it in the office. Why should he, when she would no doubt send him packing without delay?

Lady Amelia was seated at the desk as usual. She did not wait for him to approach before she began reading from a letter in her hand.

"Mr. Valcourt has lately sold his Queen's Square academy and last-known residence and fled town, it is assumed, to avoid the consequences—legal, financial, and otherwise—for reputedly seducing one of his pupils, a Miss U—of Mayfair."

She looked up at him gravely. "Do you deny it?"

An iron weight sank onto Alec's chest, squeezing the air from his lungs. Even if he told the truth, there was no escape. Neither he nor his family would leave this room unscathed. His position was gone, his excuse to spend time with Julia Midwinter gone with it. *As though I'd ever had a chance with her, scandal or no,* he thought dully. Though after that kiss he'd foolishly allowed himself to hope . . .

Alec shook his head, a bitter taste in his mouth. "I cannot deny that such a suit exists. It is not the complete truth, but I'd rather not elaborate."

"Why not?"

He looked down at the floor. Why bother to explain? If he told her everything, and by some miracle she believed him, he might come out with his reputation partially restored. But his sister? His poor mother? It would only be worse for them.

He inhaled, resigned. "Never mind. How can I expect you to believe the truth when I don't want to believe it myself?"

She said coolly, "Truth is always the best way."

Alec snapped his head up and boldly held her gaze. "Is it, your lady-ship?" His eyes bore into hers. "Can you truly say that?"

She froze, staring at him, but did not ask what he meant. Worried concern passed over her features, then was quickly replaced with steely resolve. "You give me no choice but to remove you from your position here."

Alec nodded. "I assumed as much." Alec replaced his hat. "Thank you for the opportunity while it lasted. Good day."

He turned and left the room.

Instead of saddling Apollo and going directly home, Alec walked all the way into the village center. Yes, he dreaded telling his mother and uncle that he had lost his place at Buckleigh Manor, but more than that drove him up the High Street.

Losing his job was the final straw, yet the successful dance lessons at Medlands had already stirred up the old dreams.

His restless steps led him along the walkway bordering the High Street. Past the inn, the tailor's, the public house, and bakery, to the abandoned shop with the papered-over windows. Again he stood on tiptoe and peered inside. Afternoon sunlight reflected off the large mirror and shone into the long room—onto the wooden floorboards and the mismatched chairs around the perimeter.

Hope rose. Might he yet become the successful dancing master his grandfather had been? Again he walked to the padlocked shop door and read the small hand-lettered notice.

For let. Reasonable terms. Inquire at the inn.

Alec thought again of his meager savings. Would it be enough? Would it be wise to risk the last of his savings, now that his well-paying position was gone, his steady source of income with it?

No, it would not be wise. Then why did he find himself turning and walking toward the inn to ask about the notice?

When he entered the quiet taproom, Mr. Jones looked up from behind his counter, but without a welcoming smile. Alec had not been inside since the night of the market hall cave-in and had never bought so much as a cup of tea in the place, so reluctant had he been to spend what little money he had. But tonight, he thought, one ginger beer might be a small price to pay to ease his way into asking about the notice.

Alec removed his hat. "Evening, Mr. Jones."

Washing a tankard, the innkeeper said dourly, "What can I do for ya this time? Come to use my stairs again?"

"No. A ginger beer, if you please."

The man pursed his lips in surprise. He set aside the tankard, wiped his hands on his apron, and then poured a frothy golden mug of the stinging-sweet beverage.

Two men came in while Mr. Jones poured. Alec glanced over, dismayed to see Joe and Felton Wilcox. Just his luck.

"Ginger beer?" Joe jeered. "Oh, that's a man's drink all right. Ain't it, Felton?"

Felton snorted. "Must want to forget his troubles. Or a fickle lady what done him wrong."

Without waiting to be asked, Mr. Jones put a pint of ale before each Wilcox brother.

Joe looked at Alec askance. "You know only ladies and brats drink ginger beer, right? It ain't real beer, ya know. Don't they have it up in London town?"

"Yes, they have it. I prefer it."

Joe looked over at his brother. "Told ya he was a girly man."

Alec told himself to ignore the insult. He'd heard it all before, and it would do no good to argue with these men, especially when they were drinking.

With a dismissive wave, Joe and Felton took their ales over to the inglenook and flopped into the high-backed bench near the fire.

"Friends of yers?" Mr. Jones quipped as he wiped the spigot.

"No." Alec pulled a face. "How do they get away with harassing people?"

"Easy. Felton has been a local hero ever since he beat Cornwall's wrasslin' champ a few years back. Beaworthy folk are excessively proud and willing to overlook certain other deeds. Our constable chief among them. And so far at least, they've only bothered outsiders with few locals to defend them."

"Like me."

"Afraid so."

Alec took a deep breath and changed the subject. "That abandoned shop up the street. The one with the windows covered over?"

The innkeeper nodded. "What about it?"

"I, uh, noticed the notice." Alec chuckled awkwardly at the unintentional repetition. "And I wondered about it."

"Wondered what?" Mr. Jones looked toward the door, lifting his chin to acknowledge another patron entering.

Alec glanced over. A large well-dressed man came in and stopped to greet the Wilcoxes. "Who's that?" he asked quietly.

"Mr. Kellaway. He owns the clay works."

"Ah." Alec nodded. He leaned nearer the innkeeper and hoped to appear nonchalant. "I wondered how long it's been sitting empty, why no one has let it. . . ." He wasn't ready to admit his designs on the place. Not yet. Not when it was likely far beyond his means. Nor was he eager to have the other men present overhear and scoff at his hopes.

"Oh, it's been sittin' empty many a year now," Jones said. "A chandler let it for a time, but that didn't last. Then a bookseller. But people weren't willing to support any business that dared reopen those doors."

Alec frowned. "Why not?" he asked, fearing he already knew the answer.

Mr. Kellaway stepped to the bar, laying down his hat and tugging off his gloves. Alec would have liked to retract his private questions in the stranger's presence, but it was too late. Mr. Jones had already launched into an explanation.

"Because, man, it used to be a dancing school, run by one of them caper merchants—no offense—back before, you know, dancing was done away with hereabouts."

The innkeeper poured Kellaway a pint as he continued. "The lady of the manor was so set against the place, she refused to patronize any business that opened there, and forbid her servants to do the same. Well, I don't have to tell you that Lady Amelia wields no small influence in Beaworthy, nay, the entire parish. So most other folks wouldn't patronize the businesses either, for fear of word gettin' back to her, and their Jimmy losing his place as hallboy or their Susan as housemaid, or their Tom finding no more orders coming from Buckleigh. Weren't worth the risk."

Mr. Kellaway amiably joined the conversation. "Mr. Jones here quit holding dances in his assembly room for the same reason. Didn't you?"

The innkeeper's eyes flashed at this implied slight to his manhood. "Yes, and what else was I to do? Her ladyship called for an end of public dances and removed Buckleigh support of the assembly room—no longer of paying for the musicians, the refreshments, the candles, and such. At least her butler still buys small beer from me for the servants' hall."

"I understand, man," Kellaway said. "But I for one patronized the businesses." Kellaway paused to sip his ale.

Mr. Jones slanted Kellaway a look. "Easy for you to say—you don't rely on Buckleigh Manor for employment or patronage."

"True," Kellaway acknowledged. "And glad I am of that."

He picked up his hat, lifted his glass in salute—"Gents"—and stepped away to join the Wilcox brothers.

Mr. Jones watched him walk away, then asked Alec, "Thinkin' of opening a place of yer own?"

"I . . . was just wondering. Why it is sitting empty. Asking a lot for it, are they?"

The innkeeper hesitated, chewing his lip as he considered Alec.

Uncomfortable, Alec asked, "Who owns the place?"

"The smith out at the forge."

"The smith?"

"Aye. Mr. Desmond."

"But . . . why would he let that nice piece of property in the center of town sit idle, and keep his forge so out of the way like it is?"

Mr. Jones shook his head. "You really don't know anythin', do ya? He has his reasons—that's all I tell ya. Ain't my place to say more. I'd say go ask him yerself, but I hear he's been ailing."

"Yes," Alec murmured. "I heard that too." It was on the tip of the tongue to mention that the smith's son, helping out at the forge, had told him, but he remembered just in time that Desmond didn't want his presence spread about.

"It's been a year or more since he told me what he's askin' to let the place, and yer the first to ask in some time. May have changed 'is mind since then. So you'd better ask him or the missus yerself."

"Perhaps I will." Alec finished his ginger beer and stood. "Thank you."

The movement drew the attention of Joe Wilcox, who raised his head from his pint. "One entire ginger beer? Are ya sure you'll be all right to get home?"

Felton snorted into his ale.

"Gentlemen." Ignoring their jeers, Alec tipped his hat and took his leave, hoping the inebriated men wouldn't follow him out into the street to continue their taunts—or worse.

Alec walked to the forge. From a distance, he saw John Desmond standing in the outer porch, which expanded the work space and provided shelter for waiting customers. Desmond stood, leaning one shoulder against a support post, arms crossed, a mug in his hand.

As Alec neared, the man called, "Don't tell me those two broke your blade again."

Alec shook his head. "Nothing to repair this time." *At least not a physical object,* he added to himself.

"No? Then what can I do for you?"

Alec stepped up into the porch. "I came to ask about the property in the High Street. The innkeeper said your father owns it."

"Did he now?"

Alec nodded. "Well, he said the smith, so I assume that's who he meant."

"Tea?" Desmond offered, nodding toward the kettle on the edge of the fire.

"No, thank you."

"What's your interest in the place, friend?" Desmond asked, topping off his cup.

"Wondered what it might cost to let it—that's all."

Desmond stilled. "For what purpose?"

Alec hesitated. This man had only recently returned to Beaworthy. How long had he been gone? Perhaps he did not know about the unwritten law and would not laugh and naysay as others would. Besides, he had seen the man playing his pipe for a ball, so he likely held no scruples against dancing.

"I thought I might let it to teach fencing, and . . . dancing."

The man's brows rose. "Dancing?"

Alec sighed at the man's incredulity. "That was my profession in London. I was a dancing and fencing master there."

The man held his gaze a moment, then looked down, as though suddenly interested in the tea leaves at the bottom of his cup.

"I don't think that will go over well here, friend."

"So you know about the ban on dancing?"

Desmond looked out into the distance and said softly, "Aye. I know." Then he asked quietly, "Do you know why?"

"Why no dancing?" Alec clarified. At Desmond's nod, he continued. "I know it was Lady Amelia's doing. At first I thought it went against her religion, that she was a Quaker or something, though I see her regularly enough at St. Michael's. But her daughter told me—"

"You are acquainted with her daughter?" Desmond asked abruptly.

Alec shrugged. "Yes. I worked as clerk at Buckleigh Manor for a time, and we—"

"Interesting," Desmond interrupted. "Is Lady Amelia aware of your former profession?"

"Yes. I believe that is why she offered me the post."

He tilted his head to the side, dark eyes speculative. "You don't say."

"It is also partly why she removed me from that same post earlier today."

He raised his brow in query and waited for Alec to enlighten him.

Alec winced. "She'd written to a friend in London to plumb the Valcourt reputation there. Today she received her friend's reply."

Desmond's brows remained high, awaiting further explanation. But Alec didn't have the energy to deliver one. "It's nothing that affects my suitability as a tenant, I assure you."

Desmond did not push him. Instead, he asked, "Does the daughter look like her mother?"

Alec was momentarily taken aback by the question, the change in topic. He shrugged. "There might be some resemblance, I suppose, though not a striking one. Lady Amelia's hair is darker, but I believe their eyes are similar. Though I am not the best judge of such things."

Desmond nodded his understanding.

Alec thought, then added, "Their personalities are very different— and that, I think, makes them seem less alike."

"Different how?"

"Oh . . ." Alec puffed out his cheeks in thought. "Julia—that is, Miss Midwinter—is all liveliness and changeability. Rapturous one moment and wistful the next. Given to frequent smiles and laughter. She—"

Alec broke off, aware of Desmond studying him closely. Knowingly. He felt warmth creep up his neck and changed course. "On the other hand, I don't believe I've seen Lady Amelia genuinely smile once—and certainly never heard her laugh. Granted, I don't know her well, but she certainly doesn't *seem* happy."

Alec glanced over and found Desmond staring off into the distance again. "No, I don't imagine she is."

Having no wish to be uncharitable, Alec said, "But then, she is a widow, so I suppose a certain . . . sobriety must be expected." He added, "Though according to her daughter, Lady Amelia has never been happy."

Desmond gave him a sidelong glance and shook his head. "That's not true."

"No?" Alec asked in surprise.

Desmond skirted his gaze. "I knew her when she was young, growing up here as I did. Though that was before she married, or had a child, or lost her family."

Alec regarded the man's profile with interest, wanting to ask him questions but unsure where to start. He hardly had a long enough acquaintance with the man to ask personal, prying questions.

Desmond asked a question of his own. "And how did her daughter respond when you asked why Lady Amelia was set against dancing?"

"She said it had something to do with her uncle being killed in a drunken brawl at the last village dance."

Desmond shook his head. "It was no drunken brawl. It was a duel. And both men perfectly sober."

Alec gaped. "How do you know? Were you there?"

Desmond nodded bleakly. "It did happen during the May Day dance, but the dance itself wasn't to blame." Desmond's eyes shimmered in memory. "The fault lay with the dancing master himself."

Alec stared as realization dawned. He breathed, "You were the dancing master . . . ?"

Desmond hesitated, then nodded.

"*Were* you responsible?"

A grimace of pain contorted the man's handsome face. "For her brother's death? Yes, God forgive me, I was. I suppose had I not been there, the rest might have been avoided as well."

Desmond drew himself up. "It's all last year's thatch at this point. And, friend, a word of advice? It's obvious you admire Miss Midwinter, but sheathe your heart. You would never be allowed to marry her."

Alec ducked his head. It was his turn to avoid the other man's gaze. "I know that," he said, sheepish. But did he? Did he really believe it?

Desmond turned away and bent over his workbench. Alec thought it was the end of their meeting. When Desmond turned back, however, he handed him a scrap of paper inscribed with a modest figure. "This is the rate we set some time ago, but let me talk with my father before we go any further. Come back tomorrow, all right?"

Alec nodded, though he felt little victory. Suddenly the prospect of letting the place held less appeal than it had a few minutes before.

Not to go back, is somewhat to advance, And men must walk, at least, before they dance.

—Alexander Pope

Chapter 15

The next morning, Alec rose early and volunteered to help his uncle's manservant prepare the large garden plot for planting seed potatoes and other vegetables. Old Abe was clearly surprised by the offer but did not refuse.

Pushing the wooden plow with its dull blade, Alec tilled row by row—stopping only to dig out roots or stones by hand and then continuing on until his muscles burned and sweat ran down his back. He needed the exercise, the exertion, and found the strenuous labor oddly satisfying. He finished by digging shallow trenches according to Abe's instructions. He offered to plant the sprouted seed potatoes as well, but Abe waved him away, muttering that he wasn't about to let some young buck work him out of a job.

Alec cleaned himself up and dressed to face the day.

After the midday meal, he steeled himself and walked over to Buckleigh Manor to retrieve Apollo. The weather was damp and grey fog hung low in the air, mirroring his dismal mood. As he walked, scenes from the previous day returned to him, increasing his depression of spirits. Lady Amelia's cool dismissal. His talk with Desmond at the forge. How Alec had hoped to return to his uncle's house possessing an alternate plan to present to his family, to soften the blow of his bad news.

But the trip to the forge had not resulted in the clear path he had hoped for. Desmond would discuss it with his father and let him know. Was it only the rate he was unsure of—or was it Alec's suitability as a tenant? And what of the reverse—did Alec really want to enter into any contract with a man who had killed another in a duel—her ladyship's brother no less?

His stomach soured at the thought.

Then his mood sank further when he recalled his mother's wide-eyed dismay and his uncle's stiff-lipped disapproval when Alec had confessed he'd lost his position at the manor.

"What did you do?" his uncle had asked.

Alec hesitated, then said, "She inquired into my background." But could he really blame it all on the past? Had he not provoked her into doing so by presuming to spend time with her daughter?

"And why did she feel the need to do that?" Cornelius Ramsay had asked shrewdly, giving Alec a glimpse of the keen solicitor he truly was.

His mother frowned. "Brother, I am sure Alec did nothing to—"

Alec interrupted her with a hand to her shoulder. "It's all right, Mamma. Uncle is right. I brought it on myself."

After the unhappy scene, Aurora had followed him upstairs and squeezed his arm. "It isn't your fault, Alec. Don't take it to heart."

He'd pressed his eyes shut. "Aurora, it is time I stopped blaming others for all my troubles. My position at Buckleigh Manor and my conduct there were my responsibility. You and Mamma are my responsibility, and I am done trying to pass the blame."

Now, as Alec passed through the Buckleigh Manor gate, he felt for the first time that he deserved the lion's scowl. He walked around the ornamental lake, giving the house a wide berth on his way to the stables. He should have taken Apollo back to his uncle's after he'd broken Barlow's arm, but Barlow and even Miss Midwinter had encouraged Alec to leave Apollo so they could continue to work with him. And both horse and horseman had become better trained, though Alec knew he was still far from a skilled equestrian.

Reaching the stables, Alec began to saddle Apollo on his own. Young Tommy earnestly offered to help, his sad eyes telling Alec he knew neither horse nor rider would be back. He thanked the groom, and Mr. Isaacs, for all their help and generosity in allowing him to board his horse there these several weeks.

When he led Apollo out, there stood Mr. Barlow waiting for him. Perhaps he'd seen Alec walk past from the office window or had simply anticipated his intentions.

Looking uncomfortable, Barlow said, "Her ladyship didn't go into the particulars. But if you misrepresented your character or qualifications, I cannot blame her. I trusted you, Mr. Valcourt. I hope I did not err in doing so."

"You did not err, sir. And I have never breathed a word about . . . any duty I have undertaken here."

Barlow nodded with a distracted frown, and Alec's stomach clenched at the thought of disappointing and disillusioning this man.

Alec added, "And I am deeply grateful for all your help, sir. With Apollo and . . . everything."

Again, that terse nod, and then the manager turned and walked away, hands behind his back.

Alec would have liked to shake his hand, but he doubted the gesture would have been accepted or appreciated.

Tommy brought out a pair of riding gloves Alec had forgotten, and Alec thanked the groom again. Then he mounted without trouble.

As he rode past the house a few minutes later, he looked through the office window, and there stood Barlow. Alec halted Apollo and raised a hand.

Barlow hesitated, then raised his own hand in solemn farewell.

Miss Midwinter, he noticed, had not come out to say good-bye. No doubt a wise move on her part, but still it chafed. As he trotted away from Buckleigh Manor, he determined to push her from his restless thoughts.

He glimpsed a flicker of movement over the churchyard wall and looked over, his foolish heart constricting. All he could see was something bobbing beyond the stone wall—a feather in a woman's hat as she walked past? He did not recall Julia wearing a feathered hat.

Not wishing her or anyone to witness his mortifying retreat, Alec did not investigate to see who was passing by on her way to Buckleigh Manor. Instead he set his face in the opposite direction.

He urged Apollo into a canter, as though speed would help him outrun the memories of their times together, the image of her face, her two faces—smiling lively Julia and vulnerable lost Julia. And their kiss . . . Alec knew he should regret it, but he did not. Not anymore.

Why? Why her? he asked his heart. She was unsuitable. Changeable. A determined flirt. She didn't seem to care what he thought of her—what anyone thought of her. Was that part of her appeal? Worse yet, she was expected to marry another man. How could Alec compete with wealthy, handsome James Allen?

He rode on, urging Apollo off the Buckleigh Road and across the open meadow.

Why could he not moon over a lady like Patience Allen, above him as well, though perfectly sweet in character and temperament? Or Tess Thorne—pretty, full of faith, and closer to his social equal? He must force himself to put Miss Midwinter from his mind. He must. He would.

⁍

Lady Amelia stared at herself in her dressing table mirror. She did not like what she saw. Her hair was still thick and auburn, her jaw still firm. She was three and forty, yet to her critical eye she appeared older. Widowhood did not suit her. Nor, apparently, did motherhood. Had worry for Julia caused the lines across her brow, the dull wan complexion? Or was it guilt?

Probably both.

She remembered with discomfort the scene with Mr. Valcourt over the letter and his dismissal. Her cool superiority when she'd insisted truth was always the best way.

Again she heard Mr. Valcourt's challenge, *"Can you truly say that?"* echo in her memory.

What did he know? Had Lieutenant Tremelling told him? Mr. Valcourt's uncle had been Mr. Midwinter's solicitor—might he have confided in Mr. Ramsay and he in turn mentioned something to his nephew?

Please no. Not yet. I want to tell her myself. But how? she silently asked her reflection. *She hates me as it is. . . .*

With a sigh, Amelia rose and went down to the library.

When the footman announced a caller, a slurry of irritation, dread, and guilt rained down on Amelia. She would not refuse to see the woman, though she was tempted to do so. But she knew neither of them would enjoy the meeting.

Mrs. Valcourt entered still wearing her coat. Hopefully that meant she did not plan to stay long. Amelia gestured her nearer, staying seated behind her desk, as though it might shield her from the unpleasantness ahead.

The lonely feather atop Mrs. Valcourt's outmoded hat quivered, but she did not look nervous. Rather she appeared resolute. Determined.

Amelia indicated a chair, but the woman shook her head. "No, thank you."

Amelia thought it best to take charge of the conversation straightaway. "I do hope, Mrs. Valcourt, that you have not come to ask me to reinstate your son."

"I am here only to tell you the truth." The woman spoke softly but with conviction.

"Good. Better to allow our children to face the consequences of their actions and learn from their mistakes. Do you not agree?"

"I do agree, my lady. However, in this instance, Alec is not guilty of the accusations laid at his door."

Inwardly, Amelia groaned. Had Mr. Valcourt persuaded his naïve mother of his innocence? She hated to be the one to disillusion her. Amelia clasped her hands on the desk. "Mrs. Valcourt, I realize mothers are often reluctant to acknowledge the flaws of their own offspring. But your son is a man, after all. Are you saying he is incapable of wrongdoing, of becoming involved with a female pupil?"

Mrs. Valcourt's eyes flashed. "I am fully aware that my son is not perfect. Of course he is capable of making mistakes. We are all of us guilty of some sin or other. However, this particular sin you refer to is my husband's and not Alec's."

"But the young woman in question specifically named Mr. Valcourt—" Amelia broke off in disbelief. "Don't tell me you are trying to shift blame to the *other* Mr. Valcourt, who can no longer defend himself. How convenient for everyone, except of course, the memory of your dear departed husband."

Mrs. Valcourt shook her head, thin mouth twisted bitterly. "He is neither, my lady."

Amelia stared at the woman, felt a frown pucker her face. *More wrinkles.* "What do you mean? Not dear . . . or not departed?"

"Neither, as I said. He is not dead. At least, not as far as we know."

"But . . ." Amelia sputtered, "you wear black."

The woman nodded. "Yet you have likely noticed Aurora and Alec don't. Perhaps you thought them disrespectful, not to honor their father by remaining in mourning for the full six months."

"It did cross my mind, yes."

"Well, now you know better."

Amelia searched her memory. "I am certain you told us he was dead."

"I never said so." Mrs. Valcourt shook her head. "We said he was gone, and he is. Fled the country to avoid repercussions."

"But you let us assume it."

Mrs. Valcourt nodded. "When I put on mourning in London, I had no intention of deceiving anyone. It was a genuine reaction—my husband, my marriage, my former life . . . were dead to me. But continuing to wear it here was deceitful, I own. But it was also—"

"Expedient for pretense?" Amelia suggested. "For insinuating yourselves into our society, our good graces?"

"Yes, all of that," the woman agreed, with gravity though little evidence of remorse. "But it also spared my children and me the great shame of having to explain the truth of why my husband was not with us. I thought it the lesser of evils."

Amelia shook her head, self-righteous anger simmering within. "Truth is always the better way." Those words again. She hoped God would forgive her.

Mrs. Valcourt looked her directly in the eye, held her gaze for two ticks of the mantel clock. Two ticks too long.

"Are you telling me you have never been tempted to shield your daughter from a painful truth?" she asked. "Can you not understand, at least a little, a mother's desire to protect her children from the shame caused by the wrongdoing of a parent? Their own flesh and blood?"

Amelia felt a knife of painful realization slice her heart. Yes, she could well understand the desire to shield her daughter from her parents' shame. From mistakes not of her own making. But Amelia said nothing of this to Mrs. Valcourt. *What a hypocrite I am.*

Mrs. Valcourt continued, "Well. However poorly you think of me, I am not willing that Alec's reputation should suffer. That *he* should suffer because of his father's wrongdoing. Though he and his sister have, in fact, already suffered a great deal through all of this. As have I."

What did the woman expect her to do about it? Rehire her son? Instead she stiffly thanked Mrs. Valcourt for coming and for telling her the truth.

She did not promise to keep the news to herself, nor did Mrs. Valcourt attempt to extract any such promise. As Beaworthy's leading citizen, perhaps she *ought* to tell everyone the truth about their new neighbors. Perhaps it was her duty. But the thought sickened Amelia, and she knew she would not do so.

She supposed it was a credit to the son that he did not wish to expose his mother to such mortification, that he was willing to accept the blame. Should she tell Barlow? Julia? Admit her source had been wrong in one important detail? She was loath to do so. The Valcourt family had not risen in her esteem because of this information. She still did not want Julia spending time in the handsome young man's company, nor forming an ill-advised attachment.

After Mrs. Valcourt took her leave, Amelia sat in the library for a long time, not bothering to light a lamp when the sunlight faded and the room dimmed. Her mind was otherwise occupied, revising her former conclusions. The senior Mr. Valcourt had seduced a young lady, had ruined her and left town to avoid her father's wrath and worse. In the process, he broke his wife's heart, bankrupted his family's academy, and destroyed his son's future prospects.

Had the man deserted them for good? By the looks of things, yes.

Her friend's letter had not gone into great detail about the legal recourses the injured father was pursuing in the case of his compromised daughter, but they must be grievous indeed if Valcourt felt he had to disappear. In the meantime, his wife of many years was left carrying his shame but none of his protection. Amelia shivered. Oh yes. Even if she could not approve, she could understand why Mrs. Valcourt wore black. Why she allowed them all to believe a less-humiliating lie.

As Amelia sat there, raindrops of memory began to fall. She felt as though she were gazing up into a night sky, while icy pellets spun toward earth and hit her face, melting against her one by one. Another compromised young woman. Another angry father. Another man protesting his innocence and disappearing. She heard again his desperate *"You must believe me."* Felt again the confusion. The shame. The pain of a heart breaking into jagged pieces.

No. She pressed her eyes closed, tight. Wincing away the images, the memories, refusing to allow the rain to fall on her ever again.

❦

After dinner that night, Mrs. Valcourt summoned Alec and Aurora into the sitting room for a family meeting behind closed doors. Alec had noticed her strained silence and forced smiles during the meal and wondered what was wrong. Or rather, what *more* was wrong, considering they had lost his income on top of everything else. Grimly, his mother told them she had paid a call on Lady Amelia Midwinter that day and confessed everything to the woman.

"But, Mamma—" Alec began.

She held up her hand. "I know, I know. But I could not sit silent and allow that woman to think so ill of you." She pressed her lips together. "I suppose I hoped she might reinstate you. But she made no indication that what I told her had any bearing on that decision. So"—her hands fluttered like dying birds—"I have told our secret for nothing, apparently. I've brought shame on you, on your uncle . . ."

Alec grasped his mother's cold fingers. "No, Mamma. That shame is not yours to claim. Father did this, and it is our duty to make the best of our new lives. Perhaps we ought to have told all from the outset—I don't know. But we will face this together, whatever comes."

After reassuring his mother and sister as best he could, Alec left the house and trudged back up the Sheepwash Road to the Desmond smithy. Although he still had questions about the duel, something told him Desmond was a good man, even if he had made a horrid mistake in the past. And Alec needed a friend at present. A friend who just might understand.

As the Desmond property came into view, the front door of the house opened and John Desmond stepped out onto the stoop with a lantern, as though he'd been watching for him.

"Hello, Valcourt. I was beginning to wonder if I'd see you tonight." He walked across the narrow yard to the forge.

Alec followed, stepping into the porch behind him, wondering where to start.

His back to Alec, Desmond hung up the lantern, then picked up something from the workbench. When he turned, he held an old key hanging on a loop of thick string. "I talked with my father, and we are in agreement, assuming—"

Alec held up his hand to stay him. "I need to tell you something first."

Desmond tucked his chin, brow furrowed. "Oh?"

Alec doubted the Desmonds would want to rent property to the Valcourt family after he told all. But he knew it would be better coming from him.

Alec hesitated, struggling to find the words. His gaze landed on a miniature violin lying across the wooden bench. He'd not seen it the other times he'd been there.

"Do you play the *pochette* as well as the pipe?"

Desmond glanced at it. "I used to."

The small violins allowed dancing masters to carry an instrument in a large coat pocket while instructing, and then bring it out to play while his pupils danced.

Desmond positioned the instrument against his ribs—it was too small to hold in the standard way—and picked up the bow. He struck a few experimental notes, then launched into a jaunty tune.

The door to the nearby house opened, and an elderly man stepped out, dressed in a tweed coat over a simple shirt and trousers.

Desmond stopped playing. "Papa! You're to be in bed."

"And miss hearing ye play? Does ma'old heart good to hear ye, Johnny. It does indeed. Now if I cahn but see ye dance again, then all will be well. Perhaps a Highland Fling for yer old paw?"

Alec noted that Mr. Desmond's Scottish brogue was more marked than his son's.

"Papa, go on back inside. It's chilly tonight. I don't even remember those old dances."

An elderly woman stepped onto the stoop, pushing a wool cap atop her husband's snowy head. "Yes you do, Johnny," she said.

The woman had black hair streaked with silver, and dark eyes, her skin more golden than the typical English or Scottish rose. Spanish, perhaps? Or Italian? Alec realized then where Desmond got his coloring.

"Not tonight, Mamma." Desmond turned. "Besides, tonight we have a visitor."

Alec stepped out from the shadows of the forge porch, sheepish to disrupt the family moment.

"Allow me to introduce my parents," Desmond said. "Fergus and Maria Desmond. And this is Alec Valcourt. It's his sword you helped me to mend, Papa."

"Ah yes, a fine blade." The man stuck out a thick gnarled hand. "How do ye do, lad?"

"Well, thank you, sir. A pleasure to meet you both."

"Mr. Valcourt here is also the man I mentioned who is interested in letting the old academy."

The man's bushy white brows rose. "Is he indeed?"

"Yes, a genuine London dancing master, transplanted here to Beaworthy of all places."

"Good heavens, lad," Fergus Desmond said. "I'd na'wish that on m'worst enemy." The man's eyes glinted with humor.

"I was not aware of the, um, local views on dancing when we decided to come here."

Father and son shared a knowing look.

"There must be a better place for ye to set out yer shingle, lad. Not that I'm keen to get rid of ye. Just thinking of yer future. . . ."

"My uncle resides here, sir. Cornelius Ramsay. My mother, sister, and I have come to live with him."

"Oh. I see. Your father's gone, is he?"

Alec exhaled, then began, "He *is* gone. Gone nearly six months. My poor mother wears mourning, for her heart is broken, and people here assume he died. And . . . we have allowed them to believe that." Alec admitted, "It was easier to explain—why we had to sell our home and academy, why we had to leave town. But it isn't the truth."

Three pairs of solemn eyes regarded him.

"What is the truth?" Mrs. Desmond quietly asked.

Alec swallowed. "The truth is, my father is not dead. At least as far as we know. He has left the country to avoid the suit brought against him by a girl's father. A former pupil of ours, who has named my father as her seducer."

Fergus and Maria Desmond's faces drooped in identical fashion. They looked at one another and exchanged a look of shared sadness. Beside him, Desmond gripped his shoulder.

"Is the gir-el tellin' the truth?" Fergus asked in a low voice.

Alec hung his head, ears burning with shame and guilt. "I'm afraid so. Though the girl was not completely innocent. She was an incorrigible flirt, but that does not justify his actions. She was young and foolish and vain. He should have known better. He did know better!"

"All we like sheep have gone astray . . ." Desmond murmured, shaking his head.

Alec inhaled. "At all events, Lady Amelia wrote to an acquaintance in London to inquire into my reputation, and learned of the scandal. She assumed I was the Mr. Valcourt implicated, and I was prepared to let her believe it. My mother, however, was not, and told her everything today. I imagine it will only be a matter of time before the entire village knows of the scandal, not to mention our deception regarding my father's fate."

Alec drew himself up. "I wanted you to hear it from me directly."

"Well, lad, thaht is quite a sad tale." The old smith nodded. "And I'm sorry for ya. Yer maw most of all."

"Thank you for telling us," Desmond added.

Alec stiffened his spine. "All this to say—I will understand perfectly if you don't wish to let your property to me."

He waited, the silence lengthening while the three Desmonds exchanged looks.

A crack of a smile lifted Fergus Desmond's thin mouth. "Poor lad. Frettin' over our reputations—as though they might be spoilt by associatin' with *him*. Can'e imagine?"

"Don't tease the boy, love," Mrs. Desmond gently chided.

Desmond said to his parents, "I haven't told Alec the whole sordid tale yet. Though he knows the worst of it." He turned to Alec. "Suffice it to say, we don't hold what you told us against you. In fact, we understand."

Mrs. Desmond nodded sadly. "All too well."

❧

Alec's pulse thrummed as he walked back to his uncle's. He had done it. The key even now hung heavy in his pocket. He had agreed in principle to let the former dancing academy for two months at very reasonable terms. Desmond had insisted, however, that Alec meet him at the empty shop the next evening to thoroughly inspect the place and make sure he knew what he was getting into before any money changed hands. Desmond would meet him there at eight. Alec felt satisfied—exonerated—to be counted as trustworthy, after Lady Amelia's accusations and dismissal. He would do everything in his power to prove himself worthy of John Desmond's trust.

A little voice whispered, *Is Desmond trustworthy?* But Alec found he both trusted and liked the man—and his parents.

Alec hoped he had done the right thing. How would his mother react? His uncle? Beaworthy's residents? He hoped they would not all be sorely vexed.

And Lady Amelia? He shuddered to think.

For better or worse, he would be a dancing master again. Not a clay pit drudge, not a deskbound clerk under Lady Amelia's thumb, but his own man. He dared not count on many pupils, though he prayed that eventually he could make a go of the place. Thankfully, he knew his mother and sister would not mind doing without an allowance for the time being.

Along with his worries, a low hum of eagerness, of excitement began to pulse through his body. He had done it—taken the first step toward opening his own academy. What should he call it? Valcourt Dancing and Fencing Academy, as before? Or have a new sign engraved with his name: Alec Valcourt, Dancing & Fencing Master.

He quite liked the sound of that. It had been too long since he'd heard it. Or even dared think of himself by that moniker.

Alec tossed his topper in the air, spun in place, and caught his hat before replacing it once more.

A giggle reached his ears—ears which quickly heated when he realized how foolish he must have looked. He glanced up and saw a ginger-haired girl of five or six walking hand-in-hand with her father. Eyes twinkling, she gave him a gap-toothed grin as she passed.

Alec doffed his hat to her and continued on his way.

⁓

The next morning, Julia knocked on Mr. Ramsay's door, trying to squelch a flutter of nerves. When she had not seen Mr. Valcourt the day before, she'd asked Barlow if he was ill, only to be told he'd been given the sack.

True—Lady Amelia had told Julia about the letter from her London acquaintance and warned Julia to stay away from Mr. Valcourt, but she had not said she planned to dismiss him. Julia didn't know why she was surprised. And now she felt duty bound to apologize on her mother's behalf. In her heart of hearts, she believed there must be some mistake about the story. She hoped Mr. Valcourt might confide in her the truth, and affirm her faith in him.

When the housekeeper answered the door, self-consciousness flooded Julia. She could not very well ask to see Mr. Valcourt privately. That was too forward even for her. Instead she asked to see Miss Valcourt.

The housekeeper told her to wait while she went to see if Miss Valcourt was at home to callers. What airs the woman put on. Julia hoped the girl wouldn't refuse to see her on her brother's behalf.

But a moment later, Aurora came out of the sitting room, surprise and concern on her sweet face. "Miss Midwinter. Are you all right?"

Did she look as ill as she felt? "I am well, thank you. I . . . simply wished to pay a call."

Aurora looked at her with forthright blue eyes, which were somehow innocent and knowing all at once. She took a step nearer and lowered her voice. "My brother is not here, Miss Midwinter. He has gone out."

The girl had seen right through her ruse, Julia realized. Yet she saw no condemnation in Aurora's eyes, though she must know her mother had dismissed Alec.

"I see." Julia faltered, "I . . . I only wanted to tell him, that I am terribly sorry about . . ." Had he confided the news of his dismissal to his family? She hated to be the one to do so if he had not.

Aurora said kindly, "It is not your fault, Miss Midwinter."

"No," she said bitterly. "It is my mother's." Guilt pinched her. She knew that the fault was partially hers. Had she not shown any interest in Mr. Valcourt and not insisted on spending time with him, her mother might never have inquired into his past.

Several thoughts flickered across Aurora Valcourt's face. A look of uncertainty was replaced with a snap of decision, like the throwing of a bolt.

"Miss Midwinter," she said. "Would you care to take a turn about my uncle's gardens? His bluebells are exceptional this year."

Julia recognized the glint in the younger woman's eyes. "Yes. I should like that very much."

"Just let me retrieve my bonnet and gloves."

A few minutes later, the two young women strolled around the gardens, one freshly plowed and a second, smaller kitchen garden with a few lettuces sprouting up and a border of bluebells for color.

Aurora began, "Alec would not like me discussing this with . . ."

"With me?"

"With anyone. But I don't agree with him. I told Alec not to be a martyr, but he would not listen to me." Aurora took a deep breath. "What has your mother told you?"

Julia hesitated, unsure how much Aurora knew, and cringing to say the words aloud. "She told me she learned that Mr. Valcourt had seduced a young lady—one of his pupils. I don't want to believe it, but my mother has a London acquaintance who wrote to her about it." She held her breath. Hoping the girl would not be shocked. Hoping she would vehemently deny the story.

Instead the girl nodded. "It is true. A Mr. Valcourt did seduce one of his pupils—a well-connected and vocal young woman, as it turned out. But it was not Alec."

"But," Julia blurted, "he did not deny it."

"No. Out of a misplaced sense of family duty." Aurora sighed. "Alec wasn't the Mr. Valcourt who had an affair with one of his pupils. That dubious honor belongs to Mr. Colin Valcourt. My father."

Julia stared. Shocked.

"Yes, you see—though an awful scandal either way—how much less mortifying for us all, but especially my mother, if a young, single man were to become involved with a pupil. But it was my father—married, his wife and daughter right upstairs in their apartment." Aurora shuddered. "And no recourse available to the girl's angry father—no man to work on, to convince to marry his daughter and save her reputation." Aurora exhaled deeply. "I will say this for Miss Underhill. She did not claim to be perfectly innocent in the affair. There were no charges of . . ." She could not bring herself to say the horrid word, but Julia could guess.

"What did your father say in his defense?" Julia asked.

"Not much. He left the country to avoid the civil suit and damages." Aurora added, "Can you see why we were not eager to make the circumstances of our coming known to our new neighbors?"

Aurora shook her head in regret. "How quickly word spread in London. How rapidly and thoroughly the damage was done. You don't understand, Miss Midwinter, how well known the Valcourts were. My grandfather had been dancing master to two dukes. He published books of music and dance. He spent his life building a reputation for honor and excellence. One is not invited into the homes of nobility without the highest personal recommendations.

"My grandfather passed on his academy to our father, but he was not the best manager. Money flowed through his hands like water. Under Alec's leadership the academy would have flourished. He would have been a very successful man, wealthy even, and able to marry well. Instead, with one sin, my father ruined everything. It's all gone now. The academy, the private lessons, the reputation . . . Gone forever."

Julia nodded, feeling ill. "How long ago was this?"

"About six months ago now. Before he . . ."

When she hesitated, Julia gently suggested, "Died?"

Aurora stared at her, grieved and upset, and Julia was sorry she'd asked.

The girl faltered, "Your mother did not . . . did not mention that my mother paid a call to . . . clarify the matter?"

Julia felt anger flash. "No. She did not say a word to me."

Aurora bit her lip. "I have said more than I should have. It is not my place. But I could not stand by and let you think the worst of Alec, the dearest and kindest brother in the world."

❧

Julia returned home and confronted her mother at the first opportunity.

"I cannot believe you did not tell me. Alec Valcourt did not seduce a pupil. His father did."

Lady Amelia's lips tightened. "Mr. Valcourt lost no time in pleading his case, and enlisting you to his cause, I see."

"Mr. Valcourt has not breathed a word," Julia insisted. "I went to see his sister. She told me because I asked."

"Did she also tell you her father is not dead, but has merely left the country to avoid trial?"

Julia stared. "She did say he left the country, though not that he was still alive." Aurora had seemed on the verge of saying more but had held her tongue.

"So you see," her mother continued. "I am not the only one keeping information to myself to serve my own purposes."

"What purposes? To cast aspersions on an innocent man in hopes of dashing my admiration for him? Now I only admire him all the more for trying to protect his family."

Her mother defended herself, saying, "Mrs. Valcourt came here only yesterday. I had not yet decided what to do with what she told me. I had been considering not telling anyone to avoid exposing the family to further gossip."

"I am not *anyone*. I am your daughter."

Lady Amelia stilled. "Yes, you are," she breathed, those foreign tears shimmering in her eyes once again. Then she averted her gaze and inhaled deeply. "Perhaps I should have told you straightaway. But it does not change anything."

Julia slowly shook her head. "On the contrary, Mother. It changes everything."

WANTED by a Dancing Master of the first respectability; a young man, either as an APPRENTICE, or an Assistant. Address post paid to A. B. Z. at Read's Coffee-house, 102 Fleet Street.

—*The* (London) *Times*, 1815

$\mathscr{C}$hapter 16

The next day turned ominously dark and rainy. It was too wet to go out-of-doors, so Julia and Patience sat quietly in the drawing room. Thankfully, her dear friend had arrived before the heavens opened. Julia fiddled with the locket around her neck and watched Patience work diligently on a sampler, seemingly content to sew for hours, her stitches precise and orderly.

On her lap, Julia's loop of canvas held a snarled mess of knotted embroidery thread. She just hadn't enough interest in needlework to do it justice—nor the patience. Julia sighed. Her friend was certainly aptly named.

Patience looked up at Julia's sigh, white-blond eyebrows arched. "Is something amiss?"

Everything, Julia thought, but instead asked a question of her own. "Why does your family call you Pet? I'm not sure why I've never thought to ask. I know there are such things as pet names, but could they think of nothing more original?"

Patience shrugged, tying off a thread. "I don't mind. I suppose Patience does not lend itself to many diminutives." She looked up in thought. "And when my father says, 'Hello, my pet,' it sounds so sweet, and reminds me how much he loves me."

Julia snorted.

"I'm sorry, Julia," Patience said earnestly. "I know you didn't feel close to your father, but I am certain he loved you."

"Are you? Based on what, pray? I doubt he said more than a dozen words a month to either of us." Julia tried to imagine Mr. Midwinter calling her by some fond pet name . . . but could not.

Patience considered. "Surely you exaggerate, Julia. He had been ill for a long time, remember, yet he must have loved you."

"Why?"

Patience shifted. "Because . . ." She faltered. "Because that's what fathers do."

Pain sliced Julia's heart. "Not all fathers." She felt tears fill her eyes and angrily blinked them back. She did not want her friend's pity.

Patience reached across and touched her arm. "Well, we all love you. And your mother does. It is as clear as the nose on your face."

"You and your platitudes, Pet. Ugh. Now I'm using that name."

"I don't mind. And your mother does love you."

"She may love me, but she certainly doesn't approve of me."

Patience's eyes softened. "She worries about you, Julia, and tries to protect you. Sometimes, perhaps, she tries a little too hard, but she means well, I know."

"More platitudes."

"Come now, Julia. You must admit you don't make it easy for her." Her friend's eyes twinkled. "In fact it seems to be a matter of pride to you, how skilled you are in vexing her."

"That bad, ey?"

"Oh come. You cannot pretend my words surprise or offend you."

Julia exhaled loudly. "It sounds, well, worse coming from you, Miss Perfect. Now there's a pet name for you. Perfect Patience."

Her fair cheeks dimpling, Miss Allen playfully pushed her arm. "Goose."

Lady Amelia stepped into the drawing room, and Julia stiffened as she always did in her presence lately, as though expecting a blow. Her mother had never struck her, so Julia supposed she anticipated verbal blows: criticisms or calls to tedious duty. Which would it be this time?

Then she noticed her mother was tying a hooded cape beneath her chin.

"I'm going out," she announced.

Both girls looked toward the rain-streaked windows. Outside, lightning flashed.

"In this?" Julia asked.

Her mother nodded. "I have a meeting with the Overseers of the Poor."

"Can you not reschedule?"

"Our new churchwarden is very earnest," she replied. "He says the poor go on in any weather and so shall we."

Julia laughed before she realized her mother had not meant it as a joke. She was relieved she wasn't expected to attend as well.

Patience nodded with solemn admiration. "Your work is very important. Take care not to catch chill."

"Thank you, Patience."

Julia knew she ought to say something kind as well, but the words stuck in her throat.

Lady Amelia flicked a glance at her, a glance that took in the knotted heap on her lap, before her mouth tightened and she turned from the room.

When she had gone, Julia stared out the window until the black carriage lumbered past. Then she tossed aside her embroidery and rose.

"Come, Patience. I cannot sit still another minute. Let's have an adventure."

Patience rose less eagerly, eyes wary. "What sort of adventure—on a day like this?"

"Precisely." With the lightning flashing and the thunder rumbling, Julia thought it the perfect sort of day to tiptoe up into the dry, dusty attic and search for secrets . . . or to frighten her oh-so-timid friend.

Patience followed her up the stairs with little enthusiasm. "Is there nothing else you'd like to do? Perhaps a game of draughts or cards. Or we might look at the new edition of the *Ladies' Monthly Museum*."

Julia continued up the stairs without comment.

Patience tried another course, "You know, we really ought to continue with our needlework. I don't mean to chide, but you promised your mamma you would finally finish your sampler."

"I think I shall go mad if I have to spend another second on such a tedious pastime."

"But—"

Julia hurried to reassure Patience. "I shall pick up my needle again soon, I promise. But first, just a *little* adventure. Please?"

Patience sighed and acquiesced.

Julia's candle lamp illuminated the way up the narrow attic stairs. At the top, she was surprised to find the storeroom door ajar. She turned toward Patience, warning finger on her lips.

Patience's eyes widened.

"Don't worry," Julia whispered. "It is probably just old Lord Buckleigh's ghost."

Her friend's lips parted. She gripped the stair rail and stayed where she was.

"Don't be silly, Pet. I am only teasing."

For all her bravado, Julia did wonder at the door being open. She was certain she had latched it the last time she'd been up there, but who else would come up to the attic? Was that person in there even now?

Julia grasped Patience's cold hand and pulled her along as she slowly edged open the door with a belligerent *creeaak*.

No answering flutter of bat wings, patter of earthly footsteps, or ghostly howl. Julia lifted her candle lamp higher and peered through the murky dimness to study the shapes and positions of the various furnishings—all apparently in their familiar places. Then why did her heart beat hard against her ribs?

In the light of her candle, dust motes hung heavy in the air, as though recently disturbed. She lowered her lamp and looked for footprints in the dust, or some other telltale sign someone had recently trespassed. She saw no definable footprints, but a swath on the floorboards shone dingy brown, compared to the less-trod, dustier areas of floor—a swath that seemed to lead toward the attic's back corner.

Julia peered toward the forbidden trunk there. She narrowed her eyes to better focus. Was it only her imagination, or did it look different somehow? Tentatively, she tiptoed around the first trunk toward it, ducking where the roof pitched lower.

"Julia . . ." Patience hissed disapproval.

But Julia kept walking. She swung her lamp from side to side and studied the floor. The dust had definitely been disturbed. Had her mother recently visited the private trunk? If not, who?

"Someone has been here," Julia breathed, half to Patience and half to herself. Mostly to justify what she was about to do.

Ignoring the dust, she knelt before the trunk.

"Julia, don't!" Patience hissed again.

"Come here and hold the light."

"I won't be a party to this."

"Your objection is duly noted, and you are absolved of any responsibility. Just hold the light."

Patience heaved a long-suffering sigh and tiptoed to her side. Hovering over Julia, she held the proffered lamp high.

Julia jested, "Do you suppose someone has hidden a body up here?"

"Julia!"

"Only teasing." She'd said it as much to vex her friend as to relieve her own nerves.

Julia laid her hands on the lid, held her breath, and lifted. It didn't budge. She saw no obvious lock, so she felt around for a latch. She noticed the raised filigree on the lower portion of the trunk. Ornamentation . . . or a handle? She reached lower, feeling her way around the filigree detail, and felt a slight groove beneath.

Gingerly, tentatively, she slid her fingers into the groove and pulled. It gave. She scooted back on her knees and pulled farther. *How delicious!*

"It's a hidden drawer," she said aloud for her friend's benefit.

Julia was fairly certain it had not been ajar before. Who had left it so? "Hold the light closer," she whispered.

Patience averted her face. "I am not supposed to look at anything in that trunk, and neither are you."

"It's not exactly *in* the trunk, is it? Just this lower drawer here. Not even locked."

Patience sighed and held the lamp closer.

Had something valuable lain there for years—decades? Or had her mother only recently hidden something within?

Reaching in, Julia's fingers felt fabric. Smooth and cool, like satin or silk. She lifted a small garment and held it toward the light. A tiny dress.

"A christening gown?" Patience asked over her shoulder.

"Perhaps," Julia murmured. "Though it is quite plain."

Was it mine? Julia wondered. Her heart fluttered. Did her mother hold sentimental affection for her after all, well hidden though it might be? She looked inside the neckline, but there was no embroidery to identify either the child or seamstress.

Julia set the gown on her knee and reached into the drawer once more. She felt nothing but rough wood. Wait . . . Something so flat she almost missed it. Julia peeled it up with her fingernail, pinched the folded paper between her fingers, and pulled it forth. Her heart rate accelerated.

A letter.

In the distance a door slammed, and Julia jumped.

Patience hissed a warning, "Julia . . ."

Julia shoved the drawer closed, slipped the letter down her own bodice, and crammed the gown into her friend's apron pocket.

She rose on shaky legs and quickly followed Patience to the attic door. They paused, listening. Had they heard footsteps? Was someone coming up?

Silence.

The two girls tiptoed onto the landing and Julia quietly closed the door behind them. Still no sound from below. She had probably only imagined the footsteps.

Julia squared her shoulders and took a deep breath, forcing her face into unconcerned lines. She walked casually down the stairs, Patience following nervously behind.

At the bottom of the stairs, Julia looked one way down the passage, toward the old schoolroom. Empty. Then she looked the other way, toward the servants' bedchambers.

Her stomach dropped.

There stood her mother's lady's maid. Doyle stared at Julia, her hard eyes studying Julia's face, then flicking to her empty hands.

Doyle nodded toward the attic stairs and said gravely, "Did ya find what you were looking for?"

Julia lifted her chin. "I don't know what you mean."

Again the maid scrutinized her face and her person. Did she notice the bulge in her bodice, or the lump in her friend's pocket? A knowing smirk twisted the woman's mouth.

Julia went on the offensive. "What are you doing up here this time of day?"

Doyle retorted, "I might ask the same of you, miss."

The vile woman did not even have the grace to appear sheepish.

"Let's go, Patience." Julia turned away dismissively.

Patience jogged anxiously beside her. "Do you think she knows we looked in that trunk?"

Julia made no answer, her mind reviewing the scene and the woman's odd expression. It was almost as if she did know. . . . Had she been the one to leave the drawer ajar? But why on earth would she?

They hurried to Julia's room and shut the door firmly behind them. Patience removed the wadded gown from her pocket and laid it on Julia's bed, smoothing it flat.

Outside, the storm had passed. Warm daylight filtered through the windows, illuminating the dress better than the candle had.

"It is a sweet little gown," Patience said, though Julia did not miss the question in her voice or the small line between her brows. "But I don't think it can be a christening gown. It isn't very . . ." Patience sought the right word and settled on "ornate."

"The material is rather cheap and coarse," Julia said with none of her friend's reserve. She fingered the border of rudimentary green X's embroidered at the neckline. "Looks like something I would do."

Patience chuckled but did not deny it. "Perhaps a gift from a poor relation . . . ?"

Forgetting the gown, Julia extracted the letter from her bodice. Patience's eyes widened, as did her mouth. "Julia!"

Clearly her friend had not noticed her slip it down her neckline.

The ink was somewhat faded. Julia squinted at the two small words printed on the front—*my . . . grace?*

Not *your grace*, as to a duke or duchess, but *my grace?* She stepped nearer the table, where she'd set the lamp, and bent her neck to look closer.

"The gown was one thing, but I'm not going to stay if you're going to read that letter," Patience insisted. "That is private. How would you like it if your mother read your post or journal?"

"She probably does." Julia's eyes remained riveted to the paper. "It may not be a letter at all. There is no direction or postal marking. . . ."

"Well, I shall leave you to your own conscience, Julia. Thank you for an . . . odd . . . afternoon."

Though the rain had stopped, the walk to Medlands would still be damp. Julia offered to call for the coach, but Patience declined, clearly anxious to leave and not be privy to the letter or whatever it was.

Julia walked Patience downstairs to the door, and asked the hallboy to escort Miss Allen home safely. Bidding her pensive friend farewell, Julia hurried back to her room and shut the door.

She brought the candle lamp to her side table and sat on the edge of the bed. She wasn't sure what she was expecting, beyond the thrill of uncovering a secret. An adventure.

Heart thumping, Julia unfolded the yellowed page and read.

Dear Grace Amelia,

How beautiful you are, my precious daughter. How perfect. I lie here and wish I could stay and watch you grow up, but I sense the heavenly Father calling me to himself even now. This world is fading

until all I can truly focus on is your face. Even your papa is beginning
to blur. He will fare well without me, I know. It is only you I think of.
Worry about. Pray for. Who will take care of you while your papa
is gone from home? Who dare I ask—trust—to care for my most
precious possession?

The letter ended abruptly, with no closing or signature. As if the
writer had been called from the world whilst writing.

Julia's brow puckered in confusion. Dormant suspicions whispered
in her brain, but she did not heed them. The only Amelia she knew was
her mother. Neither she nor Lady Amelia had ever been given second
names, as far as Julia knew. Had her mother ceased going by Grace
for some reason? But no. Lady Amelia's mother, Lady Buckleigh, had
lived past Amelia's coming-out days.

If not Lady Amelia, then who was Grace Amelia, and why did her
mother possess her letter? And why was it hidden in that secret drawer?
Julia was no judge, but this did not seem a recent letter, but it was not
ancient either.

Questions paraded through her mind. She told herself to wait, to
think through all the possibilities before rushing off to confront her
mother—not to mention the likely consequences of acknowledging
she'd entered the attic's forbidden territory.

Even so, she found her feet striding down the corridor and into
her mother's bedchamber, only to remember that she had gone out.

This is better, Julia told herself. It would give her time to compose
her thoughts, to decide how best to wrest the truth from her mother.

⁙

Alec and Desmond met at the old academy in the High Street as
planned. Taking the yet untried key from his pocket, Alec offered it
to Desmond. "Want to do the honors?"

Desmond waved the offer away, gesturing for Alec to unlock the
door. The lock was stiff from disuse but with a bit of rattling finally
gave. Alec opened the door and the two men walked inside. Dusty

damp air met Alec's nose. The floorboards squeaked, and something skittered away in the darkness. Mice, he guessed.

Extracting a matchstick from his pocket, Desmond stepped back out to the street, lifted the globe off a streetlamp to ignite the tinder, and carried it inside. He moved around the room, lighting several candle sconces on the walls. "You'll have to get more tapers. I'll check the storeroom. There might be some old ones still there."

The sconces gave off ample light for Alec to get a better look at the place. Much was as he'd surmised—the long room with wooden plank floor, barrels, crates, chairs in various states of repair around its perimeter, and a large dusty mirror covering one wall.

Alec glanced at the former dancing master. "So this is where you taught."

Desmond looked around the candlelit room, his eyes glittering with a hundred memories.

"Yes," he said quietly. "But that was a long time ago."

"Were you any good?" Alec asked, hoping his teasing tone was evident.

Desmond smirked. "I like to think so."

"Do you ever miss it?"

The man considered, then shook his head. "No. Too many bad memories welded with the good. There's no separating them." Desmond gestured with his hand. "Well, take a good look. Make sure you know what you're in for."

Alec slowly walked around the room, surveying its condition. The wooden floor was dirty and in need of refinishing yet would be good enough after a thorough cleaning. The roof leaked over the front bow window—a dark stain trickled down the adjacent wall, marring the yellow wall coverings. But he saw no other water damage, so hopefully the roof was otherwise sound.

Desmond lit a candle lamp and led the way into the back room. The small chamber enclosed the steep narrow staircase to rooms above. It also held a small desk with slots for receipts and ledgers, and floor-to-ceiling shelves, empty except for a half-empty box of tapers, a few pairs of shoes, and scatterings of mouse droppings.

Desmond gestured up the stairs. "There is a small apartment up there, but I am afraid it has become a refuge for cast-off furnishings and other things over the years. If you want to use those rooms as well, we could see about moving everything out. . . ."

Alec shook his head. It was premature to think about moving in. He had to see if he could make a go of the business before he even considered leaving his uncle's home. "I'm only interested in the academy for now."

Desmond nodded, his attention snagged by a pair of high-heeled dancing shoes on the shelf. "I can't believe these are still here." He picked one up, inspecting the stiff, dried leather.

"Yours?"

"No. The man who owned the place before me. I never favored tall heels, but he was quite short and always wore them when teaching."

Curiosity piqued, Alec said, "I followed my father and grandfather into the profession. May I ask how a blacksmith's son came into it?"

A ghost of a smile touched Desmond's mouth. "How much time do you have?"

"All night, if you need."

"Very well." He set the shoe down and led the way back into the main room. "I began helping my father in the forge when I was no more than five or six. You'd think it would be dangerous for a wee bairn, but one burn teaches little hands quickly. I liked being with my father. And I wanted nothing more than to be a smith like him one day.

"But when I was ten or so, my parents began allowing me to walk alone into the village now and again to buy a sweet or seek out mates for a game of cricket. One day, I heard music coming from somewhere in the High Street. I followed the sound and ended up here, at that window." He pointed to the leaky bow window. "Curious, I looked in and watched the old dancing master. He was rail-thin but quite elegant in his natty tailcoat and shiny dancing shoes. And the music he drew from his fiddle . . . Some tunes stately and beautiful, others so lively I could not help tapping my toes right there on the walkway.

"I found myself coming here as often as I could to watch him play or teach." Desmond glanced toward the corner, to where a coat tree stood. Beside it leaned a walking stick. He strode over and picked it up as he continued, "I can still see him standing here, tapping out the counts and sternly admonishing some hapless merchant's daughter or clergyman's son. But when his pupils had mastered the steps, he would lay aside the stick and play while they danced. That's what I liked best.

"One day, the old dandy startled me by opening the door and asking me if I liked what I saw. I mumbled that I did and he invited me in. He handed me a broom and asked if I was interested in earning a bit of money. So I began to help him, sweeping up, polishing that old mirror, running over to the inn for his dinner. My mother was happy with the extra money—though, looking back, I can see that my father was wary.

"I still worked with him at the forge in the mornings but began spending more and more of my afternoons and evenings here. I soon found myself trying to mimic the steps, though my partner was only a broom." He chuckled. "At all events, the old man took an interest in me. He was a bachelor—never married, no children. I think he was looking ahead to the end of his life and realizing he had no one to leave the place to. So he took me on as an apprentice of sorts, though, generously, he required no apprentice fee or formal arrangement. I think he knew my father would not have agreed, having always planned for me to work with him in the forge. I was sorry to hurt my father's feelings, but Mr. Sharp opened a new world to me. He lent me books and taught me how to read music and play the violin, along with fencing and dancing.

"I met people I never would have otherwise—gentlemen, lovely accomplished girls, and fine ladies. The forge could not compete. Eventually my father took on an apprentice, freeing me to spend more time in the academy.

"When I was eighteen, Mr. Sharp fell ill. I took over his classes until he recovered. After that, he sent me to London to learn the latest dances and acquire taste and refinement. When I returned, he began sending me out to teach his private lessons, because he no longer wanted to bother with the travel. I enjoyed getting a glimpse into the homes of the gentry, and eventually even the great Buckleigh Manor. . . ."

Desmond's gaze became wistful, and his words trailed away.

Then he inhaled and began again. "My father's apprentice finished his seven-year term and then worked for my father at full wages for a few years. Unfortunately he chose to leave Beaworthy for a more lucrative position in Plymouth. But by then, Mr. Sharp had died and had left his academy to me."

Desmond slowly shook his head. "He had no family of his own, so he made me family—treated me like his own son. How sorry I was to squander all the man's grand dreams for me a few years later, when I had to abandon the academy he had worked so hard to establish. . . ." Again his words trailed away.

With an air of solemn ceremony, Desmond leaned the walking stick back into the corner and returned to the present, looking around the room once more. "I'm afraid it's in worse repair than I guessed it would be."

"Uninhabited places tend to deteriorate," Alec observed. "It needs a few repairs and a thorough cleaning, but I expected that."

"Do you still want to try and make a go of it? You're perfectly free to change your mind."

"I don't want to change my mind."

Alec held out his hand, and John Desmond shook it.

Mr. Turner will attend at any house from 6 o'clock in the evening, on grown Gentlemen and Ladies, and assures the utmost Secrecy shall be kept till they are capable of exhibiting in high taste.

—*Boston Gazette & Country Journal,* 1774

Chapter 17

The next morning, Julia rose even before the housemaid entered and hurriedly readied for the day, choosing a simple day dress with the fewest fastenings, and pinning up her hair herself.

She was oddly nervous, but why should she be? The infant gown was probably her own, or perhaps even her mother's. And as Patience had guessed, likely a gift from some poor relation or favored tenant farmer. And the letter? Who knew. But it was unlikely to affect her, beyond the scolding she was certain to receive for unearthing it in the first place.

Julia let herself into her mother's dressing room, hoping to catch her before she went down for breakfast.

Her mother looked up from her dressing table mirror as Doyle finished pinning her hair. Julia held both items behind her back, hoping to appear at ease, though doubting she managed the feat.

Doyle slanted her a look, sweeping from her face to her hidden hands, speculation glinting in her dark eyes. She returned to her task. "How's that, my lady?"

"Lovely. As always. Thank you, Doyle." Her mother rose and turned to the door.

"Mamma, may I have a word before we go down?"

Her mother hesitated, whether more taken aback by the request or by the sweet tone in which it was delivered, Julia was not certain.

Doyle paused as well, her gaze again locking on Julia's.

Julia asked politely, "Doyle, would you give us a moment?"

Doyle glanced at her mistress, perhaps hoping for a rebuttal, but Lady Amelia dismissed her. "Thank you, Doyle. That will be all."

When the lady's maid had left, Julia held forth the infant gown like a white flag and asked quietly, "Whose gown is this?"

Her mother stared, her startled gaze flicking from the gown to Julia's expectant face. "Where did you find that?"

"In the attic."

"In the trunk I asked you not to open?"

"No. In the hidden drawer at the bottom."

"A hidden drawer? How did you—?"

"It was ajar," Julia interrupted. "You must have failed to close it properly when you were last up there."

Her mother shook her head. "I have not ventured up those stairs in years."

If she had not opened the drawer, then who had? Doyle? But her thoughts quickly returned to the more pressing question.

"Was it my gown?"

Her mother took the gown in her hands, and ran her fingertips over the green embroidery. "I . . . believe so." She hesitated. "But I have not looked at your baby clothes in years. Most we gave to the poor after you'd outgrown them."

So much for sentimental affection, Julia thought.

Julia moved on to the letter. She unfolded it and extended it toward her mother. "I found this letter in the drawer as well. Addressed to someone named Grace Amelia."

Her mother laid the gown aside and accepted the letter. Did her fingers tremble?

Julia waited while she read it, then asked, "Who is Grace? And why do you have her letter in your trunk?"

She expected her mother to become livid and rail, *"Sneaking around and reading other people's post, Julia? How could you?"* Yet her mother said none of those things. Her face grew not livid red but pale.

She rose and stepped to the window. Concocting a believable reply? "That trunk is not mine. It belongs to someone else."

Julia had not expected that. "Who?"

"No one you know. It was left with me for safekeeping—years ago—and never reclaimed."

"I don't understand. Who wrote that letter? And why do you have her things?"

The door opened, and Doyle entered without knocking, her inquisitive gaze darting from one woman to the other before lighting on the small gown.

With effort she returned her gaze to her mistress. "Forgive me, my lady," she began, "but Hutchings asked me to let you know the rector has arrived. He has put him in the library as you requested."

"Oh yes. I quite forgot." Her mother sighed and turned to Julia. "I am sorry, Julia. The rector is already here or I would postpone. I will keep our meeting as brief as may be, and then we shall talk. All right?"

Julia had little choice. Of course her mother would choose to speak to the rector, to anyone, over her. Julia swept from the room and flew down the stairs, nearly colliding with the stern butler as she rounded the rail. Forgoing bonnet and gloves, she hurried from the manor toward her place of refuge.

As she hastened across the lawn, Julia's mind felt troubled, and her spirit restless. She knew her mother was hiding something. Was she keeping it from her because she thought her an untrustworthy child, too immature to handle the truth? It reminded Julia of the other ways her mother treated her like a child. Dictating whom she could spend time with, and what pastimes were and were not acceptable. She was nineteen—not a little girl any longer.

Julia strode through the rose garden to the door in the churchyard wall. Pushing through it, she walked around the old church toward its entrance. She was about to go inside and up into the tower when she noticed a man standing several yards off, head bowed, hat in hand. He was standing, she realized, before the family plot—the graves of Buckleighs and her father.

Quietly, she walked over to him. She did not recognize the man, she did not think. He was perhaps forty or a bit older. Tall and athletic-looking, with a tan complexion and dark hair a bit long not to be held back in a queue. His clothes placed him neither as a well-dressed gentleman nor a laborer or farmer.

Her foot scuffed a pebble across the path, and he glanced up. He looked at her with an odd expression on his handsome face as she approached.

"Hello," she said.

"Hello," he replied, and then turned back to the graves.

He said nothing further, so neither did she. She stood a yard or so away from him, facing the plot as he did. She tried to figure out which grave he was there to visit. He stood nearest to the grave of Graham Buckleigh, she thought. Though the graves of her grandfather and aunt were nearby as well.

Julia was not enamored with silence. Quietly, she asked, "Did you know them?"

For a moment, he said nothing. She felt his gaze flash to her profile, and then he said in a low, melodic voice, "I was acquainted with them, aye. But long ago, when we were young."

"Then you have the advantage, sir. For I never knew them."

He nodded toward a headstone. "You remind me of her."

She followed his gaze. "Lady Anne? She was my aunt. My mother's sister."

He nodded without surprise. He apparently already knew or guessed who she was.

Glancing at the name engraved on her aunt's headstone, she said unnecessarily, "She married a Tremelling. I never met him either."

"Yes, I heard she married and had a child," he said. "Lady Amelia as well."

He glanced at her again, and she noticed how dark his eyes were. Like Liberty's.

She said, "My aunt died in childbirth, her child with her."

"I am sorry."

She shrugged. "Such things are unfortunately common."

"Yes." A moment of silence passed, and then he gestured toward the largest of the stately graves. "And Arthur Midwinter?"

She nodded. "My father."

"Him I never met. But I am sorry for your loss. Is your mother bearing up well?"

"Yes, thank you."

"Is she in good health?"

Julia glanced at him in surprise. Felt a flicker of suspicion at the personal question. "She enjoys excellent health. Why do you ask, Mr. . . . ?"

The man drew himself up. "Forgive me. I will not trespass any longer."

The man bowed, replaced his hat, and turned away. She watched him walk from the churchyard, something about his graceful gait reminding her of Alec Valcourt.

The rector's pony cart passed by, and Julia noticed the stranger pull his hat down low and look to the ground. But then Julia forgot about the man, determined as she was to continue her conversation with her mother.

When Julia returned to the house, Lady Amelia was waiting for her.

"Come up to my dressing room," she said flatly. "We can talk there."

Julia followed her up the stairs and down the corridor. Once inside the feminine chamber, her mother surprised her by locking the door. She indicated that Julia should sit in the armchair while she sat on the dressing table stool.

Julia clasped her damp hands together and waited, unaccountably nervous. Again whispers of foreboding spoke in a strange tongue in her mind, but she did not comprehend them. Her limbs felt jumpy in eagerness and . . . fear. Was her mother about to reveal a juicy scandal or chilling family secret? She had not locked the door merely to tell her there was nothing to tell.

Her mother appeared nervous as well. She rose and began to pace back and forth across the small room.

Julia longed to fill the tense silence. The conversation in the churchyard still fresh in her mind, she asked, "Your sister died in childbirth—is that right?"

Her mother's face flickered in surprise at the question, but she did not hesitate to answer. "Shortly afterward, yes."

Julia considered this, and asked, "Then, did your sister write that letter?"

Her mother looked at her, eyes watchful. "Yes."

"And the child died as well?"

Her mother again paced across the small chamber like a bird in a cage.

She picked up a letter—*the* letter, Julia realized—and shook her head.

"But . . ." Julia sputtered, "I grew up believing Lady Anne's child had died along with her."

"That is what we allowed you to believe, though we never actually said so—"

The words reminded Julia of how the Valcourts had allowed them to believe their father had died, though they'd never come out and said the words.

But if the child did not die, where was she? Julia's pulse rate quickened. *Could it be?*

"Am I . . ." Julia's words trailed away as her courage fled. Should she—could she—ask the audacious question? There was probably a simple explanation. No doubt her mother would shake her head and accuse her of having a childish imagination or of reading too many novels.

But she had to know.

Julia swallowed, pointed to the letter, and forced out, "Was I . . . Grace Amelia?"

She steeled herself for her mother's cutting rebuttal, her shocked offense, or hurt feelings over such a wild accusation.

Her mother said nothing, merely stared down at the letter.

Julia clenched her hands into damp fists. Was her mother counting to ten for patience? Hatching some story?

Julia repeated more stridently, "Was I?"

Unable to meet her gaze, Lady Amelia whispered, "Yes."

Julia's heart thudded. Her chest tightened until she could hardly draw breath. Her mind whirled back over the years and dipped into possibilities, scenarios, and fearful conclusions. Did this not explain her mother's disapproval, and her father's cold indifference?

Incredulous, Julia said, "Lady Anne is my mother."

"*I* am your mother," Lady Amelia insisted, eyes flashing. "You share my blood. My name. I raised you as my own. You are my family."

Julia glared at her. "But you did not give me birth?"

She squeezed her eyes shut. Exhaled wearily. "No."

Julia blinked, attempting to reorder her world, a part of her wanting to know every last detail, another part of her wishing she had never asked.

Lady Anne—not her aunt, buried in the churchyard, but the woman who'd given her birth. Lady Amelia—not her mother but her aunt.

"Why have you never told me?" Julia asked between clenched teeth.

Lady Amelia seemed to shrink into herself for a moment, a cocoon bereft of its moth. But then she took a deep, shaky breath and resumed her usual ramrod-straight posture.

"I have wanted to tell you for a long time. Have nearly done so on several occasions. Perhaps you recall your thirteenth birthday . . . ?"

Julia thought back. That was the year she'd been given her locket, as well as the only present she'd ever received from her father. Mr. Midwinter had been called away to Torrington that day but left behind the strange little gift in his absence.

Her mother had made a bigger fuss than usual over the occasion, she remembered, something about Julia nearing womanhood. There had been a special birthday supper for just the two of them, and Julia's favorite lemon-iced cake, but she had immediately noticed a glaring absence of wrapped parcels.

Probably recognizing her disappointed look, her mother had pressed her hand and said, "I have two things to give you, but . . . later, in my room. All right?"

Ah! Julia had thought. Perhaps she would receive that new French gown she wanted.

After dinner, they'd gone up to her mother's bedchamber, Julia eagerly but her mother oddly nervous. There were two gifts on her side table. Something wrapped in plain brown paper, and a small white box with a gauzy blue bow. Too small for a gown, Julia noted with irritation. Pearls, perhaps?

But when she'd opened the white box, all she saw inside was a plain gold locket, its scratched, dull finish telling her it was not even new.

Her mother began, "It was Lady Anne's . . ."

Doyle had come in and busied herself in the dressing room. Her mother seemed disconcerted to see her, though her lady's maid had always come and gone as she pleased.

Ignoring her, Julia tore open the brown paper and found the unusual brass mermaid on a chain. Then Julia had gone and spoiled their pleasant evening. She didn't remember her exact words but had blurted something peevish about receiving only her aunt's old locket and some cheap brass toy when she'd longed for a French gown or pearls.

Julia had lifted the small brass mermaid hanging from a slender metal tube attached to a chain too short to be a necklace. Frowning, she'd said, "I'm not even sure what this is. . . ."

Lady Amelia opened her mouth, then closed it again, her expression conflicted.

Doyle had come forward, glanced at her mistress, and then told Julia, "Why, it's a gift from your father," she said evenly. "Is that not so, my lady?"

Surprise flashed through Julia. "From Father?"

She looked at her mother for confirmation. "Is it really, Mamma?"

Her mother hesitated. "Well . . . um, yes, he wanted you to have it."

"Why in the world would he give me *this*?" Julia had scoffed, even as she was inwardly touched.

Clearly vexed, her mother extended her hand. "Well, you needn't keep it if you don't like."

"No." Julia held it to her heart. "I want to keep it."

And she had.

Now Julia felt a twinge of regret over her behavior but blinked it away. She had been thirteen after all.

She inhaled and said, "I remember. That was the year I received my locket and the mermaid from Father."

Lady Amelia blinked, then murmured, "Oh, um, well . . ."

A chill prickled over Julia, realization dawning. "Wait . . . I always thought it an odd gift, yet I was stupidly happy to have anything from him, so I never questioned. But Mr. Midwinter didn't buy it for me, did he."

Lady Amelia shook her head. "I meant to tell you then, when I gave it to you along with Anne's locket. But I didn't think you were ready. And from then on you have seemed so distant. So set against me. I could do nothing right in your eyes. So I avoided it, fearing if I told you it would ruin our already tenuous relationship."

"You thought *I* was distant? Set against *you*? You are the one who is cold and critical."

Her mother's eyes widened. "Is that how you see me?"

"Yes." She glimpsed the pain in Lady Amelia's eyes, but Julia did not waver. It was the truth of how she felt.

Julia winced and shook her head. "No wonder Mr. Midwinter never loved me. Deep down, I always knew he didn't."

"Oh, Julia. I am so sorry."

"And since he died, you seem to have taken over his role as distant, disapproving parent."

Lady Amelia sighed, looking away. "I don't mean to be disapproving, but I worry about you. So reckless. So much like . . ."

"Like who? My real mother?" Julia straightened her shoulders and demanded, "If Lady Anne lived long enough to write that letter, she didn't die in childbirth as I was led to believe. How did she die?"

Lady Amelia twisted her hands. "I don't know all the details. Anne was living in Plymouth at the time."

"Plymouth?"

She nodded. "Her husband was a naval officer and was based there."

"You say her husband. Do you mean, my father?"

Lady Amelia went on as though she had not heard the question. "I gather she contracted a fever during or after the birth. Such things are quite common, I'm afraid. Lieutenant Tremelling told me she held on for a week or so, but there was little the apothecary could do for her, and he hadn't thought, or perhaps could not afford, to call in a physician."

Lady Anne not being able to afford something? That didn't make sense.

"Why did you not help her?"

"I did not know of it. She and I had not been in contact for several months."

Julia frowned. "But she's buried here, in the Buckleigh churchyard."

"It was one of her last requests. And her husband and I honored it."

How strange to imagine the lovely Lady Anne of the gilt-framed portrait living in relative poverty in some small lodging house in Plymouth—dying there as well.

"A month or so after Anne's funeral, Lieutenant Tremelling brought you to me," Lady Amelia said. "His ship was due to depart, and although there was enmity between us, he asked me to care for you."

"What a sacrifice that must have been for you." Julia could not keep the acidic tone at bay. "I am surprised you agreed to such an onerous task."

Her lips tightened. "You are wrong, Julia. The moment I saw you, I wanted to agree. Though I needed to discuss the matter with Mr. Midwinter, of course."

"How he must have railed against it." Julia swallowed the old feelings of rejection.

"No. He left the decision to me."

Julia squeezed her eyes shut. "I don't understand. If I was your sister's child, and you took me in after her death, why the need for secrecy? Why not raise me as your niece? Buckleigh Manor is not entailed. Would it not have come to me anyway, through Lady Anne, since you had no heir?"

"It wasn't about Buckleigh."

Julia scoffed. "It's always about Buckleigh!"

"Not this time." Lady Amelia pressed her lips together, as if considering how much to say. "My sister's reputation was not all it should have been. I thought it better, for your future, if you were thought to be my own child. It was not difficult to conceal the truth. A lady did not announce she was in a family way. Such things were not spoken of in polite company. Nor were adoptions spoken of openly. Even today, families almost always keep such things to themselves, unless there is some question of entailed properties or title, which in this case there was not. There was nothing illegal or unseemly in raising you as my own, Julia. I can think of at least one other family we both know who added to their number in similar discreet fashion."

Illogical embarrassment swept over Julia. "Does everyone else know? Am I the last to learn the truth?"

"No, my dear," Lady Amelia soothed. "Some people knew or guessed, I suppose, but they certainly would never have told you, the child. And in time the matter was largely forgotten. I confided in the former rector. He understood my desire to raise you as a Midwinter, and he's the one who recorded your birth and baptism in the parish register. He was nearly like a grandfather to me, God rest his soul."

Julia thought about the date on Lady Anne's headstone. "So I was actually born—what, about a month earlier than the birthday I've always celebrated?"

"Yes."

"And did my real father agree to give me up—or did you force him?"

Again, the accusatory tone cut like a whip.

Lady Amelia grimly shook her head, her face mottled pale and red. "How you speak to me. Do you despise me so much?"

Julia made no answer.

Her mother turned away. "He was . . ." she began, then paused. She seemed to think the better of whatever she had been about to say, which made Julia suspect she was lying.

"Lieutenant Tremelling was, of course, grieved indeed to part with you. I am sure he loved you a great deal. But he felt he was unable to care for you, being so often away at sea."

"Why have I never met him? Did you forbid him to visit me? Afraid your secret would get out?"

Again the woman hesitated. "I . . . did mention the risk were he to come here."

"He wouldn't have agreed to just give me away like that. Not forever. Not unless you bribed him or threatened him or something. Look me in the eye and tell me you did not coerce him."

Lady Amelia met her eyes briefly, before her troubled gaze skated away. "I did not threaten or force him. I give you my word."

"Your word? What is your word worth after all of this?" Julia slowly shook her head. "I cannot believe you kept all this from me."

Her mother said earnestly, "I only meant to protect you."

"Protect me from what?"

"From cruel gossip. From being robbed of your rightful future—a good name, an untarnished reputation, the most advantageous marriage . . ."

Julia tilted her head to one side, reading between the lines. "Is that what you meant about Lady Anne's reputation? I was born too soon, is that it?"

She pressed her lips together. "Yes. But your mother married long before you were born. You were legitimate—have no fear of that."

"Well, everything's perfect, then, isn't it," Julia scoffed. "Legally legitimate, but in reality, some sailor's by-blow."

Lady Amelia's neck reddened. "Don't use such ugly words."

"Why not? If it's the truth?"

"Truth is a strange thing, Julia. And not as simple as the self-righteous young like to believe."

That night, Julia tossed and turned for hours, scenes from her troubled childhood spinning through her mind. She again thought of the hurtful words she'd once heard her father—Mr. Midwinter—hurl at her mother. *"You had better tighten the reins on that wild child while you still can,"* he'd said. *"The apple doesn't fall far from the tree. . . ."*

A part of Julia had relished the apparent criticism of *saintly* Lady Amelia, even though the words cut her as well.

Now that piece of Julia's history rewrote itself in her mind. Not a reference to any mistake Lady Amelia had made. But a reference to Lady Anne—the "tree" Julia had fallen from.

Fallen. How appropriate.

Captain Cook . . . wishing to counteract disease on board his vessels, took particular care, in calm weather, to make his sailors and mariners dance the Hornpipe; a dance of a most exhilarating character.

—Carlo Blasis, 1830

Chapter 18

Alec began his work in the old academy by taking stock of the situation. He wrote lists of repairs to make, tasks to accomplish, supplies to purchase, and things to clear away, like several irreparably broken chairs and clutter left from its short-lived stints as bookshop and chandler's. As he moved about the room, the clatter of baking pans from the wall he shared with Mrs. Tickle's bakery and the faint aroma of cinnamon kept him company.

On Saturday, Alec spent the afternoon cleaning the back office, and then went home for dinner. During the meal, he shared his progress and plans with his family. Aurora listened with interest, but Uncle Ramsay grimaced and launched into a litany of cautions and concerns. His mother listened to her brother's warnings with a worried frown.

After dinner, Alec returned to the academy to tackle the main room. He stood there surveying the space and trying to decide where to begin when someone knocked. Alec started, then turned and opened the door to Mr. Lug, who lit the streetlamps of which Beaworthy residents were so proud. The man said he'd stopped by because he was surprised to see light in the window of the long-deserted shop. Alec assured him all was well—he was letting the place from the Desmonds—but did not explain to what purpose. He was relieved when the old man did not press him.

Alec went back to work, carrying a few broken chairs up the office stairs to join the other castoffs stored there. When he returned to the main room, he saw a shadowy head above the still-papered lower windows, backlit by the streetlamp. Unsettled by the sight, he looked closer, and recognized the tall man's face with relief. Smiling to himself, Alec crossed to the door and opened it.

There stood John Desmond framed in lamplight, armed with a broom and a sword. He lifted both. "Thought you might need a hand, friend."

Alec eyed the sword with amusement. "Try sweeping with that and you might lose a hand."

Alec noticed the man had again waited until after dark to venture into the village. He clearly still wished to avoid trumpeting his presence.

Desmond stepped inside. "Which shall we take up first?"

Alec grinned. "Which do you think?"

With an answering smile, Desmond leaned the broom against the wall, and Alec retrieved his own sword from the back room.

The clash of steel striking steel was jarring after the quiet solitary hours working alone. Swords raised, the two men began fencing, advancing and retreating across the long room in a slow, methodical *chassé*. Gradually both the pace and display of skill increased. Desmond advanced, driving him backward, closer to the wall with every lunge.

Alec retreated, struggling to parry. Desmond's blade suddenly flashed, and he barely dodged in time. Thunder and turf, the man was fast. Thank heaven they were using practice tips. Once Desmond had improved his physical condition, Alec doubted he would be able to keep up with him for long. He would enjoy the advantage while he could.

Finally, Alec's practice tip hit its mark, and Desmond touched his chest in acknowledgement.

"Touché," he panted, wiping a hand across his brow. "That's two for two, lad. I'll best you next time."

Alec didn't doubt it.

After they caught their breaths, they set aside their swords in favor of less manly—and less taxing—brooms. Together they swept the cobwebs from the ceilings and walls, and the dirt from the floors.

"Ever thought about reopening the place yourself?" Alec asked.

"No. Those days are over for me."

"Where did you go when you left? Did you teach somewhere else?"

Desmond shook his head. "I left that part of my life here in Beaworthy—buried with Graham Buckleigh. I threw in my lot with the crew of a merchantman and sailed the world. Tried to forget the past by filling my days with backbreaking labor, exotic ports, and the occasional sailor's hornpipe."

Alec smiled at that. "Is there where you learned to handle a sword?"

"Aye, though I learned a bit of fencing from Mr. Sharp when I was young."

"A man who can repair a blade as well as wield one. A rare combination."

Desmond nodded. "I've spent the last few years working with a sword cutler in Plymouth. That was where I was living when my mother wrote to tell me my father was ill."

"You had not been back before?"

He shrugged. "I slipped into the area to visit my parents when I had leave now and again over the years. But never long enough to make my presence known."

Alec paused in his work, leaning against his broom handle and studying the man. "They must have missed you."

Desmond paused as well, his mouth turned down in a sad smile. "Yes, and I missed them."

Alec took a breath and said tentatively, "Do you want to tell me about the duel? You told me you felt responsible, but something tells me there is more to the story."

Desmond looked down, then met his gaze. "I was wondering when you would ask. In fact, I am surprised you didn't ask before."

Alec waited. Not sure the man would confide in him. Not sure he wanted him to.

Desmond inhaled, then began. "Lady Amelia's brother, Graham, challenged me. I tried to talk him out of it, but he wouldn't listen. He came to kill me, and I suppose I should have let him. But in the end my will to live was too strong."

He paused to gather his thoughts, then continued, "His valet handed me a note during the May Day dance. It demanded I meet him in the upper room of the market hall. I went only to talk—not to accept his challenge. I went unarmed and took no second."

He grimaced. "But Graham came armed with a pair of dueling swords. He tossed me one and raised the other. I only meant to defend myself, to parry his attack. But he feinted at the last second, and . . ." Desmond shook his head, eyes distant and pained.

"I can still hear the sickening sound of punctured flesh. Like air and spoilt wine bursting from a ruptured wineskin. Still see the shock in his face when he realized . . ."

Desmond swallowed. "You can't imagine how many times I have rehearsed the scene in my mind, asking myself what I could have done differently. There must have been some way to change the outcome." He lowered his head. "But, God forgive me, I don't know what else I could have done."

"Did you leave directly afterward?" Alec asked, thinking of his own father.

Desmond replied, "Soon after. The constable began asking questions, which made my parents nervous. I had Graham's note and the valet's testimony, so he hesitated to charge me with murder outright. Still, duels are illegal. And even if juries are reluctant to convict gentlemen in such situations, I was not exactly a gentleman, was I? Graham was the earl's son. I could easily have been convicted and hanged. My parents begged me to leave before charges were pressed. They said it would break their hearts to see their only son imprisoned or hanged."

Desmond sighed heavily and picked a dust wad from his broom.

Alec asked, "Is that why you come here only at night? Are you afraid you might be arrested?"

Desmond shook his head. "No. My mother spoke to the constable before she wrote to me, to make certain there was no warrant out for my arrest. But that doesn't mean people here will welcome me back, or ever again take lessons from me."

Then he looked at Alec and braved a grin. "Now, don't feel sorry for me, Valcourt. I am happy to help my father. And I like working with my hands, though I admit the hilts and scabbards are more enjoyable than horseshoes."

"Perhaps you ought to advertise," Alec suggested. "I'm sure many gentlemen would like a fine sword—a dress sword, if nothing else."

"I don't know. I haven't advertised since my dancing master days. I doubt it would be wise to put my name in print again."

A thought came to Alec unbidden and unwanted—his uncle's assertion that Lady Amelia may have been with child before her marriage. He hesitated, then asked, "Why . . . did Graham challenge you in the first place?"

Desmond's mouth twisted. "Graham accused me of seducing his younger sister, Lady Anne."

Alec's mind whirled in a dizzying sense of having lived through this before. *Wait . . . Lady Anne?* Alec stared at the man, dumbfounded. Uncle Ramsay said nothing about Lady Anne.

Desmond glanced at Alec, then looked away. "He said I'd ruined his sister, and left her with child."

Alec's stomach soured. "Why did he blame you?" Once again, the image of Miss Underhill flashed in Alec's mind. He guessed why. "Simply because you were the dancing master?"

Desmond shook his head. "No," he said, expression bleak. "Because Lady Anne herself named me as the father."

Alec stared. "But I thought—"

A knock sounded on the door, startling Alec and Desmond both. Alec could see no faces appearing in the upper windows, but he glimpsed the top of a feather bobbing in the breeze.

"Hang on. I think it's my mother."

He opened the door an experimental crack. His heart lifted. Both his mother and sister stood there, pails and scrub brushes in hand.

Aurora said, "We thought you could use some help."

He gestured them inside, especially relieved to see his mother, who had been concerned about his plans, and her brother's reaction.

Now she looked with polite interest toward Desmond, while Desmond stood awkwardly awaiting introductions.

"Forgive me. Mother, Aurora, may I introduce my new friend, Mr. John Desmond. Desmond, my mother, Mrs. Joanna Valcourt. And my sister, Miss Aurora Valcourt."

He bowed. "Mrs. Valcourt. Miss Valcourt. A pleasure."

"Mr. Desmond, how nice of you to help Alec."

"No great act of charity, I'm afraid, ma'am," Desmond said humbly.

Alec explained, "Mr. Desmond owns this property."

"Ah. I see."

"And as I'm in great part to blame for its neglected condition," Desmond added, "it's the least I could do."

"Nonsense." Alec smiled at his mother and sister. "Mr. Desmond has only recently returned to Beaworthy after living in Plymouth and before that traveling the world. His father runs the forge outside of town. He has been ill, and Desmond has returned to help him."

"That is very good of you, Mr. Desmond," Aurora said, eyes warm with approval.

"Yes, you are a good son," their mother added.

"You are very kind to say so," Desmond said pleasantly. "But I cannot allow you to call me *good*, for I am not. Please, call me Desmond. Or John, if you prefer."

"And," Alec announced, "I have a great secret, but you both must promise never to tell anyone. . . ."

Desmond stiffened as though expecting a blow. Did he think Alec was about to share his confession?

"What is it?" Aurora grinned, reading Alec's teasing tone and anticipating a joke or happy surprise.

Alec clapped Desmond on the shoulder. "Desmond here is a former dancing master and has promised to teach us all the dances he learned in his travels."

Desmond's dark brows rose, and his mouth quirked in a lopsided grin. "Have I indeed?"

⁓

Julia and Patience spent the afternoon in Julia's bedchamber, sitting on the half tester bed, legs tucked beneath their skirts like the childhood playmates they once were. Instead of dolls between them, the latest fashion magazines lay in haphazard disarray across the white counterpane. Julia had confided to Patience all she had learned about her parentage, and now the magazines lay forgotten.

Julia ended with a plaintive, "I told you he didn't love me." She believed the words more than she ever had before, and saying them aloud caused her chest to ache. "He wasn't my father and was glad of it." She tossed the brass mermaid back into her drawer and shook her head, detesting the tears filling her eyes. "Why? Was it really only because I was his wife's niece and not his own flesh and blood? Am I so unlovable?"

"No, of course not." Patience squeezed her hand. "Your mother loves you, and she's known all along."

"Not my mother. My aunt." Julia shook her head, stunned all over again. "Had you any idea?"

"No. But I think it wonderful—Lady Amelia, raising her sister's child as her own. How generous. How kind."

Julia looked up from beneath her lashes. "Must you always be such an optimist?"

Patience shrugged. "Why not?"

"I wonder what James would think if he knew," Julia mused. "I suppose he would no longer be interested in me—my birth being 'too early' and all."

"It's possible." Patience tucked a stray wisp of white-blond hair behind her ear, then added thoughtfully, "James *is* the most fastidious of us all."

Julia flashed her a hurt look.

"Oh, don't take it to heart, Julia. You and James are friends, yes.

But you've never wanted to marry him. You've always said marrying James would simply be exchanging one cage for another: Buckleigh Manor for Medlands."

"Did I say that? How rude."

"I thought so," Patience agreed. "But honest too."

Julia thought. "You know—it is strange. James will have Medlands one day and I shall have Buckleigh Manor. Lady Amelia doesn't want me to leave here, so I am almost surprised she hasn't urged me to marry Walter instead."

Patience ducked her head shyly. "I have a theory about that."

"Oh?"

"Perhaps it's because she knows Walter is adopted. Not a natural son of our parents. Not that it has ever mattered to us, though it might to your mother."

"It should matter to her least of all, but— My goodness," Julia exclaimed. "Is he?"

"I should not have mentioned it. But considering all you've learned, I thought it might ease the sting a bit, to know you are not alone."

"Does Walter know?"

"Oh yes. He's always known. But it's not something we talk about. We're a family and we love each other and that's that."

Julia shook her head in wonder. Then she said, "You're right that I've never wanted to marry either of your brothers, because they are like brothers to me as well. But I admit James was my 'if all else fails' plan."

Patience elbowed her playfully. "Then marry for love and you shan't need any such desperate plan."

Julia sighed. "I don't know if I *can* love anyone but myself. And you, of course."

"Of course you can." Patience squeezed her hand once more. "Raise your eyes from yourself for a few days and you might surprise yourself."

Julia felt her mouth fall ajar. Meek Patience Allen had just chastised her. No doubt the chastisement was well deserved, but she was taken aback nonetheless.

"Patience Allen. I am surprised at you." She grinned to soften her words. "In fact, I am rather proud of you for standing up to me." Julia winked. "But I do hope you don't plan to make a habit of it."

⚬↶

Alec held his first unofficial lesson in the High Street academy. The day had turned grey and rainy, and Walter Allen had walked into town for their fencing bout instead of waiting to meet him in the Buckleigh churchyard as usual. The warmth radiating through his wall from Mrs. Tickle's ovens and the smell of baking bread were welcome on such a chilly day.

They fenced for a time, Alec demonstrating the flèche and balestra after reviewing the fundamentals. Walter was improving, but Alec admitted to himself that the man would likely never be a graceful competitor. Though dancing might help—both in fencing and in winning Miss Thorne's admiration. . . .

The door burst open behind them and both men started. The stout constable stood there, pistol drawn.

"Mr. Lamont," Walter said, lifting both hands until his sword nearly brushed the ceiling.

Alec asked, "Is there a problem?"

The constable looked from one to the other. "Heard swords. No one's supposed to be in here."

Alec said, "I should have thought to let you know—I've let the place from the Desmonds."

"For what purpose?"

"Fencing lessons, as you see. And . . . dancing, perhaps."

"Dancing? In Beaworthy?"

"My uncle assures me it is not against the law."

"Doesn't mean it won't get you into trouble." Lamont glared at him, then opened the door. "Watch yourself, Valcourt. For I'll be watching you."

When the door had closed behind him, Alec walked over and made sure it was secure, sighing in relief.

After they'd sheathed their swords, Alec said, "Speaking of dancing. How about a dance lesson to cap off our fencing?"

Walter's face wrinkled as though he'd smelled something foul. "And ruin a perfectly good day? I could understand following fencing with shooting or hunting. But not prancing about. No."

"You don't think dancing is manly—is that it?"

"That's right. Not the mincing, courtly steps you've taught us, at any rate."

"Perhaps I did not choose wisely in our previous lessons. Allow me to show you a real man's dance, danced by tough-as-iron seamen—men who sailed with Captain Cook around the world, suffering hardships and savages and storms."

Walter scowled. "Men like that don't dance."

"But they did. They do. Sailors invented a dance called the hornpipe for exercise aboard ship, since it requires only a small space and no partner. Captain Cook himself ordered his crew to dance the hornpipe to keep the men in good health."

Walter narrowed his eyes. "Is that a cock-and-bull story?"

"No. The dance steps come directly from sailor's tasks. . . ."

Alec demonstrated with his right hand to his forehead, then the left. "Looking out to sea."

Then he bent his knees and lifted one leg high in a side kick and then the other. "Lurching in foul weather . . ." He gestured with his arms. "Pulling in the ropes . . . And giving a tug to his breeches both fore and aft."

"That's a real dance?" Walter scoffed. "You're hoaxing me."

"Not at all." Alec began dancing the steps in half-time. "One-two-three hop, step-hop, step-hop . . ."

"There are some sixteen steps in all, and as many variations as there are men to dance them." Alec brought the dance up to tempo and asked, "Does this look like a minuet?"

Walter shook his head, eyes widening as Alec danced—legs flying, springing from one foot to the other, shoes rat-a-tat-tatting the floorboards in rhythmic percussion.

Walter watched Alec's whirling feet in amazement. "Hang me, that's fast."

Alec paused to catch his breath, wiping the sweat from his hairline with the heel of his hand. He grinned slowly at his friend. "Your turn."

But Walter was spared when the door burst open behind them.

There stood Mrs. Tickle, face flushed from her hot ovens, or was it . . . alarm?

"Goodness heavens!" the baker exclaimed. "Are you all right?" She looked around the room. "I thought the world was coming to an end, or an earthquake struck, like I read about near Inverness last year."

"No," Alec assured his neighbor. "We were only dancing. Sorry, Mrs. Tickle. Did we disturb you?"

"It isn't me I am thinking of, but I do worry for my jellies and cakes." She pressed an emphatic hand to her generous bosom. "Thank heavens the day's bread has already risen! Do be a lamb and promise not to, um, stomp about like that before seven in the morning?"

"Yes, of course. I promise."

"Well, good. That's all right, then. As long as the world hasn't ended . . . and my cakes don't fall."

After Walter took his leave, the day continued grey and drizzly. Even so, Alec found himself drawn out-of-doors, longing for fresh air after the hours spent in the still-stale academy. Longing to see Miss Midwinter again.

He walked out of the village and down the Buckleigh Road, hoping to catch a glimpse of her at her favorite place—the churchyard.

When he reached the Buckleigh church, he automatically looked up at the tower. He was both relieved and disappointed to see it vacant. He was about to turn back when he noticed a solitary figure with her back to him, standing before a cluster of headstones. The hooded cape disguised its wearer, but somehow, he knew it was her.

He slowly walked over, his feet quiet on the spongy turf until he kicked a stone and set it skittering over the path.

She glanced over at him, then quickly averted her face. But not before he saw the tears on her cheeks. His heart twisted at the sight.

"Mr. Valcourt," she acknowledged in a voice thick and tremulous.

He glanced at the grave. It was not fresh. In fact the lichen-cankered headstone appeared to have stood there for decades. He read the birth and death dates—the woman had died nearly twenty years ago.

Lady Anne Tremelling. The name struck Alec like a fist, and he recalled what Desmond had told him about the duel, and what he had *begun* to tell him about Lady Anne before they'd been interrupted. What about this grave had upset Julia Midwinter now? It seemed a strange coincidence that she should stand before this particular grave, so soon after Desmond's confession—if confession it had been.

Alec asked gently, "Are you all right?"

She didn't respond immediately. But then she began shaking her head, over and over again. "No," she whispered.

He looked again at the headstone. "Lady Anne was your mother's sister. Is that right?"

She opened her mouth, then closed it, apparently thinking the better of what she'd been about to say. Then she said, "Lady Amelia's sister, yes."

He nodded, musing aloud, "Your aunt, then."

Julia gave a bleak little laugh. "So I thought."

Confusion filled him.

She turned her head, glancing at him from beneath her hood. "Are you good at keeping secrets, Mr. Valcourt?"

He thought of Miss Underhill, his father, and now Desmond. "Very."

"Yes, I suppose you've proven that already."

She said nothing further for some time, and he began to think she would not confide in him after all. But then she looked about the churchyard as if to assure herself they were alone and began quietly, "Lady Anne was not my aunt. She was my mother—the woman who birthed me."

Alec stared, mind whirling. *Lady Anne. Desmond. Julia?* His uncle had it wrong, then, about the reason for Lady Amelia's rushed wedding. He hoped his expression showed none of the shock he felt, only interest and concern.

She flicked him another glance—to gauge his reaction? "She died shortly after I was born. I have only just found out." She gave a rueful laugh. "What an idiot I am. Can you believe I never knew? Never guessed?"

He blinked. Faltered. "I . . . believe such things are normally kept quiet. For the child's sake, and the family's."

Her gaze fixed on the headstone, Julia snorted quietly but said no more.

He swallowed and asked, "So . . . Lady Amelia and Mr. Midwinter decided to raise you as their own child?"

Another bleak sound, more scoff than laugh this time. "Lady Amelia, yes. But Mr. Midwinter barely tolerated me. At least now I understand why. Why he didn't . . ."

Her face contorted with anguish that tore at his heart, and he had to resist the urge to take her in his arms. She again averted her face, scrubbing at her eyes with the back of her hand.

He whispered, "She told you?"

Julia shook her head. "Only after I found a letter Lady Anne had written to me before she died."

Alec could not begin to imagine what that must have felt like.

"Don't," she said, eyeing him fiercely.

He stepped back. "Don't what?"

"Don't pity me, or judge me."

"Very well."

She looked down, kicking at a little clump of moss with her slipper. "I suppose you will look at me differently now."

"How so?"

"Now that you know I am not who you thought I was. Who I thought I was."

"Oh, are you not human after all?" he teased. "Are you actually a woodland sprite or a famed West Country piskie?"

"No."

He took a step nearer. "You are still Lady Amelia's pride and joy. Still headstrong, still a bruising rider and righter of wrongs, still the bravest and most foolish woman I know, still determined to lead every dance, and still an incorrigible flirt. Is that not true?"

She hesitated, torn between offense and amusement. "Yes, I . . . suppose it is."

"Then you are still the woman I thought you."

"Very funny," she said dryly.

She sent him a covert glance, then inhaled deeply. "I suppose you've never had any doubt about who you are?"

He smirked. "About my role on this earth? Daily. But about my parentage, no. No room for question, I'm afraid."

"Why 'afraid'?"

He shifted his weight, suddenly uncomfortable, wondering what all Lady Amelia had told her. "I am afraid I am a great deal like my father. Look like him, and share many of his weaknesses . . ."

When he trailed off, Julia suggested, "And his strengths?"

Again he shifted. "I . . . don't know that either of us are as strong as we should be. Should have been."

Julia regarded him, then said quietly, "Aurora told me, you know . . . how you accepted the blame for your father's wrongdoing."

Foolish, loyal Aurora, Alec thought. He pulled a face. "I do blame myself. The young woman started with me. Flirting and flattering. She was a very pretty girl, and I admit I was taken in by her charms for quite some time. I thought she really admired me. But slowly I began to see she was only playing with my affections—she knew her father would never approve of a match between us. I realized no good could come of it. The wisdom and warnings of my grandfather had been drilled into me from youth. So I began to pull away—tried to reestablish a professional distance between us. At first she tried harder. But when she realized I would not yield, she felt snubbed and grew angry. I did not realize at first just how angry. Or that she planned to take revenge on my family.

"She turned her attentions toward my father. Twice her age, though still handsome, I suppose. I tried to warn him, but he scoffed at me. Who was I to tell him anything? Had he not withstood the flirtations of a hundred schoolroom misses in his day? Even daughters of nobility?"

Alec shook his head. "I should have tried harder. Should have made certain they were never alone. But we each had our own private lessons to teach, often in pupils' homes. I could not be with him—with *them*—every time they were together. . . ."

Alec inhaled sharply. "The worst of it is, I really believe my father had been devoted and faithful to my mother until that point. Oh, he might have admired a beautiful woman or fawned over some fine lady in hopes of acquiring her children as pupils, but I had never seen him look at a woman inappropriately until Miss Underhill sank her claws into him."

He sighed. "He had reached a certain age, you see. Felt his years— and wanted to feel young again. I suppose it made him vulnerable. Not that I excuse him. But nor do I think Miss Underhill some innocent taken advantage of by a cunning older man. No matter what she told her own father about the affair."

Again he shook his head. "Well, you can imagine what tales the gossips spun. No parents would send their daughter to Valcourts after that."

"No," Julia agreed. "Understandably so, I'm afraid."

"Yes."

Julia tilted her head to look at him. "Why didn't you tell Lady Amelia this, when she confronted you?"

"I would not add to my mother's mortification for the world."

"Only your own—by taking on your father's blame?"

He shrugged. "A small price to pay." More than a small price—almost all of his income, but he did not say so.

Julia looked at him earnestly. "I think you're wrong, Mr. Valcourt. I think you are strong. Very strong in the face of such a loss. In becoming the man of the family. Uprooting your mother and sister and settling with them here in this . . . godforsaken place."

He raised an eyebrow. "Beaworthy . . . godforsaken?"

She looked at him, aghast. "Do you mean to tell me you like it here?"

"Except for the small matter of it crushing my dreams and avowed profession, you mean? Then, why yes, it's charming."

She laughed. "Thank you, Mr. Valcourt. You have cheered me, and not just anyone could have done so today. I sincerely appreciate the effort."

"My pleasure."

He looked at Lady Anne Tremelling's headstone once more. A part of him knew he should leave well enough alone, but another part of him—the selfish part—wanted to extend this small bubble of intimacy, of empathetic conversation, as long as possible.

"And where is *Mr.* Tremelling?" he asked.

Her face clouded, and he instantly knew he had chosen the wrong course.

"It is Lieutenant Tremelling, actually," she said.

Lieutenant Tremelling . . . the name rang in his memory. The man he had met in Plymouth in Mr. Barlow's stead. *That* was Julia's father— or, at least, the man Lady Anne had married? But while he was still pondering this, Julia continued.

"I've never met him, that I can remember. He's gone to sea a great deal. For years on end, apparently." Again that bleak, heartbreaking little laugh. "Twenty years without a single day of shore leave, poor man."

Her sarcasm didn't fool him. He said soothingly, "Perhaps he thinks it's for the best. Especially if he knows you believe yourself to be some-one else's daughter." *And perhaps she is*, Alec thought.

"I never felt like Mr. Midwinter's daughter. Not the way Patience feels about her father. Or the obvious love and affection Sir Herbert feels for her."

She glanced at him. "You will think me cruel and cold. But I felt no great grief when Mr. Midwinter died. My deepest sense of loss was for myself. I thought, All these years, I've tried to be worthy of him. Tried to be good—make him love me. And when that didn't work, to at least make him notice me." She spoke matter-of-factly, without maudlin self-pity. "When he died, I thought, It's finally over. I shall never know a father's love, but at least I can quit striving."

She shook her head, agitated. "Now to discover I have a father I've never met? It scares me." She pressed a hand to her abdomen. "I'm frightened to death by this sprout of desperate, pathetic hope. . . ."

Was Tremelling her real father? Alec wondered. He knew Desmond had been accused of seducing Lady Anne, but Julia didn't know that. And it certainly wasn't his place to tell her, especially as he wasn't certain it was true. Either way, his heart ached for her. And Alec felt a pinch of guilt for all the unloving and uncharitable thoughts he'd had about his own father. His father was not a perfect man—not by any means. But Alec had grown up with no shadow of doubt that his father loved him.

"I am sorry, Miss Midwinter."

"Don't. You promised. No pity."

"Very well. But I shall pray for you. You cannot stop me." He gently pressed her hand.

She looked at him, almost shyly, and braved a wobbly smile. "I shouldn't want to stop you."

On with the dance! let joy be unconfined;
No sleep till morn, when Youth and Pleasure meet
To chase the glowing Hours with flying feet.

—Lord Byron

Chapter 19

After dark that evening, Desmond again joined Alec in the academy for a bout with the practice foils. After twenty minutes of rigorous fencing, the two men stopped to catch their breaths. Alec wanted to ask him about his relationship with Lady Anne but hesitated to pry. Nor could he share Julia's revelation, when he'd promised to keep her secret.

Behind them, the door latch clicked. Alec stiffened and turned to see who was entering. He relaxed when he saw Mrs. Tickle pushing open the door with her elbow, her hands full, holding a plated cake. Alec was glad to see the woman—and the cake—but hoped they hadn't been too noisy, as he and Walt had been.

He smiled at his generous neighbor. "Good evening, Mrs. Tickle. I hope we didn't disturb you."

"No, not at all. I—" Her gaze shifted to Desmond and she froze, smile vanishing. She inhaled a breathy gasp. "Well, I . . . I find I am disturbed after all." Backing toward the door, she shifted the cake to one arm, smearing icing on her apron, and yanked the door open before Alec could move or offer to help. He'd been stunned stupid by the woman's reaction.

"You probably don't know any better, Mr. Valcourt," she said. "But I will not have you sharing one of my cakes with the likes of him!" She let the door bang shut, taking the cake with her.

Beside him, Desmond sighed. "Sorry, Valcourt. I should not have come. I don't want to cause strife between you and your neighbors."

"No, *I'm* sorry," Alec said. "I don't know what to say." He looked at him squarely. "But you are welcome here, Desmond. Always."

"In that case . . ." Desmond raised his sword to eye level and gave him a crooked grin. "I've seen what you can do with a sword in hand, Valcourt, but what about when it's beneath your feet?" He lowered to his haunches, laid the sword on the floor, and looked up at Alec, one brow arched in challenge.

Alec grinned in reply. Understanding Desmond's intent, he reached down and laid his own sword across his.

If the man wanted a sword dance, he'd be happy to oblige.

⁂

Julia walked into the village alone after dark. It was a very daring thing to do, which is of course why she did it. She hoped to see Mr. Valcourt. Walter had mentioned he'd been meeting him for fencing lessons in the village.

The lamplighter walked by with his wick and pole, and Julia stepped behind one of the columns of the deserted market hall, hoping not to be seen out walking alone at night. Glancing about her, she saw that repairs had begun on the market hall, but the ceiling was not yet completed. Evidence of workmen—scattered nails, footprints in masonry dust, and anthills of sawdust lingered in the stalls.

As she stood there waiting for the lamplighter to pass, she found her gaze drawn to the devil's stone between the village church and inn. It somehow struck her as symbolic of her own situation. Trapped in Beaworthy like that stone that didn't belong there. Caught between the church and the devil? She thought again of how the bell ringers had been unable to turn the stone last November, and the resulting predictions of doom.

She shivered.

A sound drew her attention across the High Street. Music. Near the end of the street, in a long-abandoned shop, light streamed from the top of half-covered windows. She stared. Now and again, a shape bobbed in the upper windows. A head . . . jumping? Were the Bryanites now using that old shop for their meetings, since the collapse of the market hall? She supposed it made sense. But the music she was hearing . . . it didn't sound the sort to be played at a church meeting, "ranters" or no.

Looking both ways and seeing no one about, Julia crossed the street and tiptoed closer. She was not tall enough to look over the covered lower windows, but she did find a tear in the paper and bent to peer in, feeling foolish, yet unable to resist the tug of curiosity.

Inside the lamplit room, a man with his back to the window played a lilting tune on a pipe. On the floor were crossed two swords. Over them Alec Valcourt danced, his feet flying in steps, hops, and leaps from one quadrant of the sword-cross to another. He danced in shirtsleeves and waistcoat. The snug buff trousers showed his muscular thighs and calves in high relief.

"My goodness . . ." Julia breathed.

A voice startled her. "Miss Midwinter?"

Julia jerked upright, her face heating. Aurora Valcourt and her mother stood on the walkway, looking at her expectantly.

"I . . . heard the music," Julia stammered. "I was only curious. . . ."

Aurora smiled. "Would you like to come inside?"

Julia glanced from Alec's friendly sister, to his more cautious mother—for the first time noticing a slight resemblance to her brother, Mr. Ramsay.

"If you don't think they'd mind," Julia said.

"Not at all." Aurora opened the door, and Julia followed Mrs. Valcourt inside.

"All right, Desmond. Let's see you try it," Alec said. He turned at the sound of the door closing.

"Hello, Mother, I . . ." Mr. Valcourt's mouth parted in surprise. "Oh . . . Miss Midwinter. Um . . . welcome." He cleared his throat self-consciously and spread his arms. "Welcome to the Valcourt Dancing and Fencing Academy, soon to open." He added dryly, "And likely soon to close as well."

"Good for you," Julia said, all admiration.

"But please do keep it under your bonnet for now. We are not quite ready to announce our grand opening."

"Of course." She gestured toward the crossed swords. "I am sorry to interrupt. Don't let me stop you." She smiled at Alec, noticing how handsome he looked, his color high, his dark hair tousled. She ran her gaze over his white sleeves and close-fitting waistcoat. Without a coat, his broad shoulders angled to his narrow waist in a masculine V.

Mr. Valcourt touched his own arm, as if only just realizing he stood in his shirtsleeves. He reached out and snagged his coat from a nearby chair. The man behind him set aside his instrument and helped him on with it like a skilled valet.

Her gaze moved to the musician. She recognized him with a start. The stranger from the churchyard.

"You're not interrupting anything important," Mr. Valcourt said. "We were just . . . fencing."

He must have noticed her looking at the other man. "Oh, forgive me," he said. "Miss Midwinter, have you met Mr. Desmond? Mr. John Desmond, Miss Julia Midwinter."

"Mr. Desmond and I have met before," Julia said. "In the Buckleigh churchyard. Though . . . we were not introduced."

"A pleasure to see you again, Miss Midwinter." The man bowed.

"Mr. Desmond has only recently returned to Beaworthy," Mrs. Valcourt kindly explained. "He has come home to help his ailing father in his forge outside of town."

"Ah, I see." The name Desmond sounded vaguely familiar. Had that not been the name of the elderly couple she had seen dancing in the High Street two years ago? Julia thought so but couldn't be certain.

"I am sorry to hear your father is not in good health," Julia said. "And sorry you have had to return to Beaworthy. Had you been away long?"

Alec stepped forward and abruptly changed the subject. "I must say I am surprised to see you, Miss Midwinter. What brings you into town this evening?"

"Oh. I . . ." What could she say? She was too ashamed to confess she had been hoping to see him, especially at night. Not with wronged widow Valcourt looking at her so respectfully, not to mention innocent-eyed Aurora. How their looks would change if they knew!

"Just . . . out to take some air," she said.

She felt Mr. Desmond studying her face and wondered why. Did he somehow know about her . . . her unsavory past?

It was Julia's turn to change the subject. "Don't worry, Mr. Valcourt. I shan't go rushing off to Lady Amelia to report your clandestine dancing."

Alec turned to Mr. Desmond. "Miss Midwinter has joined us at Medlands for a dance lesson or two, you see." He drew himself up with a single clap of his hands. "Well, Desmond, I believe it is your turn."

The man held up his palm. "No thank you, Valcourt. My dancing days are over."

"Oh no," Alec said. "You'll not get out of it that easily. After all, you're the one who laid down the challenge."

"I'm afraid I've been completely distracted by the arrival of the ladies." Mr. Desmond hedged, "I doubt I'd recall a single step." He picked up his pipe as though a baton to ward Alec off. "I'll play again and you dance. You ought not miss an opportunity to perform for such a lovely audience."

With a sheepish glance at her, Alec ducked his head but relented. "Very well."

Alec positioned himself in the sword-cross. Mr. Desmond began to play, and Alec danced. If anything his steps were faster, his leaps and hops higher than they had been before. Julia watched, entranced. She had never seen such dancing.

Finally both dancer and musician ended with a flourish.

When Alec bowed, Julia joined Aurora and Mrs. Valcourt in hearty applause. His face flushed with exertion and pride.

"And I thought keeping up with you in *fencing* would be difficult," John Desmond said with a grin.

Behind them, someone knocked on the door. They all froze, then looked from one to the other. Mr. Desmond, she noticed, stepped into the shadowy threshold of the back room.

Squaring his shoulders, Mr. Valcourt strode to the door.

Julia's stomach clenched. If she had heard the music, it was likely others in the High Street had as well. She hoped it was not someone who would report her whereabouts to her mother.

But when Alec opened the door, there stood the disapproving lady herself.

She looked from Mr. Valcourt, to the swords, to his mother and sister, to her. "Pardon me, Mr. Valcourt, but I have come for my daughter. Julia, let us go."

"Why have you come?" Julia asked.

"Why? Because I could not find you at home. I grew worried and came out looking for you."

"I am perfectly well, as you see." Embarrassment singed Julia's neck and ears. She detested being treated like a wayward child. Especially in front of Alec Valcourt.

Suddenly her mother's gaze flicked from Julia's face to the backroom doorway, to the tall man standing partially hidden by the shadows.

She gasped, paled, and seemed to sway.

Surprised, Julia looked from her to Mr. Desmond, noticing his stricken expression as well.

Her mother's face reddened at an alarming rate. "How dare you . . ." she breathed, nostrils flared.

Mr. Desmond said only, "My lady."

"Julia, we're leaving." Eyes flashing, she took two long steps, hooked Julia's arm with a claw-like hand, and all but dragged her from the room.

"Mother!" Julia hissed in mortification. "How dare *he*? How dare *you*!"

But Lady Amelia had already pulled her through the door and out into the street, where the Buckleigh carriage awaited.

The footman helped them inside. When they were seated and the door shut, Julia demanded, "Why did you do that?"

Her mother asked almost fearfully, "Did he seek you out? Ask to meet you?"

"What are you talking about? Mr. Desmond? I don't even know him. I only learnt his name five minutes ago. Neither he nor Mr. Valcourt had any idea I would show up there tonight."

"Then why are you here? What possessed you to leave the house at night?"

As the carriage started to move, Julia said, "I . . . happened to meet Miss Valcourt and her mother. They were on their way to see Mr. Valcourt, and they showed me the . . . shop." She was sorely tempted to tell her mother what he planned to do with it but remembered his plea to keep it quiet for now. Though, knowing how clever—and connected—her mother was, she probably already knew.

"What did he say to you?" Lady Amelia asked.

"Mr. Desmond? I don't recall him saying much of anything."

"No? Well . . . good."

"Why *good*?"

"Because I don't want you associating with him—with any of them. Mr. Desmond is not to be trusted."

"Do you know him?"

She turned a hard face toward Julia. "Of course I know him," she snapped. "He's the man who killed my brother."

Julia gaped. "That man? Why? Why would he? You told me it was a duel, right?"

She gave the barest begrudging nod.

"What, or shall I say whom, did they fight about . . . ? You?"

"No." Her mother gave a bitter little snort, very unlike her normal ladylike reserve.

Julia narrowed her eyes. "What are you not telling me?"

Her mother said carefully, "I mentioned there were . . . rumors . . . before Anne married, but—"

Julia interrupted, "Are you referring to the rumor that Lady Anne may have been with child before she married? What has that to do with Mr. Desmond?"

Her mother's mouth tightened into stern lines. "I have said more than enough. No good can come from discussing this further." She turned and stared out the window the rest of the way home, refusing to say another word on the subject.

෴

The next afternoon, Julia sought out Doyle. She found the lady's maid tucked up in her mother's dressing room, sewing a tippet around the collar of a walking dress. As she sewed, she sipped a glass of sherry from the bottle Julia had given her earlier.

Startled, the woman made to slide the glass behind a powder box, but seeing it was only Julia, relaxed. "Miss."

"Hello, Doyle." She handed the woman a small box of sweets. She'd bought them for Patience's upcoming birthday but could always buy more.

"Thank you, miss." Doyle set aside her sewing before opening the box of sticky sweets.

Julia sat on the stool of her mother's dressing table and watched the servant nibble on the candy with evident relish. Then she began, "Doyle, you've been here for a long time. So you knew Lady Anne well, did you not?"

"Oh yes. I was lady's maid to both Lady Anne and Lady Amelia. And to their mother before them."

"I found that letter in the trunk," Julia said conspiratorially, but she didn't come out and accuse the woman of leaving the drawer open. "After that, Lady Amelia told me . . . you know . . . about Lady Anne and me."

Doyle's eyes widened and she set down the box of sweets. "Did she now?"

"Yes. You knew, I assume. I imagine a lot of people knew. At least among the servants."

"Yes. Servants usually know more than their masters realize about the goings-on in a house."

"Why did no one ever tell me?"

"And why would we do that? Eager to lose our posts, were we? No. Wasn't our place. Besides, people don't talk about such things. Not to the child herself, at any rate. It's private-like. In the family. And we are loyal, most of us, even if we don't always agree with what goes on."

"You didn't agree?"

"I didn't say that, miss. I don't always see eye to eye with her lady-ship—that's no secret—but I did think it were right decent of her, considering."

"Considering . . . what? Lady Anne's putting the cart before the horse?"

"I wouldn't say it in so many words. Not to you, miss. But yes."

"How did my . . . Mr. Midwinter react? Did he resist the arrange-ment?"

Doyle hesitated, head tilted to one side. "What did *she* tell you about that?"

Julia hesitated. If she admitted Lady Amelia had said nothing beyond "He left the decision to me," would the servant seal her lips as well? Julia poured herself a glass of water from the carafe on the dressing table and proceeded with what she knew from personal experience. "Mr. Midwinter was not keen on the arrangement but made no objec-tion." *Apparently,* she added to herself.

"Oh, he had objections, all right," Doyle said. "But he washed his hands of the whole matter and said she could do as she pleased, because he knew she would regardless."

Her throat suddenly dry, Julia sipped her water and nodded en-couragingly toward Doyle's glass.

Doyle picked it up. "Besides, Lady Amelia had been in a deep de-pression of spirits for months. Kept to her room for the most part." She sipped the sherry. "Having a child to care for was the one thing that seemed to help her over her grief. And though I don't say it was a love match, Mr. Midwinter was not a cruel man and no doubt preferred a content companion to a melancholy one."

Julia felt certain that, if she revealed her ignorance, the conversation would quickly end. She needed to tread carefully—pretending to know all, while subtly seeking more information.

"Of course she was grieving," Julia said. "Her father and brother dead, her sister . . . lost."

"Oh, but it was more than that." Doyle pulled a face. "What a hullabaloo. Mr. Midwinter was tempted to refuse the match with Lady Amelia altogether to keep out of the family scandal."

"My grandfather did not approve of Lieutenant Tremelling," Julia suggested.

"No. Nor did Master Graham. At first they forbade Anne to marry the man, threatening to cut her off from the family without a farthing or even a dowry. So, she broke things off with Tremelling, or so she claimed."

So she claimed? Julia wondered, but did not ask.

"Then a few months later, she comes cryin' to Lord Buckleigh, confessing she was with child. But insistin' the child was *not* Lieutenant Tremelling's doin'. Said it couldn't be—he'd been away at sea."

Julia felt her mouth slacken. "Did my grandfather verify her story?"

"That I don't know. I do know he and Master Graham put a lot of pressure on Lady Anne to reveal her lover."

Julia wanted to ask what Anne said but made do with a nod of sage understanding.

"And when she finally did," Doyle continued, "her brother was quick to believe her. But I didn't. Not at first." She slowly shook her head, eyes distant.

"Who?" Julia asked, unable to restrain herself. "Who was it?"

Doyle shrewdly narrowed her eyes at her, and Julia knew she'd tipped her hand.

In her mind's eye, Julia again saw Lady Amelia's stricken face, her shock at seeing Mr. Desmond, her refusal to talk about the duel. *The duel—of course!* Aloud she ventured, "John Desmond?"

The maid's wiry brows rose. "Ah! So you have heard of our infamous dancing master, ey?"

Dancing master? she thought, but merely said, "Only recently." For some reason Julia hesitated to mention she'd met him.

Doyle continued. "He denied it flat. But Master Graham didn't believe him. How could he, when his little sister had named the man?"

Julia's heart thudded. *Could it be?* Was John Desmond her father?

"But I wanted to believe him innocent," Doyle said. "He always seemed so respectful and gentlemanlike. He treated Lady Anne more like a silly girl than a lover. I sometimes chaperoned their dancing lessons, you see. And between you and me, I thought he was more interested in Lady Amelia than in Anne. And Lady Amelia was certainly smitten with him—that I can tell you. Though I probably should not. I doubt she told you that, ey, my girl?" She drained her glass.

Julia gave a noncommittal shrug.

The servant shook her head. "Poor Mr. and Mrs. Desmond. They made a great show of defending their son, but that's what parents do, I suppose. Against all reason. Lost most of their Beaworthy customers over it too. Most of their business comes from Shebbear or Bradford these days, I gather."

"Why do you say they defended him against all reason?" Julia asked. "I thought you didn't believe him guilty?"

"Not at first. But then there was that awful duel, and your uncle's death, and the earl's apoplexy. Dark days indeed for Buckleigh Manor." She shuddered. "Johnny Desmond left the village soon after, and that seemed to confirm his guilt. And as the gossips said, he was the dancing master, after all—and everyone knows better than to trust their daughters with that lascivious lot."

Julia frowned, trying to tie all the knotted threads into a comprehensible pattern. Footsteps sounded in the passage, though Julia barely heard them. "So Lieutenant Tremelling is *not* my father, but the former dancing master is?"

The door latch clicked, and Doyle jumped, her gaze darting toward the dressing room door and back to Julia. She hissed, "I didn't say that. And if you heard it, you didn't hear it from me."

Lady Amelia stalked into the dressing room, her troubled eyes shifting from Julia's face, to Doyle's flushed face, and back again. "What has she been telling you?"

How much did she overhear? Julia wondered. "It isn't her fault," she said. "You would not tell me everything, so I asked Doyle to fill in the blanks of what I already knew—or guessed."

For a moment her mother hesitated, then said flatly, "Leave us, Doyle. My daughter and I must talk."

The sheepish lady's maid rose a little unsteadily. "Very good, my lady. Sorry, my lady."

"And take your sherry with you," she called after the woman.

Head lowered, Doyle returned, snatched up the glass, and scurried from the room. Lady Amelia closed the door behind her and locked it.

She sighed. "I would rather you had let it lie, as I asked, Julia. Or if you could not do that, that you would have come to me with your questions."

"I tried."

Her mother inhaled, pressed her hands together, then exhaled. "I know you have." She squeezed her eyes shut a moment, then asked, "What more do you want to know?"

Julia took a deep breath. "Was John Desmond Lady Anne's lover, and my . . . father?" How strange to say the words aloud, especially to the woman she had always known as her mother.

"So they said."

"Who said?"

"My father and brother. They put a lot of pressure on Anne to reveal her lover, so they might *work* on the man." Her complexion took on an ashy hue. "I have sometimes wondered if that's why she finally named him." She slowly shook her head, her eyes hollow and distant, as though reliving the scene.

"Mr. Desmond denied her claim. But I don't think anyone believed him. Even those who desperately wanted to."

"Who do you mean?" Julia frowned.

Her mother blinked, as though returning to the present. "I . . ." She swallowed. "I mean his parents, of course."

She twisted her hands. "Graham was incensed. He'd trusted the man and felt betrayed for his sister's sake as well as his own. He challenged Mr. Desmond, but it was no fair fight, not when one party was a fencing master. Graham was killed. And then Mr. Desmond left the village soon after, sealing his guilt."

Julia had never seen such emotion on her mother's face. It unsettled her. She asked in a timid voice, "So . . . who is my father?"

Lady Amelia winced as though in pain. "I don't know!" she cried, her voice high and plaintive. Then she exhaled to regain control of her emotions. "My sister named John Desmond. But I've never been absolutely certain she told the truth. I was not well acquainted with Lieutenant Tremelling, yet there are times I look at you, and I think I see a resemblance, some of his features. . . ."

Julia found herself hungry for answers, for connection. "Which features?"

"Your smile. Your fair hair and eyes."

"But," Julia protested, "people have always said I have *your* eyes. . . ."

"Well, I am your aunt, after all, so some resemblance is not surprising. A blessing, really."

"And Lady Anne?" Julia asked. "How do I resemble her?"

Lady Amelia barely contained a grimace. "In personality—you seem to share her reckless ways."

Later, on her way across the hall, Julia paused before Lady Anne's half-length portrait, which she so often glanced at in passing. The background was black oil paint, setting off the woman's fair skin and golden brown hair in high relief.

Her hair was arranged in a high mound atop her head in the style of decades past. She wore a rich overdress of coral satin with puffed elbow-length sleeves over a belted gown of ivory. She did not smile, yet the pose seemed coy, now that Julia looked at it again. Lady Anne sat sideways but looked toward the painter, chin resting on her hand. Her large eyes were framed by well-defined brows far darker than Julia's. Julia leaned nearer. Her eye color was not terribly distinct—a dark blue, perhaps.

Julia stepped back once more to regard the whole. Was there a resemblance? Yes, in the shape of her nose and her lips, perhaps.

And that gold locket around her neck . . . It was *her* locket, the one she received for her thirteenth birthday. Lady Amelia told her it had been Lady Anne's when she gave it to her, but now it was truly significant. Julia had possessed her mother's locket all these years without knowing it.

The locket was empty—no miniature graced it, no lock of loved one's hair. How apropos, Julia thought, that this token from her former family was a hollow shell. As empty as she felt.

Those Gentlemen and Ladies who propose sending their Children to be instructed may depend the best care will be taken as to their Behavior.

—dancing master advertisement,
Boston Gazette & Country Journal

Chapter 20

Amelia felt adrift. Awash in a murky mire of fears and regrets. How stunned she'd been to see John Desmond standing in his old academy, only a few yards from her precious Julia. For years, she'd wondered if he would return, but as time went by she began to assume he would stay away forever, to avoid prosecution for the illegal duel, to avoid her, to avoid the stigma of it all.

She still remembered the awful scene, the day before May Day, though she'd done her best to forget it.

Desmond had come to teach a dancing lesson as previously arranged, only to be met by Amelia, stunned and undone.

"There will be no more lessons," she'd said stiffly, desperate to control her emotions.

His dark brows rose. "Oh? What's happened? What's wrong? You're clearly upset."

"How can I not be"—she struggled to get the words past her tight, scorching throat—"when this very day my sister has named you the father of her child."

"What?" He frowned, thunderstruck. "Lady Anne is . . . with child?" His incredulity seemed so authentic, so believable.

Her chin trembled. She stood there, nostrils pinched, eyes stinging, but determined not to cry. Not trusting her voice, she managed a nod.

"Dear Lord," he breathed. "And she names *me*?"

"As I said." She pointed toward the library door. "Anne is in there with Father and Graham, confessing all as we speak."

She risked a glance at his face—jaw clenched, eyes troubled—and saw a storm of emotions. But guilt? She was not certain.

Heartsick, Amelia followed behind as John Desmond strode into the library to confront the accusation head on. Graham and their father whirled on him furiously, but Anne remained sitting, face averted.

"I don't understand this, Lady Anne," Mr. Desmond said, mouth tight. "You know I am not the man."

But she had only ducked her head.

Instead he appealed to her father. "I have never been intimate with your daughter, my lord. I give you my word." He sent a pleading glance to Amelia, but she looked away, blinking back tears.

"Then why does she name you, Mr. Desmond?" Lord Buckleigh challenged.

"I can only suppose she is frightened out of her wits, and the man responsible is unable or unwilling to do his duty."

Lady Anne began to cry aloud. And Amelia felt nauseous. She knew John Desmond, knew what he would do.

He took a step nearer the youngest Buckleigh. "Anne, are you certain nothing can be done to bring the man around?"

"I . . . What? No, you are the man. You know you are!"

He stared at the desperate, tear-streaked face as if she were a creature from another world.

"I know no such thing," he repeated evenly. Again he looked at Amelia, his dark eyes begging hers for understanding. He said quietly, "But as a man of honor, I offer to marry her."

The words were a blow to Amelia's chest. She could hardly breathe. Her mind railed against it. No, it was not fair. No!

"I don't want to marry him," Anne screeched. "Don't make me, Papa. Don't make me."

Confusion swamped Amelia. Why accuse Mr. Desmond, then refuse to marry him? She was both relieved and stricken, for if Anne did not marry soon, she would be beyond hope. *Please, God, let her marry anyone but this man.*

Graham narrowed his eyes at his teacher and former friend. "Why is my sister afraid of you? And if you claim innocence, why offer for her? Why would you want her if another man has ruined her?"

Again Anne wailed.

Their father added, "It hardly helps your case."

Desmond drew back his shoulders, clearly steeling himself. "I realize that by being alone with Lady Anne during our lessons, only irregularly chaperoned, I may have contributed to such rumors. That being the case, I am willing, as a gentleman, to rescue her reputation."

Graham's eyes flashed. "You mistake yourself, Desmond. You are no gentleman. I will not give you my sister, but I give you this." He yanked off a glove and threw it to the floor in flagrant challenge.

"Graham, no!" Amelia cried, terrified of what would come next.

But John Desmond ignored the thrown glove, not picking it up to accept the challenge. Instead, he turned and left without another word. Amelia had been tempted to hope, but she should have known John's calm denial would only inflame her brother all the more.

The next day, the first of May, Amelia emerged from her bedchamber with bloodshot eyes and a battered heart, and went through her morning routine in a haze. Just before midday, she realized she had not seen Graham all morning and began to worry. She stopped in his room but did not find him, nor his valet.

None of the family planned to attend the May Day dance or surrounding festivities—not after the wretched scene of the day before. She supposed John Desmond would attend. As dancing master, he was probably obliged to be there, to support his pupils.

Amelia found her father in the library and asked if he had seen Graham.

Her father straightened, instantly alert. "Is he not in the house?"

"Not that I can find. I cannot find his valet either."

"Devil take it," he muttered. "I told him not to go."

Amelia tensed. "Do you think he went after Mr. Desmond?"

"I hope to God not." He rose and yanked the bell cord. When the footman entered he barked, "Have my horse saddled immediately."

But Amelia was already running. Out of the house, across the grounds, past the church, and up the Buckleigh Road. Side stitching, lungs burning, she ran into the village. She heard the music, saw the crowd, the people dancing around the green. There were Mr. and Mrs. Desmond. Where was their son? Amelia looked this way and that but saw no sign of John or her brother. That was a good sign, was it not? Then again, if they meant to duel, they wouldn't do so in front of all these witnesses. . . .

Suddenly from down the market hall stairs, thundered Perry, Graham's valet.

"Perry!" she called. "Where is my brother?"

The man's face was pasty white, nearly green. He blinked and stammered, "He . . . I . . ." He swallowed, then made do with pointing up the stairs. "I'm to get the surgeon."

Her heart pounded. "Then go, man. Make haste!"

Amelia ran up the stairs. She burst through the door and saw John Desmond on his knees, leaning over Graham's body.

Her brother's eyes were glassy and lifeless. Blood seeped through his waistcoat and onto the floor.

John Desmond looked up at her and froze, his expression cracking like shattered glass. "Amy . . ."

Her stomach seized, turned to ice. She whispered, "Is he . . . dead?"

John winced and nodded. "I tried to talk him out of it, but he would not listen. . . ."

She shook her head, throat burning. "*You* were the master. He was your pupil. And so was she. . . ." Amelia sucked in a ragged breath. "How could you?"

John rose and started toward her, but she held up her hand and backed toward the door. "Stay away from me."

Stricken, he protested, "Amy, you can't believe I would hurt you—"

"Ha!" She half laughed, half cried. "You have killed us all."

She stumbled back down the stairs, fearing she was about to retch. Glancing around in a nauseous daze, she saw all the people still blithely dancing, unaware. The musicians were still playing. The world continued on, as if life had not just ended.

The cheerful music hurt her ears. Her vision tilted—puffing musicians, clapping crowd, and happy dancers with skirts whirling, spun like a dizzying carousel before her eyes. Amelia's emotions tightened like a fiddle string and then snapped.

"Stop," she shouted. "Stop dancing! My brother is dead, and John Desmond has blood on his hands. How can you dance?" Tears clogged her throat and flowed down her cheeks.

Nearby, Maria Desmond gaped in shock and grasped her husband's arm. The musicians squeaked to a halt, and people stopped and stared.

Amelia was beyond caring what they thought of her. Body trembling, she cried, "Dancing masters can't be trusted—isn't that what people say? But I never listened. Why did I not listen? They smile and charm, and all the while they are seducing your sister and killing your brother."

She shook her head, blinded by tears and grief. "No more dancing masters, and no more dancing. Not here. Not ever. Not as long as I live."

Her father rode up, and dismounted in ungainly fashion. He took one look at her and his knees buckled. "Where is he?"

"Above the market hall."

Her father's face and body spasmed. He clutched his chest and lurched for the stairs. Mr. Hopkins, the constable, ran after him. From out of the crowd, the surgeon, followed by Graham's valet, hurried up the stairs as well.

Later, much later, the constable, surgeon, and valet carried down two bodies. The dead body of her brother, and the crippled body of her father, who'd suffered his first apoplexy there in the market hall, while weeping over his one and only son.

Lord Buckleigh suffered a second attack after the funeral, one that laid him low indeed. Though bedridden, he went on to live for several months. Long enough to confirm Amelia's edict that dancing and dancing masters were no longer welcome in Beaworthy. Long enough to see her safely married to an influential, responsible man. And to see Anne married to a man he didn't approve of but could no longer refuse.

He had two closed-door meetings with the magistrate, and Amelia assumed they were drafting formal charges against John Desmond. Yet before the constable could act, John Desmond had quietly closed his dancing academy and left Beaworthy without telling anyone where he was going. He stayed away for many years, until most everyone thought he would never return.

But now, he had. . . .

Amelia blinked back to the present. Why had John Desmond returned now of all times? She had heard his father was ailing. Was that the reason? Or had fate arranged to bring the man here at this critical time when Julia learned the truth about her mother, and was asking questions about her father? If so, she did not appreciate God's interference.

What was so important that he would risk returning now? Were there not charges still pending against him? She deeply hoped his return had nothing to do with her daughter.

Setting aside useless conjecture for action, Amelia sent for her estate manager.

When Barlow entered, she began, "I would like you to call on Mr. Arscott."

"The magistrate, my lady? And what business have I with him?"

She swallowed. "I have discovered that Mr. John Desmond has recently returned to Beaworthy." She slanted him a look. "I suppose you knew already and I am the last to learn of it?"

He pursed his lips and blustered, "Oh, well, I . . . may have heard a rumor. . . ."

"Never mind. I assume he was charged with the crime of my brother's death. I wish to know the status and specifics of those charges."

Barlow looked at her askance. "After twenty years?"

She sent him a frosty look, and he hesitated, then offered obsequiously, "I shall see what he says."

She nodded and waved her hand in dismissal, yet Barlow remained where he was.

Clasping his hands, he grimaced in thought and said, "But in asking, my lady, might I not inadvertently bring the fact of Mr. Desmond's return to the magistrate's attention?"

"What of it?"

"Are you . . . certain . . . that is what you wish to do?"

Barlow looked at her with sad, knowing eyes. He had been with her family for more than thirty years. He was there when it all happened. He knew the horrid, mortifying tale all too well.

When Barlow returned late that afternoon, his expression was that of a messenger who knew he came bearing unwelcome news.

"Well?" Amelia asked, steeling herself.

"Mr. Arscott says there are no charges against John Desmond that he is aware of."

"Why not?" she snapped. "There is no statute of limitations on murder."

Barlow was clearly taken aback by her outburst and looked to the floor.

Amelia was embarrassed to have lost her composure and took a deep breath to calm herself.

Apprehensive, Barlow continued, "Moreover, Mr. Arscott tells me that formal charges were never lodged against John Desmond."

She stared, angry and confused. "I don't understand. Duels were illegal then and they're illegal now. Nothing has changed. My brother is still dead. I know my father spoke to the magistrate. He would not have let his son's death go unpunished. We had a different constable then, but Mr. Arscott was magistrate then as he is now."

"Yes."

"Did he say why charges were never pressed? Was Father afraid Graham's reputation would be tainted if people knew he'd taken part in an illegal duel?"

"That might have been part of it, I suppose. Though Mr. Arscott hinted there might be more to the story."

"What more? What did he say?"

"He said he would prefer to speak with you privately, should you wish to pursue the matter, or press charges yourself. Unfortunately, he is occupied with the Easter quarter sessions, and then departs for London for a few weeks. But he said he could see you when he returns, if you'd like to call."

Botheration. She didn't want to call on old Edward Arscott. To dredge up and rehearse the awful day, and answer questions about why she still cared after all this time. . . . She was almost relieved she could not see him straightaway.

But did her brother not deserve justice?

The thought of demanding that John Desmond be punished made her feel nauseous. She knew it was her duty, and she would do so. But it would not be easy. She feared that if she started stirring those old embers, she might rekindle a flame. One that would burn them both.

◦⁄◦

Julia sat waiting atop Liberty when Desmond stepped out of his parents' house the next afternoon. He seemed surprised to see her but not unhappily so. A good beginning, she hoped.

"Hello, Miss Midwinter." He looked at her, then shook his head. "My goodness, staring me down like that, you remind me very much of your mother."

She frowned. "You needn't say such things, Mr. Desmond. I know now that I am not Lady Amelia's natural daughter. I am Lady Anne's daughter, as I believe you already know."

His brows rose. "Are you indeed?" He stood stock-still a moment, then strode toward her. "May I help you down?"

He helped her dismount from the sidesaddle. Then she looped Liberty's rein around a nearby tree limb with plenty of slack for the horse to nibble grass.

"Come now," she said. "You knew Lady Anne was with child before you left Beaworthy, and that she named you as the father. Do you deny it—when you killed my uncle in a duel over it?"

"I . . . don't deny knowing the charges against me, but—"

"But you deny me?" A stew of anger and rejection simmered to a boil until she thought she would explode. "Even though Lady Anne said—"

"I know what she said," he interrupted firmly. "But it wasn't true."

"You claim innocence? Or are you too ashamed to admit the truth?"

"I don't claim to be innocent, Miss Midwinter. I am guilty of many things." He stepped into the forge and calmly began stoking the fire. She followed him inside, stomach churning.

He said, "To this day, I wish I had managed to meet Graham's challenge without killing him. I know what shame is. I have carried it with me these twenty years. But I have no reason to be ashamed where you're concerned."

She lifted her chin. "That is my shame to carry alone. Is that it?"

"That is not what I—"

"Well, you lost no time in disabusing me, did you? In making sure I don't try to claim you. Why should I be surprised? The man I thought my whole life was my father didn't want me. Lady Anne's husband apparently doesn't want me, and now you don't want me either. I'm sorry to have wasted your time."

She turned away in a swirl of skirts and hurts, but he gently caught her arm.

"Wait, Miss Midwinter. You have not wasted my time. Come and sit here. I want to talk with you."

She allowed him to lead her to the bench and meekly sat.

"I'll make tea, shall I?" He began pottering about with kettle and cups. "Tell me, when did you find out?"

"I've learned it in bits and pieces over the last week or so. Lady Amelia kept it a secret from me all these years."

He nodded. "No doubt she wanted to protect you from all the rumors flying around back then."

"She protected me from nothing and exposed me to worse. I should have known Mr. Midwinter was not my father. That cold man could never have fathered a child."

He looked up sharply, clearly taken aback at her coarse words, but did not correct her. "Their marriage was not . . . close?"

"Hardly. I never saw him display any affection toward her, nor to me."

"Yet you feel sorry for yourself but not for her?"

She recoiled as if slapped. "How dare you? You know nothing about it."

"Forgive me." He filled the kettle and set it on the fire.

Julia said, "I suppose you like hearing that Lady Amelia has not been happy. Serves the Buckleighs right after running you out of town."

"You are mistaken." He shook his head soberly. "I take no pleasure in learning she has been unhappy. I would never have wished that for her."

"I find that difficult to believe. I saw how harshly she spoke to you that night in the academy."

He audibly exhaled. "I have given her reason to despise me."

"Because of her brother?"

"Yes, and because she believed her sister's word over mine. And who could blame her for that?"

"I could."

He regarded her. "You two don't get on?"

"That is an understatement."

"I know Lady Amelia well enough to know she loves you. And no doubt Lady Anne and her husband loved you as well."

"Loved me? Lady Anne denied I was his. And he hasn't bothered to visit me once since he dumped me at Buckleigh Manor so he could sail away, unfettered by a brat he didn't want, who was his in name only."

"I'm sure that wasn't the reason."

"Then why has he never come to see me?" She lifted a palm. "No, don't answer. I know why. Lady Amelia forbade him. Afraid her secret would get out, and she would lose her plaything, her puppet."

He said gently, "Or perhaps he doesn't want to confuse you. Especially since you've grown up as Julia Midwinter."

"Sometimes I tell myself that. That he doesn't come because he thinks I don't know. He thinks we want him to stay away." Her chin trembled but she was powerless to stop it. "And I convince myself that he wants to come. That he thinks of me. Often. Misses me. And longs to see me again."

He nodded and said cautiously, "It . . . could be." He added, "I am sure he wants only what's best for you."

She shook her head. "But if he is my father, how could he stay away so long? Especially now that I am grown."

Desmond hesitated. "What has Lady Amelia said about . . . your father?"

Julia shrugged. "She said she doesn't know for sure."

Desmond's lower lip protruded. "Well, that's something." He spooned in tea leaves. "Have you or Lady Amelia written to Tremelling now that you know? Asked him to visit?"

Julia blinked, chest tightening. "No."

"Well then, my girl, maybe it's time you did."

"Perhaps you're right," she murmured, head lowered in thought.

He slipped a long finger beneath her chin and lifted it. "But first we need something to put a smile on that pretty face."

She rolled her eyes. "Good luck."

He hesitated. "Did Lady Amelia ask you not to return to Mr. Valcourt's after she found you there the other night?"

Julia thought back. "No." Her mother had said next to nothing about Mr. Valcourt. In fact, she'd seemed concerned only about what Mr. Desmond might have said to her.

"Well then." He grinned. "I know just the thing."

❧

Alec had yet to hold his grand opening, but he was about to teach his first official dance class in his new academy. He was eager and apprehensive at the same time.

At least the group was a friendly one: James, a nervous Walter, a self-conscious Mr. Pugsworth, Tess Thorne, Patience, and Aurora as third lady. He had hoped Julia might join them, or Desmond stop by to lend a hand, but he had yet to see either of them.

He first taught them an English country dance and was in the midst of teaching a Scottish reel when the door opened behind them. Alec turned, his abdomen tightening as it often did since reopening an unpopular establishment. He was relieved to recognize the caller as friend and not foe.

Desmond entered with a broad smile. He held the door for none other than Julia Midwinter. Alec's mood lifted. His happiness was dampened, however, by the redness of her eyes and her blotchy cheeks— she'd been crying. But she braved a smile and greeted everyone. Alec wondered if Desmond had said something to upset her but doubted it of the kind man. As much as he trusted Desmond, he found himself looking from man to young lady. He saw no resemblance between the two and was glad of it.

The lesson resumed, and with the addition of another couple, they moved on to a longways dance for eight.

While Alec instructed, Desmond walked through the steps, partnering Julia. But when it was time to dance to music, he stepped aside. "You dance, Valcourt. I prefer not to. I'll play."

Having previously noticed his friend's reluctance to dance, Alec did not press him. He happily took over as Miss Midwinter's partner while Desmond played the Scottish tune "Broom, the Bonny, Bonny Broom" on Alec's fiddle.

When the dance ended, Alec said, "Come now, Desmond, teach us some exotic dance you learned in Spain or the Indies."

Desmond smiled fleetingly, then became reflective. "Actually," he said, "I would rather teach you a dance I learned not in some distant place, but in my own home, my hands in my mother's, my father playin' his pipe. A dance every Beaworthy lad and lass once learned, to dance on one special day of the year."

"The May Day dance," Miss Midwinter breathed.

Desmond looked at her in surprise. "Do you know it?"

She shook her head. "No, but I shall never forget seeing an older couple dancing it all alone around the green two years ago."

He nodded. "My parents. They decided to renew the tradition on their own, I'm proud to say, despite ridicule. Though with my father's health, I doubt he shall manage it this year."

"I am sorry to hear that."

Desmond raised both hands. "Come. I'll teach you the dance."

He asked them to find partners and form a line.

Walter looked longingly at Tess, but when she met his gaze, he ducked his head, face reddening, and snagged his sister's hand instead. This left Milton Pugsworth to partner Tess, while James danced with Aurora, and Alec remained with Julia.

"Gentlemen, offer your fair partner your right hand. Ladies, place your left hand in his. Now stand side by side and walk slowly in a step, shuffle-step. That's right. Sixteen counts. Now, join both hands and turn in a circle. The footwork is: step, step, step, hop. All the way around. Excellent."

They repeated the simple steps until everyone, except for Walter, was proficient.

Lifting an "aha" finger, Desmond crossed the room, hefted the old coat tree, and placed it in the center of the room. He explained that it would represent the fountain on the green beside the market hall.

"Now, imagine making your way down the High Street, villagers in pairs ahead of you and behind. Lining the street, a happy crowd of onlookers clap and cheer you on. Musicians play near the market hall, the music growing louder as you near the fountain. Fiddle and pipe raised in cheerful celebration.

"Neighbors you have barely seen through the dim winter months, now dance beside you in the spring sunshine, calling greetings to those they know, and remembering those not present that year. Dancing *for* them. Thankful for life while we have it, for our community and neighbors and friends."

The eight of them danced around and around that old coat tree, changing partners and dancing again as Desmond played.

As Julia and Alec danced past him, she smiled at Desmond and said, "You were right. This was exactly what I needed."

Dancing adds graces to the gifts which nature has bestowed upon us. . . . And, if it do not completely eradicate the defects with which we are born, it mitigates or conceals them.

—Pierre Rameau, *The Dancing Master*, 1725

Chapter 21

In the library, Julia faced her mother, steeling herself for a fight. "I wish to meet Lieutenant Tremelling. To ask him for myself if he is my natural father, and what he viewed the arrangement between you to be."

Julia imagined Lady Amelia had warned him to stay away, perhaps even paid him a great deal on the condition of his absence. He must have to support an ailing mother or father, and that was why he could not come and risk losing the money. For himself, he would not care. A man like him, a lieutenant in His Majesty's Royal Navy, must do quite well on his own. . . .

Julia imagined herself standing on the deck of his ship, the wind in her hair, a refreshing mist dampening her face, watching the rolling sea. Seeing the coast of England, the former limits of her life—Buckleigh Manor, Lady Amelia—growing smaller and smaller, farther and farther away, until they released their choke hold on Julia's throat and disappeared from view.

Ahead of them lay unknown horizons, new worlds to explore, new adventures. Her father stood at the helm, tall and handsome in his uniform with fair hair like hers. He smiled at her, pride evident in his eyes. He had conquered the objections of a few superstitious salts not keen on having a female aboard. And already she saw their begrudging admiration as she gained her sea legs so quickly, helped her father chart their course, and wasn't ill once.

Lieutenant Tremelling—or Captain Tremelling, as he was certain to become under her influence—had been surprised and delighted when she'd contacted him. How he'd missed her over the years, but he had stayed away, obeying Lady Amelia's edict. Of course she was welcome to live with him and share his life. Had that not always been the desire of his heart, though he'd never dared believe it possible?

Lady Amelia had begged and pleaded and threatened. But she could not forbid her. For he was her father, and she his beloved daughter, and they had years to make up for. Her rightful place was by his side. . . .

"Very well."

Julia blinked, awoken abruptly from her dreamy, idealistic reverie. "What?"

"I said, very well," Lady Amelia repeated. "I can see you are determined. And whether or not he is your father, he *was* Lady Anne's husband. If you wish to meet him, you shall. Will you write to him or shall I?"

Julia stared, felt her lips part. The confidence of her imaginings faltered, and a rare feeling—fear—tingled down her spine. "Perhaps it would be better coming from you the first time—so he knows you approve."

"As you wish. I don't say I approve, by the way, but I agree. I know you shall never be content otherwise."

Lady Amelia slipped a piece of stationery from the desk drawer and dipped a quill. "Anything particular you wish me to express?"

Julia considered. "Make sure he knows that meeting me won't obligate him to anything—that any further relationship between us will only be if he wishes it."

Lady Amelia held her gaze a moment longer, then bent to write.

Several minutes later, she blotted the ink and, without being asked, handed her the letter.

By way of preamble, Lady Amelia said, "I have attempted to word it in such a manner, that if the letter were to be misdirected, a stranger would not learn *all* our private family matters."

Julia nodded vaguely and read.

To Lieutenant Thomas Tremelling,

Miss Julia Midwinter, the young woman in my care, has been acquainted with her history and wishes to meet you. Note that a meeting does in no way obligate you or Miss Midwinter in any way. Any future involvement will be left to your discretion and mutual agreement.

Please come to Buckleigh Manor on the 12th, between three and five in the afternoon. Or if that is not possible, on a Saturday afternoon at your convenience as soon as may be. I trust that with the war over, you will have leave to travel to us. If not, please send word of a time and place of your preference and we shall come to you.

We await your reply.

> *Lady Amelia Midwinter*
> *Buckleigh Manor,*
> *Beaworthy, Devon*

Amelia waited for Julia to read the letter, praying she would not come to regret writing it.

Julia looked up at her, eyes troubled. "Does he even know my name?" she asked, sounding nearly panicked. "He may not realize you are referring to me, for Julia Midwinter was not my birth name."

"He'll know," Amelia assured her.

"Did he agree to your changing it? Does he even know?"

"Yes, Julia," she assured her again. "He agreed."

For the most part, Amelia added to herself.

She remembered very well the entire conversation, though she didn't often think of it. But after Julia left to prepare for bed, Amelia allowed the memory to come.

A footman, long since dismissed, had shown him into the drawing room. In one arm, Lieutenant Tremelling awkwardly held the infant bundled against the January cold. His dark blond hair was slicked back like a schoolboy's whose harried mamma had smoothed it with a spit-dampened palm. He was in uniform—dark blue wool tailcoat with a double row of brass buttons, buff waistcoat with stand-up collar, and boots over buff breeches. Under his other arm he held a large cocked hat of beaver felt with gilt trimmings. She wondered what sort of official navy business warranted his calling in uniform but made no comment.

The man exuded masculinity, and his face was undeniably handsome with prominent cheekbones, deep-set eyes, and a strong slightly hooked nose. But personally, Amelia had never found him attractive, nor had she ever especially liked the man. She had seen him about a month prior, at Anne's internment in the Buckleigh churchyard. Amelia had spoken to him only briefly then, enough to learn Anne's child—a girl—had survived but had been left in Plymouth with a nurse. Lieutenant Tremelling had made no mention of calling again, and his return filled her with surprise and not a little misgiving.

He looked stiff. Nervous. Like a young man paying his first courting call. But Amelia steeled herself. She had never trusted the man completely and didn't mean to start now.

He glanced down at the cradled child, perhaps five weeks old. "I've come to introduce you to your sister's daughter." He exhaled. "And . . . to ask you to care for her, now Anne's gone."

Amelia felt her palms begin to perspire. She looked down at the little face, her skin so pale and translucent that blue veins shone through. The child was bald save for the fairest fuzz atop her round head and, at the moment, asleep. Amelia had no idea what to say. Instead she asked, "What do you call her?"

The man looked down, uncomfortable. "Anne named her Grace Amelia."

Amelia's stomach clenched. It was quite common for mothers to name their daughters after themselves—but after a sister you'd hurt terribly?

He glanced up and must have seen her look of disbelief. He held up a placating palm. "I'm not saying that to try to persuade you or flatter you. Here." He set aside his hat and reached awkwardly with his free hand into an inner pocket. Amelia made no move to relieve him of the child.

"Here's a letter Anne began for the child. Before she . . ." He swallowed. "See for yourself."

Steeling her heart anew, Amelia read the brief letter in her sister's shaky hand.

Dear Grace Amelia,

How beautiful you are, my precious daughter. How perfect. I lie here and wish I could stay and watch you grow up, but I sense the heavenly Father calling me to himself even now. This world is fading until all I can truly focus on is your face. Even your papa is beginning to blur. He will fare well without me, I know. It is only you I think of. Worry about. Pray for. Who will take care of you while your papa is gone from home? Who dare I ask—trust—to care for my most precious possession?

Amelia's heart tightened into a fist until it physically ached. She had closed her heart to her sister. Could she open it to her sister's child? Foolish Anne. Had she been up to her old ways even so near the end of her life, on the surface so charming, but all the while calculating to manipulate others to do whatever she wanted? Amelia inwardly chastised herself for thinking ill of her sister, so recently departed.

"I would not feel comfortable calling her by that name."

"I understand," the man said. "And I think Anne would understand as well. From her letter, you can see she was mostly concerned about finding someone to care for the child."

Amelia searched the letter once more. "You don't think she meant for you to find a nurse or a neighbor to care for her while you were away at sea? But that you would care for her yourself as much as possible?"

He lowered his head. "She may have done. I don't know. But I've got a new commission—my ship sails on Friday. And I can't afford to keep our little place—not and pay a full-time nurse in the bargain." He looked up at her from beneath golden brows. "Speaking of expense. There has been quite a bit of late. What with the apothecary for Anne, new things for the babe, and the wet nurse I—"

Amelia interrupted, "Did Anne ask you to bring the child to me?"

He grimaced. "Not . . . exactly. Near the end she made me promise not to let the child suffer want. She said, 'My sister will take care of her, if worse comes to worst.'"

"I see," Amelia said dryly. "How long do you expect to leave her with me?"

He shifted from foot to foot, and rubbed the back of his neck. "Truth is, m'lady, with the war on, I don't know when or *if* I'll be back. And certainly not regular-like. I was hopin' you'd take her on permanently."

"Permanently? How permanent? Until you change your mind? Until the war is over? Until you remarry?"

His face slackened. "Hang me, m'lady. Whatever you think of me, I did love Anne. I've no thought of remarrying."

"And after the war?"

"*If* this war ever ends, I'll still be an officer. And that's if I make it home. War is deadly business. It would greatly ease my mind if I knew you would keep her. That she would be raised here. How could a man do better for his daughter?"

Was the child really *his* daughter, in spite of Anne's claim? Perhaps he was simply eager to be rid of the dancing master's child now that his unfaithful wife had died. Should she come out and ask him? Even though to do so would be to accuse him, or at least Anne, of lying? Amelia could see no definite resemblance to either man, though the child's coloring certainly resembled Tremelling's more than Desmond's. But the infant was Anne's as well, and so small. Amelia was not likely to see a resemblance to anyone for months or even years. And by then it would be too late. She would have lost her heart all over again.

Inhaling deeply, Amelia drew herself up. "If I am to raise her here and give her every advantage, as you suggest, then I should like to raise her as my own."

"Yes, m'lady. As I said."

"I mean, as my own daughter, in name and understanding."

He winced in confusion. "I'm not sure I follow."

"Surely you remember the scandal." Amelia hesitated, then forged ahead, "Or are you saying this *is* your child, even though Anne alleged otherwise?"

His face stiffened. "I'm not saying anything. I married your sister, and we planned to raise the girl as our own. That's all I'll say. But . . . does it matter, m'lady? Will it affect your decision?"

Would it? Amelia considered. If she did raise the child, would it not color her perception of the girl—bias her? Did she really want to know?

She exhaled, then replied, "No. But you understand that I would want to protect her from that scandal if I could."

"Meaning . . . she would grow up not knowing about Anne and me, thinking she was your natural daughter—yours and Mr. Midwinter's? But you've only been married, what . . . ?"

"Six months. We could keep her here in the manor until she is older. Some will know or at least guess she is not ours, though most won't question. And in time, people will forget. Accept."

"I shall never forget." He shifted the child to his other arm, and picked up his hat once more. "But if you think it best, I shan't object."

"I will need to speak to my husband, of course. Give me two days and return for my answer."

"Two days?"

"You said your ship did not sail until Friday, did you not?"

"Yes, but . . . Oh, very well. Of course you need to talk with your husband."

The child woke and began to chafe and complain in Tremelling's embrace. Amelia should have known right then, that there would be trouble ahead.

As soon as Lieutenant Tremelling took his leave that day, Amelia had instructed Barlow, then her coachman, to follow the man back to his lodgings in Plymouth.

Barlow returned the next day and reported seeing Tremelling enter a dilapidated inn and kiss a frowsy woman who looked none too pleased to see him return with squalling babe in arms.

It had settled things for Amelia. Though she had her doubts about her own maternal inexperience, doubts about her ability to love Anne's daughter, and doubts about Mr. Midwinter's ability to love anyone, she knew she would raise the child far better than Lieutenant Tremelling ever could. She would do her best. And prayed God . . . and the child . . . would forgive the rest.

Arthur Midwinter offered little protest. "If you feel you must take in your sister's child, I won't forbid you. Better than having you moping about in your rooms all day. Why do you want to give her the Midwinter name? Ah yes, the rumors about your sister and that caper merchant. Well, we might spark a few rumors of our own, having a child appear so soon after marrying, but I don't care for the good opinion of these rustics hereabouts. I can easily bear it if you can."

Amelia chose to ignore his insult about her neighbors. Instead she had thanked him with genuine gratitude. It was the closest thing to affection she had ever felt for the man.

When Lieutenant Tremelling returned two days later, she was ready for him.

"You'll take her?" he asked.

"Yes."

Clearly relieved, he had unloaded a small trunk containing the child's few things as well as Anne's belongings—including her locket, which he wanted the girl to have.

Then he asked, "What will you call her?"

"I have given that a great deal of thought," she began. "As I said, I would not be comfortable calling her Grace Amelia."

"What about just Grace, then?" he suggested. "That's what I call her. My Gracie girl."

Amelia hesitated at the affection in the man's voice, and a stitch of caution pricked her. "Are you certain you want to do this, Lieutenant? Decide now, for the girl's sake. Don't upset her life by coming back for her in a year or two. Nor mine."

"Of course not. I am not a clod, no matter what you and your family thought me." He inhaled and nodded decisively. "No. This is what's best for her. I see that. I won't change my mind."

Amelia said more gently, "If you do want to see her someday, I ask that you contact me first. That way I can prepare her for it. Explain. I would hate to see her shocked and upset. But promise me you won't ever come storming in or try to steal her away. That would be cruel indeed—very hard on us all."

"What kind of man do you think I am?"

A *selfish opportunist,* Amelia thought, but she refrained from saying so. Instead she asked, "Will you sign something to that effect? To protect her, you understand."

"If you like."

He looked at the paper she handed him, which a London solicitor had drawn up for her. He paused, looking up at Amelia in question. "Julia Midwinter?"

"Yes. Julia was our mother's name, Anne's and mine. I think Anne would approve. Do you object?"

"No, I suppose I don't. I'm just accustomed to calling her Grace." He grimaced. "But as I won't be here to call her by one name or another, I suppose it shouldn't matter. Hurts a bit though, I admit." He chewed his lip. "I can understand about Amelia. But could you not at least keep one of Anne's names for the girl, and call her Grace?"

The name struck her as wrong, and Amelia didn't want to agree. Grace. How hypocritical the name felt. That Anne should want to name this child, conceived out of wedlock, allegedly fathered by the man Amelia had loved. The man she thought loved *her*. The man who broke her heart, killed her brother, and abandoned them all? Grace?

"I would be willing to list Grace as her second name in the baptismal record, if you like. But we shall call her Julia."

"Thank you, m'lady. It means a great deal."

A body of Bryanites, a sect lately sprung up from amongst the Wesleyan Methodists, made their appearance at the time of the Cornish hurling contest, and attempted to put a stop to the diversion by commencing their devotional exercises. . . .

—*The West Briton,* 1823

Chapter 22

Alec looked around the academy in satisfaction. Thanks to the help of his mother, sister, and Desmond, the academy was ready for business. And just that day he'd hung the old sign: *Valcourt Dancing & Fencing Academy.*

He had decided to offer a grand opening dance, in which he and Aurora, along with James and Patience Allen, would demonstrate a country dance or two, then invite those watching to participate.

Alec went to see the nearest printer, in Holsworthy, and had notices printed, announcing the grand opening of the academy and offering his services for private lessons as well. *In for a penny, in for a pound.*

Mrs. Tickle had hung a notice in the bakery window and placed a stack on her counter, which pleased Alec greatly. She had even offered to donate an iced cake for the occasion.

Desmond would not attend—insisting his presence would hinder Alec's chances of success. He also confided that someone had paid a nighttime visit to the forge, and painted *Killer* on the wall. Apparently word of his return had begun to spread, despite his efforts.

Alec had yet to hear from Miss Midwinter one way or the other, but Sir Herbert had promised to be on hand, to lend visible support. He and Lady Allen also reiterated their offer to host a ball at Medlands, perhaps after Alec's first crop of students had learned an evening's worth of dances.

Alec began to dream of success, even while he reminded himself that with Lady Amelia remaining staunchly against dancing, Mr. Jones turning down his request to use his assembly room, and word of his own dismissal from Buckleigh Manor likely making the rounds, there was no guarantee any pupils would show. He thought he could at least count on the few families who had expressed interest during his initial round of calls.

He hoped.

༄

As soon as her mother sent the letter by messenger to Plymouth, Julia's nerves began to fray to thin, taut threads. Outwardly, she pretended not to care, insisting Lieutenant Tremelling would not come or that he would send a reluctant reply. Inwardly, of course, she hoped for an eager one—confirmation. Affirmation. Answers. She became moody and snappish—even more so than usual, as her mother was quick to point out. Julia paced the house like a caged animal, unwilling to leave for fear of missing Lieutenant Tremelling should he call, though she would never admit it.

She had planned to attend Mr. Valcourt's upcoming grand opening. But then Doyle gave her mistress a printed notice she'd picked up in the village. When Lady Amelia saw it, her mouth thinned to a hard line and she forbade Julia to attend, which only worsened her mood. The grey, rainy weather didn't help either. They were experiencing one of the wettest springs in recent memory, according to Barlow.

Easter arrived and Julia declined her mother's offers to visit the millinery for a new bonnet, or to take hot cross buns from Mrs. White's kitchen to their needy neighbors. Even attending divine services on that holiest of days did nothing to improve Julia's spirits.

The next morning, her mother declared she'd had enough. Julia had stewed about indoors too long. She told Julia to gather her bonnet, wrap, and gloves—they were going out.

Her mother had not forgotten about the deceitful call Julia had paid to Patience Allen's grandmother as a ruse to attend the ball in Holsworthy. As part of her daughter's penance, she decided, they would pay another, this time sincere, call.

‹⁄›

On the day after Easter, Alec returned to his academy to finalize preparations, carrying with him a potted plant. For the grand opening itself, Nancy from Posey's had offered an arrangement of hothouse flowers, which would brighten up the place even more. The High Street was unusually quiet, Alec noticed, and many of the shops were closed. Then he remembered why—proprietors and patrons alike had gone to watch the hurling match. Alec had heard men eagerly discussing it after church the day before. Alec would have liked to see the match as well, but instead placed the plant in the bow window and set to work.

A short while later, Desmond knocked on the academy door. Alec glanced at his watch, surprised Desmond would stop by during the daytime. He usually avoided doing so. Alec opened the door and instantly noticed the tension in his friend's face.

"There's going to be trouble," he said. "The Bible Christians are marching down the road as we speak—they plan to protest the hurling match."

"The Bryanites?" Alec asked.

Desmond nodded. "Your friends the Thornes are among them. Someone's bound to get hurt."

Alec grabbed his coat and tugged it on. "What can we do?"

Desmond grimly shook his head. "I don't know. But we can't sit by and do nothing."

❧

Carrying a basket for Mrs. Hearn—with another jar of rose hip jam and a quartern loaf of bread—Julia sullenly followed her mother out to the carriage, and they were soon on their way. They passed through Beaworthy, then turned west, following the road out of town.

Suddenly the carriage lurched to a halt. Julia heard voices, loud shouts, and a curse from Isaacs, the coachman. Her mother drew back the window curtain and Julia followed suit, looking out with mild trepidation. Had Isaacs driven them into the middle of a strike or bread riot?

The road bordered an open field. A crowd had gathered along the verge, overflowing onto the road itself. People jostled to see over those in front of them. Children sat on men's shoulders. From their relatively higher vantage in the carriage, Julia could see over most of the crowd into the field beyond. Wooden posts had been planted in either end as makeshift goals. Muddied men fought for possession of a small ball. Half the men were dressed in formerly white shirts, now mud-grey. The others were stripped to the waist.

As Julia watched, the men separated into sides. Standing between the two teams, a man in black threw the ball into the air. With a roar, the men all surged forward, shoving violently at their opponents in pursuit of the ball.

A man in stained white caught the ball and was quickly grabbed around the midsection by a member of the opposing team. The first man let the ball fall, but a teammate picked up the ball and ran with it, butting opponents with an outstretched fist as he ran. About to be tackled, he tossed the ball sideways toward another teammate, but before that man could catch it, he was set upon by a hairy, shirtless man, like a wolf upon a lamb.

To Julia, the shouts and grunts and surging men seemed like a scene from battle, foot soldiers engaged in hand-to-hand combat.

"It's a hurling match," Lady Amelia said. "In-hurling, I believe. Graham used to sneak off to play."

Julia gestured emphatically toward the window at the scene beyond. "You denounce dancing as dangerous and immoral, but *this* is acceptable behavior?"

"It's an old West Country tradition. Like wrestling."

"It's uncivilized."

Judging by the rapt fervor of the cheering crowd, Julia was alone in her opinion. Or was she?

From across the field came a cluster of people in Sunday best—women in dark frocks and bonnets, and men in black coats and snowy neckcloths. Their voices preceded them across the field. These people were not cheering. They were singing.

> "Jesu's tremendous name
> Puts all our foes to flight. . . ."

As the group of a dozen or more neared, Julia recognized the Thornes among them. These then were Bryanites.

The supposed "ranters" marched onto the playing field, voices raised on the final words of the hymn.

> ". . . and conquering them,
> through Jesu's blood,
> We still to conquer go."

For several moments the players unclenched their holds on their opponents, or paused where they were, staring dumbfounded at the odd collection of men and women, young and old, singing reverently amidst their game.

"A strange place for devotional exercises," her mother observed.

"They're trying to stop the match," Julia said.

The singing trailed away, and Mr. Thorne stepped forward. His powerful baritone voice boomed across the field, over the murmuring crowd, and into the Buckleigh carriage.

"Stop this riotous display, brothers. Have we not just celebrated the resurrection of our Lord? The great John Wesley, God rest his soul, spoke against the violence of wrestling and hurling. And of their insidious power to turn our hearts and minds from what we ought be devoting our time—the worship and service of our great God."

The crowd's murmurings increased, but Mr. Thorne spoke louder. "He is a God of love and peace, yes. But He is also a God of judgment. Turn, my brothers. Leave behind worldly diversions for that which truly satisfies, for that which eternally saves."

The onlookers began to grumble and complain of the delay of the game. A few shouts of "Go home" and "Leave off" rose in vexation. One of the players took advantage of the stupefied inattention of his opponent to swipe the ball from his grasp.

"Hey!"

And just that quickly, the game surged back to life. The players leapt for the ball en masse, knocking down a young Bryanite as they did so. During the pileup, the ball squirted loose. The writhing mound dove in the other direction, taking down two others who had rushed forward to stand in front of the women.

Ben Thorne, leaping to shield his sister, was knocked from his feet as well. Julia gasped.

From out of the crowd, two dark-haired men ran—John Desmond and Alec Valcourt. Julia pressed a hand to her mouth. They ran across the field, dodged players, and tried to help the fallen victims to their feet before they were trampled further.

Without consciously deciding to do so, Julia threw open the carriage door and leapt out. Ignoring her mother's cries of alarm, she ran across the field. Had she not stopped the Wilcox brothers singlehandedly when they'd harassed Tess Thorne? If she could handle two champion wrestlers on her own, certainly she could help now. The players wouldn't dare touch her. Righteous indignation swelled in her breast that these overgrown schoolboys would trample peaceable men and women in their heedless wake.

Reaching the mass of players, she raised her arms and shouted, "Cease this instant!"

But blinded by competitive fervor, the rushing pack didn't recognize her. She realized with sudden panic that they didn't even really see her, for all her waving of arms. Her demands fell on deaf ears.

The blow struck so unexpectedly, she didn't even see who collided with her before she was knocked breathless and thudded to the ground. *Jesus, help me.*

The rushing men in crushing boots charged at her like bulls with sharp hooves. Julia winced and braced for impact.

Suddenly she was lifted up and whirled out of harm's way by a pair of strong arms. She opened her eyes, and saw the grim-set face of John Desmond, carrying her across the field. Relief and gratitude flooded her. She glanced back over his shoulder and saw Miss Thorne in Alec Valcourt's arms, while Ben Thorne draped an older man's arm around his neck and helped him limp from the field.

A part of Julia was disappointed that she was not the one in Mr. Valcourt's arms, that he had once again rescued pretty Tess Thorne. But another part of her was deeply moved to be held by a man whose feelings for her were purely paternal.

Amelia had watched in horror as her reckless, impetuous daughter leapt from the carriage. She'd reached out to try and stop her, but her fingertips brushed muslin and lace and could not gain hold. It was just as in her dreams, when Amelia couldn't reach Graham in time to save him.

"Julia!" she'd cried. But she was gone. Her brave avenger of wrongs. This time she would get herself killed.

"Isaacs—stop her!" Amelia shouted, rising and tripping over her long gown. The coachman clambered down none too nimbly and was soon lost in the surging crowd.

Amelia untangled her skirts and braced herself in the open carriage door. She focused on Julia amidst the players, until she was suddenly knocked off her feet. Amelia cried out and prepared to jump, but when she glanced up, what she saw filled her with relief and a dizzying sense of unreality.

John Desmond held Julia, her Julia, in his arms. He carried her daughter toward the carriage—to safety, to her. In an unworldly, dream-like moment, Amelia saw three paths split before her like the tines of a fork. In one, she rushed to them, demanded he set her daughter down, and scolded Julia. In the second, she rushed to them, threw her arms around them both, and thanked him profusely. In the third, she some-how changed places—and was herself held in his arms. Amelia squeezed her eyes shut and felt herself sway. She was clearly not well. The shock. The fear.

She sat back heavily onto the carriage seat, and when she opened her eyes a moment later, John Desmond stood before the carriage, her daughter in his arms like an offering.

She swallowed her pride and started to thank him, but Julia began talking, and her opportunity was lost.

"You may put me down, Mr. Desmond," Julia insisted. "I am not hurt."

He set her down none too gently, eyes flashing. "You might have been worse than hurt—you might have been killed. What were you thinking, rushing into the mob like that?"

Julia's eyes brightened with tears. "I only wanted to help."

Defensiveness rose in Amelia. How strange to hear this man pre-suming to reprimand her daughter.

But before she could protest, he inhaled through flared nostrils, clearly struggling to control his temper. Amelia remembered that look. How many times Anne had provoked it.

"I'm sorry, lass," he said. "I don't mean to scold. But you gave me a devilish scare. And your mother as well, no doubt."

The two of them looked at her through the open carriage door. Amelia found herself uncharacteristically tongue-tied.

She faltered, "I . . . I am just glad you are safe."

She braved a look into John Desmond's face and forced out words she could never have imagined saying to him again. "Thank you."

They were the first kind words she had spoken to the man in twenty years.

Suddenly a man she recognized as the innkeeper grabbed John Desmond's arm.

"Better get out of here before the match ends, Johnny. Ya don't want this lot to lay eyes on ya—not while they're all worked up."

Mr. Desmond glanced around at the people nearby. Amelia followed his gaze. Most spectators watched the match with rapt attention, but two men she didn't know stared at Desmond with narrowed eyes. One elbowed a companion, and he turned and scowled as well.

John Desmond smiled wryly at the innkeeper. "Thank you, Mr. Jones. I was just leaving."

Every savage can dance.

—Jane Austen's Mr. Darcy,
Pride and Prejudice

Chapter 23

The night before the grand opening, Alec slept fitfully, dreaming all sorts of tedious, disconcerting dreams: He came prepared with dances for eight couples, but only two showed. He tried to play the fiddle while he taught, but the fiddle had only one string. Mrs. Tickle's cake with its purplish icing was tiny, and the resulting slices were embarrassingly minuscule. He could not remember a single step. . . .

It was a relief to awaken and realize he had merely been dreaming. *I am prepared,* he told himself. Even if he made a few mistakes, the day could not be half as bad as the dreams.

He washed and dressed with care in his dark blue coat, light breeches, and patterned waistcoat. He carefully tied his cravat in an elegant mail-coach knot and then pulled on his highly polished shoes.

He picked up his grandfather's walking stick, used to mark the tempo for the last three decades, and once again today. He kissed his mother's cheek, asked his sister to arrive by ten, waved off breakfast, and shook his uncle's hand.

"My boy, I know how hard you've worked," Cornelius Ramsay

began. "And I wish you every success, I really do. Remember that if nobody comes, it is more Beaworthy's fault than your own. Old ways die hard."

Alec reminded himself his uncle meant well and warmly thanked him.

Alec left the house, strolled into the village, and crossed the High Street with a decided spring in his step. Today was the day. The Valcourt Dancing and Fencing Academy, defunct in London, was about to be reborn in Beaworthy.

He could do this.

When he looked ahead and saw the cluster of people standing outside the academy door, his heart gave a little leap. A crowd, at this hour? Had they misread the notice, or were they so eager?

He quickened his step. But as he neared, doubts flashed like fireworks over London's St. James's Park. All men? And unlikely suspects for dance lessons. Mr. Jones; Mr. Gilbert, the tailor; Mr. Vanstone; Mr. Lug, the lamplighter; Joe Wilcox; and Uncle Ramsay's younger clerk . . .

Why had the word *suspects* come to him? The men's expressions were a mixture of headshaking grimace and knowing smirk. These were not prospective pupils. What were they looking at?

Mr. Jones saw him hurrying up the street, and nodded in his direction, drawing everyone's attention to his approach.

The other men stepped back to allow him to pass.

"Sorry, Valcourt," Jones muttered. "Afraid something like this would happen."

Something like what? Alec's stomach clenched. His heart followed suit.

Then he saw.

The academy door had been kicked in. Several panes of window glass smashed. Draperies slashed. Glass lay like hail on the newly refinished floor, now scuffed and soiled. The mirror—the big, beautiful, *expensive* mirror—had been cracked. Dirt, muddy water, and torn plants were strewn over the room like a flower shop after a storm. Or a graveyard.

Disbelief, anger, and grief shuddered through him in waves. He felt as if someone had died—or something. His dream. Gone. And the last of his savings with it.

Even the cake Mrs. Tickle donated had been taken—leaving behind only a telltale smudge of puce-colored icing.

Who had done it? Why?

Mr. Jones stepped inside, crunching over broken glass. "Warned ya folks don't take kindly to dancing round here."

"Which folks? Who did this?"

The man avoided his gaze.

Alec pushed. "You didn't see anyone? Hear anything?"

Mr. Jones shook his head, yet a wary gleam in his eye told Alec the innkeeper may have seen someone, or at least had his suspicions, but wasn't about to say so and risk a similar visit to his own establishment.

That afternoon, Julia stepped gingerly over the broken glass, stunned by the cruel vandalism. Alec Valcourt and John Desmond stood in the corner, discussing what to do first—board up the broken windows, or sweep up the glass before someone got hurt.

Julia shook her head, sickened. "If my mother did this, I shall never forgive her."

Alec looked up from the debris to frown at her. "Do you really think a lady like her would stoop so low?"

His look, his words chastised her. Yet she stubbornly lifted her chin. "I don't say she did it herself. But it would be the work of a moment to send someone. Or simply to hint to a tenant or a servant that something like this should be done—to send a message."

Mr. Desmond shook his head. "I would never believe it of her."

"Then who?" Julia challenged.

"Unfortunately," Alec replied, "I can think of two possibilities."

He squatted to his haunches and picked up a jagged chunk of clay brick, which had apparently been thrown through the window.

"China clay," he observed and tossed it aside.

Julia stared. "You think the Wilcox brothers did this?"

"Probably, though I can't prove it."

Mr. Desmond, she vaguely noticed, disappeared into the back room, likely to give them a moment alone.

Alec rose and laid a reassuring hand on hers. "Don't fret, Julia. My uncle—others—warned me something like this might happen."

"But . . . all your work. Your grand opening . . ." Her words trailed bleakly away.

He sighed. "I know. And I am deeply disappointed, of course. But at least no one was hurt, and eventually, perhaps, I might try again."

He did not sound very confident. Why should he be, if he assumed the vandals would simply strike again?

"What has the constable said?" she asked.

"Mr. Lamont is sorry, but there is nothing he can do."

I'll kill them, Julia thought. Well, not actually kill them, though she would give the Wilcox brothers a setdown they would never forget.

Alec must have seen the look in her eye, for he slowly shook his head. "Julia . . . don't. Don't confront them. And certainly not alone. Don't put yourself in harm's way. It's not worth it."

"Yes, it i—"

"No," he said fervently, pressing her shoulders with both hands. "You—your safety and well-being—are far more important to me than any dancing academy."

Alec's words, his touch, warmed Julia deeply.

Soon after, Julia returned to Buckleigh Manor, planning to change into clothes more suited for clean-up work, and to request Barlow's help in putting Mr. Valcourt's academy back in order. But first she was determined to confront her mother.

Julia found her in the library as usual, writing letters. She looked up at her approach and set her quill back into its holder.

Watching the woman's face carefully, Julia said, "Tell me you had nothing to do with what happened at Mr. Valcourt's academy."

Her mother looked at her blankly. "What happened?"

Her reaction, her question, seemed genuine enough.

"Someone broke in, smashed windows, broke the mirror, chairs . . ."

"Did they indeed . . . ?" Her lower lip protruded.

As though she were impressed? *Heaven help me,* Julia thought, struggling to control her temper and her tongue.

"You don't look very sorry to hear it," Julia said. "Or surprised."

"I am not surprised."

Julia gaped. "Why? Because you—"

"Because I expected something like this might happen," she interrupted. "It is one of the reasons I didn't want you there."

Julia said, "I know you think you have cause to despise Mr. Valcourt as well as Mr. Desmond, who owns the property, but—"

"True."

"What?"

Her mother held up her hand. "Julia, I had nothing to do with any vandalism in the High Street. How could you even think such a thing? Do you know me so little?"

Julia hadn't really believed it, yet she was relieved to hear it from her own lips.

"I certainly don't approve of Mr. Valcourt's profession," she added. "But I approve far less of destruction of personal property."

"But you are glad it happened, are you not? I suppose you see it as a sort of poetic justice—fate righting wrongs. Or God's judgment on dancing masters everywhere."

"I won't lie and say the thought didn't briefly cross my mind, but no, I don't think God had anything to do with this. I doubt He assigns vandals the lofty roles of fate or justice."

After dinner that evening, the maid helped Julia change into more appropriate attire: a day dress, apron, and gardening gloves. Julia found Barlow and asked him to join her, but his face sagged in regret.

"I am sorry for Mr. Valcourt, of course. But my loyalties lie with her ladyship."

For once Julia was not able to persuade the man to do what she wanted.

As twilight fell, she slipped from the house alone and walked into the village, planning to join the clean-up work in progress there.

Julia had meant to heed Mr. Valcourt's warning and stay away from the Wilcox brothers. But when she saw Felton Wilcox, lounging against a column of the deserted market hall, her anger boiled, and she could not let the injustice stand unchallenged.

She stalked over to him. "You did it, didn't you."

A self-satisfied grin was his only reply.

She longed to slap the grin from his face but resisted. "Why? What has Mr. Valcourt ever done to you?"

He shrugged. "Don't like outsiders comin' in here, thinkin' they're better than us and changin' things."

She shook her head. "But to jeopardize a man's livelihood? I would have thought you'd have some respect for that, if for nothing else."

Felton's eyes flashed a warning, but Julia plowed ahead.

"Some champion you are. This is low—even for you."

He grabbed her chin. Hard. "Watch it, miss. For I can do far worse . . . to him and to you if you push me. Don't think I won't."

Fear shot through Julia. She should have listened to Alec. She forced herself to meet the man's searing glare.

From the shadowy recesses of the market stalls, his brother, Joe, lurched forward.

"Felton? What are you doing?" he asked, his voice quiet but strained. "That is Miss Midwinter. From the great house. I don't think we ought to, uh, bother her."

Felton frowned. "Then she shouldn'ta struck me with that whip of hers. Or stuck her nose where it don't belong."

"Let her go," someone called.

Alec's voice. Relief swept over her.

Felton turned his head, but kept his stinging grip on her chin. "Well, well. If it ain't the pretty caper merchant. Has the mincing dance-man come to save the fair lady?"

She glanced over and saw the fire in Alec's eyes, heard the steel in his voice when he said, "Unhand her. Now."

Oh Alec, Julia thought, *be careful.* She feared he would end as damaged as his academy, and that she could not bear.

"Or what?" Felton scoffed. "Will you dance me to death? Give me a good waltzing? Egad, I'm shaking in my boots."

Alec began stripping off his coat. "That's not what I had in mind, no."

Joe Wilcox stepped to his brother's side, adopting a ready stance—knees bent.

Alec snorted. "Two against one, is it? Very well."

Ben Thorne crossed the High Street. "Alec? Is, um, everything all right?" Ben looked over and saw her in Felton's grip. His face went rigid. "What are you doing, Felton? Let her go!"

"You're just in time, Ben," Alec said. "Set this aside for me, will you?" He tossed the young man his coat, and pushed back his sleeves, exposing muscled forearms.

With a nervous swallow, Mr. Thorne laid the coat over a nearby stall.

Joe Wilcox gestured in Ben's direction. "That's yer idea of evening the numbers? Pummelin' that pole bean won't be any fun. Them ranters has to turn the other cheek and can't hit back."

"But I can," Walter Allen said, stepping in front of Ben.

Thank you, God, Julia thought. How fortunate that these loyal friends were on hand—no doubt helping Alec restore his academy. Walter, tall and brawny, gave the two Wilcoxes pause. The Allens were a leading family, well known and well connected for all their secluded ways. Julia guessed Felton Wilcox wouldn't want his "secret" crime becoming widely known.

Felton formed an unconvincing smile. "Mr. Allen, isn't it?"

"Yes, Mr. Wilcox. Walter Allen of Medlands. And when you bother my friends here, you bother me."

"And me," Mr. Desmond said, stepping onto the adjacent green and into the fray.

Joe Wilcox scowled and stepped forward menacingly. "Well, if it ain't the coward who pulled a gun on us. Where's your gun now?"

In a low voice, Desmond replied, "I won't be needing it." He glanced meaningfully down at his sheathed sword, eyes glinting.

"Good to see you, Desmond," Alec called over to him, not removing his gaze from the Wilcox brothers.

"Desmond? John Desmond?" Felton said, looking disconcerted now.

"From the forge?" Joe asked. "Isn't he the fellow what killed Graham Buckleigh years ago?"

"The same," Desmond acknowledged.

"I heard you were back," Felton said. "But I didn't believe it."

"Believe it." Desmond then nodded toward Julia. "Mr. Valcourt asked you to release Miss Midwinter. Now, are you going to comply, or shall I find some way to encourage you?" He lifted his hand nearer the sword hilt. The scabbard glinted in the light of a nearby streetlamp.

Felton roughly released Julia's chin, thrusting her from him. "With pleasure. The jade's a nuisance, as everyone knows."

Desmond's jaw clenched. Mr. Valcourt, she noticed, fisted his hands.

Felton lifted his palms. "I don't wish to fight, not with Mr. Allen here. Out of respect for his . . . lovely sister."

Julia gasped. If he dared come anywhere near her sweet friend!

Walter narrowed his eyes and took a step forward.

Alec said to Felton, "Perhaps your *little* brother might chat with my friends here, and leave you and me to settle matters between us on our own?"

Joe shook his head. "I ain't goin' nowhere."

Alec grasped Desmond's sword and lunged forward, but Desmond gripped his arm.

"Don't," he hissed. "Take it from me—it's not worth it."

Without removing his focus from Felton, Mr. Valcourt said in a low, terse voice, "Ben, escort Miss Midwinter home safely, please."

Ben looked about to object but, seeing Alec's rigid jaw, apparently thought the better of doing so. He walked forward, gently but firmly took Julia's arm, and led her away.

Alec waited until Ben and Julia were a safe distance away. Around him, the men stood—tense—looking from one to the other, awaiting Alec's cue, or to see who would make the first move. Alec was torn, longing to strike back even as his conscience told him Desmond was right.

Suddenly Mrs. Tickle came marching across the street. "What is the meaning of this? What are you boys doing?"

Everyone froze. Apparently even the Wilcox brothers were hesitant to fight in front of a woman—or at least, this particular woman.

As Mrs. Tickle neared, her gaze snagged on Joe's arm. "Joe Wilcox!" she scolded. "Is that puce icing on your sleeve?"

Joe's mouth fell open. He lifted his wrist and blinked at the stain there. "I . . . don't think so. . . ."

"Well, I do. That's the icing from the cake I made for Mr. Valcourt. I was trying for a nice lavender color, but it went off to a brownish-purple. Very unusual, Joe. Very telling."

"I . . . don't know what you mean."

"It means you took my cake. And likely helped your brother here vandalize Mr. Valcourt's academy. What have you got to say for yourself?"

"It wasn't my i—"

"Shut up, Joe," Felton snapped. "Don't let 'er fluster you."

"I'll do more than fluster you," she said. "I'll refuse to serve you in my bakery."

Joe blanched. "But, Mrs. Tickle . . . you wouldn't. I'm yer best customer, you always said."

"Not after this."

Nearby, the door to the public house opened. The constable, Mr. Lamont, strode reluctantly across the cobbles toward them. "What's going on here?"

Felton gestured toward Alec. "This man pulled a sword on us for no reason. I could take the lot of 'em, of course. But now you're here, I won't have to."

"Mr. Lamont, you are just in time." Mrs. Tickle propped a pudgy fist on her hip. "Felton and Joe here have some explaining to do. Joe has icing on his sleeve from the cake stolen from Mr. Valcourt's. It doesn't take a genius to put one and one together and figure out these two were behind the vandalism last night."

The constable rocked back on his heels. "Is that so?"

Felton shrugged, unconcerned. "Can't prove it. Besides, why are you harassing us?" He nodded toward the others. "Valcourt's threatening us with a weapon. And John Desmond's a killer. You ought to be arresting them and leave us champions in peace."

Lamont jerked a thumb toward the public house. "From where I was sitting, it almost looked like you were threatening Miss Midwinter, of all people."

If he saw that, why on earth did he not come out sooner? Alec wondered.

Lamont added, "Or were my eyes playing tricks on me?"

"That's right." Felton nodded. "You were seein' things, George."

Joe began to sweat. "I told Felton not to bother her. She—"

"Hush, Joe," his brother interrupted. "Ol' George here is just flexin' his flabby muscles. He won't forget who we are."

"No, I won't forget," the constable said. "In fact, I shall be keeping my eye on you from now on. Off with you now—unless you'd like to go and see the magistrate directly?"

Joe tugged his brother's arm. "Come on, Felton," he pleaded. "Let's go."

Felton hesitated, then shrugged off his brother's hand. "Fine. We were about to leave anyway." He pinned Alec with a malevolent glare. "But this ain't over, Valcourt. You mark my word."

Mrs. Washington and myself have been honored with your polite invitation to the assemblies. . . . But, alas! our dancing days are no more.

—George Washington, 1799

Chapter 24

The next day, Julia returned from Mr. Ramsay's house and handed her wet umbrella to Hutchings.

Lady Amelia stepped from the library into the hall. "Where have you been?" she asked.

"Attempting to help Mrs. and Miss Valcourt sew new draperies for the academy—the others were slashed and trampled beyond repair. I wish there was more I could do. I feel so helpless." She followed her mother into the library, removing her bonnet and gloves as she went.

Lady Amelia stood at the wall of windows, her head tilted to one side as she often did when thinking. "How is Mr. Valcourt taking the setback?"

"He puts on a brave front, but I can see he is discouraged," Julia replied. "His mother and sister are upset as well. His pain is theirs. They wanted so much for him to succeed."

"That speaks well of their family loyalty."

"Can you not do something to help him?" Julia asked.

"Help Mr. Valcourt?" Lady Amelia shook her head. "I am sorry for him. But it isn't my role to come to his aid."

"Why not?" Julia snapped. "You help everyone else in the parish."

Her mother turned to face her. "Julia, I wouldn't want to encourage Mr. Valcourt, either in his profession or in his relationship with you. You know I've never approved of your spending time in his company. Your behavior has certainly suffered since you met him—lying, dancing, leaving the house at night without a chaperone, or even my knowledge. . . . No, I cannot help but conclude he has been a bad influence. And I will have nothing to do with him or his academy."

Incensed, Julia threw caution to the wind. "I cannot stand to hear you blame Mr. Valcourt for all our problems, *Mother*. I had been sneaking out alone and flirting with men long before he came to town. Mr. Valcourt has made me see what a gentleman really is. And how it feels to be treated, respected as a true lady, in every sense of that word. If you had seen how I flirted with him, and all but begged him to kiss me on several occasions. Yet he resisted my many offers." *Well, all but one,* she silently amended.

Lady Amelia weakly shook her head. "I don't believe it. You are only saying this to try to make me change my mind about him."

Julia huffed. "Fine. Continue blaming Mr. Valcourt. He has made a convenient scapegoat."

Lady Amelia frowned suddenly and leaned closer. "What's happened to your chin? Is that a bruise?"

Julia gingerly touched her chin, still tender from Felton Wilcox's grip the day before. She had meant to powder it but had forgotten to do so. "Mr. Valcourt came to *my* aid last night, or I should have much worse than a bruised chin."

"What do you mean? Who dared touch you?"

"The same man who vandalized Mr. Valcourt's academy," Julia said, bristling. "Not that you'd care about that."

After Julia had left in a pique, Amelia retreated to her room, feeling nauseated. Her daughter had been sneaking out alone . . . flirting . . . offering kisses? Thankfully it hadn't gone further than that. She hoped. And now . . . confronting dangerous men as well?

When Amelia thought back, she was forced to admit that Julia had been acting rashly and pushing the boundaries of propriety—and her patience—long before the Valcourts arrived in Beaworthy. She had been fooling herself to think otherwise, to try to cast blame elsewhere when it belonged solely, soundly, with her.

Kneeling beside her bed, Amelia beseeched God for forgiveness, for wisdom to guide her daughter and to show her how much she was loved and valued.

❦

On Saturday the twelfth of April, Amelia met with the housekeeper first thing in the morning, including Julia in the staff meetings as usual. Amelia informed the woman they were expecting a possible caller to be arriving between three and five that afternoon and asked her to have tea, a light meal, and a cake ready.

When the housekeeper had taken her leave, Julia lifted her chin. "I don't know why you bother, Mother. He won't come."

Amelia had noticed that Julia had begun addressing her with a cold, formal *Mother* instead of her usual *Mamma*. It stung, but she made no comment.

Julia waved dismissively. "Ah well, the servants shall enjoy the cake."

Amelia knew her daughter well enough to realize she was trying to protect herself from disappointment in the event Lieutenant Tremelling did not come. But she also noticed the extra care Julia had taken with her appearance. She wore a modest, pretty gown of her favorite color—a morning-glory blue that flattered her complexion, brought out the blue in her changeable eyes and the gold in her honey-colored hair. And Doyle had confided that Julia had agreed to the hot iron, and endured the tedious hair dressing without a word of complaint. Unusual indeed.

At five minutes before three, Amelia and Julia rose by silent agreement and crossed the hall to the drawing room. Julia sat on the settee across from Amelia's armchair. She affected a casual posture and feigned interest in a novel, but Amelia noticed she failed to turn its pages, and her eyes often strayed to the mantel clock.

Amelia was nervous as well, though she tried not to show it. For her own sake, she hoped the man would not come—would never come—and never take Julia from her. But for Julia's sake she wished he would appear any second and show an interest in the vulnerable girl, whether related by blood or not.

Three came and went. Then a quarter past. Then half past three.

"I knew he would not come," Julia said flippantly. "Did I not tell you?"

"Perhaps he has been unavoidably delayed, my dear. Let us wait a bit longer."

Four. Half past four.

When the clock struck five, Julia tossed aside her book and stalked from the room. Amelia might have chastised her, but she'd seen the sheen of tears in her eyes, and knew Julia fled in hopes she would not notice.

With a sigh and a prayer for wisdom, Amelia slowly rose and followed Julia upstairs to her bedchamber. There she knocked, steeling herself for a harsh refusal. When Julia made no reply, Amelia slowly opened the door.

Inside, Julia lay across her bed, that old mermaid in her hand, crying into her pillow. Amelia's heart twisted. She had not seen her daughter display such grief in years—anger, yes, but not sadness. It reminded her of the long-ago incident with the rouge. Would Julia push her away as she had then?

She gingerly approached the bed and said in her gentlest voice, "Remember, my dear, Lieutenant Tremelling is a naval officer. Perhaps he is away at sea." She smoothed a lock of hair from her daughter's temple, surprised Julia didn't jerk away.

"The war is over" came Julia's muffled retort.

"True," Amelia said. "But perhaps he has been taxed with patrol duty or is away on some other Royal Navy business. In our letter, we *did* say if the twelfth wasn't convenient, he was welcome to come another time. No doubt that is what he plans to do—come as soon as he is able."

Amelia was lying.

At the last minute, she had dispatched Barlow to follow the hired messenger to Plymouth—to verify the messenger located the lieutenant and delivered the sensitive letter into his hands. She had asked Barlow to be discreet, not to allow Tremelling to see him. She knew Julia wanted the man to come of his own volition, without undue persuasion, because he *wanted* to see her.

Upon his return, Barlow had reported that he'd stood at a discreet distance while the messenger knocked at a lodging house not far from the docks. He had seen Tremelling answer the door, half dressed and in need of a shave, though it was nearly noon. The young man had handed over the letter, then waited for him to read it. Tremelling had offered the messenger a coin but no reply.

So Amelia knew very well Lieutenant Tremelling was not away at sea.

Though usually a stridently honest person, she found the lie slipping easily from her tongue. She wished the words were true. She longed to protect Julia, as she had failed to protect others she had loved.

She found herself remembering Mrs. Valcourt's falsehood— allowing people to believe her husband dead, for her sake, yes, but for her children's sake as well. How judgmental Amelia had been.

Seeing her disappointed child now, Amelia's heart ached, and she wished she'd asked Barlow to extract a promise from the man, or to drag him back by the ear.

But then Amelia wondered if she judged Lieutenant Tremelling too harshly. Perhaps he had been stunned by the letter, intimidated to meet the girl he left behind all those years ago. After all, Julia was his wife's child, whether she was his daughter or not. If so, she would not blame him for nerves. But a military man should find the courage, even if it took a few days to muster.

Perhaps he really had been called to duty after he received their letter, and was unable to come. But if so, could he not have written to tell them? Surely for Julia's sake, he could have eked out a few lines in reply.

He had written before, after all, to keep them informed of his various changes in direction so they could send money. Amelia thought of the last reply she had sent, before Julia asked her to invite Tremelling to call. Was he now reluctant to come because of what she had previously written? Was it her fault he stayed away?

All the following week, it tore at Amelia's heart to see Julia's eager gaze follow the silver tray upon which Hutchings carried in the day's post.

Nothing.

◦

Needing time away from his repairs and worries, and from his family's long faces, Alec decided to take a walk and enjoy the sunny day, rare amid all the rain they'd been having. He strolled into the countryside, then veered from the road along the woods, recalling seeing Miss Midwinter there his first Sunday in Beaworthy.

As he walked along the stream, he saw that very woman in the distance, standing on the bank. His foolish heart banged against his chest at the mere sight of her.

Julia looked at something in her hand, then reeled back and tossed it away in a long arc. It glinted in the sunlight, then splashed into the water downstream.

He quickened his pace to join her. As he neared, he saw the hard lines of her face suddenly crumple. She ran downstream and jumped onto a rock jutting above the current, then to another farther out.

"Miss Midwinter!" he called and jogged to the bank. "Are you all right?"

"I've lost something." She bent toward the water, searching.

Lost? "What is it? Can I help you find it?"

"Yes, please. It's a mermaid. On a chain."

"A mermaid? What color is it?"

"It's made of brass, I think."

Tears glistened in her eyes and her chin trembled. For some reason the mermaid was important to her. He wondered why she had thrown it in the first place but did not ask. Gauging where he'd seen the splash, Alec jumped nimbly onto a rock a little farther downstream, then to the next, searching the shallow water.

He glanced over at her and saw her face pinched in grief. "We'll never find it. How stupid of me. I was just so . . . so . . ."

The shiny glint of metal caught his eye—well beyond his perch. With a resigned look at his boots, Alec stepped into the calf-high water.

"Do you see something?" she called eagerly.

Not wanting to raise her hopes, he said, "Not sure." He leaned low, raking his fingers through the water, and snagged the object—an antiquated figurine on a slender metallic tube. It looked like a whistle to him. He gave an experimental blow, and a gurgling shrill pierced the air.

Her face brightened. "You found it!"

She splashed over to him and carefully grasped the offered mermaid by its chain. "Oh, thank you!" She beamed, then rose on her toes to kiss his cheek.

Alec took a deep breath, relishing the sweet gesture and the sweet satisfaction of coming to her rescue.

He helped her from the stream and walked her back toward Buckleigh Manor, both of them wet from the knees down.

She dangled the mermaid whistle from its chain. "This was a gift from my father," she began. "I've always thought that meant Mr. Midwinter, but recently I learned Lieutenant Tremelling sent it."

"Ah." Alec nodded his understanding. "Then I am glad we were able to find it."

She sent him a sidelong glance. "You may be shocked to learn that for a time I thought our friend John Desmond might be my father."

"Oh?" Alec looked at her, unsure what to say or how much she knew.

"I learned he was accused of seducing Lady Anne," she continued. "Sparking the infamous May Day duel and his departure. Everyone believed him guilty, apparently. Except for his parents."

"But you don't?"

She shook her head. "He told me he is not my father."

"You asked him?"

"I did. I wish . . ."

"Wish what?"

She sighed. "Oh, never mind. At least we know now why Lady Amelia is so set against dancing masters."

They reached the Buckleigh Manor gate and paused before it. She turned to him and said, "Well, thank you for coming to my rescue. I had better go and change out of these wet things."

"Me too. And how will you explain your soggy frock?"

"I shall just say I went fishing, and caught . . . a mermaid." She winked at him, then turned and passed beneath the gate.

Alec looked up, the lion above warning him that he had gone far enough.

❦

Alec knew what was coming and braced himself. He had been asked to dinner at Medlands, yet he knew Sir Herbert had another reason for wanting to see him and speak with him privately. But first the man coddled him with a good dinner and good conversation, in an attempt to cushion the coming disappointment.

After dinner, the ladies rose and withdrew to leave the men to their port and pipe.

Alec partook of neither but waited while Sir Herbert lit his pipe and poured himself, James, and Walter a small glass. He pulled the pipe from his lips and fiddled with the stem. "I am sorry, Mr. Valcourt. But in light of what has befallen your academy, I cannot in good conscience proceed with plans for a ball here. I cannot invite destruction to dear Medlands. Nor subject my wife and daughter to danger."

Walter protested, "But, Papa, we—!"

Alec laid a hand on his friend's forearm. "No, Walter. It's all right." He met the older man's troubled gaze. "I understand perfectly, sir. And I could never live with myself if any harm were to come to your home or family."

Sir Herbert nodded in evident relief.

"But it isn't right to give in to a few bullies," Walter insisted.

James smiled at his brother. "And what would you have us do, Walt? Challenge them both to a duel?"

"That is no joking matter, James," Sir Herbert gently chided, all of them thinking of Graham Buckleigh, no doubt.

"There must be something we can do," Walter said, face screwed up in thought.

"Don't hurt yourself, there, Walt," James teased.

But for once Walter did not smile at his brother's teasing. "No, James. It isn't right. We shall have to think of something. Alec must have his dance one way or another."

"I appreciate that, Walt," Alec said. "But at present I think it best to let things lie."

Or at least his uncle thought so. Uncle Ramsay had advised Alec not to attempt another grand opening or any public dancing which might rouse more ire. And when Alec thought of how Julia had been threatened by Felton Wilcox, he was ready to agree. Ready to give up.

His father's voice echoed in his mind. *"You'll never succeed, Alec, unless you push harder. Learn to be more aggressive. . . ."* Perhaps his father had been right about him all along.

⁖

Alec walked to the inn the next evening, looking for a little solace. He knew he would not find it at the bottom of a glass, but the company of his fellowmen sounded appealing.

After his conversation with Sir Herbert, Alec decided he would reopen the academy quietly without any fanfare. He would likely have to find a second source of income as well.

He was back where he'd started. No—worse off, for he'd spent most of his savings preparing for his ill-fated grand opening.

When he entered the inn's taproom, he hesitated in the doorway, surprised to see Mr. Barlow sitting at the counter in low conversation with Mr. Jones. Alec had not seen Barlow since his dismissal. *Maybe this is not the best idea,* he thought.

Both men looked his way before he could retreat.

"Valcourt," Jones acknowledged with a nod. "We were just talking about you."

Uh-oh. "Shall I leave?"

"No. Sit yerself down. A ginger beer?"

"Yes, please."

When Jones turned away to pour, Barlow began somberly, "I am glad to see you, Valcourt."

Alec thought the man's expression indicated otherwise, but said, "And I you."

"I regret how your time at Buckleigh Manor ended," Barlow said. "Her ladyship eventually confided in me the particulars—I hope you don't mind. I was sorry to hear the tale, but I must admit relieved as well—relieved to learn I had not trusted you in error. I am only sorry I didn't know it at the time."

"That's all right, Mr. Barlow."

Jones set his ginger beer before him.

Barlow said, "On my tab, please, Jones."

Alec began to protest, but Barlow insisted. "Come on, lad. Allow me this small thing."

"Very well, thank you."

"How is Apollo?" Barlow asked.

"Doing well. Though I admit I haven't ridden him much lately with all the preparations...." Alec allowed his words to trail away and sipped his drink without tasting it.

"I was sorry to hear about the vandalism at your place."

Alec nodded. "Well, I was certainly warned something like that might happen."

"Still a dashed shame, Valcourt." Jones frowned. "A man ought to be able to establish whatever lawful business he chooses without fear of retaliation. I doubted anyone would patronize yer academy, but I certainly didn't expect anything as bad as that. In Beaworthy, of all places."

"Might help if we had a competent constable," Barlow muttered.

"Or one who wasn't quite such a wrasslin' enthusiast," Jones added, then excused himself to check things in the kitchen.

A new thought struck Alec. He looked at Barlow and began, "If her ladyship ever decides to hire another clerk..."

Immediately, he noticed a wary light in Barlow's eyes, his hand tighten on his glass.

Alec quickly continued, "I hope you will consider Ben Thorne. An excellent young man." And Alec would love nothing better than to help Ben escape the clay works—and the Wilcox brothers' clutches.

"Thorne, you say?" Barlow pursed his lips in thought. "I shall consider it."

Alec knew better than to ask for his old job back. And, truth be told, even though he feared he would never resurrect his academy or his career, he had no wish to return to the Midwinters' employ.

Mr. Jones returned and leaned an elbow on the counter. "So are ya going to try again?" he asked Alec. "Plan another grand opening?"

Alec shook his head. "I don't think so. My uncle advises against it."

The innkeeper's lower lip protruded. "I'm sorry to hear it. What will ya do?"

Alec shrugged. "Reopen quietly. Teach a few private lessons." He sighed. "And hopefully avoid more trouble."

If in the ballroom a lady asks any favor of a gentleman, he should under no circumstances refuse her requests. Well bred gentlemen will look after those who are unsought and neglected in the dance.

—*Rules of Etiquette & Home Culture*

*C*hapter 25

Fergus Desmond insisted on coming into the village to repair the academy door latch and lock but would accept no money for his work. "The least I cahn do, lad," he'd said with a sad smile.

Alec made what other repairs he could on his limited budget and began teaching dance to a few local children and Mr. Pugsworth. He resumed fencing lessons with Walter, which Sir Herbert had insisted on paying for.

He was teaching a lesson to young Timothy Strickland when his own mother entered, white-faced. She walked directly to the back room, gesturing for Alec to join her.

He felt Timothy Strickland's puzzled gaze on his profile.

"Sir? Was that the left foot or the right?"

"Right," Alec mumbled vaguely. "Um. Pardon me a moment, Tim."

He followed his mother into the office. She stood there, unmoving, porcelain features brittle and hands clasped. She reminded him of a bone-china figurine. Breakable. Or perhaps, already broken.

She looked up at him with red eyes. "I am sorry to disturb your lesson."

"That's all right, Mamma," Alec said gently. "What is it?"

"I've had a letter. From your father."

Alec's heart thumped. "What did he . . . ? Wait. Give me a moment."

Alec stepped from the office and addressed his young pupil. "I am sorry, Tim. Something has come up. May we reschedule your lesson for tomorrow? No charge for today, of course. Be sure and tell your mamma."

"Very good, sir. Good-bye, sir."

The boy grabbed his hat and turned toward the door. Spying a few boys on the green, he jogged off to meet them.

Alec returned to his mother. "Now, what did he say?"

"He writes that circumstances have changed."

"How so?"

"Miss Underhill is Miss Underhill no longer. Apparently, your father was not her only conquest last year. The other fellow was a bachelor and offered to marry the girl, and he convinced Mr. Underhill to dismiss the civil case."

"The suit has been dropped?"

"Begrudgingly, but yes. It seems the new husband didn't want his marriage to be the talk of London." She lowered her head and uttered a bleak little sigh. "Unlike mine."

She extracted the letter from her drawstring bag and handed it to him. Alec read it without eagerness. His father explained that he had spent the last several months living in a hovel in France, afraid to reveal his citizenry lest he incur wrath over the war. He thanked God the French he'd learned at his father's knee had not failed him altogether.

His father's sheepish tone surprised Alec. He seemed more remorseful and repentant than he had been initially.

I know I did wrong, Joanna. And I am sorry. Deeply sorry. But I
have never strayed before and never shall again. Can you forgive me?
Perhaps you think me a coward. Perhaps I ought to have stayed

and faced the civil trial. But the damages he was seeking! I had nowhere near that amount. It would have ruined us.

We were already ruined, Alec thought. He read on.

I never meant to stay away forever. Only 'til the thing died down— as I knew, or at least hoped, it would. But I realize it would be presumptuous for me to show up there now, to presume you would be ready and willing to accept me back into your life. Especially since you are, I assume, living under your brother's roof and his protection.

I am enclosing my direction—my solicitor's letter reached me here without trouble, so apparently the post is getting through unimpeded at last. I will await word from you.

Alec looked up. "What do you want to do, Mamma?"

She hesitated, twisting her hands. "I don't know. He wants me to forgive him, but I don't know if I can." Her eyes filled with tears. "In time, perhaps. If I felt he was truly repentant. But even were I to forgive him, I am not sure I could ever trust him again." She pulled a handkerchief from the sleeve of her bombazine gown and dabbed at her eyes. "I . . . need time to think."

Alec nodded. "Of course you do." He briefly embraced his mother and then walked her home.

Together, they told Uncle Ramsay about the letter. The man listened somberly and confessed himself torn. On one hand, he was tempted to advise his sister to refuse the man outright, and let his assumed demise rest as it was, since Lady Amelia had apparently not told anyone. Joanna Valcourt had weathered enough scandal already and was due to suffer more gossip and recrimination if her "dead" husband showed up in Beaworthy.

But when he looked at his sister in black, face wan and growing thinner by the day, he could not deny that her mourning—though quite real—was doing her looks and her health no favors.

In the end, he left the decision to her, and said he would support her in whatever course she chose.

She promised to think about it, and to pray.

⚬⁄◯

Nearly a week had passed since Julia's hoped-for meeting with Tom Tremelling, but there had still been no word from him. Alec Valcourt was busy with his academy and seemed to have little time or inclination to seek out her company. Meanwhile, her mother had redoubled her smothering watchdog efforts, even though Julia had not tried to venture out again at night.

Finally she managed to leave the house one afternoon when her mother was busy meeting with the parish clerk. She put on sturdy walking shoes and sought out John Desmond.

She found him beside the forge, painting over the outside wall. Even so, she could still see most of a word someone had scrawled there in red paint. *Killer.*

Jackanapes. She inwardly cursed the culprit, whoever it was.

She said, "You've had a visitor, I see."

"Yes. Unfortunately it's a repeat performance." He held up the pail. "At least we already had the paint on hand from the last time." He smiled gamely. "And how are you today, Miss Midwinter?"

"You may call me Julia, you know. You have before."

He paused in his work. "I don't know that your mother would approve of my taking that liberty."

"Well, she is not here to complain, and *Miss Midwinter* seems too formal, considering our relationship."

"Oh?" He eyed her somewhat warily, she thought, one brow quirked.

She said briskly, "I took your advice. I asked Mother to write to Lieutenant Tremelling, inviting him to visit. But he has not come, nor even bothered to write back."

"I'm sorry to hear it. Perhaps the letter did not reach him, or duty keeps him away."

"So Mother says. But I know better. I think if he really were my father he would come—would have come ages ago."

He set down the brush and pail and turned to face her. "I told you, lass. I'm not the man."

"But"—she ducked her head—"you risked your own safety to rescue me that day at the hurling match. And stood up for me with Alec Valcourt against the Wilcox brothers. . . ."

"I did, yes." He wiped his hand on a cloth. "Though any man would have done the same."

She shook her head. "Not any man. But a father would. Would you tell me if you were? Or did Lady Amelia extract a promise of secrecy from you?"

"No, lass. No secrets."

He looked at her, a deep sadness in his eyes. "I'm sorry you don't know who your father is, but you know who you *are*, don't you, lass?"

"Pfff." Julia scoffed. "Not who I thought I was."

"But you know whose child you are?"

"If I'm not yours, I suppose I am the daughter of a lieutenant who prefers shipboard life to me."

"No, Julia. You are a child of the king."

"Did King George have an affair with Lady Anne as well?" she quipped.

Desmond shook his head, eyes troubled. "Do you really not know what you're worth, lass? To your heavenly Father?"

She looked at him, uncertain, then shook her head. "You say that now. But if you knew me—my temper, my thoughts. How I've treated my mother. How I've flirted with men . . ."

"I don't need to know. But God already does."

Julia shrugged off the uncomfortable thought as if it were a shawl of itchy wool.

He continued, "God created you for a purpose from the beginning of time, Julia. And He sacrificed His beloved Son to redeem you for all eternity."

She shook her head. "If my heavenly Father is anything like my earthly one, He doesn't want anything to do with me. I have no doubt greatly disappointed Him."

"Haven't we all?"

"Are you saying it doesn't matter?" She sneered. "That we can do whatever we want and God still loves us?"

"It does matter. Sin grieves God's heart and our own as well. Can you honestly look back and not regret those wrong things you've done?"

Julia was tempted to give a flippant answer, to ignore the hollow ache inside, and lie. Instead she felt her chin tremble. "I do regret them."

"Then turn from those things, and ask God to forgive you. He will. He has. And yes, He loves you in spite of it all. He loves *you*, Julia. No matter what."

She shook her head. Her throat tight, she said, "I don't deserve it."

"No, of course you don't. None of us do," he said gently. "That's why it's called grace: unmerited favor."

Grace? Julia's attention was snagged by the word. The name . . . Her name.

Desmond fell silent, looking at her with those kind, knowing eyes. She grew increasingly uncomfortable as the silence stretched between them, with nothing to distract her except her own thoughts. Her conscience.

She said, "I would not have taken you for a religious man."

He winced. "No doubt, considering my past. Even now I don't know how *religious* I am, but I know I'd be lost without Christ."

"That's how I feel. Lost."

"Then, my girl, are you ready to be found?"

Still Julia's heart resisted. "How do I know you are telling me the truth about Lady Anne? Can you prove it?"

"No, I can't," he said. "But let me make two things plain to you."

She looked up at him, struck by his earnest tone.

He took one of her hands in his larger one. "I am not your father. I could not be. I never touched Lady Anne beyond the chaste contact of the ballroom."

Petulant, Julia began to pull away. "So you said—"

But he held her hand fast. "And the second thing. If I were your father, I would never deny it." His eyes held hers. "And you would never need doubt your father loved you."

Julia's heart pounded at his words.

He squeezed her hand and released it. "Now, best head on home, lass. Lady Amelia would not be pleased to know you've spent more time in my company."

"Do I really remind you of Lady Amelia? You said so the last time I was here."

He glanced at her. "Yes, your bearing and your voice remind me of her a great deal. Though now that I've spent more time with you, I can see similarities to Lady Anne as well."

"How so?"

"In temperament. Lady Anne was a charming girl. Quite gregarious."

"Lady Amelia said something similar, although from her it was not a compliment."

He nodded. "Amelia was quieter. Thoughtful. Intelligent. Yet she had a dry wit which never ceased to catch me off guard. She was unaware or at least unaffected by her own beauty, whereas Anne was very aware of hers. Lady Amelia was generous and graceful." He grinned. "And an excellent dancer."

"*My* Lady Amelia?" Julia asked, incredulous.

"Ah . . . well. Don't tell her I told you." He winked.

Julia shook her head in disbelief. "Are you trying to tell me that, in her younger days, she was . . . amiable?"

"Very."

She narrowed her eyes. "If it were not unfathomable, Mr. Desmond, I might think you were in love with her."

He looked down at his work-worn hands, then met her gaze once more. "It was all a long time ago, Julia. Lady Amelia has married and raised a fine daughter and lived an entire twenty years since then."

"And you?"

He looked somewhere beyond her, and Julia saw pain flicker across his eyes. "I have lived twenty long years as well."

Julia waited for him to say more, but he did not. He only stood there, staring off into the distance, or into the distant past.

Her mother was pacing the library and pulling on gloves when Julia returned. Her hat and reticule lay on the desk nearby.

"I was just coming to look for you," she said. "I've been worried sick. Where have you been?"

Julia looked at Lady Amelia with new eyes, trying to see what Desmond saw—that quiet, modest woman full of wit and kindness and grace.

Her mother added, "Tell me you were not off somewhere with that dancing master again."

"I was talking with a dancing master—but not Mr. Valcourt."

She stilled. "Then who?"

"I think you know."

Her face paled. "Why would he . . . ? Is he trying to ingratiate himself? To win your trust?"

"I went to see him, Mother. Not the other way around."

"Why would you?"

"Because I wanted to learn the truth."

"The truth according to him is not necessarily the truth, Julia."

"One could say the same of you, my lady. Or your sister."

She frowned at that. "What did you tell him? Does he know who you are?"

"He knew only that I was your daughter, until I relieved him of that misapprehension."

She paled all the more.

"Twice now I've asked him if he is my father, which is quite humiliating now that I think of it. . . ." Julia flopped into a chair.

Her mother asked in a shaky voice, "And what did he say?"

"He said he is not, insisted that he never touched your sister except to hold her hand while dancing."

She exhaled a jagged breath. "And you believed him?"

"Yes. Eventually. Though I did not want to." Julia smiled a little sadly to recall the scene, and her heart throbbed with the resounding bleak conclusion. "So Lieutenant Tremelling really is my father, but he has no interest in seeing me—even though we've written and asked him to come. Does he think coming here would be admitting Anne lied all those years ago?"

"Perhaps." Her mother exhaled a long breath. "But I've thought of another possible explanation." She paced across the room once more.

"Go on," Julia prompted.

Lady Amelia pressed her lips together, then began, "Lieutenant Tremelling wrote to me more than a month ago. That in itself was not unusual, for he wrote regularly over the years to keep us apprised of his whereabouts."

"Why?"

"I sent occasional notes about how you fared."

"And money?"

"Yes, Julia, I sent money. But I never saw it as a bribe. Not directly. My father had made no provision for Anne in his will, beyond her dowry. Yet I'd always thought that if she and Father had lived, he might have softened in time, and done something for her. And Lieutenant Tremelling would have benefited as well. That's how I justified it. And, yes, I thought if he found himself destitute, he might very well show up here and demand more, or try to take you away . . . so Barlow or I sent a little something whenever he wrote."

She paused to draw breath. "But this letter was different. With the war over, he wrote that he was feeling uncertain about the future, and proposed a change. . . ."

"What change?"

"He laid out two possible scenarios for his future after the navy. In the first, he would relocate here to Beaworthy. He asked if there might be some position for him here on the estate, where he might have the opportunity to make your acquaintance without insinuating himself into your life. But I already had Barlow as my manager, and at the time Mr. Valcourt was our clerk. Tom Tremelling was a lieutenant in His Majesty's Royal Navy—was I to offer him a place as a footman?

A groom? And I admit I did not welcome his presence here—or the inevitable questions that would arise about the fate of his and Anne's child. Besides, you had already elevated Barlow to iconic father figure. How much more so would you have idealized Lieutenant Tremelling?"

"He wouldn't have been a father *figure*. If he *is* my father."

"But remember, we had been told otherwise."

Julia said, "You mentioned two scenarios. What was the second?"

Her mother nodded. "That he would open a public house there in Plymouth, if I would provide the start-up funds."

"So you sent him the money?"

"Yes, I directed Barlow to deliver a significant sum. Though in the end Mr. Valcourt delivered it."

"Mr. Valcourt?" Julia blinked. "He never told me that."

"Then that is to his credit. For he was asked not to speak of it."

Julia scowled. "You sent the money to keep Lieutenant Tremelling from coming here and meeting me, didn't you."

She sighed. "Yes, but keep in mind this was before you found Anne's letter and began asking questions."

"Then, is it any wonder he hesitates to come here now?"

"I did write to him again, remember, and asked him to come. You saw the letter."

Julia looked directly into her mother's eyes, daring her to lie. "You didn't only pretend to send the letter, did you?"

"No. You may ask Barlow if you don't believe me."

"He sent the messenger?"

"He personally made sure it was delivered, yes."

Julia threw up her hands. "Then why has he not come?"

"I don't know," her mother quietly replied. "But I intend to find out."

Coup de grâce. A finishing stroke; a stroke of mercy.

—Noah Webster

*C*hapter 26

At Walter's urging—he insisted it wasn't good for man nor beast to stay indoors so long—Alec took the afternoon off and joined him and James for a ride.

The three men had not ridden far, when they were joined by Patience Allen and Julia Midwinter, apparently out for a ride of their own.

Apollo trotted ahead, matching his gait to that of Julia's brown mare. Alec took pleasure in riding with Miss Midwinter, though he knew he was an inferior horseman. Walter hung back with his siblings, apparently giving him and Julia time to talk alone.

Alec glanced at her but noticed she kept her face averted. There was something about her raised chin and compressed mouth that made Alec wary.

He asked tentatively, "How are you, Miss Midwinter?"

"I'm well," she replied. "Except that Lieutenant Tremelling refuses to meet me."

He thought back to his meeting with the man. Alec was under the impression that Lady Amelia had communicated in the letter—and by way of a bank note—that she'd wanted him to stay away.

"Does he know you wish to meet him?" Alec asked. "Has Lady Amelia agreed?"

"She wrote to him on my behalf," Julia said. "I saw the letter. And Barlow assures me it was delivered."

Apparently Lady Amelia had changed her mind, Alec realized, now that Julia knew about her past. Yet perhaps Tremelling was skeptical. Again Alec was tempted to tell Julia he'd met the man, but Barlow had asked him to keep that to himself.

He tread cautiously. "May I ask what outcome you hope for from such a meeting?"

She nodded, jaw pulsing. "I want to see him with my own eyes— see the resemblance Lady Amelia mentioned. Ask him why he stood silently by while Lady Anne blamed John Desmond." Her voice tightened. "Ask why he gave me away. And why he did not want to see me . . ."

She turned to him, eyes glinting. "Do *you* know why? Mother tells me you delivered money to him when you were our clerk."

"Did she?"

Julia nodded.

Alec was surprised but relieved to be able to tell her. "Yes, when Barlow broke his arm and was unable to ride, he sent me to Plymouth to deliver a letter to Lieutenant Tremelling in his stead."

"I can't believe you didn't tell me."

"I promised not to speak of it. Besides, I didn't want to drive a wedge between you and your mother."

"Too late, I'm afraid. I can't believe it. Lieutenant Tremelling has even met our former clerk but cannot be bothered to see me." Her voice rose. "Did he tell you why? Does he still deny he is my father?"

"We didn't talk long. At the time, I didn't even know what his connection was to your family."

Apparently Julia wasn't even listening. She shook her head, small nostrils flaring. "If he won't come here, I shall go to him. I'll ride to Plymouth myself, if I have to, and demand answers."

Foreboding flooded Alec. "Julia, don't do anything rash. . . ."

But Julia lifted her crop, urged Liberty to speed, and galloped away.

Abruptly Apollo lurched wildly forward and raced after Liberty.

Alec reared back and nearly lost his seat. He made a mad grab for saddle leather and held on, pulling on the reins.

"Whoa, Apollo. Whoa!" he called desperately over the pounding of hooves.

To no avail. Apollo galloped full out, as though a hound after a fox.

God in heaven. His horse was determined to follow Julia's—straight toward the high stone wall ahead. The stubborn gelding gave no heed to Alec's yanks on the reins or his commands to stop, which floated away, futile, on the wind.

The stone wall loomed nearer and nearer. *High. Too high.*

Ahead of him, Julia's horse leapt, lifting its muscular forelegs over the stone wall, its rear hooves skating over the stone with a spray of rubble. Horse and rider landed, hooves thundering, on the other side of the wall.

Alec breathed a prayer for her safety and for his.

A few seconds behind, Apollo tossed his head against Alec's pull and jumped. Apollo's forelegs hit the wall with a sickening snap, the sheer momentum pushing the horse over the wall. One moment Alec was atop the careening horse, the next he flew over Apollo's head. He landed beyond the wall with a bone-jarring thud, and felt the wind slammed from his lungs. His mind blacked out, then came to, dazed.

As though from far away, he heard a woman scream. Julia? Patience?

He opened his eyes a slit and glimpsed Julia cantering back, then half pushing, half jumping from her sidesaddle. Her legs became twisted in her long skirts, and she stumbled but quickly regained her feet. Eyes wide, Julia ran to where Alec lay, one cheek pressed to the turf, legs sprawled. He angled his head a few painful inches and saw Apollo on his side, legs bent unnaturally, whining and snorting in a futile attempt to rise.

Julia dropped to her knees by Alec's side and gently laid a hand on his shoulder. "Mr. Valcourt? Alec? Can you hear me?"

"Yes," he managed in a reedy voice. "Apollo?"

Julia looked over her shoulder and her eyes filled with tears. "He's injured, I'm afraid."

Alec winced. "How bad is he?"

Tears spilled down Julia's cheeks. She managed a breathy whisper, "Bad."

Walter came riding around through the gate, followed by James and Patience. Walt leapt from his horse and ran toward his fallen friend. "Alec! Are you all right?"

"I don't know."

"We shouldn't move him," Patience called, still atop her horse. "James, go and fetch Papa—quickly. He will know what to do."

Julia glanced again toward the fallen horse, then looked up at her friend with tear-filled eyes. Her voice hoarse, she pleaded, "Patience, please go find Barlow."

Ten minutes later, Sir Herbert came riding through the gate on the back of James's horse. He dismounted with his old army bag and hurried over, grim-faced but calm. He knelt and began examining Alec's spine and limbs, asking questions in low tones about his level of pain and sensation in each appendage.

Barlow jogged onto the scene a moment later. He sent Julia a worried look before kneeling beside Apollo, talking in soothing tones and running his hands along the forelegs, which to Alec suddenly seemed as fragile as tinder sticks compared to the girth of the horse.

A litter for Alec was sent for, and while they waited for it, all the men consulted together in somber tones about the injured horse.

"Can you help him?" Julia asked in a frightened little voice Alec had never heard before.

Barlow looked at her, sadness mingled with anger. "I am afraid not, miss. The breaks are too bad." He shook his head, frustrated and upset. "What were you thinking, Valcourt? To try a jump like that?"

Julia's chin trembled. "It wasn't his fault. His horse must have decided to follow mine."

"You jumped that wall?" Barlow's face darkened. "That was a very stupid thing to do."

Julia blinked against a new flood of tears, and Alec's heart twisted. He doubted her beloved Barlow had ever spoken to her so harshly.

She walked solemnly over, knelt by Apollo's head, and stroked his forelock. "I am sorry, Apollo. I never meant for you to get hurt." She attempted a chuckle, but it died in a sob. "You cheeky thing. Who would have guessed you would even try? Not I. And not Mr. Valcourt, no doubt. What a brave boy you are. Shh . . . I'm sorry you're in pain. So sorry . . ."

Lady Amelia strode onto the scene, looked about her grimly, and demanded to know what had happened.

Julia explained, not attempting to divert blame from herself.

"You jumped that wall?" Lady Amelia echoed. "Knowing full well an inexperienced rider was behind you?"

Alec grimaced to hear the words. Insult added to injury.

"It didn't cross my mind his horse would follow."

"Do you not see how you lead people astray? How your recklessness endangers others? What if Mr. Valcourt had died? What then? Will you never learn?"

Barlow and the other men rose in accord. Barlow walked over to where Alec lay and dropped to one knee. "It's your horse, lad. I can't tell you what to do, but . . ."

Alec understood, though deeply saddened. "Do what you think best."

Barlow nodded, rose, and extracted a pistol from his pocket.

Eyes wide, Julia asked in alarm, "Is there nothing else you can do?"

"I am afraid not, miss. Best head on home."

"No." Lady Amelia spoke up, her voice carrying across the distance. "Miss Midwinter will stay and witness the consequences of her actions."

"But . . . my lady!" Barlow objected.

Lady Amelia held up her hand. "She needs to face this. It might have been a man lying dead on the ground, instead of his horse."

Julia lowered her head, blinking fiercely. Then she rose and backed away a safe distance, keeping her eyes averted as Barlow took aim.

Hand on the trigger, Barlow faltered. "Are you sure you ladies want to be here?"

"Of course we don't want to be here," Lady Amelia snapped. "But don't let that animal suffer any longer. Do what must be done, and quickly."

Alec could not turn away, not while two ladies stood there so stoically. He lowered his eyes to the ground and waited, dreading the shot as he had dreaded each piteous whinny moments before. He would miss the troublesome horse, as one missed any creature one had taken the time to tame.

The shot rang out, an echoing crack, and the horse whinnied no more.

Alec could not see Julia's face, but he risked a glance at Lady Amelia, standing nearby. Tears glittered in her eyes, and her expression convulsed as she looked from him to her daughter.

"She might have died," Lady Amelia whispered. "You both might have died."

☙

In the meadow behind the churchyard, Julia bent and laid a clutch of forget-me-nots on Apollo's grave. She had insisted the horse get a proper burial, like other beloved Buckleigh horses and hounds before him. Mr. Ramsay made no objection, but nor did he or Mr. Valcourt accept Lady Amelia's offer of financial recompense for the horse. It was not Miss Midwinter's fault, both insisted, but Julia knew better.

Again her eyes filled with hot tears as she looked down at the mound of dirt.

"I'm so sorry." Her throat burned and tightened, and she said no more.

Thankfully, Mr. Valcourt had escaped the ordeal without serious injury. Yet somehow she felt very sure she had lost his friendship and any possible future between them with the loss of his horse. The fall, the death, felt heavy with significance. With finality.

God might love and might even forgive, she realized, but that did not mean He erased the natural consequences of her actions.

She became aware of a figure quietly approaching. She looked up and saw John Desmond. Her heart ached at the thought of how disappointed he must have been when he'd learned what she'd done.

He stood near her and reverently removed his hat. "I heard what happened," he said.

She hung her head. "Then why are you here?—unless you've come to chastise me. I deserve it, I know. I shan't mind."

"No, that's not why I've come. I imagine you've been chastised enough."

Julia nodded, chin trembling. "Mother is so angry with me. She's threatening to sell my horse. . . ."

"I'm not surprised. Jumping that wall was dangerous—you must have scared the life out of her. You know losing a child is a mother's worst fear."

Julia shook her head. "No, her worst fear is that I leave Buckleigh Manor."

He looked at her earnestly. "Julia, don't forget—Amelia has lost her parents, her brother, her sister, and her husband. She is alone except for you. Daughter or niece—you are the only family she has. Can you not understand why she might hold on a little tightly, try her utmost to protect you, and worry about losing you?"

Julia considered. "I had not really thought of it that way."

"Please do." He added, "For both your sakes."

Julia nodded thoughtfully, then she said, "You still haven't told me why you've come."

With a sad smile, he stood beside her, put his arm around her shoulder, and squeezed. "For this."

It was as if he'd squeezed her heart. The words *unmerited favor* whispered in her memory, and tears filled her eyes once more.

Unfamiliar with such displays of affection, she stood stiffly in his one-armed embrace, not daring to breathe. Gradually, bit by bit, something deep within her unfurled and began to expand, drawing in comfort like a dry sponge. Slowly, tentatively, Julia leaned her head against his shoulder and breathed deep.

To be fond of dancing was a certain step towards falling
in Love. . . .

—Jane Austen, *Pride and Prejudice*

Chapter 27

At his doting mother's insistence, Alec sat propped with pillows on the sitting room settee. His head ached and his previously injured ribs throbbed once more, but he was thankful it was nothing more serious. Nothing like Apollo had suffered.

Mrs. Tickle had visited that morning and brought pies. The Desmonds stopped by to check on him, and the Thornes stopped by to pray.

Later in the afternoon, Miss Midwinter and Miss Allen came bearing chamomile tea and plain biscuits as though he were an invalid. Also a new edition of the *Gentleman's Magazine and Historical Chronicle* he could read while he rested.

He was pleased to see both ladies, though ill at ease to be found reclining in the middle of the day as though he were on his deathbed—or a man of leisure. His mother excused herself to take the gifts to the kitchen and help Mrs. Dobb prepare a tea tray. Patience sat with Aurora on the other side of the room, and the two began a game of draughts.

Miss Midwinter sat on a chair near him and clasped her hands on her lap. "Are you certain you are all right?" she asked. "We will happily pay Mr. Mounce's bill, you know, if you wish to consult him."

"I am quite well, Miss Midwinter. I promise you."

She bit her lip. "Again, I am sorry about Apollo. Deeply sorry. I—"

"Miss Midwinter," he interrupted, reaching over to press her hand. "There is no need to keep apologizing. I am sorry as well, and I know you are. All is forgiven."

She nodded, blinking away tears. "Thank you."

Alec glanced at the magazine and grinned. "If you mean to treat me like a proper invalid, perhaps you might read to me? I should enjoy hearing your voice."

Her eyes brightened. "If you'd like. In fact, I've marked a section here in the editor's preface I thought might encourage you."

"Go on."

She opened the journal and found the place. Alec enjoyed gazing at her lovely profile and listening to her clear, unaffected voice as she read.

"I call to mind here the pleasing account Mr. Sterne has left us in his *Sentimental Journey* of the grace-dance after supper. I agree with that amiable writer in thinking that religion may mix herself in the dance. . . . It is a silent but eloquent mode of praising Him. . . ."

She paused and looked up at him earnestly. "I hope you won't give up, Mr. Valcourt. Your academy will succeed. I know it."

Though he struggled to believe her, he could not deny her visit was a balm to him, body and soul.

❧

His headache receded two days later, and Alec returned to the academy. As he prepared for his first lesson of the day, he thought back to Miss Midwinter's visit, her earnest face and encouragement when she'd said, *"Your academy will succeed. I know it."* He certainly hoped she was right.

With that in mind, he once again pondered his father's letter, and what it would mean for them all if he came to Beaworthy. Would he waltz back into their lives, and take over the academy as though it were his? Would he understand that Alec didn't have enough pupils to keep himself busy, let alone two dancing masters?

At that moment Desmond stepped inside the academy.

Or three masters, Alec thought wryly.

Desmond removed his hat. "Hello, Valcourt. Busy?"

"I have a pupil coming soon, but I have a few minutes. How are you?"

"I came to ask the same of you. Feeling all right?"

"A little sore. That's all. A little heartsore too."

Desmond nodded. "I imagine you are. Miss Midwinter is quite tormented over it."

"Yes, I know she is. But she came to see me, and I assured her all was forgiven."

"I am glad to hear it. And if you ever have the need, you are welcome to borrow my horse."

"Thank you. But I am in no hurry to get back in the saddle."

Deciding to confide in Desmond, Alec told him about his father's letter and his desire to rejoin the family. "As you know," Alec finished, "there was some question of his . . . fate when we first arrived, and should he return—what in the world would we tell people?"

Desmond inhaled and slowly shook his head. "That's quite a quandary, friend. I haven't any easy answers to offer you, I'm afraid. But if you need anything else—a listening ear or a spare bed—you need only ask. And of course you have my word that I will keep what you've told me to myself. I hope that goes without saying."

"Indeed it does." Alec smiled at the understanding man, grateful for his friendship.

The door opened behind them and Mrs. Strickland walked in, bringing her son Timothy for another lesson.

"Hello, Mr. Valcourt. Here is Master Timothy, ready for his—" She broke off, staring at John Desmond. "What is he doing here?"

"What do you mean, ma'am?" Alec asked. "Mr. Desmond is—"

"I know very well who he is. Infamous—that's who he is." She grabbed her son's hand and jerked open the door. "And we'll have no part in any business he's involved in."

Great, Alec thought. Another setback. At this rate, how would he ever succeed in bringing dance—and life—back to Beaworthy? *God, please help me. I can't do this on my own.*

◌╱◌

It rained all night, but the morning broke clear and sunny. Alec walked into the village, determined to enjoy the beautiful April day. He saw Nancy from Posey's perched on a stepladder, transplanting flowers into the baskets hanging from the lampposts. Cheered by the sight, he waved to her. She smiled and lifted a dirty hand in reply.

When Alec reached the academy, he was stunned to see that the glass in the broken, boarded-up windows had been replaced. He had not done so, nor had he placed another order with the glazier. He would have to ask the man what he owed. He walked down the street and around the corner to the glazier's workshop, but the man insisted he owed nothing, saying only, "We take care of our own here in Beaworthy."

Perplexed but grateful, Alec thanked the man and returned to the academy, brighter now with light shining through every windowpane.

Later, Aurora led the Millman twins through the figures of the minuet. The Millmans were a merchant family from nearby Shebbear whom Alec had met during his initial calls.

Julia Midwinter stopped in, supposedly on an errand for her mother. Alec doubted the excuse but was happy to see her nonetheless. She wore a pink-and-white walking dress with a matching bonnet. The colors favored her complexion. Her skin glowed, and she looked feminine and sweet. Alec found himself longing to stroke her cheek, and to kiss her. He was glad they were not alone together in the academy. Well . . . mostly glad.

She glanced across the room, taking in Aurora and her young charges. "I am happy to see you have pupils, Mr. Valcourt," Julia said. "I feared that after the vandalism, people might stay away."

"Business is not exactly thriving, Miss Midwinter. But we have a handful of pupils, thank goodness. In fact, a few have signed up for lessons *because* of the vandalism, to show their support." He added teasingly, "You really ought to see Mrs. Tickle dance the Highland Fling."

She smiled, then asked, "No thought of rescheduling your grandopening dance?"

He shook his head. "No. Small, quiet lessons will hopefully attract less negative attention."

"Unfortunately, less positive attention as well," she said. "It's too bad there isn't a way to spread the word without increasing the risk of certain parties taking notice."

Aurora looked over at them, greeted Miss Midwinter, then asked, "Alec, would you mind bringing out the appointment log, so I may schedule the Millmans' next lesson?"

"Of course." He turned to Julia. "Excuse me a moment."

But Julia followed him into the back office with a great show of nonchalance.

Inside the small room, she glanced at him and whispered almost shyly, "I've been thinking . . . Is what happened with that Miss Underhill the reason you've been so uncomfortable when we've been alone together?"

He nodded. "That, and mortal fear of your mother." He grinned, but she did not return the gesture.

Instead she looked down, embarrassed. "Then, how low your opinion of me must be, when I have acted such the flirt."

"You are wrong, Miss Midwinter. Though I may not have approved of everything you've done, it wasn't because I didn't admire you but because I did."

She looked up then, a tentative smile brightening her face.

He went on, "And as sorry as I was to have to come here to Beaworthy in the first place, meeting you has certainly eased that disappointment."

"Has it?" She leaned toward him slightly, invitingly.

For a moment he stilled, his gaze lingering on her mouth. Oh, to kiss those lips again . . . But then he stepped away and busied himself at the desk, the open door firming his resolve.

"You say something like that, yet you still pull away," she said, vulnerable and incredulous at once.

He picked up the appointment log, then set it back down. He took a deep breath and faced her. "Miss Midwinter," he began, "as much as I admire you and want to . . . be with you, I am trying to be realistic. You know your mother would never countenance a courtship between us. I doubt she would have at all events, but as I have not yet proven myself—"

"I don't care if you succeed or not."

"But I do. And pretending there is a future for us, allowing myself to hope, to"—he reached out and ran a finger over her soft cheek—"kiss you again, would only make it more difficult for me when the inevitable happens." He held her gaze, willing her to see all the sentiments he knew he should not express.

"The inevitable?" she asked.

He sighed. "When you marry someone else." There. He'd said it. What would she do now, now that he had taken her no doubt light flirtation and carried it out to its logical conclusion like a killjoy?

"Who says that's inevitable?" She pouted, and he saw a glimpse of the adorable little girl she'd once been.

He smiled indulgently. "I do." He leaned near and pressed a soft kiss to her cheek. "And it's time you accept that fact as well."

He resolutely stepped to the door and gestured for her to precede him from the room.

That afternoon, after his last lesson, Alec stopped at the inn once more, pleased to again see Mr. Barlow there, even as guilt struck him. He hoped the man didn't blame him for Apollo's death.

"Afternoon, Valcourt. Good to see you up and about." Mr. Jones poured him a ginger beer without being asked. Alec felt a wave of pleasure sweep over him at this sign that he'd become a regular.

"Yes, I'm very glad you're all right," Barlow said. "Even as I am sorry about Apollo."

Alec ducked his head. "I am sorry as well. Sorry I was not skilled enough to prevent it."

"Not your fault. There's no talking sense to a male when he's bent on chasing after a certain female . . ."

Alec felt his neck heat. Did Barlow know how he felt about Julia? He said, "Well, I was glad you were there at the end. Thank you. I know that was difficult for you."

"Yes. It always is."

They sat in silence for several minutes, each left to his own memories.

Mr. Deane entered, removing his hat and greeting the other men. He took a seat near Alec and asked, "Planning another grand opening now that you've got your place fixed up?"

Mr. Jones tipped a glass under the spigot. "Says his uncle advises against it. Just gonna limp along with a few quiet lessons."

Mr. Deane nodded. "Probably wise."

Mr. Jones set the pint before him. "I'm not sure I agree. . . . I'm thinking it's time to get the Beaworthy musicians back together."

Mr. Deane gaped at him, then shared a look of surprise with Barlow.

Alec looked from one to the other, then asked, "Do you mean . . . you would play for the grand opening if I planned another?"

Alvin Deane frowned. "I haven't agreed to that, Mick. That's risky for a businessman like me. And Barlow here works for the lady, don't forget."

"True," Barlow said with a nod. "It would be a problem."

Mr. Deane added, "Besides, I pawned my flute."

"Yer brother owns the shop, man," Jones scowled, wiping the counter in agitation. "It's not like he's had any offers on the thing."

"Even so," Deane said. "I haven't played in ages."

"I can't play for any dance, I'm afraid," Barlow said. "But Fergus Desmond might, if he's feeling up to it."

"And John Desmond plays as well," Alec added. "Pipe *and* violin."

The men shared uneasy glances.

Jones's cloth stilled. "Not sure that's the best idea, son."

"And no offense," Deane said. "But your place isn't big enough for musicians and dancers to boot."

It would be a crush, Alec realized. The other men were silent as well, sipping from their pints or thinking.

Suddenly Mr. Jones slapped his cloth against the bar. "That's it, then. Rot it all—let's do it."

They all turned to stare at him. Mr. Deane asked, "Do what?"

"Let's have Valcourt's dance upstairs. Get the assembly room out of early retirement. About dashed time, I'd say."

Mr. Deane's brows lowered in concern. "Mick, are you sure?"

"Why not? Only live once. Might as well live like a man, ey? Better to die a stallion than suffer a gelding. Oh. Sorry, Valcourt."

"That's all right. No offense taken."

"If we agree to play," Jones challenged him, "will ya let off with this 'reopen quietly' business and do it up proper?"

Alec smiled, hope lightening his heart. "If you're quite sure, Mr. Jones, then I shall indeed. Thank you."

Barlow, ever the voice of reason, said, "Hold on, now. Before you go getting the man's hopes up, we ought to see if we old codgers can still play."

"I agree." Deane nodded. "I'll have to run it by the missus first, but if I were to play, I would need a great deal of practice first."

"My sister could play the harpsichord," Alec offered. "Though if you wish to limit the group to gentlemen, I understand."

"Tell her she is most welcome, Valcourt," Jones said. "None of us can play the blasted thing, and it's a shame to let 'er sit idle. Though I would guess she's terrible out of tune. The harpsichord, that is, not your sister."

With cautious excitement, they set about planning their first—and hopefully not last—rehearsal.

❧

Rehearsal time had been set for four o'clock the following afternoon, when light would still be sufficient to see by without the expense of candles. Alec walked over from the academy, enjoying a chorus of birdsong, a warm breeze, and the colorful sight of baskets overflowing with red, yellow, and white flowers up and down the High Street.

He saw Mr. Deane's wife coming out of the greengrocer's with a crate of imported lemons, her expression indicating she'd sampled liberally of the fruit. He called "Good day" to her, and she replied with a sullen "Hmph."

He did not see Mr. Deane and hoped that meant he'd decided to join them.

Entering the inn, Alec nodded to Mr. Jones's cook, who was tending the tap for him while they practiced. Alec climbed the stairs by threes, eagerness and hope lightening his step.

He was the first to join Mr. Jones in the assembly room. Jones greeted him, then reminded him not to raise his hopes too high—he wasn't sure which men would actually show and which would decide it was too risky.

Mr. Jones brought out his bass viol, well oiled and in pristine condition.

"She's a beauty, Mr. Jones," Alec said.

"That she is, son. That she is."

Mr. Barlow entered next, violin case in one hand, other hand raised aloft. "I don't say I will play for the dance itself, but I could not resist the opportunity to play with you lot." He sat down and drew out his instrument.

Alec took his out as well and checked the strings. He said, "I spoke to Mr. Desmond, Senior. He said he would be here if he is feeling well enough. And my sister should be here any minute." He noticed that Mr. Jones had removed the dust cover from the harpsichord in preparation.

Alec hoped he and his sister knew enough of the older pieces, for he certainly did not expect these hardworking men to take the time to learn new ones. He'd consulted his grandfather's books to review the fashions of twenty years ago, and had brought sheet music for some of the older, traditional scores.

Mr. Desmond arrived, winded. Maria Desmond held his arm.

"Good to see you, Fergus," Mr. Jones said. "Mrs. Desmond."

"Where's John?" Alec asked.

"Minding the forge. Didn't think he'd be welcome."

The other men exchanged sheepish looks.

Aurora strolled in with Julia Midwinter. "I hope you don't mind," Aurora began. "But Miss Midwinter asked to come along and watch."

The men all looked at each other in alarm.

Julia held up her hand. "Don't worry, gentlemen. I applaud your efforts to support Mr. Valcourt. You have my word, I shall not say a word about this to my mother or anyone else, but please let me stay and take part."

"Very well, miss," Barlow answered for them all, and he and Julia shared a smile.

Aurora sat at the harpsichord and flipped through the sheet music. Mrs. Desmond helped her husband into a chair, where he mopped his brow with a handkerchief, and then brought out his pipe.

Mr. Deane had yet to show.

They waited a few more minutes, then began an old-fashioned minuet by Mozart. The instruments squeaked and squawked. At one point, Alec noticed Julia wince, one eye squeezing shut in apparent pain.

Mr. Barlow laid aside his violin and rose. "I'll attempt to conduct if you don't mind. Some of us are out of practice, I see. Not you, Miss Valcourt. You play beautifully."

Aurora smiled and dipped her head.

Standing before them, Barlow lifted his hand and signaled the musicians to begin all together. Alec and the others followed his lead. The estate manager was quite a good conductor, Alec realized. For several minutes, the man's hand swayed side to side, to synchronize their playing in three-quarter time.

Then Barlow surprised them all by turning to Miss Midwinter and offering his hand, a hint of challenge on his hound-dog face.

Julia hesitated, confessing, "I don't know what to do."

"And I've no doubt forgotten," he said. "Just mirror my steps as best you can."

Barlow bowed in elegant fashion. She curtsied. He bowed to the musicians. She followed with another curtsy. Then Barlow led her to the middle of the room and released her hand.

Most of the minuet was performed separately side by side, with the partners passing one another, joining hands, and then separating again. Barlow began the stately mincing steps. He rose to his toes in the balance steps, and performed the crossover steps with surprising grace.

Impressive, Alec thought.

Julia did her best to mimic Barlow's movements, and what she lacked in accuracy, she more than made up for with beauty and eagerness. A smile of self-conscious delight spread across her face, and Alec's heart warmed to see it.

"And . . . that's all I remember," Barlow said, as he bowed again before halting.

Mrs. Desmond applauded. "Bravo!"

Barlow waved his hand. "Valcourt, come over here."

Alec laid down his instrument while the others played on.

Mr. Barlow took Julia's hand, and then—with a meaningful look—laid it into Alec's.

"Thank you, sir," Alec whispered, conscious of the moment's significance. He looked at Julia, pleased to see her sparkling eyes, her dimpled smile.

Together Alec and Julia danced the minuet. The queen of dances. The dance that had opened more royal balls than any other. And now, the first dance to be performed in the Beaworthy assembly room in more than twenty years.

❦

Later Julia walked home, the afternoon's melodies still playing in her mind. She would have to be careful not to hum them aloud in her mother's presence.

Strolling up the Buckleigh Manor drive, she was surprised to see the constable leaving the house. She wondered what business had brought him there and hoped nothing was wrong.

He tipped his hat as he passed. "Miss."

She dipped her head in acknowledgement. "Mr. Lamont."

Entering the house, she went directly to the library. When she opened the door, her mother started, inhaling a gasp.

Julia hesitated. "Are you all right?"

"Yes. Sorry. I am on edge today for some reason."

Julia felt suspicion rise. She asked, "Something to do with Mr. Lamont? I saw him leaving just now."

Her mother fluttered her hand. "No, not him. I asked him to call about a few village matters—that is all."

Was that all? Julia wondered. Or was her mother hiding yet more secrets?

Considering Julia had just danced with her estate manager in the village assembly room, she decided not to press the matter.

Amelia did feel nervous and on edge. A few days before, she had again dispatched Barlow to Plymouth to call on Lieutenant Tremelling, firmly request he visit, and assure him that doing so would not jeopardize the funds she had sent, nor any future stipends.

She had half hoped Barlow would find Tremelling incapacitated or shipwrecked to explain his absence to her heartbroken daughter. Instead, when Barlow returned, he reported he'd located Tremelling in the same state as before. This time Barlow spoke with the man personally, and assured Lady Amelia that he had stated their case plainly and emphatically.

Satisfied they had done all they could, Amelia anticipated the following Saturday afternoon with more hope and dread than she had in several weeks. In the meantime she steeled herself for her meeting with the magistrate, who'd sent word he'd returned from London and would receive her at her convenience.

❧

On Thursday afternoon, Amelia entered the magistrate's study and took the seat he offered.

"Mr. Arscott, thank you for seeing me."

"A great pleasure, my lady," the thin, silver-haired man said. "It has been too long. How are you keeping?"

"I am well, thank you. And you, sir?"

"Well enough. A little lonely, but that is what old age brings, I'm afraid. I have outlived too many of my friends, including your dear father. And how is that spirited young woman of yours?"

"She is . . ." Amelia began, nodding as she searched for honest words that would not reflect poorly on Julia, "growing up. But those years are not without their trials, as you may recall from your own youth. I know I certainly do."

His eyes glinted with understanding, and maybe his own memories. "Yes. As do I."

He folded his hands on his desk. "Well, I assume you are here to discuss the matter your Mr. Barlow brought to me a few weeks ago. He intimated you might wish to lodge charges against John Desmond, who, I understand, has returned to the parish."

"Yes, that is—that *is* the matter I am here to discuss. But as far as charges, I have not settled on what is best to be done. I must say I was quite shocked to learn charges had not been pressed at the time."

He nodded. "I spoke with your father about this on two separate occasions, after his first apoplexy, and again after he'd been laid low. Though he was in deep grief, of course, I do believe he was sound in mind and judgment."

"Then, why?" she asked. "What reason did he give for not bringing the man to justice? Did he not wish to besmirch Graham's reputation?"

"That may have been part of it. He saw no reason to cast any shadows on his son once he was gone. No good could come of it, he said."

"But certainly justice—"

"Your father wasn't convinced punishing John Desmond was just."

Amelia swallowed. "No?"

Arscott shook his head. "He doubted the allegations against him."

"But there was no question he was the man my brother fought. The man who ended his life." After all, Amelia had seen him leaning over her brother's body, bloody sword in hand.

Mr. Arscott nodded. "And that would have been enough to charge Mr. Desmond with manslaughter. And had Lord Buckleigh believed the young man guilty of . . . of the breach of honor your sister accused him of, I have no doubt he would have directed me to pursue the man to the full extent of the law."

Amelia stared. "He didn't believe Anne?"

The older man hesitated. "I have no wish to speak ill of the dead."

"Of course not. But . . . I am surprised. Father never said so to me."

"He had reason to doubt her story—that I will say. Even before . . ."

"Even before what?" Amelia prompted.

The man looked at her, then away, clearly pondering some weighty matter. Then he straightened his shoulders and looked at her again, a resolute expression firming his face. He unlocked his desk drawer, riffled through the files there, and pulled one forth.

"Your father left this with me. He knew he wasn't long for this world and didn't want it found among his personal effects. I don't think he intended for me to show it to anyone, unless Mr. Desmond's fate depended on it. But I think, given the circumstances, I should show it to you. God forgive me if I am wrong to do so."

He extracted a letter, yellowed with age, the once-red seal darkened to nearly black.

"What is it?"

"A letter your sister wrote to your father, not long before he died."

Her gaze flew to his, then back down to the letter. Anne had written to their father? He had never mentioned it. She reached out shaky fingers to take the paper.

"If you still want to press charges after you read it, come back and see me."

Amelia hesitated. "I may take it with me?"

"Yes. I trust you. And it is something you may wish to read in private."

Good heavens, Amelia thought. What was in the letter?

[Queen] Victoria had displayed no great disapprobation of the duel. Cardigan was a personal favourite of hers, and prior to his trial, she had hoped that he would "get off easily."

—Stephen Banks, *The Duel and the English Gentleman*

Chapter 28

Amelia made haste home and went directly to the library and shut the door. There she sat at her desk, opened the letter with trembling hands, and read.

Dear Papa,

I have committed a grievous sin and am deeply sorry for it. I know I cannot rectify the past, or bring my brother back, or restore your health to you, but I had to try, at least, to make peace with you, and with God, and with my own conscience. The apothecary advises me not to travel in my delicate condition, so this letter will have to suffice.

I have not confessed the truth to Amelia, or to anyone else. I have no wish to cast more shame and scandal on the family name, or add to my sister's heartache; she has suffered enough. And now that she is engaged to marry a man of your choosing, there seems no point.

I saw it in your eyes, Papa. You never believed my claims of Lieutenant Tremelling's innocence. Not completely. I think you knew or at least suspected I had lied about the father of my child.

I never meant to name John Desmond. But he was the easy choice. The obvious choice. The dashing dancing master with whom I had flirted during lessons, though he never encouraged me. With whom I had spent a great deal of time—usually in the company of my brother and sister, or at least a servant, but not always. It was not out of the question.

I never intended to name any man. But after you and Graham worked on me for days upon days, pushing and prodding and threatening . . . I grew weary and desperate.

It was wrong of me. Very wrong. I knew how Mr. Desmond felt about Amelia. And how she felt about him. But I did it anyway. To protect the man I loved. I knew you would be furious, but I underestimated how murderously angry Graham would become—that he would challenge Mr. Desmond in a duel, not to first blood but rather to the death.

So you see, in one sense I was right. To name Lieutenant Tremelling as my child's father would have assured his death, or at least our poverty. For you had already forbidden me to marry him, and threatened to withhold my dowry if I did.

But Tom Tremelling is not the sort of man to give up what he wants. He convinced me that if I were compromised, my family would have to allow us to marry. Yet I feared for his life. When I suspected I might be carrying a child, I made him leave, pretend to go to sea, so he could not be blamed.

I planned that later, after no man could be produced and made to marry me, only then would Tom come home and say he still loved me and was prepared to forgive my indiscretion and marry me.

I was so stunned when Mr. Desmond offered to wed me, though he and I both knew he was innocent. That was never part of the plan. Logically, you and Graham should have accepted on my behalf, though I was relieved you did not.

After the duel . . . I could not believe what I had done. I am ashamed to think of it now. I was so focused on my selfish plan, I did not consider the potential consequences.

By the time Tom returned, Mr. Desmond was nowhere to be found (What other choice did I leave him?), your only son was dead, Amelia had lost her will to live, and you had lost your health and the strength to object to our marriage. So Tom Tremelling came out the hero and Mr. Desmond, the villain.

Tom is not a hero. He is far from perfect, as I have learned. But he is my husband, and I love him. And together we will love our child, soon to come into this world and make us a family.

But I could not rest until I wrote this letter. I will leave it to you to decide if and when to share this confession with Amelia or anyone else.

I don't ask your forgiveness, I know I don't deserve it. I know Desmond and Amelia will never forgive me either. But God has forgiven me, and that must be enough.

Your repentant daughter,
Lady Anne Tremelling

Amelia stared, her mind struggling to come to terms with the words she had read. Words that tilted her world on its head. Had she not told Julia she doubted her sister's story? That she thought Julia resembled Lieutenant Tremelling? John Desmond had been telling the truth all along.

Amelia's eyes filled. *Anne is right,* she thought. *I have never forgiven her. But I should have. . . .*

At that moment Julia walked into the room, and instinctively, Amelia slid the letter into her lap, out of view.

Julia narrowed her eyes as she walked forward. "What is it you don't want me to see? More secrets, Mother? Really? Will there never be an end to them?"

Amelia hesitated, seeing the challenge written on her daughter's face. "What is it?" Julia repeated.

Amelia pressed dry lips together. "A letter Lady Anne wrote to my father, not long before he died."

"Lady Anne?" Julia's eyes brightened with interest. She held out her hand, palm up. "Show me." Julia's gaze held hers. "Trust me."

Heart pounding, Amelia slowly brought forth the letter and laid it in her daughter's hand. It would give her some of the answers she desperately sought, but likely none of the answers she wanted. *Oh, God, am I doing the right thing?*

Julia read the lines, and then read them again. Certain phrases leapt out at her, branding themselves on her mind and heart.

"But he is my husband and I love him. And together we will love our child, soon to come into this world and make us a family. . . ."

Tears filled Julia's eyes, but she blinked them away. She would not cry over a few sweet words, not when floating in a sea of treachery. Her stomach soured. To be the offspring of such a mother and father, to be conceived in such a scheme, with such heartbreaking results! She wanted nothing to do with these people.

But at the same time another sentence cut like a knife:

"Tom Tremelling is not the sort of man to give up what he wants."

Yet he had given *her* up. His child. Had she not always known she was not wanted?

"Why did you hesitate to show me this?" Julia asked, refolding the letter.

Lady Amelia sketched a noncommittal shrug. "I had only just read it myself. And I didn't want . . ." She winced, perhaps thinking the better of what she'd been about to say.

"You didn't want me to think poorly of my real parents?" she suggested. "Or were you afraid I might think too well of Mr. Desmond?"

"I did not think you would like its contents." Lady Amelia held out her hand for the letter, and Julia returned it, noticing her mother avoided her eyes.

"Will you show it to anyone else? To Mr. Desmond?"

Lady Amelia shook her head. "It's all ancient history now."

"Is it?"

"I am only glad it can answer a few questions for you. I have no interest in opening old wounds."

"But don't you see? This could heal old wounds."

"I don't know, Julia. Let me think about it, all right? Promise me you won't go running off to report this to . . . anyone."

"But I—"

"You asked me to trust you. And now I need you to trust me too."

Amelia took the letter—and her lingering questions—and returned to Mr. Arscott's house the next day.

When his housekeeper showed her into his study, the old magistrate pulled a face and set aside his newspaper.

"My lady, I cannot say I am happy to see you. I had hoped that after our last meeting, you might have changed your mind about pressing charges against Mr. Desmond."

She reached into her large reticule and pulled forth the folded letter. "I can't understand why my father did not show this to me."

"Can you not?" Mr. Arscott asked gently. Sadly.

Confusion filled her.

He said softly, "Your father did not wish you to marry Mr. Desmond, did he?"

Amelia's heart hammered within her. Could it be? Would her father have allowed her to believe Desmond guilty of all, to keep her from marrying the man? As if she ever would have married the man who killed her brother! But had she known he'd been falsely accused, that Graham had challenged an innocent man . . .

"Now, my lady," he said, watching her closely, "before you judge your father too harshly, remember he did not press charges against Mr. Desmond, though he had every right to do so. Letter or no, duels are illegal. And he could have seen to it that John Desmond was convicted of manslaughter."

"Then why didn't he?" she whispered, though she suspected the answer.

"Your father knew how you felt about the man. And wanted to spare him for your sake." Mr. Arscott winced and added, "I think he also wished to avoid the additional unpleasantness and scandal were the matter to come to trial. I advised him that in prosecuting Mr. Desmond, the accusations leading to the duel would necessarily come to light. Witnesses who may have seen Lady Anne meeting a man alone, a man not yet her husband but not John Desmond either . . ."

Amelia's stomach cramped at the thought of seeing such accounts in the newspapers.

Mr. Arscott sighed. "I was an old friend of your father's, and I understood his wish to avoid further embarrassment and grief for the family, and for you, so I saw to it that the matter was quietly dropped."

Amelia whispered, "I see. . . ."

Resolved, Amelia handed him the letter. "I wish you to keep Lady Anne's confession in your records. After you and I are gone, I don't wish anyone else to attempt to lodge charges against John Desmond."

He nodded gravely. "I understand."

Amelia took her leave, mind still whirling. The day's knowledge was a double-edged sword. In her heart of hearts, Amelia had always been relieved that John Desmond had not been hanged or transported. But had she known all . . . Had her father confided his doubts, or shown her Anne's confession, would Amelia still have given in to her father's deathbed request that she marry Arthur Midwinter?

She still recalled his plea, that he could die in peace if only he knew she was well settled and had a man's protection before he died. Now Mr. Arscott had revealed that her father had known how she felt about John Desmond, though she had not admitted it to anyone, knowing their differences in station were a significant impediment. Still, she would not have married a man she knew full well did not love her, had there seemed any possible hope of a future with one who did. A man she had loved with every fragment of her broken heart.

When Amelia returned to the house, she found Julia sitting idly in the drawing room, making a halfhearted attempt to work stitches in her sampler. A pastime she knew the girl despised.

"Would you not rather go riding?" Amelia suggested. "It is a lovely day."

She expected Julia to retort with something like *"I thought you meant to sell my horse"* or to brighten at this sign that Amelia didn't intend to follow through on her threat. But Julia only shrugged and said nothing.

"I've been thinking," Amelia said, trying again. "It has been too long since we have had the Allens to dine. You would like that, would you not? I know you enjoy James's company, as well as seeing Patience, of course."

"If you like," Julia said listlessly, which only increased Amelia's concern for her. She nearly preferred outspoken, snappish Julia to this quiet melancholy girl who reminded her too much of her own depression of spirits after her long-ago heartbreak and the death of her brother.

Amelia prayed again that Lieutenant Tremelling would come on the morrow, especially after the letter's confirmation that he really was Julia's father.

⁓

A rainstorm pelted down all morning, and Amelia feared that even if Tremelling planned to come, the weather might delay him. Thankfully, the skies cleared after midday. Amelia found her gaze straying often to the library windows, which faced the drive. Just before three, she rose from the desk and went to stand near the windows. She saw no carriage or horse approach. As she turned away, however, movement caught her eye. She looked again. There to the side of the drive, near the garden wall, hovered a figure. A man in a dark blue uniform and cocked hat.

Nerves jangling, she rang for Barlow, and he was at her side in less than a minute, loyal man.

She nodded toward the figure, and he peered in the direction she indicated. Then he drew his shoulders back, turned on his heel, and marched from the room to do her unspoken bidding.

Meanwhile, Amelia walked quickly to the windows in the drawing room, much closer to the drive, and open several inches to allow in the temperate spring breeze. From there she could see the man fairly well. She immediately noticed that his coat, with its double row of brass buttons, hung rather loosely over baggy breeches. His face was still handsome, though his features—especially his protruding brow and cheekbones—were accentuated in his current gaunt state.

Barlow appeared and crossed the drive toward the man. Amelia hoped he didn't spook like a flushed quail and take flight.

Or did she?

"Thank you for coming, Lieutenant," Barlow said, his voice carrying through the open window. "You are welcome at the front door, if you like. Or I would be happy to show you inside through the garden door there."

The man looked trapped, uncomfortable. "I . . . don't know."

Barlow said, "I know one young lady who will be happy to hear your name announced."

"It's all so formal, isn't it?"

"Doesn't have to be." Barlow assured the edgy man as he might calm a frightened horse.

"Might I not stay out here?" Tremelling asked. "Could you not mention to the girl that I am here, and she might come out and speak to me, if she likes?" He looked down and chuckled nervously. "Probably take one look at my old buss and run the other way."

"I doubt that, sir." He paused for a moment, then continued, "Very well. I'll see what the lady says."

"Lady Amelia, do you mean, or . . . ?"

Amelia knew he had little interest in seeing *her*.

"It's Miss Julia you are here to see, is it not?" Barlow verified.

"Yes, but I imagine Lady Amelia wants to preside over our meeting."

Amelia cringed at the edge to the man's voice. But it was true. She would like to be there. To make certain the man didn't say anything hurtful. Or propose anything life-changing for Julia.

And devastating for her.

Amelia went upstairs and found Julia in her bedchamber, and gave her the news.

"He's here?" Julia asked, her voice a timid squeak.

"Yes," Amelia said, and helped her smooth back her hair and straighten her skirt. Together they walked down the stairs.

Barlow waited in the hall below.

"He's asked to speak to you alone," Amelia explained to her. "Outside. But if you have any hesitation at all, I shall go with you."

Julia considered, then said, "It's all right. I want to speak to him alone."

Amelia bit back the warnings and worries that rushed to her lips. She sent Barlow a look, then said as calmly as she could manage, "Very well. I shall be in the drawing room if you need me. And Barlow shall walk you out."

"Thank you," Julia said in a small proper voice, hands tightly clasped.

"If it helps, my dear," Amelia said softly, "he looks very nervous. Perhaps you might try to put him at his ease."

Julia nodded, solemn eyes wide.

Personally, Amelia didn't care a fig if Tremelling was at his ease. He had no right to be. But she knew it might soothe her daughter's nerves to know she was not alone in her anxiety.

Pulse racing, Julia led the way to the side door. There she paused with her hand on the latch. She squeezed her eyes closed and prayed for strength, and calm, and for the meeting to go well. Beside her, Barlow pressed her arm in silent reassurance. She glanced at the dear man, and they shared a tremulous smile.

Taking a deep breath, she pushed open the door and let herself outside. As she crossed the drive, her heart beat hard and loud with every step. She was certain Lieutenant Tremelling would hear it.

She saw him standing near the garden gate, hands behind his back, fidgeting. He wore his uniform, just as he always did in her imaginings, when he had appeared so dashing and competent—dark wool tailcoat with brass buttons over light breeches. A knapsack was slung over one shoulder, and under his arm, he held a large cocked hat with brass trimmings.

He turned as she approached.

Palms sweating, she braved a look at his face—weatherworn yet handsome, with strong nose, sharp cheekbones, and deep-set eyes.

His jaw slackened when he looked at her. "Grace . . . er, I mean, Miss Midwinter."

"Lieutenant Tremelling." She dipped her head but offered no curtsy. She doubted her trembling knees would manage the feat.

"How strange to hear you address me so formally."

Julia met his gaze. "I think it's a little late to start calling you Papa." She forced a little chuckle that sounded false in her own ears.

She turned to the manager, hovering behind. "It's all right, Barlow. You may leave us."

"I'll be just inside, miss. You need only call and I'll be right here."

She nodded, then turned back to the visitor. Was he really her father? She stared at him—his build, his face, his hair. At closer range now, she noticed that the dark coat hung rather loosely and the white breeches were dingy. The stand-up collar of his buff waistcoat was sweat stained and his limp cravat spoke of neglect. His hair was darker than she had imagined. What had Lady Amelia once said—she had his fair hair? Lieutenant Tremelling's hair was a nondescript ashy color that might once have been blond, but no longer. His tanned face showed early signs of dissipation—loosening jowls and broken blood vessels marring his cheeks and nose.

From a distance, she had caught a glimpse of the officer who had cut an impressive figure in his naval uniform and turned Lady Anne's head. But Julia was standing too close now, and the sun was unforgiving. In its light, his eyes were translucent as bottle glass, not quite green or blue. Changeable, like her own. The people who'd told her she had her mother's eyes had never met this man.

Yes, she saw a hint of herself in his face. Or did she only imagine what she so badly longed to see?

"I must look ancient to a young girl like you," he began, self-conscious under her scrutiny. "The years have not been kind to me, I'm afraid. But you have grown into a very pretty girl. Though I wager you know that well enough."

"Do I look as you thought I would?" Julia asked.

He tucked his chin, considering, "When you walked out here, I thought, hang me, she looks like Lady Amelia but with lighter hair."

"Do you see any of Lady Anne in me?"

Twisting his lip, he studied her face. "A bit. Her nose and chin, perhaps. And I see you're wearing her locket. But I confess my memory isn't all it should be, and I haven't seen her in twenty years, remember."

"I see her every day," Julia said, feeling foolish even as she said it. "Her portrait hangs in the hall inside."

He didn't seem to hear her but continued to stare, shaking his head in awe. "Hard to believe you are the same wee babe I brought here all those years ago."

Julia hoped he wasn't disappointed. How had he imagined her? Or had he bothered to imagine this reunion at all? Even if he had, likely nowhere near the hundreds of times she had done so.

Lieutenant Tremelling turned and lifted his chin toward the old church. "That's where I met your mother. In the Buckleigh churchyard. Do they still hold services there?"

Julia shook her head. "Only on special holidays and the occasional wedding or funeral."

He nodded. "That's why I first came here—for a wedding of a shipmate. His bride had grown up nearby. I was sure I'd be bored out of my wits at a small country wedding. Instead I took one look at Lady Anne Buckleigh and set my sights on winning her. Weren't no easy task either, I can tell you."

Apparently not—I hear lying and manipulation were required, Julia thought, biting back the words. She didn't want to embarrass or pressure him, but remaining silent went against her tendency to speak her mind and worry about consequences later. She waited to see if he would tell her his version of events without having to wrest it from him.

Julia prompted, "Lady Amelia told me she thought I had *your* hair. And your smile."

"Did she now?" He smiled at this.

In that flash Julia could see her mother had been right. When he smiled, she caught another glimpse of the dashing man he'd once been.

"Yes." He nodded. "I had yellow hair like yours as a younger man."

Suddenly his smile faded. He winced in confusion as though looking into the sun. "Lady Amelia told you that . . . ? That you had my smile and all?"

That's right, Julia reminded herself. *He probably thinks Mother still believes John Desmond—the man Anne named—is my real father. But he would assume Lady Amelia would never mention the dancing master to me.*

"It's all right," Julia said quietly. "I know Lady Anne was with child before the two of you married. I also know that you are my father, even though she originally claimed you were not to"—*overcome Grandfather's objections without losing her dowry*—"spare your life."

Julia tensed, fearing he would deny it. Instead he asked, "How do you know all that?"

"Lady Anne wrote a letter confessing all. I've read it."

"Did she? When?"

"Not long before her father died, I gather."

He looked down, chewing his lip in thought. "I ought to have guessed. I knew Anne felt guilty, about the duel and her brother's death. I admit I wasn't keen on losing the dowry, though it was her idea to claim I wasn't your father. She was afraid of what her brother would do to me. I wasn't. But in the end, I went along with it. I told her a dozen times it wasn't our fault. Still, she couldn't rest. Awful dreams she had about it."

"My moth— Lady Amelia has bad dreams about it too."

He shook his head. "A sorry business all around. But that's all water under the bridge now. Does no good to torture oneself with *what ifs* and *should have dones.*"

Had he tortured himself with second-guessing and guilt? Somehow she doubted it. But Lady Anne had. That was something.

He pulled a face. "What's important is that we married as soon as we could. We meant to give you a proper family and a proper home. And we would have too, had Anne lived."

Julia wondered if they would have been able to do so even had Anne lived, with Lieutenant Tremelling so often away at sea, and Anne left to fend for herself for months on end.

"Why did you give me away?" Julia forced herself to ask, though she detested how vulnerable her voice sounded.

"You know why," he said. "Your mother died. I could not raise you on my own."

"Why?"

"Why? Because I am a naval officer. Gone to sea for months on end."

"Was there no other profession you might have turned to?" Why had she bothered to ask? Did she really want to hear him say the navy was more important to him? That he didn't care enough to seek a change in occupation?

"I couldn't have done that," he said. "The navy is all I know. Anne knew that when she married me. I couldn't change for her, and I . . ."

"Couldn't change for me?" Julia finished for him.

He lifted his hands. "What would I have taken up? I was too old to learn a new skill, to start over as someone's apprentice. I might have found some lowly post, but how then would I have provided for you and a nurse?"

Julia snapped, "As it is, you didn't provide for me at all."

His brows rose. "Now I see a bit of Anne's temper in you. That I do recall. But I did provide for you, didn't I? I swallowed my pride and came to Lady Amelia, who'd never made any secret of how she felt about me—that I wasn't good enough for her sister."

"But had you no money saved? What of Anne's dowry?"

He winced. "Gone, I'm afraid. A 'can't fail' investment that did just that. Anne warned me, but I would have my way."

"So Lady Amelia gave you money in return for me. Is that it?"

He clearly hadn't expected the question. His mouth parted, then he closed it, and started again. "I wouldn't say that. I own she helped me get back on my feet after Anne's death. And yes, she's sent money now and again over the years, when times were hard."

Even if his motives had been self-serving, Julia realized he *had* provided for her, in his way. Otherwise she might have grown up in a shabby pair of rooms in the hustle and bustle of a port city, with a dead mother, an absent father, and some paid nurse to keep her alive until her father's next shore leave. Her education would have been

piecemeal at best. Her speech, her health—even her complexion—
would have suffered.

She asked, "Have I any half brothers or sisters?"

"Not that I know of." His laugh died before it started, ending in
an odd choked sound—no doubt realizing his poor taste in saying
such a thing to a young lady, let alone his daughter. "That is, I never
remarried. Not—official-like. I do have a . . . woman friend I've been
with for years now."

"What about other family?" she asked. "Have I grandparents or
aunts, uncles, or cousins on your side? I haven't any relatives on the
Buckleigh side, nor the Midwinter. At least, none close."

He shook his head. "My parents are long gone, I'm afraid. I did have
a brother, but last I heard he'd moved to the West Indies to work for
a planter there. I don't know if he ever married or had children. Not
much of a writer, Dick wasn't."

"That seems to run in the family."

"Ha. Yes, well. I know I'm not much of a letter writer either. And
even if I were, I knew Amelia intended to raise you as her own. I didn't
think she'd even tell you about me."

"Is that why you didn't come sooner?"

He shrugged. "I didn't think Lady Amelia wanted me to. Not really.
And even after Mr. Barlow came to convince me . . . I don't know. I
took a look at myself, my life . . . and I didn't think you'd like what you
saw. Heaven knows I don't most days."

Ever since Julia found that letter to *Grace Amelia*, she had wondered
where she had come from and what her life might have been like.
She had imagined a happy family with an affectionate mother given
to smiles, embraces, and laughter. And a doting father who teased
her and took her on adventures. Perhaps a little brother and sister to
look up to her, to sing around the fire at Christmas, and join in lively
conversation around the dinner table. A picture far more warm and
jovial than the life she'd lived instead.

But now those images floated above her like glistening soap bubbles,
popping one by one.

Julia pressed her lips together, then said, "I still have that mermaid you sent me."

"Do you indeed?" His brows rose in surprise. "A silly thing to send a young girl, I suppose. It's a boatswain's whistle, actually. But when I saw it in a shop in France, I thought of you. I doubted Lady Amelia would ever give it to you."

"She did, though I believed it to be a gift from 'my father.' I did not yet know about you."

"Ah." He nodded his understanding.

"I only learned the truth recently. I found the letter Lady Anne had written to me. Apparently you delivered it to Lady Amelia when you delivered me."

"Did I? I forgot about that letter."

"It's where I first saw my real name. My original name."

"Grace," he said.

Julia nodded. "Yes, Grace Amelia."

He waved a dismissive hand. "That's right, but I always called you Grace. My Gracie girl."

"Did you?" Julia breathed. Hot tears filled her eyes.

He looked stunned. "I . . . didn't mean to upset you."

"No. No, I like hearing it." *A pet name at last.*

"Do you? Good. I like saying it." He smiled tentatively. "But I don't like seeing my girl cry. Come on, Gracie girl. How about a smile for your old man before I go?"

She blinked. "Leaving already?"

"Aye. Told the missus I'd be back tonight, and the coach leaves in half an hour."

"Oh. I see."

"I've got something to give you before I go." He slid the knapsack from his shoulder and pulled out a book tied with a crude twine bow. "I feel foolish even giving it to you, seeing how grown up you are. In my mind, you were yet a little girl."

"That's all right. I still like to read."

"Thought you might. Never went in for books myself, but Anne did." He self-consciously fingered the cover of *Gulliver's Travels*. "You probably read this long ago."

She had. But she would never say so and hurt his feelings. She would read it to the girls at Miss Llewellyn's. "It's perfect," she said. "I adore stories—especially adventure stories. Thank you. I shall treasure it."

He exhaled in relief. "Good. I'm glad."

He made no offer of a future meeting, and she did not ask for one. She found, deep within herself, a slowly rising feeling of contentment, like bread rising in a warm kitchen on a lazy summer morning.

It was enough.

Impulsively, she stuck out her hand. "Thank you, Lieutenant Tremelling. I appreciate your taking the time to come here and answer my questions."

He took her hand. Held it. "My pleasure. As it turns out."

She said abruptly, "If you'd like to see Lady Anne again, you're welcome to come inside and see her portrait."

He hesitated. "No, that's all right. I remember her in my heart, and that's enough for me. Besides I don't think I'd want her seeing me now, washed-up salt that I am." A corner of his mouth quirked. "Let her keep her memories, and I shall keep mine."

"Very well." She extracted her hand from his. "Take care of yourself."

"I shall, more or less. And you do the same."

Julia started to walk away, then turned back. "You did right, you know. In bringing me here to Lady Amelia."

"Did I?" he asked.

She nodded. "I haven't made it easy for her, but she's been a good mother to me."

"I am glad to hear you say so."

Julia formed a wobbly smile. "So am I."

Returning to the house, Julia walked to the drawing room. Finding the door halfway open, she quietly crossed the threshold and paused. Apparently her mother had not heard her enter. For a moment Julia remained just inside the doorway, taken aback to see Lady Amelia standing at the window, head bowed in grief, or in prayer. She looked so fragile, so vulnerable, that Julia's heart softened toward the woman she'd so often battled against.

Julia reached out and pushed the door a few inches, and the hinges obliged with their customary creak.

Her mother's head snapped up, and the guard fell back over her eyes. She straightened her shoulders, but Julia did not miss the clenching of her hands at her sides.

"Well?"

"I am glad I met him."

"Are you?" Fear flashed in her eyes.

In that moment Julia felt a perverse sense of power. She held the upper hand and knew it. She could likely ask for anything she wanted with her mother worried as she was—likely fearing Julia might announce her plans to go off and live with Lieutenant Tremelling or something even less likely.

But Julia found she felt no pleasure at the thought. No desire to manipulate or provoke, only to assure.

How foreign.

"And?" her mother prodded, trying to mask her anxiety. "Have you made plans to see him again?"

Julia inhaled and shook her head. "No. He didn't offer. And that's all right with me."

"Is it?"

Julia thought, then nodded. "Yes, I find that it is."

Give us grace, Almighty Father, so to pray, as to deserve to be heard, to address thee with our Hearts, as with our lips. Thou art every where present, from Thee no secret can be hid.

—Jane Austen

Chapter 29

That Sunday in church, Amelia could barely sit still. As thankful as she was about Julia's visit with Tremelling, her mind still churned over her conversation with Mr. Arscott the Friday before, tormenting her with what might have been. She was tempted to leave things lie as they were and silently justified doing so. She was not obligated to reveal the new evidence in John Desmond's favor, she told herself. There were no charges against him, and she had made certain none would arise in future. That was enough, surely. There was no point in resurrecting the past, the awful events and swirling scandal some in the village were too young to even recall. No. She had done her duty—to him and to the Buckleigh name.

She leaned back against the hard wooden pew and drew in a long breath, telling herself to be calm. It was already time for the sermon, and she had barely heard a word of the service so far, not a single prayer or hymn. *Pay heed,* a small internal voice whispered. *Listen.*

The dear curate, Mr. Evans, was officiating the Sunday service in the rector's stead. He climbed gingerly into the high pulpit, opened his black book, and read from the book of Matthew, chapter five.

And every word was like an arrow straight to her heart.

"'But I say unto you, That whosoever is angry with his brother without a cause shall be in danger of the judgment. . . .'"

Had the clergyman somehow read her mind?

Almighty Father, have mercy, Amelia prayed. *I am sorry, but—what was I to think? Was I to believe Desmond's word over my own sister's? And what about Graham?*

"'Therefore if thou bring thy gift to the altar, and there rememberest that thy brother hath ought against thee; Leave there thy gift before the altar, and go thy way; first be reconciled to thy brother, and then come and offer thy gift.'"

Abruptly Amelia stood, as though the pew were on fire.

The curate looked up from his text, mouth ajar.

Around her the congregants swiveled and stared.

All those eyes focused on her, people who looked up to her as the lady of the manor, who followed her lead in so many ways. How she had led them astray. . . . But John Desmond was not in attendance. Before Graham's death, he used to attend regularly but now did not risk public outcry by joining his neighbors in worship. Another thing her family had taken from him.

"I need to say something," she blurted, before thoughts of saving face could triumph. She owed it to him and so much more. "I . . . have a confession to make." She licked dry lips.

Around the nave, some people exchanged nervous glances while others leaned forward, eager to hear titillating gossip.

She took a steadying breath. "Many of you know that I blamed Mr. John Desmond for . . . several . . . calamities and losses in my family years ago. Recently, I have learned that he had been falsely accused. Yes, he was involved in a duel with my brother—one my brother did not survive. My brother wrongly believed his cause just and challenged Mr. Desmond, attacked him for something Mr. Desmond did not do."

She swallowed. "Now I realize many of you—out of misplaced

loyalty to me, or mistaken prejudice—have not welcomed Mr. Desmond back to Beaworthy, and worse have treated him and his parents unkindly or not patronized their forge. That is my fault, all because of the false charges my family laid at his feet some twenty years ago."

She looked around the assembled faces—some well-known, some barely—willing them to believe her and take her words to heart, whatever they thought of her. There were the Valcourts. And Mr. Arscott. The schoolmistress, Miss Llewellyn. And farther back, many of her own servants and tenants.

"And so today," she said, "spurred by the Scripture Mr. Evans read, I could not sit here, silent, and let you go on believing the worst of him. It is not true. It has never been true."

She paused for breath, and noticed the woman from the bakery clap a hand across her gaped mouth. And in the pew beside Amelia, Julia sat with tears in her eyes.

Amelia picked up her prayer book and concluded, "So, if you will excuse me, I will go and see if I might be reconciled to him."

Amelia asked Isaacs to drive her directly to the Desmonds' forge. Her heart still burning and convicted within her, she knew she would not rest until she had spoken with him and made things right.

When she reached the Desmonds', Isaacs helped her down.

Pulse racing, she looked toward the forge, and there he was on the porch. Not working on the Sabbath, but sitting on a bench, reading from the leather-bound Bible in his lap.

Seeing her approach, he rose, surprise and concern etched across his handsome face.

Lady Amelia looked at the man and could hardly breathe.

"Hello, Amy . . . sorry. Lady Amelia."

Her throat suddenly dry, she wordlessly indicated the bench he'd just vacated.

"Do you mind if I sit?"

"No, of course not." He glanced around the well-used porch. "But your gown . . . Shall we go into the house?"

She shook her head. "No thank you. I would rather speak to you here. Privately."

He moved aside his teacup, and she silently sat down.

He stood waiting, clearly feeling awkward. He asked, "Did church let out early this morning?"

She shook her head but said nothing, her mind racing yet blank at the same time.

He pressed the Bible in his hands, waiting for her to speak, expression growing increasingly concerned. "Has something happened?" he asked. "Is Julia all right?"

"I think she is all right, yes," she replied. "Her father finally came to see her."

"Oh . . ." The air seemed to leave him.

Was it the fact that Tremelling had come at last, or her outward acknowledgement that Desmond was not Julia's father?

"And . . . how did that go?" he asked gently.

She drew in a deep breath. "I wasn't privy to much of their conversation. He wouldn't come inside, so she went out to him."

"Did he stay long?"

She shook her head, lip pursed. "Half an hour, perhaps a little more."

"What did she say about it afterward?"

"That she was glad he came. That he answered her questions."

"That's good. Does she plan to see him again?"

"I don't think so. She said he did not ask for another meeting, and neither did she. I own, I was selfishly relieved. I feared he might want to take her away with him. But at the same time, I was sorry for her sake, that he did not at least express interest in seeing her again. She said she did not mind, but I fancied I saw hurt in her eyes. Disappointment."

Amelia blinked away sudden tears and averted her face. "And you will think me ridiculous, but just for a moment, I found myself wishing you *were* her father. For you would not have hurt her or disappointed her."

She risked a glance at him and saw his eyes widen in surprise. For several moments he stood, apparently stunned into silence, and she began to regret her rash words.

But then he said in quiet wonder, "That is a great compliment, my lady. And you're right. I would not hurt her for the world."

He cleared his throat and humor lit his eyes. "But I don't think any parent can expect to escape this life without disappointing his child at some point. And the same could be said the other way around. We all of us fall short now and again, and disappoint someone dear to us, or ourselves. Thankfully, my parents have always been the forgiving sort."

She looked up at him, nerves quaking, throat tight. "And . . . are you? The forgiving sort, I mean?"

He nodded. "I hope so, yes. Though there are three things for which I've never been able to forgive myself."

She lowered her eyes, afraid to ask, longing to know. She whispered, "Three things?"

He sat on the bench beside her. "Aye. Hurting my parents. Hurting you. And ending Graham's life."

He ran an agitated hand through his hair. "You never would let me apologize or explain. And how could I? When I knew I had done something unforgivable in your eyes."

His face puckered in fresh grief. "I never meant to kill Graham. And I am so sorry he died that day. I can tell you all the things I've tried to tell myself over the years: 'He tossed me a dueling sword and came at me. What was I to do? I reacted in self-defense. Instinct. There was no time to think . . .'

"How I wish I could go back and change the events of that day. Do it all over again, even if it meant I was the one to die instead of Graham. I cannot forgive myself, so I don't expect you to forgive me either."

The pain in his expression softened her heart all the more. "I have spent years blaming you," she said. "For Anne, for Graham, for Papa . . . But it wasn't fair. It wasn't your fault."

He looked at her, dark eyes shimmering.

For a moment she was tempted to sink into those eyes, but she looked away, determined to follow this through.

"I went to see the magistrate, and he gave me a letter Anne wrote to my father not long before he died. Confessing everything."

Desmond's eyebrows rose. "Did she?"

Amelia nodded. "But I should have believed you without any letter." She took a deep breath. "I misjudged you—in so many ways. In my misery I was all too quick to believe the worst about you. It was wrong of me." She swallowed. "And I am sorry."

His mouth parted. He stared at her, stunned.

She pushed out the final words over a painful lump in her throat. "Will you forgive me, John Desmond?"

Slowly he began to shake his head, and for a moment she feared he was refusing her request.

Then he said, "You are asking *me* to forgive *you*?"

Chin quivering, she nodded.

He rose and reached down a hand to her. She placed her trembling fingers in his, and he gently tugged her to her feet.

Keeping hold of her hand, he looked into her eyes, one corner of his mouth quirked in a sad smile. "Dear Amy, don't you know I forgave you years ago?"

Heart squeezing, Amelia drew a shaky breath. "Julia told me something you said to her—that if you *were* her father, you would not deny it."

"Aye. And did she tell you what else I said?"

She looked into his intense dark eyes, and managed a little shake of her head.

He captured her other hand as well. "I told her if she were my daughter, she would never need doubt I loved her." His gaze nearly fierce, he added hoarsely, "And neither would her mother."

⟳

Alec left church that morning with his mother and sister, all of them quiet and reflective. Alec had been astounded when Lady Amelia had absolved John Desmond, especially in such a humble public way. He was touched—and sorry for every uncharitable thought he'd ever had about her.

Ahead of them, he saw Miss Midwinter, striding down the church path, planning to walk home, he guessed, since her mother had taken the carriage when she left during the service. He excused himself from his family and quickened his pace to catch up with her.

"May I walk with you?" he asked, coming alongside.

"Of course." She seemed relieved to see him. "What an extraordinary service!"

"Indeed. No one was tempted to fall asleep today."

"Can you believe she stood up in the middle of church, and pronounced Mr. Desmond's innocence?" Julia shook her head. "I was amazed. And I confess, quite proud of her."

"As well you should be. You ought to tell her so."

"I shall. I wonder how her meeting with Mr. Desmond is going."

"I wonder as well. I spent the rest of the service praying for them both."

"Did you? That was kind."

For a few moments, they walked along the High Street without speaking, past the Sunday-silent shops.

Then Julia said, "I finally met Lieutenant Tremelling yesterday."

He looked at her, interested but wary. "How . . . did it go?"

She briefly summarized the encounter, and then Alec asked, "Not the outcome you'd hoped for?"

Her shoulders lifted in a self-conscious shrug. "I suppose a foolish part of me hoped he would take me away with him, and we would sail the high seas together. But that did not happen, so I shall be anchored here in boring Beaworthy for the foreseeable future." She sighed. "Still, I am glad to have met him."

As they turned onto the Buckleigh Road, she sidestepped a puddle, then asked, "How go plans for the grand opening dance?"

"We rehearse again tomorrow. We have yet to announce a date, but we're looking at the second Friday in May." The musicians had decided it would be wise to wait until after May Day, with all its somber connotations.

Alec added, "I worry the Wilcoxes will again try to spoil our plans. I had thought to sleep in the assembly room the night before, with sword at hand, but the constable assures me he will stand guard himself this time."

Julia's fair brows rose. "Does he indeed? I am surprised."

"Did Lady Amelia light a fire under him, do you think?" Alec asked.

"That sounds unlikely—though I did see Mr. Lamont leaving Buckleigh Manor recently, now that you mention it."

There was so much more he wanted to say to her, but at that moment the Buckleigh barouche rattled up the road behind them, slowing down to collect Julia, no doubt.

Knowing his time was short, Alec asked quickly, "Any chance you can get away tomorrow?"

"Certainly."

"Will you meet me at the fountain after my last lesson—say, three o'clock?"

Her eyes shone with curiosity. "Very well. I shall look forward to it."

When the carriage halted, Alec glanced through the window at Lady Amelia, hoping to see a change there, some sign that the meeting with Desmond had gone well, but her expression was impossible to decipher.

❧

On the last day of April, Julia stood outside the market hall, waiting for Mr. Valcourt to finish his final lesson of the day. Her mother had said little upon her return from the Desmonds' forge. Julia didn't press her but hoped she had made peace with the man Julia had grown fond of.

While she waited, she found herself staring at the fountain. She had paid it little attention before, dry as it had been for as long as she remembered.

She felt someone's presence and stiffened, dreading to find Felton Wilcox leering over her. But it was only Mr. Evans, the kindly old curate.

"It's unusual, isn't it?" he asked, eyes on the carved fountain.

"Yes, I suppose it is." She again surveyed the draped female figure reaching upward with head bowed. The broken chains at her feet. Then she looked back at him, comforted by his familiar presence. "Who built it?" she asked.

He glanced at her in mild surprise. "Has your mother not told you the story?"

Julia shook her head.

"It was commissioned and designed by Lady Katherine Buckleigh, nearly a hundred years ago. I believe she would be your great-great-great grandmother or something like that." He chuckled and then returned his gaze to the fountain.

"Lady Katherine had always been a proud, hardhearted woman—" He lifted his forefinger. "Her words, mind. But she stood up in church one morning and declared she'd found peace with God."

He gave her a sidelong glance. "There's an account of it written in the church records, if you'd like to read it for yourself sometime."

"Perhaps I shall. Go on."

He nodded and continued, "She said she'd had a vision of herself, bound in chains, a prisoner of sin and misery. Then she saw our Lord Jesus, holding the key, ready to free her if she would but turn to Him. Then Lady Katherine saw her chains falling away, her downcast head of shame becoming a bowed head of worship. She lifted her freed hands to praise Him, and to point the way for others." Mr. Evans lifted his own hands to demonstrate, paralleling the figure above them.

Then he said, "Afterward, she drew a figure based on her vision. She commissioned the fountain and oversaw the work herself. It was her way of commemorating the moment. To thank Him for the grace He had given her—had given everyone."

Julia studied the fountain. "I don't see her name anywhere."

"No, but there's a plaque somewhere. . . ." He studied the base of the fountain, then pointed. "There, all but grown over." He began to bend cumbrously down, but she laid a hand on his arm.

"Allow me." Julia sank down on her haunches. "Where?"

"That small rectangle there. See it?"

Julia brushed away the dead leaves that had gathered around the base, and began pulling up muddy overgrown grass. In her effort, she yanked out a long, woody root as well and nearly lost her footing.

Finally she uncovered the plaque, but its inscription was unreadable, the engraved words encrusted with dirt, moss, and lichen.

Julia picked up a twig and began to scrape away at the letters.

"That's it," Mr. Evans encouraged.

The letters revealed themselves, and Julia smiled up at the curate. She ran her gloved fingers over three engraved words.

Love and Grace.

Mr. Valcourt emerged from his academy and walked toward them. Rising, she observed with pleasure his athletic stride and excellent bearing. He looked the picture of a confident, successful gentleman. He would be all that and more if she had anything to say about it. Once again Julia breathed a prayer of thanksgiving that he had not been seriously injured in the fall—and that he would have his grand opening after all.

He tipped his hat. "Miss Midwinter. Mr. Evans. A good day to you both."

The curate remained long enough to greet him, then went on his way.

Mr. Valcourt stood a respectable distance from Julia, clasped his hands behind his back, and looked up at the fountain in silence. He waited until Mr. Evans was out of earshot, then began, "I have been thinking, Miss Midwinter—how often you say you don't like Beaworthy..."

Julia looked at his profile, his inscrutable expression. "That's correct."

"May I ask why?"

"I've told you. Because it's boring here. Small, insignificant, stifled by the past."

"Are you describing the village, or yourself?"

She gasped, irritation flaring.

He lifted a placating hand. "Tell you what. If you don't like Beaworthy the way it is, let's change it."

"What do you mean?" she asked. "Are you talking about your grand opening?"

"No. Not specifically. Let's not wait 'til then. Let's throw off the rules that aren't scriptural or helpful and bring back life and celebration."

Her eyes widened. "How?"

A small grin stole over his face. "I don't know everything such a change would require, but I do know one way to start. . . ."

Julia listened to his plan with interest. Then, before going their separate ways, she reiterated the details one more time. "You will meet me here tomorrow, right here by the fountain?"

"Yes."

"You won't leave me standing here alone? Looking foolish?"

"No, I shan't," Alec said firmly. "I will be here."

"At twelve?"

"Right. The traditional time." He started to walk away, then turned back. "If I am a few minutes late, don't worry. Don't assume I've abandoned you. I'll be here."

She nodded, his words pinching her heart. Was it an unintentional choice of words? Or did he know her so well that he recognized, deep in her heart, she feared any man she cared for would abandon her?

She forced a smile. "Very well. I shall wait for you."

As Mr. Valcourt strode away, the girl from the flower shop saw Julia, curtsied, and said timidly, "Good day, miss. Will you and your mum be by in the mornin' for your posies as usual?"

She smiled at the girl. "I believe so. After all, it is tradition."

Lady Amelia's May Day ritual was not something Julia looked forward to, but she did look forward to the plans for afterward. If only her mother would not spoil them . . .

Alec went first to Uncle Ramsay's office. He knew his uncle wouldn't participate, but he at least wanted to respectfully inform him of his plans, and hoped he would not object, or at least not forbid them.

Entering the law office, Alec greeted the clerks, Mr. Pugsworth and Mr. Bixby, then stepped to the door of his uncle's private office.

There on his desk, littered with sheaves of papers, sat a large iced cake. A generous wedge lay on a plate before him, and his uncle was chewing a forkful as he read a legal document of some sort.

"Hello, Alec," he said around a mouthful. "Forgive me, I was just having a bite. Care to join me?"

"Is that one of Mrs. Tickle's cakes?" Alec asked, realization beginning to dawn.

He nodded, and wiped his mouth. "Silly woman brings one by nearly
every other day. Says I'm doing her a favor by helping her dispose of
her unsold goods."

Favor, indeed. Alec bit back a smile. The mystery of Cornelius Ramsay's portly figure had been solved.

After speaking with his uncle, Alec walked over to Medlands and
discussed his plans with the Allens. All were eager to be involved,
except for Walter.

"Sorry, ol' chap," Walt said. "You know I'd do anything for you. But
I can't dance in public. I'd end up embarrassing us both. But I shall be
there, of course, to support you."

"No. You shall learn the dance, Walter Allen, if it's the last thing I
accomplish on this earth." Alec considered Walter's predicament for
a moment and then said, "I have an idea. . . ."

He asked for pen and paper and sat at Sir Herbert's desk, while
Walter looked on. Alec began to draw a diagram, sketching two shoe-
print shapes in each position of the dance, then numbering the steps,
the movements for both feet, *L* and *R*, in a series of drawings.

Walter's eyes widened as he watched. "Is *that* what I was meant to
be doing?"

The light went on in Walter Allen's eyes. And in Alec's heart.

Alec had seen the method attempted with notable success only once
before. His grandfather had been engaged to teach a man of science, a
noted fellow in the Royal Society who was marrying above himself and
wished to add dancing to his otherwise scholarly accomplishments.
The man might have been a genius, but when it came to dancing he was
completely befuddled. It was the only time Alec saw his patient, gentle
grandfather throw up his hands in frustration. In desperation, he had
painstakingly drawn a series of numbered diagrams—feet connected
with dotted lines at the various angles and intervals required of each
dance. Somehow the diagrams had opened the man's eyes and allowed
him to master the steps that had previously eluded him.

Alec could only hope the same method might work for his friend.

The drawings took far longer than Alec had expected and he returned home barely in time for dinner. There, he shared his plan with his mother and sister.

His mother, in turn, wanted to discuss her decision. Over the last few days, she confided, she had begun several letters to her estranged husband—some railing and refusing, the next full of stipulations. She had torn and wadded each in turn. For now, she decided, she would send no letter. And that would be answer enough. Alec was disappointed but did not argue, still hoping that, in time, she would have a change of heart.

After the talk with his mother, the hour was late. Alec decided to wait until morning to talk to Desmond and finalize the day's arrangements.

To every thing there is a season, and a time to every
purpose under the heaven: A time to be born, and a time
to die; . . . A time to kill, and a time to heal; . . . A time to
weep, and a time to laugh; a time to mourn, and a time
to dance.

—Ecclesiastes, chapter 3

Chapter 30

Julia and her mother set off earlier than usual the next morning. Grey
clouds were gathering in the west, and Lady Amelia wished to carry
out their May Day tradition before the rain reached them. Taking
the barouche into the village as usual, they purchased flowers, laid a
bouquet of forget-me-nots at the market hall in Graham's memory,
and visited the family graves. The rain held off, but her mother did
not seem inclined to tarry in either the High Street or churchyard that
year, which suited Julia's plans perfectly.

They returned to Buckleigh Manor sufficiently early for Julia to
enjoy a late breakfast with her mother. After the meal, she would slip
away and walk back to the village in plenty of time to meet Mr. Valcourt at twelve.

∽

In the morning, Alec dressed with care, and put a sprig of lily of
the valley in his buttonhole. Then, taking his grandfather's walking

stick with him, he strode into the village to call on the Thornes, Mr. Jones, Mr. Evans, and Mrs. Tickle, though he didn't think his neighbor would take part, after her reaction to seeing Desmond in the academy. Afterward, Alec walked to Miss Llewellyn's school, then out to the forge to speak with Desmond, missing Apollo more with each step. As he went, he glanced up at the sky, hoping the amassing grey clouds wouldn't turn into a midday downpour and spoil their plans.

When he arrived at the forge, Desmond was not there. He knocked at the Desmonds' door and his mother invited him inside.

Mr. and Mrs. Desmond gestured toward their small dining table with raised-brow expectation, awaiting his response.

"Cahn you believe it, lad?" Mr. Desmond asked. "Ever seen such a fine, big cake in yer life?"

Alec regarded the yellow-and-white iced cake in surprise. "It is indeed impressive," he agreed, noticing a decorative border of peppermint candies. "Is it one of Mrs. Tickle's?"

"Yes," Mrs. Desmond said, eyes wide in wonder. "She delivered it here yesterday. For Johnny."

"Aye. Fer all of us."

Mrs. Tickle has been busy, Alec thought. He smiled, his heart lightening to see their happy expressions and to know what the gift meant.

The Desmonds told him their son had been called away to the Strickland place, to repair an iron rail or some such. But they promised to deliver Alec's message as soon as he returned.

The Stricklands lived several miles away, and Alec feared his friend would not return by twelve. But there was not sufficient time for Alec to make the trip out there and return by noon himself. He sighed, reproaching himself for not walking out to the forge last night. Oh well, it was too late now. He would have to return to the village without him and hope Desmond could join them later.

He thanked the Desmonds and began the walk back to Beaworthy. A quick look at his pocket watch assured him he had plenty of time.

Ahead of him, two figures appeared on the road and stopped, blocking his way.

Thunder and turf. Not these two.

Joe and Felton Wilcox stood, legs spread, arms crossed over their chests.

"Well, well," Felton said. "If it ain't the caper merchant. What's your hurry, caper merchant? Late for your beauty treatment?"

Beside him, Joe guffawed. "Good one."

Alec's hands fisted on their own accord, ready to defend himself. If only he had thought to wear his sword.

Abruptly an odd sense of acceptance stole over him, shrouding him in illogical calm.

"You know what, gents?" He smiled and spread his hands. "I am a caper merchant, as you call it, and proud of it. Yes, I like to dance. I am graceful and gentlemanlike and dress well. I am not cut out for work in the clay pits as you are, and I am not, nor will I ever be, as good a wrestler as either of you. Nor will I ever smell half as bad, and that's all right with me."

Joe nodded along, enjoying Alec's apparent praise.

But Felton narrowed his eyes, catching the insult. "Speaking of clay pits, Valcourt, there's a nice mud puddle right there." He gestured toward the roadside sludge left by recent rains.

Joe looked over and smiled. "Well, ain't that convenient."

"Perhaps we ought to do Mr. Fancy Pants a favor and acquaint him with its pleasures?"

With a glance of silent agreement, both men charged with a great roar.

Alec waited until the last second, and then leapt to the side with a move that would have made his grandfather—or any bullfighter—proud.

Meeting with no collision to slow his momentum, Joe flew toward the mud puddle. His feet flew out from under him. He made a wild grab for his brother and almost took Felton down with him. Felton skidded through the mud, arms windmilling, but Alec knew it was only a matter of seconds before he attacked again.

For one of those brief seconds, Alec looked at the mud, then his fine suit of clean clothes. With an inward shrug he tossed down his stick and launched himself at Felton, still off balance, and managed to knock the larger man off his feet.

Splosh. Squilch. Down into the mud they went. Felton fell on his back. Alec landed atop the man's broad torso. Mud splattered onto Alec's face. His shins sank into damp sludge. Alec rolled to the side, narrowly evading Felton's bear-like grasp.

Joe heaved himself up none too gracefully, slipped again, and landed on his knees.

Alec snatched up his walking stick. "Listen, gents. There is somewhere I need to be. So let's postpone this little mud fight for now. In the meantime, what would you say to a few pints down at the public house, and hefty slices of Mrs. Tickle's famous pork and apple pie, ey? My treat?"

"Well . . ." Joe said, with a hopeful look at Felton.

Felton shook the hair from his face, eyes narrowed. "Nice try, macaroni."

"Oh, come on, Felton," Joe whined eagerly, lumbering to his feet once more.

Alec slapped the walking stick against his palm. "And if you still want to pummel me after you've eaten and drunk your fill," he added, "I shall meet you wherever and whenever you like, all right?"

"Seems very fair, Felton," Joe said, licking his lips.

"You would think so, Joe," Felton sneered, rising and brushing himself off. "Anything for a free pint."

Felton eyed Alec—and his stick—with distrust. "Very well, Valcourt. We know where you live, and can always find you another time. But if yer buyin', we're drinkin.'"

Alec was surprised though relieved Felton Wilcox had agreed. Had the man recognized the painful possibilities presented by the stout walking stick in Alex's grip? He could only hope so.

Alec tossed Joe a silver crown. "I have to go home and change first. But you two get started without me."

On the green before the fountain, Julia looked at her watch pin with trembling fingers. It was foolish to be nervous, she told herself. Still three minutes before twelve. *Mr. Valcourt said he would come and he will. He'll be here.*

How self-conscious she felt, standing there in the midst of the High Street, alone before the fountain of Love and Grace.

Love and Grace. So beautiful together carved in limestone. Such uneasy companions in Julia Midwinter's soul.

Perhaps her watch pin was fast. She looked up at the church tower, wishing it had a clock. But Beaworthy had no striking clock. Beaworthy had bell ringers who rang, not every hour or even every day, but on special occasions. And the first of May at twelve o'clock had been marked by the ringing of bells for twenty years, and would no doubt be marked again today. She wondered which bell ringers were on duty.

Julia felt someone's gaze on her and turned her head. Mr. Deane, the greengrocer, paused before the crates of produce and baskets of spring berries on display before his shop, no doubt wondering what Miss Midwinter was doing, standing there alone.

Did he have any idea what day it was? Had they all forgotten?

Mr. Evans, the curate, came down the street toward St. Michael's, walking beside Mr. Clark and Mr. Rogers, two of Beaworthy's bell ringers. All three men looked over, no doubt surprised to see her standing there. They tipped their hats and disappeared into the church.

Birdsong and silence on a day when there should be happy music, clapping, and dancing feet. Friends and neighbors calling to one another. Hands and voices raised in greeting. She remembered Mr. Desmond's words about the old tradition and missed the community she'd never embraced. Missed Alec too.

Where was he?

He isn't coming, she thought. Like Mr. Midwinter, like Lieutenant Tremelling, even like Lady Anne—they had all left her. In the sky above, grey clouds passed overhead like a portent.

The church bells began to ring, each clang a fist to her heart. *Where is he?*

The innkeeper stood in his doorway, watching her. And there was Mrs. Tickle, the baker, polishing her display window. How would Julia explain herself if the woman came over to chat? Perhaps she should give up and go home.

Suddenly elderly Mrs. Desmond appeared, and Julia's heart lifted. She recalled seeing the small woman standing near this very spot two years before in graceful pose, waiting for someone. Then Mr. Desmond, Senior, had jogged into view, though she hadn't known his name then. He'd tossed aside his apron and took the woman's hand.

Together they had danced around the fountain and down the High Street, their hobbling steps made beautiful by their lingering grace, their smiles, and the love in their eyes as they shuffled away into the afternoon sunlight. . . .

"Mrs. Desmond," Julia now hailed. "Have you come to dance again this year?" She smiled hopefully.

But the small woman's face did not break into an answering smile. "Oh, my dear, I'm afraid not. Have you seen Johnny? Johnny Desmond? I fear his father has taken a turn for the worse."

"Oh no," Julia said. "Shall I find the surgeon?"

"No need. Mr. Mounce is with him already."

"I haven't seen your son, but if I do, I shall send him home directly."

"Thank you, my dear." Knobby hands clasped, Mrs. Desmond looked agitatedly up and down the High Street one last time and, with a regretful glance toward the fountain, turned and hurried away.

Now Julia was alone again. The appointed time had come and gone. Was there any point in staying?

As if to further discourage her, the grey cloud above her opened. A sudden downpour chased her under the market hall.

Alec's words echoed in her mind, his reassuring voice surprisingly deep for his trim frame. *"If I'm a few minutes late, don't worry. Don't assume I've abandoned you. I'll be there."*

Standing there, damp and chilled, she decided she would wait one more minute. After that, rain or no rain, she was going home.

The thought gave her pause, and she realized Buckleigh Manor really was home, in spite of all the negative things she had said about the estate—and its mistress—over the years. Lady Amelia, for all her rigid, overprotective ways, did love her. She was her mother, her family, the only family she had ever really had. And remembering Mr. Desmond's words, Julia was the only family Lady Amelia had as well.

Julia knew she ought to have been grateful. She ought to have been kinder. She would start, she decided, then and there.

The bell rang again, startling her. *Clang, clang, clang.* That was strange.

She looked up, her gaze tracing the bell tower upward to the spire. She felt her eyes drawn to the cross atop the pinnacle, arms outstretched. How many times had she glanced at the village church without really noticing the cross? Without acknowledging what it meant?

Now she faced a difficult truth. All her life, she had been seeking a father's love and approval. . . . And if she could not have a father's love, then any man's approval would do. She had strived so long and so hard to gain attention in the wrong ways and from the wrong people. All the while ignoring her heavenly Father, and His Son.

She closed her eyes and asked God to forgive her. Then she thanked Him for His love and mercy. For grace.

The sun shone through a break in the clouds, a sliver of sunlight, of hope, shining down on that cross. Julia stepped out from under the market hall and felt the warmth of it on her face, through her skin, and into her soul. It was as if God himself had reached down, touched her cheek, and whispered, *"I will never leave you."*

Suddenly Alec came jogging into the High Street from the Buckleigh Road. Her heart leapt. She released a breath she barely realized she'd been holding.

Vaguely she noticed he was wearing freshly pressed trousers rather than the breeches he usually preferred, and a green coat in place of his favorite blue. He was still tying his cravat as he hurried over. She knew he was something of a dandy, but had he really left her standing there simply to change clothes?

Then she noticed a speck of mud along his jaw and another near his ear.

"What happened to you?"

"Sorry I'm late. I hope you didn't worry."

"Are you late?" She fluttered her lashes. "I had not noticed." She sent him a sidelong glance, and they shared a grin.

He held out his hand to her, and she placed her fingers in his. He gave a squeeze that she felt all the way to her heart.

"May I have the honor of this dance, Miss Midwinter?"

She felt her neck heat, self-conscious to be standing there in the middle of the High Street, hand in hand. It felt somewhat . . . daring, she decided. And she liked that. Liked too the warm way Alec Valcourt looked into her eyes.

"I should enjoy it above all things," she said, her grin widening.

They turned, both facing down the High Street side by side, their inside hands joined. Julia feared she'd forgotten the steps, simple though they were.

But Alec, ever the dancing master, murmured reminders as they progressed. "Step, shuffle-step. Step, shuffle-step. Very good, Miss Midwinter. Sixteen counts."

He turned to her and took her other hand as well. "Now, we turn in a circle. Step, step, step, hop . . . All the way around. Perfect. What a natural you are."

Julia warmed at the praise, perhaps more effusive than the simple dance deserved but boosting her confidence nonetheless.

"Now, forward once more."

From somewhere nearby came the sound of a reedy pipe being played.

Julia swiveled her head, surprised to see John Desmond standing on the walkway outside the dancing academy, playing the May Day tune. Mrs. Tickle came out of the bakery and smiled up at him. Julia was about to excuse herself to tell Desmond that his parents needed him, when that very couple hurried around the corner, both looking spry and eager.

"Mr. Desmond, are you all right?" Julia called.

"Right as a trivet, miss." He patted his wife's arm. "The old love here worries for nothing. I choked on a peppermint from one of Mrs. Tickle's cakes, that's all. Mrs. Desmond was sure I was having an apoplexy."

"The old fool lives to frighten me to death, you know."

Julia smiled. "I am so glad you're all right."

"Wouldn't miss this year's May Day dance for the world," Mr. Desmond said.

He bowed to his wispy wife, and she curtsied in return, a fond smile creasing her lined face. Julia noticed the sprig of lily of the valley in his buttonhole and another tucked into his hat band.

Julia and Alec would not dance alone after all. They fell into step behind Mr. and Mrs. Desmond as their son played on.

The innkeeper, Mr. Jones, disappeared within his establishment. But a few minutes later, he returned, striding out of the inn with a bass viol. Behind him came dear Mr. Barlow, fiddle in hand.

John Desmond looked up, surprised and pleased to see them. A moment later, they were joined by Mr. Deane on a flute, his first few notes shrill and out of tune, but quickly finding his way into the melody.

Desmond met her eyes across the distance, and Julia felt that all— well, almost all—was right in her world.

She and Alec shared a smile and danced on.

Alec hummed along with the May Day tune, relishing the dance and his partner. His heart felt lighter than it had in months. Drawn by the music, people began stepping out of shops to see what was going on. Including, unfortunately, the Wilcox brothers from the public house. But even they could not spoil this moment for Alec.

The Medlands carriage rattled up the High Street. James and Walter hopped out, then reached back to hand down Patience and their mother. Sir Herbert brought up the rear. Alec was especially surprised to see Lady Allen, who so rarely went anywhere, disinclined to leave the happy surroundings of Medlands.

Sir Herbert and Lady Allen hurried over and fell into place behind Alec and Julia, giggling like carefree children.

"I hope I remember the steps," she said.

"Of course you do, my love. We danced this every year when we were young. Just follow the others. It does not matter if we stumble once or twice. It's being here that counts."

"Exactly so," Alec agreed.

The curate, Mr. Evans, appeared, with his wife in tow. Behind him came Miss Llewellyn, and a band of bell ringers and their spouses. Tess Thorne and several others came from the direction of the Green Street tenement.

Soon the High Street around the fountain and market hall was filled with dancers, and the walkway became crowded with onlookers, who clapped or tapped their toes to the music.

Alec's mother and sister appeared, wearing tentative smiles. Alec noticed with a start that his mother was out of mourning at last—she wore a lovely blue-and-ivory gown—and looked years younger. For some reason the sight gave Alec hope.

From his law offices across the street emerged Uncle Ramsay, who surveyed the scene with cautious concern. Mr. Pugsworth followed him out. His eyes lit when he saw the schoolmistress, and he walked over to ask her to dance. Miss Llewellyn hesitated but then agreed with a toothy grin.

Walter pulled a folded diagram from his pocket, consulted it one last time, then bowed before Tess. "Miss Thorne, may I have this dance?"

Her dark eyes widened in surprise, and if Alec was not mistaken, pleasure. "Yes, Mr. Allen. I would be delighted to dance with you."

James Allen turned dutifully to his sister. But Patience, Alec noticed, tilted her head significantly toward Aurora. James complied, leading Aurora out to join them.

Then Patience shocked everyone by walking over and standing before the Wilcox brothers. Joe's mouth drooped in surprise. Beside him, Felton straightened to attention, his Adam's apple traveling up and down his throat. He pushed the curtain of blond hair from his eyes and stared at the young woman before him.

As Alec danced past, he heard Patience say, "Mr. Wilcox, you don't intend to threaten or harm my friend Alec Valcourt any further, I trust?"

"Uh . . . no, ma'am. I mean, miss. Miss Allen."

She gave him a lovely smile. "Then shall we join the dance, Mr. Wilcox?"

Felton's mouth fell ajar, but he stuck out his elbow and Patience took it. As the two walked toward the dancers, Nancy from the flower shop claimed hulking Joe as her partner.

Uncle Ramsay stood back, at the periphery, though Alec had expected nothing else. But then Mrs. Tickle grabbed the solicitor's arm and pulled him along behind her into the fray, like a fish on a line.

Alec and Aurora sought out each other's gazes of long habit and shared a laugh of surprised delight at the sight, before returning their attention to their partners.

Other couples joined in. Around them, the sounds of community, of celebration, filled the High Street and village green. Water trickled from the fountain for the first time in years. Alec saw it as a good sign for his future.

Suddenly a second carriage rattled up the High Street. Big, black, and ominous. The Buckleigh Manor barouche.

Alec groaned. Lady Amelia Midwinter had come to put a stop to their celebration before it had barely begun.

The groom hopped down with an umbrella but, seeing the rain had stopped, set it aside. He let down the step and unlatched the carriage door. Then Lady Amelia herself came into view, head bowed to watch her step as she alighted.

The music squeaked to a halt. The crowd hushed. A few onlookers retreated back into shops, hoping not to be seen or associated with the forbidden goings-on.

Lady Amelia looked up, and Alec caught his first full glimpse of her face. She wore an intense expression, part frown, part concentration, as she scanned the crowd, looking for someone—Julia, he supposed. Her gaze tripped over Desmond, then skittered on.

Resolutely, Julia stepped forward, shoulders back, head held high. Not guilty, yet not defiant either.

"Are you looking for me?" she asked evenly.

Lady Amelia blinked. "Um . . . yes. I didn't know where you'd gone. And then it started to rain. . . ."

Lady Amelia again looked around the High Street, taking in the frozen dancers, the startled onlookers, the idle musicians. Mr. Barlow, he noticed, sheepishly ducked his head.

She asked, "What is going on?"

"We're celebrating May Day," Julia explained. "The old Beaworthy tradition."

When Lady Amelia made no reply, Julia added, "It's been far too long since we have done so."

Lady Amelia looked again at the assembled, wary faces. "Well then, don't let me stop you."

No one moved.

"Go on with what you were doing," Lady Amelia urged. "Pray don't stop on my account. I am only one person, after all."

Still no one moved. A few exchanged questioning looks. Was she being sarcastic or sincere?

The elder Mr. Desmond stepped onto the walkway and gave his son a significant look, nodding toward Lady Amelia.

Understanding, Desmond surrendered his pipe to his father and stepped down into the street.

"One person, perhaps," he said across the distance. "But a very important one. Highly influential."

He crossed the paving stones. "We would be more likely to believe you won't hold it against us if you'd join in." He held out his hand to her.

Brave man, Alec thought.

Or stupid.

With all eyes on her, Amelia felt nervous and self-conscious. "Oh no," she said. "I have no intention of dancing. But all of you go ahead."

No one moved.

She swallowed, then continued, "You have every right to celebrate the old traditions. I know I said otherwise years ago, but I was wrong. You are free to dance, all of you. Free to live as you please." She looked at her daughter, willing her eyes to communicate all the love she felt. "Even you, Julia. I have tried to shelter you for far too long. You are free."

Julia came and stood at Desmond's side. "Come, Mamma. Just once around the green for Beaworthy? For me?"

Amelia's heart squeezed to hear the cherished moniker, the affectionate *Mamma* Julia had avoided using the last several weeks. She had missed hearing it.

"Remember, my lady," Mr. Evans began, stepping forward. "Even the Good Book says there is a time for everything. Even a time to dance."

Desmond bowed before her. "May I have this dance, my lady?"

Amelia's breath caught. How startling to see this man bow before her, to hear him ask her to dance as he had done so many years before. . . .

Knowing the crowd awaited her response, Amelia felt wary and ready to flee. She did not want to dance. Not here. Not now. It would be a blow to her pride, humbling after maintaining her stance against it for so long. How self-conscious she would feel dancing in the middle of the street with the whole village as witness. She didn't even remember the steps. She should just leave. Without her stifling presence, she told herself, they would return to their celebration.

But then she looked once more at Julia, saw the hope and concern in her beloved face, and could not resist.

She swallowed, then forced a smile. "Very well, Mr. Desmond. I would be honored."

Gasps and excited whispers were soon followed by applause, intermixed no doubt with a few judgmental whispers behind hands.

Mr. and Mrs. Desmond beamed at them, clearly overjoyed to see their son about to dance again. Fergus Desmond launched into the tune on the pipe, his wife standing at his side. The other musicians closed their gaped mouths and joined in.

John Desmond led Amelia to a place in line behind Julia and Mr. Valcourt, and gave her a reassuring smile. "Just follow my lead."

Amelia did so. And after a few hesitant missteps she found the rhythm and mastered the simple steps.

For a minute or two, only a few of the original couples danced, most still watching Lady Amelia cautiously. Then, with looks at one another, shrugs of acceptance, and game smiles, the other couples, and several new ones, joined in.

Together the inhabitants of Beaworthy danced around the village green hand in hand. The clouds had passed, and the fountain of Love and Grace flowed steadily at last.

Epilogue

ONE YEAR LATER
MAY 1, 1818

W e observed the first of May much as we always did. We dressed gaily and drove in the barouche from Buckleigh Manor into Beaworthy. It was tradition, Lady Amelia said. But I knew she had another reason for wanting to visit the village on this particular day. She wanted to make sure no one forgot.

We drove first to the flower shop and there bought a large bouquet.

But Lady Amelia did not lay forget-me-nots at the place where her brother died. She decided it was time to forgive and forget. She would remember the man, the good, but not the regrettable details of his death. Instead she placed the forget-me-nots at the foot of the fountain of Love and Grace. Two things she wanted never to forget.

This past autumn, she and I went to London for the "little season." Mamma had decided it was time I finally saw and experienced all I had been missing. At the same time, she planned to introduce me to many suitable gentlemen, hoping one of them would win my heart where James Allen had failed. I enjoyed London, and I am glad we went, but her plan did not succeed. For I had left my heart with a certain dancing master in Beaworthy.

We returned in early November, in time to watch the bell ringers turn the devil's stone, this time without incident. However, this did not signal the end of change for our village. For with the arrival of spring this year, new life has budded all around. Romance has budded as well.

Mr. Ramsay, Alec's uncle, has wed the widow Mrs. Tickle and now shares her snug house, where the rooms are ever warm and he is ever well fed. Last I saw him, he was happier and more portly than ever. The new Mrs. Ramsay has decided, however, not to change the name of her bakery, for Mrs. Tickle's pies and pasties are world famous, you know, and Mrs. Ramsay's are not.

Alec's mother and father now live in Mr. Ramsay's former cottage. Mr. Valcourt returned and has succeeded in earning his wife's trust and winning her heart all over again. When he arrived in Beaworthy and those first, awkward introductions had to be made, flabbergasted pupils and neighbors invariably sputtered, "But . . . I thought you were dead."

In response, Colin Valcourt had nodded solemnly and said, "The man I once was is dead. I was gone many months, and they had no word of me. They feared, even assumed, the worst. And can you blame them? Trapped in war-torn France as I was? But I am back, through the grace of God. Whole and healthy and reunited with my family. Is that not what is important?"

And eventually people accepted him as they had the rest of his family.

Mr. Valcourt, Senior, now assists his son in the dancing academy, which began prospering soon after the grand-opening dance. In fact, these days he teaches more lessons than his son, who is occupied with other endeavors.

Alec Valcourt still teaches the occasional dancing or fencing class, but also devotes time to a new book of dance instruction and etiquette he will soon publish. He is also quite busy arranging our wedding trip. He and I are engaged to be married, and he plans to leave the academy in his father's sole charge for a few months while he and I see more of the world together.

Walter Allen has begun courting Tess Thorne, and has learned to praise and dance with the best of the Bryanites. James Allen is not courting anyone, as far as I know, though his eyes still linger admiringly on Aurora Valcourt whenever he sees her, especially as she is blossoming more and more into a beautiful young lady, now in her eighteenth year. Perhaps James is waiting to find a more suitable match. Or perhaps for the match of his heart to become a little older.

My dear friend Patience is not being courted at all, I'm afraid. But she seems content with that. She is happy to be . . . patient.

The olive branch she'd extended to the Wilcox brothers had been only that. She'd never held any romantic feelings for either man, which is little surprise. However, I will say, her chosen method was quite effective, as the brothers have not given Alec any trouble since.

John Desmond is on his way to becoming a renowned bladesmith, making dress swords and fencing swords for gentlemen and noblemen. He does it for the satisfaction of working with his hands, of creating something functional and beautiful. But these days he spends less time admiring hilts and scabbards than he does admiring a certain woman's auburn hair and dainty figure, her quiet smile and fine eyes.

At midday this first of May, the church bells ring, not in somber memorial of a long-ago death, but in annual celebration of life.

Hearing the much-anticipated signal, the inhabitants of Beaworthy come out of their respective shops and homes and join in the May Day dance. This year we are also attempting a new dance Alec has composed. It is called Upon a Spring Day—a dance of new life. The steps are simple, but some of us will take longer than others to master them: Turn. Bow. Reach high. Clap. Honor your neighbor. Join hands with your partner and walk forward, hand in hand.

Author's Note

I learned to dance the box step standing atop my father's size 15 triple E shoes. I danced the polka with uncles and cousins at family weddings, then went on to take every ballroom dance class I could sign up for during my university days. My dear, long-suffering husband has taken various dance classes with me over the years, and most recently English country dancing at the Tapestry Folkdance Center in Minneapolis. It *was* research, after all! We learned a lot and had a great time. You may want to try English country dancing for yourself sometime if lessons are offered near you.

Now for a few historical notes.

My version of 19th century Beaworthy is a compilation of a few villages. Residents of Shebbear, Devon, turn a "devil's stone" every year. It is also the place where a man named James Thorne built the first Bryanite (Bible Christian) chapel in 1817. Beaworthy's May Day dance was inspired by Helston's annual "Furry Dance," which I'd love to attend someday. And fictional Buckleigh Manor was inspired by Buckland House, in the village of Buckland Filleigh, Devon. Many thanks to Madeline Jane Taylor for her helpful book about the area, *Buckland Filleigh, A Continuous Thread.*

Mr. Valcourt's dancing instructions come primarily from *Lowes' Ball-Conductor and Assembly Guide* by the Lowe brothers, teachers of dancing, Edinburgh, 1820. (Joseph Lowe went on to become dancing master for Queen Victoria's children.) Other dance instructions and steps come from various sources, some of which are quoted in the chapter epigraphs. I hope historical dance aficionados will forgive the liberties I took to simplify the dance descriptions for modern, nonexpert readers (myself included).

I would like to thank the Manchester Area Historical Society, and Kenneth Schwarz, Blacksmith and Master of the Shop in Colonial Williamsburg, for answering my questions about blacksmiths and sword repair. Any mistakes are mine.

I would also like to thank my English friend Anne Rogers—photographer, author, and bell ringer—for answering my questions about church towers and bells. Originally, I described Julia standing atop a battlemented church tower, but Anne informed me that battlements are usually slanted, making them nearly impossible to stand atop. She "talked me down" to a parapet, which is still plenty dangerous. So even though reckless (and fictional) Julia Midwinter managed the feat, please don't try it yourself, okay?

Appreciation also goes to those who shared their joys and struggles of raising adopted children. Their descriptions of adoptee anger inspired my character's struggles in the book.

Warm gratitude and hugs to author Michelle Griep and my agent, Wendy Lawton, for their helpful suggestions for improving the manuscript at the eleventh hour.

As always, thanks to my husband and sons, my first reader, Cari Weber, and everyone at Bethany House Publishers, especially my editor, Karen Schurrer. I couldn't do this without each and every one of you.

Discussion Questions

1. Do you like to dance? Did you grow up in a dancing or non-dancing family? In your opinion, how has dancing—or views about dancing—changed over the years?
2. Did you enjoy the novel overall? What was a favorite moment or scene?
3. Did you have a favorite character? Least favorite? Did your feelings toward any of the characters change as the novel progressed?
4. How would you say Julia changed throughout the course of the novel? What about Lady Amelia? Alec?
5. Did anything in the novel take you by surprise? What made it surprising?
6. Do you know someone who has dealt with adoption anger or abandonment issues in their family? How did it play itself out?
7. Did the quotes at the beginning of each chapter add to or detract from the enjoyment of the story for you? Can you recall a favorite?
8. What was the most interesting historical detail (about dance, dancing masters, Bryanites, etc.) you learned in reading this story?

9. How would you describe the theme(s) of the book? Did anything you read apply to something you are going through in your own life?

10. Near the end of the book, Julia faces a difficult truth: *All her life, she had been seeking a father's love and approval. And if she could not have a father's love, then any man's approval would do. She had strived so long and so hard to gain attention in the wrong ways and from the wrong people.* Can you relate to this—if not now, perhaps at an earlier point in your life? How would you advise a young woman struggling with these sorts of feelings and her sense of self-worth?

JULIE KLASSEN loves all things Jane—*Jane Eyre* and Jane Austen. A graduate of the University of Illinois, Julie worked in publishing for sixteen years and now writes full time. Three of her books, *The Silent Governess, The Girl in the Gatehouse,* and *The Maid of Fairbourne Hall,* have won the Christy Award for Historical Romance. She has also won the Midwest Book Award, Christian Retailing's BEST Award, and has been a finalist in the Romance Writers of America's RITA Awards, Minnesota Book Awards, and ACFW's Carol Awards. Julie and her husband have two sons and live in a suburb of St. Paul, Minnesota.

For more information, visit www.julieklassen.com.

More From Julie Klassen

To learn more about Julie and her books, visit julieklassen.com.

Emma and her father have come to the Cornish coast to tutor the youngest sons of a baronet—but all is not as it seems. When mysterious things begin to happen and danger mounts, can she figure out which brother to blame...and which to trust with her heart?

The Tutor's Daughter

To escape marrying a dishonorable man, Lady Margaret Macy temporarily disguises herself as a housemaid. Soon entangled in intrigues both above *and* belowstairs, will she sacrifice a chance at love in order to preserve her secret?

The Maid of Fairbourne Hall

When Captain Matthew Bryant leases Windrush Court, he is intrigued by the beautiful girl who lives quietly in the gatehouse. But is he willing to risk his future plans for a beguiling authoress shadowed by scandal?

The Girl in the Gatehouse

◊BETHANYHOUSE

Stay up-to-date on your favorite books and authors with our *free* e-newsletters. Sign up today at bethanyhouse.com.

Find us on Facebook. facebook.com/bethanyhousepublishers

Free exclusive resources for your book group! bethanyhouse.com/anopenbook

anopenbook

If you enjoyed *The Dancing Master*, you may also like...

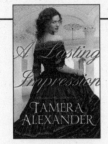

Claire Laurent longs to create a lasting impression with her art. Attorney Sutton Monroe is determined to reclaim his family's land and honor after losing both in the war. But will their ambitions come at too high a price?

A Lasting Impression by Tamera Alexander
A BELMONT MANSION NOVEL
tameraalexander.com

When Miss Felicia Murdock stumbles into Grayson Sumner's life, he'll have to decide whether he wants to spend the rest of his life keeping this lively young lady out of trouble.

A Talent for Trouble by Jen Turano
jenturano.com

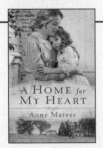

Sadie is torn when she is offered the position of matron at the orphanage where she works. She loves her job, but she also loves her beau, Blaine—and tradition dictates that she cannot have both...

A Home for My Heart by Anne Mateer
annemateer.com